DRAGON SPEAKER

BOOK I OF

THE SHADOW WAR SAGA

To Richard,
    Thank you for your support,
and congratulations on your
achievements of the evening! Keep
writing, and keep dreaming. I hope
you enjoy the story!
            Love,
                Elana ♥

SHIVNATH PRODUCTIONS

FILM & PUBLISHING

DRAGON SPEAKER
Book I of
The Shadow War Saga

This book is a work of fiction.

www.allentria.com

Dedicated to the heroes who made this book possible:

Paul Hobbs Wilson, Lynn McCune, Russ Johnson, Megan Burby, Walter Mugdan, Vivienne Lenk, Brandon Hart, Willow Belden, Bernie Richards, Maggie Chatterton, Matthew Fields, Matt Warren, Christine Arcidiacono, Nick Rucker, Debra Fricano, Gary Ow, Marshall Honorof and Celey Schumer.

And to Skylo and Oreo – my little lost heroes. I did it all for you.

CONTENTS

Prologue	7
Map *of Aeria*	18
Chapter One *Ten Ages Later*	19
Chapter Two *The Ceremony*	24
Chapter Three *The Dragon God*	31
Chapter Four *Witch Hunt*	40
Chapter Five *Into the Mountains*	47
Chapter Six *Argos Moor*	56
Chapter Seven *Allentria*	66
Map *of the Smarlands*	76
Chapter Eight *Cezon's Scheme*	77
Chapter Nine *Magic and Mayhem*	82
Chapter Ten *The Road to Noryk*	89
Chapter Eleven *The Imperial City*	96
Chapter Twelve *The New Quest*	104
Chapter Thirteen *The Vale Room*	113
Chapter Fourteen *The Plan*	123
Map *of the Galantasa*	130
Chapter Fifteen *The Fifth Companion*	131
Chapter Sixteen *The Bargain*	136
Chapter Seventeen *The Summoning*	143
Chapter Eighteen *Dragon Speaker*	152
Chapter Nineteen *What Wisdom Dictates*	159
Chapter Twenty *Priorities*	166
Chapter Twenty-One *Captured*	176
Chapter Twenty-Two *Darksalm*	187
Chapter Twenty-Three *The Rescue*	197
Chapter Twenty-Four *The Princess and the Peasant*	206
Chapter Twenty-Five *The Dragon and the Darkness*	215
Chapter Twenty-Six *Desertion*	223

Chapter Twenty-Seven *The Palace in the Lake*   229
Chapter Twenty-Eight *Shivnath's Chosen*   238
Chapter Twenty-Nine *The Ball*   248
Chapter Thirty *The Foresight*   259
Chapter Thirty-One *The Monster*   266
Chapter Thirty-Two *Good Business*   274
Chapter Thirty-Three *On The Run*   282
Chapter Thirty-Four *Best Friends*   289
Chapter Thirty-Five *Into the Shadows*   299
Chapter Thirty-Six *Demons*   306
Chapter Thirty-Seven *The Secret of the Sword*   317
Chapter Thirty-Eight *The Greatest Battle*   325
Chapter Thirty-Nine *Necrovar's Side*   331
Chapter Forty *The Shadow Lord*   340
Chapter Forty-One *The Hero*   347
Epilogue   356
Glossary & Pronunciations   360
About the Author   366

"You are already everything you need to be."
~Arisse Chardreilas, Twelfth Age

PROLOGUE

GROUGE WAS A SECOND-RATE DEMON AT BEST, but he took pride in guarding his Master's citadel. It perched near the summit of Mount Arax, so Grouge would be able to spot approaching enemies from leagues away . . . not that any enemies would dare approach in the first place. The fortress's black walls rose from the steep cliffs of the volcano, and its arches, turrets, and spires were all laced with defensive wards.

Grouge was supposed to be guarding the citadel with his life — or, more accurately, afterlife — but he was secure in the knowledge that it was impenetrable. He curled his barbed tail around his squat, feline body, closed his black eyes, and rolled onto his side for a well-deserved nap.

A loud thud jolted him awake and he sprang back to his feet, whiskers aquiver. He looked for the source of the disturbance, but the winding steps below were empty. There were no patrols circling the skies overhead either, which was odd because there were always patrols.

Just when Grouge had managed to convince himself everything was fine, a sharp edge pressed against his throat.

"Don't make a sound." A voice, soft yet resonant with power, breathed in his tufted ear. "Nod to show you understand."

Taken off-guard, Grouge whimpered and managed to nod. The blade was removed from his neck and his attacker stepped into view.

It was a human warrior, garbed in tattered brown robes that marked him as one of the rebels. Though he looked young, his head was haloed by a mane of white hair. Volcanic drafts blew back a few stray strands, revealing a pale face set with glowing purple eyes. He was a *rheenar*, one of the deadliest foes a demon could encounter.

"You were a manticore when you were alive, yes? Can you speak?" the man asked. Grouge nodded again. "Speak, demon. I won't hurt you."

"Yes." His fear of annihilation began to ebb away, only to be replaced by the fear of what would happen when the Master discovered this human had breached the citadel's defenses.

"I wish to meet with Necrovar. I come in peace."

"You've a strange way of showing it," Grouge muttered. Surprisingly, the mortal sheathed his sword and raised his hands, as if in surrender.

"There. Now will you please bring me to your master? According to the rules of war, you must allow me to speak with him."

Grouge hesitated. He didn't want to admit it, but he didn't actually know the rules of war. Surely there were no rules in war?

A shudder whisked across his blackened withers as he studied the warrior. There was something off about the man's angular visage—it was too symmetrical, too perfect. The more he stared, the more it seemed this human didn't look human at all. Still, he'd asked nicely to be brought to the Master. He'd said he was there in peace. Nobody so polite would lie about their motives. Would they?

"Fine," Grouge grumbled, ignoring his misgivings. "Follow me, flesh-rat."

He turned and led the man down the citadel's pillar-lined entryway, proceeding through heavy doors that swung open for them. They were in the stronghold.

Unfortunately, a patrol squad was also there.

The squad captain appeared to have once been human. Now, he was something both more and less than a human. He'd died and had been resurrected as a demon, complete with midnight flesh and vacant eyes, their whites and irises swallowed by darkness.

"What's the meaning of this?" the captain demanded of Grouge. His troops gaped at the *rheenar*, shocked to see a rebel walking about freely in their home.

"Uh . . . well, I'm bringing this man to the Master," Grouge replied nervously, his tail curling between his back legs. "He has requested a meeting, as per the rules of war."

"Necrovar is expecting me," the human added. "And if he is displeased with my presence in his domain, that is my problem. Not yours."

"It certainly is," said the captain. He made a show of standing tall before the mortal but failed to disguise the crease of fear upon his brow. After a moment's consideration he turned back to Grouge. "Very well, soldier. You may proceed. We wouldn't want to keep the Master waiting."

Grouge and the warrior set off again. Grouge remained silent as he led the man through the maze of halls, but he burned with curiosity. What made the flesh-rat so certain he would survive this visit? Granted, he was doing a good job so far, but what trick did he have up his sleeve?

Grouge couldn't take the suspense. "Why must you talk to the Master?"

"I have something to offer him."

Grouge was sure this warranted a follow-up question, and he wracked his tiny brain to come up with something suitably clever. "Why are you offering it?"

"Because he would take it from me anyway. Not all of it, but . . . " The man trailed off, glancing away. The gravity of his statement was lost on Grouge.

They rounded another corner, and there it was. The arched entrance to the Master's lair was engraved with jagged runes. Two demon direwolves stood guard on each side of the door, and the moment they spotted the intruder, they charged.

In an attempt to appear as powerful and commanding as the warrior, Grouge stepped forward and cried, "Halt!" The guards slowed to a walk, snarling and snapping their jaws. "This man is here in peace. He has requested a meeting with the Master. Let him through."

The direwolves grudgingly moved aside, yet their eyes

remained fixed on the warrior as Grouge guided him to the arch. Skeins of shimmering necromagic cobwebbed across it, and while demons could pass through without harm, Grouge wasn't sure the human could do the same.

"I'll go ahead and—" Grouge cut himself off as the warrior drew his magnificent sword and sliced through the dark threads. The necromagic fizzled and spat as the barrier vanished.

"Right, then. Stay here until I announce you."

"I need no announcement. As I said, Necrovar is expecting me." With a twirl of his cloak, the man vanished into the throne room.

Grouge considered fleeing. If the foolish mortal had come looking for a fight, it would be best to get as far away as demonly possible. But the warrior had said he had something to offer the Master. Something the Master wanted.

Though Grouge knew eavesdropping was rude—not to mention treasonous, when one was eavesdropping on one's superiors—he crept through the antechamber on padded paws and peeked into the obsidian room beyond. Golden, claw-shaped brackets clung to the walls, clutching torches that illuminated the high, vaulted ceiling. Cast-iron urns of blue fire flickered upon a raised dais at the head of the hall, flanking a great dragonbone throne. Seated on that throne was the Master.

Like His demons, He had once been something else: a human. There was no humanity left in Him now. His rotted black skin was too taut for His skull, and His flesh ripped when His features moved too drastically, revealing pitted bone beneath. Pinpricks of yellow-orange light danced in empty eye sockets, serving as His pupils. Like a raging wildfire or a bloodthirsty hurricane, He was a wonder and a terror to behold.

". . . that is why you're here, not for any noble, self-sacrificing reasons—and don't delude yourself otherwise." The Master spoke down to the warrior, who stood alone in the middle of the room. Grouge quaked at the sound of His rich baritone.

"I know what I'm doing. This is no mistake."

"So you think," was the snide reply. "I wonder what your

mother would say?"

"I couldn't tell you," the warrior said stiffly. "For all I know, she's dead."

"Ahh . . . if you only knew the truth, Valerion."

Grouge's stomach plummeted. Valerion? He'd brought Valerion of the Unknown Lands into the citadel, the evil, murderous lightmagic-wielder who led the mortal races of Selaras in rebellion against the Master?

Grouge was a dead demon.

"You've been stuffing your head with those stories your followers tell. You so desperately want to believe *you* are the hero the world has been waiting for."

"Do you want what I've offered, or not?" Valerion's voice was tight with anger.

"Obviously I want it. And I will grant your request. When you die, I shall resurrect you — not as a demon, but as your own, true self."

Grouge was dumbstruck. What had Valerion offered as payment for such a reward? Grouge had paid dearly when he'd made his own deal with the Master, but for some reason, he couldn't remember what he'd given in exchange for a second chance at life.

"Then take it," Valerion growled.

"That's not how it works. It will revert to me when you die."

"But surely," the mortal persisted, "you have the power to take it now."

The Master's eyes narrowed. "Why the rush?"

"Why the hesitation? If you do this, you'll be the most powerful wielder in the world."

"I am the most powerful wielder in the world." There was no trace of arrogance in the Master's voice. He was merely stating a fact.

"But this way, you could restore the balance between the magics and bring us peace," said Valerion. "Isn't that what you've been fighting for all this time?"

The Master stood and descended from the dais, approaching

the warrior with the fluid grace of a serpent. "So demanding. So presumptuous. What *would* your mother say?"

He began to wield His magic. With a single gesture, He wrenched the shadows from their resting places and directed them toward Valerion. The human stood still as wisps of darkness encased him, his eyes glinting through the gloom like two purple stars in an empty universe.

The Master summoned the shadows from the antechamber next, and Grouge felt horribly exposed. A wintery wind filled the air, howling and wailing in horror. It was bright, it was dim, and then . . . it was silent. The shadows, exhausted, slunk back to where they belonged.

"You know this means I've won?" The Master sounded breathless, as if the spell had cost Him a great deal of energy. "If you sign a surrender treaty now, I vow no more blood will be spilled."

Valerion said nothing.

"Fine. Your stubbornness is of no consequence to me. I have what I need, and those who choose to fight deserve the deaths that await them."

Still no reply.

"I could kill you, Valerion," the Master murmured. "I *should* kill you." But He made no move to do so.

Grouge stewed in anticipation; why didn't He strike down His most dangerous enemy?

"We are finished here. You may see yourself out, but rest assured, I will not be so merciful the next time we meet."

"We won't meet again," said Valerion. His voice was faint and weak, an echo of its former glory.

"No? Do you think you can hide from me, you foolish child? I own your soul now — you have no more magic. You cannot fight me."

Valerion had given the Master his *soul*? If he had relinquished the source of his life and magic, then how was he still alive? Without a soul, you were little more than a hollow husk, though Grouge had no idea how he knew that. This deal — a soul in exchange for a life—felt eerily familiar.

"I don't need to fight. This war is over." Valerion turned his back on the Master and strode away. Grouge's paws scrabbled against the stone floor as he tried to scamper off, but it was too late. Valerion entered the antechamber. The warrior's calm eyes met Grouge's terrified ones for a heartbeat, and then he was gone, off to fight his way out of the citadel with only his sword to defend himself.

"Grouge," hissed a voice that he knew as well as his own. Oh no. The Master knew he was there. "Come in here, Grouge."

Grouge had no choice but to obey. His belly filled with dread as he crawled into the room and forced himself to look upon the Lord of Shadow Lords.

"Well?" said the Master. "What did you make of that?"

"I . . . I think—I think it will serve you well to have Valerion's magic," Grouge spluttered.

The Master nodded, tapping the tips of His clawed fingers together. "For the first time in a long time, I am not certain I've done the right thing. Valerion has literally handed me victory. It doesn't make sense. Did he say anything to you?"

"Nothing, Master. Except . . . when I asked why he was offering his gift, he said you would take it from him anyway—"

The Master grinned, ripping the skin around His mouth.

"—but not all of it."

The Master stopped smiling, and that alone frightened Grouge too much to say anything else. He didn't know how long the Master stood thinking. It felt like ten ages passed them by.

A shuddering noise broke the stillness, a noise that pierced Grouge to the marrow of his shadowy bones. It reminded him of a ceaseless dying breath slipping from someone's lips.

The Master's fiery gaze flickered toward the far end of His chamber. Grouge turned and saw a purple vapor shimmering through the Master's private exit. One curious tendril peeked into the throne room, as if it were searching for something.

"What is that, Master?" Grouge whispered, his hackles rising.

"Someone is wielding against us."

It was a testament to the Master's power that He didn't sound disturbed by the appearance of the strange spell. He strode forward and the vapor directed its attention toward Him, its aimless swirls coalescing into a focused point. The Master flicked His hand in a gesture of banishment, counter-wielding to dispel the smog.

It was not dispelled.

Grouge's jaw dropped. He had never seen the Master magically bested. The Master tried again, waving His hand in an arc and contracting His fingers, as though attempting to catch the spectral entity.

It had no effect. The vapor swayed and reared up in a sinuous strand, a misty cobra preparing to strike. The Master gestured again, retreating from His foe ever so slightly.

In that movement, Grouge saw defeat. The corded muscles of his body tensed and he catapulted from the throne room. He raced past the direwolves and careened through the warren of corridors.

He was forced to stop when he reached the great hall. The lethal haze was there, too, and scores of demons were snared in its clutches. Where the mist touched them, they melted. Creatures big and small were being liquefied, their flesh, bones, and muscles pooling into gobs of black ichor on the floor.

"Master!" One desperate demon cried out for her sovereign, her scream gurgling away as the vapor wrapped around her neck, turning her to slush. She was dead. No, worse than that—she was *nothing*.

Grouge bolted again. Hugging the edge of the room, he wove his way through a treacherous tangle of mist. If he could escape the citadel, he'd be fine. Through the doors, down the corridor, finally free and—

"No," he gasped, coming to another grinding halt. Outside, glowing purple raindrops fell from the sky. Demons streamed from the citadel in a mass exodus, but the rain was melting them much like the mist had. Those who had magic were shielding themselves, but the spells of the less powerful creatures were already being chipped away by the deluge.

Grouge would die if he went out there.

He was trapped.

Then a *necrocrelai*, one of the born-demons, ran by. It was Shädar, second in command to the Master. He wasn't flying because his bat-wings had been torn in the last battle with the rebels. Seizing his chance, Grouge raced under the protection of the general's necromagical shield and followed him.

Shädar took the path to the summit of Mount Arax. His whiplike tail lashed behind him, belting Grouge in the face as he struggled to keep up with the longer strides of the humanoid demon.

They crested the flat lip of the crater and Grouge spotted the Master standing at the edge of the mountain's gaping volcanic maw. Not many had made it this far. Even the stronger demons were succumbing to the toxic rain.

An ear-splitting thunderclap sent Grouge into hysterics. He looked up and saw that the sky was opening — *opening!* — just tearing itself apart, leading away into an unknown void. Purple lightning crackled around the edges of the rift, lancing out in all directions, illuminating the peaks and valleys of boiling black clouds.

"My liege," Shädar growled when he reached the Master's side. "What is this? Are the dragons finally fighting us?"

"One dragon is." An alien expression crossed the Master's features — was it sorrow? "Or two, depending on how you look at things."

With a deafening crack, an arm of purple fire lashed out from the hole in the sky, arcing toward them like some terrible, wayward solar flare. The Master wielded to repel it and the two magics met in an explosion that knocked Grouge clean off his feet.

"Try and claim me, Valerion," the Master bellowed. "You will fail! I am the balance! I am omnipotent! *I have your soul!*"

He drew His sword from its scabbard and gestured violently with the weapon. Again, His movement had no effect.

"Master?" Shädar's single word was filled with all the questions Grouge longed to ask.

The Master was silent for a time, staring down at His hands.

When He finally spoke, His words were barely audible over the agonized screams of dying demons. "I cannot wield his magic."

Shädar's red eyes went round with panic. "What? Why?"

"If a soul is not complete, it cannot be wielded," the Master explained, His flimsy skin cracking as His expression contorted. The image of the almighty, invincible wielder crumbled before Grouge, revealing a broken human in its place.

"That conniving, evil little monster. Valerion split his soul before coming to me . . . and she let him." The Master's lips curled into a snarl. "Shivnath," he hissed, with the vehemence of a curse.

Grouge never had a chance to ask who Shivnath was. A tingling sensation seeped into his body. He looked around to find a tongue of purple flame had snuck up on him. The fire didn't burn or melt him — it tightened around his middle and lifted him off the ground.

"Master! Help!" Grouge shrieked. But another fiery arm had grabbed the Master, and though He struggled and wielded, it seemed all His power was nothing compared to the unearthly energy that held Him.

He had finally, inexplicably, been defeated.

Grouge and the Master were pulled toward the hole in the sky alongside thousands of unfortunate others. Grouge's vision narrowed and dimmed as he approached the gaping fracture in reality. The world around him dissolved. Sound and touch faded away.

Then everything was nothing.

It was gone.

He was gone.

And after a moment, an eternity of waiting, suspended, neither conscious nor unconscious, neither living nor dead . . .

The rift in the sky reopened, and Grouge dropped down with the familiar inky blackness of necromagic, which was so unlike the cruel black void that had held him prisoner.

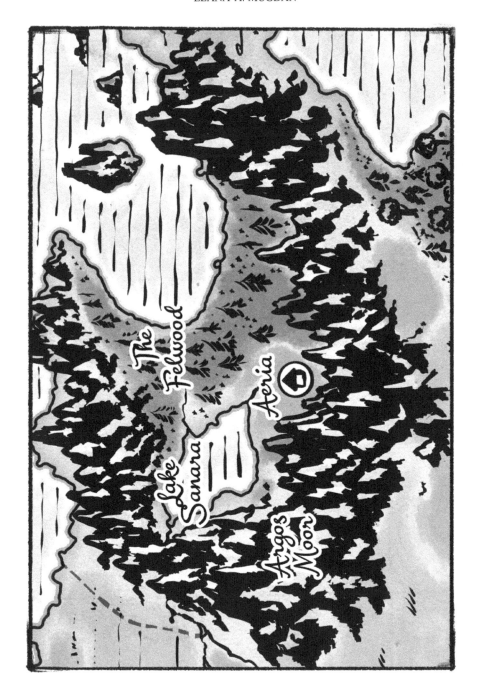

CHAPTER ONE

TEN AGES LATER

"Heroes are not born; they are made."
~ **Nyela Veridicae, Sixth Age**

Keriya Nameless took a deep breath to calm her nerves. She'd been disobedient plenty of times before, but what she was doing now was especially bad. She swept her flyaway bangs from her forehead and put an eye to the crack between the ill-fitting storage room door and its frame.

In the hall beyond, diluted light drifted through thin windows onto the wooden platform where stood Holden Sanvire, Head Elder of Aeria. The immense stone tablet next to him bore the names of all the children who were eligible for the Ceremony of Choice. A bubbling sensation, not altogether unpleasant, filled Keriya's stomach as Elder Sanvire cleared his throat. This meeting would decide her future.

"First to be considered is Sven Aablum," said Sanvire, his words echoing in the vast chamber. "I shall speak for Sven. He's done well in his studies and his magic is strong. He's expressed interest in being a Harvester, and we are in great need of Harvesters."

None of the Elders made any objections, so Sanvire picked up a piece of chalk and made a mark next to Sven's name, indicating he'd been deemed worthy. "Keep that in mind when you interpret Sven's sign, Erasmus."

Keriya craned her neck to catch a glimpse of Erasmus, the village Healer and — for lack of a better word — her father. He sat in a small alcove near the back of the hall, watching the proceedings. His silver beard, which stood out stark against his dark skin, glinted as he nodded.

"I shall, Head Elder."

Hearing his familiar serene tone calmed Keriya, and the flutterings in her stomach stilled for a moment. Erasmus had taken her in after her mother had died during childbirth, and had raised her and taught her his trade. Though he was an attentive guardian, he had never been a particularly affectionate one—but that suited Keriya just fine. She liked that Erasmus wasn't sentimental. He didn't coddle her. Most importantly, he didn't pity her.

Sanvire offered Erasmus a curt nod in return. "Very good. Next to be considered is Selina Abersae. A hard worker, but she still struggles with creation magic. Who will speak for her?"

Selina Abersae was eventually found worthy, as were many others; but when the Elders reached Fletcher Earengale's name, nobody was willing to vouch for him.

Keriya twisted her fingers through her long hair, which she kept tied back on either side of her head. She prayed someone would speak up for her best—and only—friend.

"The goddess Shivnath, blessed be her name, gave Fletcher's father a vivid sign during his ceremony," one Elder offered halfheartedly. "Fletcher may have the same—"

"Tomas Earengale was killed by the dark forest spirits on a salting expedition," Sanvire interrupted. "He was unworthy, which means his son is unworthy. Besides," he added snidely, "Fletcher's magic is as weak as we've ever seen."

It didn't take much arguing before Fletcher's name was stricken from the list.

Keriya's heart sank. Fletcher would be so upset to hear he hadn't made the cut. And if *he* hadn't been deemed worthy, what chance did she have? This ceremony was her one chance to be accepted into Aerian society, and if she wasn't allowed to participate . . .

She shook her head to clear it of that unpleasant thought.

The Elders slogged through the rest of the names. The sun had long set behind Shivnath's mountains by the time they determined that Brock Zyvlan was worthy.

"That," said Sanvire, making his last checkmark, "concludes our work. We are dismissed."

With the creaking of old bones, the Elders began to rise from their wooden benches. Keriya had known it might come to this, that she might be omitted from the list. She had to act. It was now or never. She stood and pushed through the storage room door. "Wait! I'd like permission to speak."

Outraged gasps filled the air as she ran onto the platform. Gazing at the field of livid faces, she was reminded again of everything that made her different. Compared to the earthy coloration of the Aerians, she looked like a ghost with her pale skin, gray eyes, and waxen hair, which was white and wispy as snowflakes.

"Permission denied," Sanvire roared. "And you will be punished for this!"

Though she was shorter than average for a girl of fourteen, Keriya stood her ground before Sanvire's imposing bulk as he stalked toward her.

"I've never been allowed in any of your ceremonies," she argued, prepared to accept a hundred punishments if it meant getting on that list, "and you judged me unworthy to attend school, but I learned everything I need to know from Erasmus. I don't always do as I'm told, but I shouldn't be condemned for—"

"Of course you should," boomed a particularly grumpy Elder. "And you ought to have been condemned many times before now. Elder Sanvire, I move to whip her into penitence and lock her in the stocks until the ceremony is over—with a gag in her mouth."

"That won't be necessary," said Erasmus. "Keriya will accept your decision in peace." He swept toward the podium to collect her, his robes billowing out behind him. But Keriya had come too far to give up without a fight.

"The Ceremony of Choice is supposed to be a time of new beginnings," she said. "You decide if someone is worthy based not on what they've done, but on their potential."

"And your potential is zero," growled Sanvire. "All of our professions require the use of magic, even the basest, tiniest grasp of magic. You are a cripple. You have nothing."

Her jaw clenched. She'd known they would bring this up. She'd promised herself she wouldn't let it hurt.

It hurt anyway.

"I . . . I could still do something useful," she stammered, fighting to keep the quaver from her voice. "I know you need more Harvesters. I could help with that. Or I could work with Erasmus. I know how to make medicines and — "

"And nothing, Nameless," Sanvire snapped.

Keriya cringed away from the hated epithet. *Nameless.* That was all she'd ever be to them: a useless, crippled bastard child.

"You are the only person ever to be born without magic, and that alone makes you unworthy to hold a position in our society," the Head Elder continued. "We hardly need to mention your inability to follow even the simplest of rules, or go into the shameful details about your parents."

Keriya felt her cheeks flush as she looked down at the floorboards. Why had she thought this was a good idea? She shouldn't have bothered coming. Her mother had been unwed and her father was unknown. She'd been born without a family name, and she lacked the one thing that mattered above all else.

Her fate had been decided long ago.

Still, she forced herself to look back up and meet Sanvire's gaze. If she didn't do this, she would regret it forever. She had nothing left to lose.

"Please," she whispered. "All I need is one chance."

"If you participate and Shivnath finds you unworthy, you will die in the forest by her divine will. Or you will return without a sign, in which case you will be named a Lower," said Sanvire. "You'll be made to live and work as a slave. Is that a risk you're willing to take?"

"I'm willing to take it if you are," she countered. "Even if I die, that wouldn't be so bad, right?"

She was trying to be lighthearted, but the Elders took her

seriously. They nodded to one another and conferred amongst themselves.

"I see you're not in a joking mood," she mumbled, fiddling with the loose, fraying sleeves of her brown wool dress.

Sanvire spoke privately with Elders Remaine and Fleuridae, which Keriya took as a bad sign. Fleuridae hated her more than Sanvire did—if that was even possible—and Remaine hated everyone.

"We have reached a verdict," Sanvire announced at length, turning to address the room once more. "Keriya Nameless, you may participate in the Ceremony of Choice. We'll see what Shivnath wants to do with you."

"What?" A disbelieving grin split Keriya's face. She'd hoped and wished and prayed this would happen, but never had she fully believed it would come to pass. She had taken the first step to becoming one of the Aerians. This was huge.

Brimming with jubilation, she jumped down the steps of the platform and ran to Erasmus, garnering affronted glances from the Elders for her flagrant and inappropriate display of emotion. "Erasmus, I can participate!"

"I heard. Now it's time for us to leave, Keriya. We've kept the Elders long enough."

The Healer escorted her to the heavy oak doors at the end of the hall. He made an effort to shield her from the whispers that followed them down the aisle and the venomous looks the men cast her way, but Keriya was impervious to their scorn. Nothing could ruin this moment.

For the first time in her life, she had been deemed worthy.

CHAPTER TWO

THE CEREMONY

"The beginning is far ahead of us, but we will reach it in the end."
~ **Uhs Broadvayn, Twelfth Age**

The rosy glow of morning was stretching across the sky and Keriya hadn't slept a wink. She'd given up trying long ago, and had started reading to distract herself from worrying about the ceremony.

'The dragon-god Shivnath is the ruler of all that is good and just, and the evil god Helkryvt is her worst enemy. The two have been locked in conflict since the time before time, Shivnath fighting for balance, Helkryvt for power.

In the beginning, Shivnath created Aeria by raising land out of the sea. She took stone and made it fertile; she took saltwater and made it fresh; when she was done, she appeared to her people and gave each of them a portion of her earthmagic. She allowed them to cross over from the wasteland beyond, and they built their village at the foot of her mountains.'

Keriya drank up the words from her favorite book, though she'd read them countless times before. At the bottom of the age-softened page was an illustration of Shivnath herself, illuminated by the beeswax candle that flickered on the wooden table. She traced her finger over the dragon's outline, wincing in pain when she bent her palm.

"Careful," Erasmus said as he set a shallow clay dish before her. "You'll make it worse."

Keriya placed her hands in the dish and sighed as aloefern

medicine seeped into her wounds. Last night, the Elders had announced the names of those who were worthy to participate in the Ceremony of Choice, and her name had been included. However, they'd also seen fit to discipline her by whipping her hands with a pine branch.

They'd claimed this was punishment for her intrusion upon their meeting, but Keriya knew it had really been an attempt to mollify the furious parents who didn't want her to participate with their children. She was used to the poorly-disguised abuse; her arms and back were peppered with little white scars, all marks of disciplinary beatings past. Occasionally she did something to deserve it, like the time she'd filled Elder Sanvire's rain bucket with worms. Mostly, though, the beatings were for things like 'not speaking with a respectful tone,' 'laughing too loudly in a public space,' or 'skipping.'

"You must be on your best behavior for the send-off," Erasmus was saying. "Stay away from the other participants. Don't speak to anyone. Don't even look at Elder Sanvire."

"I get it," she muttered. *Don't be yourself, Keriya.* She knew Erasmus was trying to protect her, but it was a disheartening sentiment.

Her eyes were drawn again to Shivnath. "What do the Elders know, anyway?" she asked the picture. "Bunch of wrinkled old trolls. Can't tell their tops from their bottoms."

"Watch your words. They'd banish you if they heard you speaking that way."

"Sorry," she lied. She refrained from pointing out that if she were banished, she wouldn't have bloodied hands and bruised forearms all the time.

"The sun is rising," he said. "It's time to go."

Keriya stood and snuffed the candle flame between her fingertips, but lingered over her book before closing it. She stared down at the delicate inked lines of the dragon god.

"I'll show them all, Shivnath," she whispered. "They'll be sorry."

Keriya and Erasmus were the last to arrive at the ceremonial hilltop. The other participants awaited in shivering silence, huddled together against the morning chill. At their backs, the first rays of light broke upon the crests of Shivnath's mountains, promising bright sun in the future—a rarity for the gray and stormy Aerian climate. Before them, the evergreens of the Felwood loomed like an army of giants glaring down upon their next victims.

Keriya took her place among the children, over two-hundred in number. She'd been hoping to see Fletcher, but realized he wouldn't even be allowed to watch the ceremony since he hadn't been deemed worthy.

Erasmus, who was the ceremonial officiant, walked to the head of the forest path to address his audience. "Congratulations, young Aerians. You have been deemed worthy to become part of our society, but before you are accepted among us, you must first receive a sign. You have seven suns to wander on your own, during which time Shivnath will send you a vision that will show what you are to become in life. You know of the dangers within the Felwood. We are plagued by the darkness in the forest, and many who have gone in have never returned. Shivnath is the master of life and death, and she may claim some of you as sacrifices. Your death will serve to appease her, and your survival will mark your transition into adulthood."

"I know who won't be coming back this time," someone whispered.

Ignore it, Keriya told herself, gritting her teeth. *Best behavior.*

"Hey, Ghost-Girl!" the whisperer continued. "It's too bad you're gonna die in the forest. We haven't named a Lower in two cycles."

Keriya shot a glare at Penelope Sanvire, daughter of the Head Elder. She stood a few heights away, surrounded by her friends, twirling a strand of curly black hair around her finger.

"Shut up," Keriya growled through the corner of her mouth.

"Make me. Oh wait, you can't." A cruel smirk crinkled Penelope's plump cheeks. "You have no magic."

The fiery hand of shame tightened around Keriya's throat, and she blinked rapidly to stave off the tears that had sprung into her eyes. Those four words hurt more than anyone could know.

She wasn't able to pay attention to Erasmus' send-off, and she didn't join in on the group prayer to Shivnath. She kept her mouth shut and her head down.

When the prayer was over, Erasmus stepped aside to allow the children to enter the trees one by one. He presented each of them with a sheepskin waterbag, the only thing they were allowed to take on their rite of passage.

Keriya didn't embrace the Healer when she reached him, for physical contact in public was forbidden, and she didn't speak, for she had no idea what she should say. He had raised her, fed her, clothed her, tried to teach her the art of magic—yet she couldn't find the words for a proper goodbye.

Erasmus had nothing to say to her, either; he handed her a waterbag wordlessly and gestured for her to get going. She offered him a fleeting, brave smile, though she didn't feel particularly brave, then hurried into the forest.

There was only one footpath that snaked through the Felwood—well-worn by the Salters when they made their trips to the sea—but multiple game trails branched off from it. While the trails were smaller and more dangerous, Keriya would rather risk running into wild animals than risk running into Penelope Sanvire.

The first chance she got, she veered onto a narrow rut that meandered through the undergrowth. She relaxed in the cover of the trees and even felt good enough to start humming a tuneless melody.

She uncorked her waterbag and took a small drink to quench her thirst. It was filled with water from Lake Sanara, which was said to have powerful healing properties. Though the lake had never actually healed anyone, clean water was essential for survival in the wilderness and Keriya had to do everything she could to survive this ceremony. She *would* survive, if only to spite the Elders.

She walked until purple tendrils of twilight wended their way through the forest. The shadows on the ground seemed to come to life as a cold wind stirred the leaves above. Keriya quickened her pace. She had never believed the stories of the dark spirits that plagued the Felwood, but here, alone and possibly lost, it was hard not to imagine evil things lurking behind every tree.

A branch snapped behind her. In the silence it was deafening. Keriya gasped and whirled around.

"Who's there?" she whispered.

There was a long, painful pause.

"I'm sure it was just the breeze," she explained to a nearby shrub, which seemed like it was in need of reassurance. She crept toward it and crawled beneath its branches to take shelter, scooping up handfuls of damp, smelly leaves and piling them over herself in the vain hope they might keep her warm. It took some time, but eventually she fell into a fitful, dreamless sleep.

Keriya woke to a misty drizzle at dawn. Grumbling to herself, she scrounged around for something to eat. Erasmus had taught her to identify edible mushrooms and berries, but there were none to be found. Hungry, wet, and still tired, she walked until it grew dark again. She found a rocky cave that kept her dry as she slept, but the uneven stone floor was the furthest thing from comfortable.

On her third sun of travel—another rare, bright morning—the trees began to thin. A dull roar reached her ears, and finally she was out of the forest. She had come to the edge of a cliff that overlooked an impossibly vast body of water.

"The sea," she murmured, gazing around in awe.

The roar came from waves crashing against craggy rocks below, tossing up droplets that sparkled and drifted like jeweled dragonflies in the sun. A mist-wreathed, mountainous island loomed in the distance. It was the only interruption in the unbounded horizon, where the blue of the cloudless sky faded into the azure waves.

Keriya felt small, but it wasn't a bad feeling. There was more out there. The world was a larger place than she'd believed. *So maybe*, she thought, as her heart leapt at the thought of new people and faraway lands, *there's a chance I could find a place in it.*

She spotted a path that led to the shore and descended to the soft sand. Though the sea was beautiful, she was far more interested in the island. Something about it seemed strange, perhaps even magical.

For a moment, Keriya was seized by the idea that she'd been destined to come here, that this was where she would find her sign. Entranced, she waded into the water, drawn toward the island.

Then the sunlight vanished.

She snapped out of her reverie to discover that ominous clouds had rolled in overhead. Keriya wheeled around and began sloshing back to the shore. She was in past her knees — what had she been thinking? She didn't know how to swim! Had she thought she could just stroll over to the island? How could she be so stupid?

The water tugged against Keriya's shins as it sucked backward, the only warning before a huge wave crashed upon her. She crumpled beneath it and hit the ground. Her face scraped against the sand, which no longer felt soft, but sharp and abrasive. She struggled to stand, but a ruthless undertow dragged her from the shallows.

Keriya's head broke the surface. She barely had time to inhale before she was submerged again. She kicked and flailed, and managed to surface for one more breath — an inadequate breath, a breath that seemed more water than air — before another wave wrapped her in its arms.

She fought against the tide, but she was no match for the sea. The further she got from land, the more frantic her thrashing became, and the less effective it was at keeping her afloat.

This was all wrong — she was supposed to survive, to prove she deserved a place in Aeria. She wanted this, *needed* this more than anybody. She clamped her mouth shut, drew short, searing breaths through her nostrils, and fought to keep her head above the whitecaps.

Then, as if guided by Shivnath herself, a black wave swelled and forced Keriya underwater, pushing her into the midnight depths. Her heart, which was already thumping madly against her ribs, doubled its frenzied pace as the light faded.

This isn't happening! It can't! I won't let it!

Her white hair swirled around her like spectral seaweed, spiraling upwards weightlessly even as her legs grew heavy. The sea drew her deeper into its dark embrace. She clawed at the water, trying with all her might to climb back to the surface. She could do it. She *had* to.

Shivnath, Keriya prayed, *help me! If you let me live, I'll always behave. I'll do whatever the Elders say. I'll never put poison ivy in Penelope Sanvire's bed again!*

Her entreaties grew more desperate, but if Shivnath was listening, she wasn't doing anything about it. Keriya's lungs were on fire. Her chest felt as though it would burst.

Her body spasmed of its own accord, and Keriya opened her mouth and breathed. Frigid liquid stung her nose and flooded her lungs. She tried to cough and found she couldn't—her throat was constricting, closing up in an effort to keep the salt water out.

The chilling shock of drowning brought one last surge of desperate hope. Keriya had done as her body required: she had breathed. Maybe now she could get back to shore.

She kicked again with renewed vigor . . . at least, she tried to. Something was wrong. Her brain was no longer communicating with her legs. Or her arms, she realized, as she tried to lift them.

Keriya went still and her vision grew dark.

Shivnath . . .

She didn't have time to finish her last thought before she died.

CHAPTER THREE

THE DRAGON GOD

"Choice is not the same thing as freedom."
~ *Gorkras Shädar, Second Age*

She was surrounded by darkness. She didn't know who she was, where she was, or how she'd gotten there. Her mind was blank and she herself was no more than an empty shell, bereft of feeling, desire, or purpose.

She looked around. The darkness was open and infinite, so huge it almost felt confining. Worry began to tickle the corners of her pleasantly vacant brain. She turned to get some sense of direction and found herself facing a phantom shape shrouded in shadow. The figure, which was nearly four times her size, gazed at her with eyes so black they banished all memory of light. Their sable depths were slashed by purple slitted pupils.

"We meet at last, Keriya," the phantom whispered.

The words sparked recognition within her. Tiny drops of her identity came trickling back, slowly filling the blankness within her.

"How do you know my name?" said Keriya.

"I know everything about you."

A deep, primal instinct filled Keriya with the desire to run, but an even deeper curiosity overpowered it.

"Who are you?" she asked, ignoring her unease.

The phantom raised its head and was suddenly illuminated by a sourceless, fey light. Wonder bloomed in Keriya's chest. One stray recollection returned to her, flaring up like a flame on a pile of dry tinder: she was sitting at a table in a hut, reading a book. She was looking at a page with a picture of a dragon.

That dragon stood before her now.

"You know who I am." Shivnath's voice resonated in Keriya's chest, making her ribcage hum and her heart quiver with fearful excitement. It held the promise of greatness and the threat of destruction all at once.

No picture could ever do justice to the god's grandeur. She had dark emerald scales, each one edged with a lustrous sparkle. Pearly spikes marched up her spine from the tip of her tail to the base of her reptilian skull, where they met noble horns that curved out and down. Muscular wings protruded from her shoulders, ribbed with clawed fingers like those of a bat.

"I've been trying to decide how to deal with you for a long time," Shivnath admitted. "There was always some reason I couldn't do as I pleased."

"Oh," said Keriya, too awestruck to be appropriately articulate. "Why's that?"

"All gods are bound by magical laws. As such, I am unable to meddle in mortal affairs. I may perform earthmagic that indirectly affects every creature in my domain, but I cannot tamper with individual mortals and their problems."

"Aren't you kind of tampering with me right now?"

"I'm good at finding the loophole in every rule. But I am not here to talk about the binding laws; I am here because you are dead."

Keriya stifled an incredulous snort. "That's not possible."

"Isn't it?" said Shivnath, offering a smile that held all the warmth of a glacier. "Why would I lie to you?"

The laughter died on Keriya's lips.

"You lost your memories when you left your body. I shall return them."

A rush of visions surged through Keriya's mind. They were vivid enough to blind her from her surroundings, and so vibrant they made her head ache. She jerked backwards to escape the overwhelming deluge, but they were inside her, burned into the backs of her eyes. She saw her lonely childhood. She saw herself growing up. She saw herself in the Felwood. She felt herself thrashing in the water. She tasted the burning salt. She was sinking. She was suffocating. And then . . .

"Oh . . . I'm dead?" It was the strangest feeling. Terror gripped her, yet at the same time she felt consumed by a numb, almost complacent hopelessness. In her struggle to make sense of it, her first instinct was to argue.

"If I'm dead, how can I be talking to you? Seeing you? How can I perceive myself?"

"While your body may expire and rot away, there will always be an essence, a tangle of magicthreads—your soul—which can never be unraveled," Shivnath explained. "It is what makes you who you are."

Keriya hugged her arms to her stomach. She couldn't be dead, could she? Of course not. The very notion was ludicrous! She was alive and breathing—at least, that was what it felt like. But Shivnath would never lie to her.

I'm dead.

"I have a question for you," said Shivnath. "What possessed you to leave my domain and enter the Chardons' territory? Why did you go into the sea?"

"I'm dead," Keriya murmured in a hollow voice.

"We've already established that. Now answer me."

Keriya drew a ragged breath and tried to focus. Why had she gone into the water? She examined her newly returned memories, struggling to rearrange them.

"I saw something," she said slowly. "An island. I wanted to go there. I thought it was magic, though I'm not sure what magic feels like. It just felt . . . different."

"You *are* an interesting creature," Shivnath mused. "I've decided that having you dead is unacceptable. Thanks to certain powers of mine, I have the ability to restore life; and thanks to certain loopholes in the binding laws, I will give you back yours. But before I do such a thing, I would ask that you do something for me."

A surge of relief, so strong it nearly shattered her, swept

through Keriya. "Yes. Anything!"

"What do you know of the far side of my mountains?"

"Only that it's a wasteland."

"Wrong," Shivnath replied flatly. "Beyond the mountains is a country called Allentria, and Allentria is on the verge of war."

"What's *war*?"

"Ah, to live such a sheltered life as an Aerian. War is a state of violent conflict between two or more opposing factions."

"Like an argument?"

"A big argument." The corners of Shivnath's scaly lips twitched, as if she wanted to smile. "Ten ages ago, my brethren sought to destroy the most powerful dark force our world has ever known—and they failed. This was Necrovar, the physical manifestation of evil. His war has lasted since the dawn of mankind, for humans are inherently evil."

Keriya frowned but, reflecting upon how the Aerians treated her, decided she did not particularly disagree.

"In the Second Age, Necrovar took mortal form and began his conquest. He attacked the mortal nations before setting his sights on the creatures who posed the biggest threat to him: the dragons. He nearly wiped out their race and destroyed the world of Selaras. Then, at the height of Necrovar's power, just as he was poised for victory, he was defeated by the leader of the World Alliance." Shivnath paused before she spoke the name: "Valerion."

"Valerion," Keriya echoed softly.

"Valerion beseeched the gods to help him end the war, and we agreed. Using his magic, we bypassed the binding laws that keep our power in check. We wove a spell that imprisoned Necrovar in a place where he could no longer hurt us, a parallel universe called the Etherworld. In order to preserve the magical balance, the spell also imprisoned the dragons."

Keriya remained silent, captivated by the tale, waiting for Shivnath to continue. The god's nostrils flared. A subtle change came over her sculpted features, like twilight creeping across a valley.

"But one dragon escaped. And now Necrovar has torn the magicthreads that separate our world and his prison."

"Ah," said Keriya. There was the catch she'd been waiting for.

"He is in our world once more, and he is going to finish the war he started. It is his intention to kill that dragon, while the Allentrians seek to use the dragon as a weapon—and I cannot allow either of those things to happen."

Keriya nodded. "Of course."

"So in order to save the dragon, I need you to go to Necrovar in its place."

Keriya paused mid-nod and stared up at Shivnath, trying to process what she'd just heard. "You want *me* to . . . ?"

"That's right."

Keriya frowned. This seemed like a dangerous sort of adventure—which was admittedly the best kind—but she was in no way fit for the job.

"I've read enough stories to know where this is going," she said. "I'm guessing you need me to fight Necrovar for you?"

"More or less."

"You do know I'm a cripple, right? I don't have any magic."

"I know exactly what you are, which is why I am going to weave some of my magic into your soul."

The words pierced Keriya's haze of confusion, bringing with them the light of clarity and elation. Magic. She was going to have magic! And not just any old magic, but Shivnath's magic.

"Be warned that I will not allow you to freely access the power within you. It will be veiled until the right moment. Then it will be gone forever."

The elation drained from Keriya as quickly as it had come. What good was magic if she couldn't use it whenever she wanted?

"Magic is not to be abused," Shivnath growled, as if in response to her thoughts. "It is not a tool for your foolish human whimsies."

"I—I'm sorry," Keriya stammered, shrinking away from the dragon's wrath. Shivnath wasn't anything like the benevolent, loving guardian the Aerians claimed her to be.

"You trust what the Aerians say, do you?" Shivnath sneered. Yes, she was definitely reading Keriya's mind. "They know nothing. You cannot trust anyone, Keriya. The sooner you learn that, the better."

"Then how do I know I can trust you?" she asked, trying to inject some levity into the increasingly unnerving conversation.

"You don't."

A chill trickled down Keriya's spine and spread throughout her limbs.

"Shivnath, that was kind of a joke."

"I do not joke," Shivnath told her stiffly.

"Right. I'll keep that in mind."

There was another stretch of silence. Keriya opened her mouth, and one question of the millions she pondered slipped out, almost unbidden.

"Why should I do this?"

The words hung in the air between them, ringing in the stillness, and at once she wished she could take them back.

"Why should you do this?" The god's voice was no longer cold and angry; now it was slow and calculating. She drummed her talons on the invisible ground. "You mean aside from the fact that you will remain dead if you don't?"

Keriya winced. Why couldn't she have kept quiet? It wasn't like she had a choice in the matter.

"There is always a choice, Keriya," said Shivnath. For the first time, the god's hard face was softened by a glimmer of compassion. "The trick is not to choose the lesser of two evils, but to rise above the evil once chosen. The ninth binding law states that I cannot force you to do anything against your will. You alone must decide where to go from here."

It wasn't so much the advice, but the unexpected kindness with which it was given, that made Keriya relent.

"I'm sorry. I don't know why I asked that. I didn't mean it."

"Oh, I think you did . . . but that's all for the best. I expect you'd want to do this because if you save that dragon, you will be a hero. Heroes are important and powerful. They are brave and they do great deeds," said Shivnath. "And the best thing about heroes is that everyone loves them. Isn't that what you want?"

Yes, sang a tiny voice in Keriya's head. But wanting something and deserving it were two very different things.

"Why me?" she whispered.

"Because," said Shivnath, "I chose you."

This was not the grand explanation Keriya had hoped for, nor the cryptic prophesy she had expected. It seemed to be the truth—albeit a truth so simple that it couldn't be the whole story.

"If you consent, I will weave my magic into your soul. You should know that it is a painful procedure."

"I'm not afraid of pain," Keriya boasted. That was a lie, but she was more than willing to brave pain in order to gain power.

"Very well." Shivnath raised her right paw and drew her claws through the air. A rip in the void appeared, as if she was tearing the fabric of space itself. It led away into some unknown place: a world beyond worlds, outside of time and beyond comprehension. From this opening, a shimmering purple vapor misted toward Keriya. It settled on her skin, cold and damp, and soaked into her.

For one wonderful instant her body surged with energy. Magic, sweet and delicious, lived within every fiber of her being. It wormed its way through her veins until it burned her from her skin to her core. She felt she might explode from the sheer volume of power coursing through her. Though she was already dead, she feared this would destroy whatever was left of her—her soul, as Shivnath had called it.

But the feeling faded, and she remained intact. The rip in the void shrank to nothing, mending itself neatly. All that was left of the pain was a memory and an itchy feeling in Keriya's eyes.

She blinked and rubbed them until they watered.

"It is done," whispered Shivnath. "Time for you to return to your world."

Keriya stared down at herself. Though she didn't feel any different, she knew somewhere deep within her a great power was waiting to be set free.

A sphere of light faded up before her and a shoreline swam into view within its depths. A small figure lay on the beach, bedraggled and limp. Keriya recognized it as her own body and her stomach twisted. She wanted to live again, to leave the darkness of death far behind.

The light grew, swirling around her and wrapping her in white-gold tendrils. Before it engulfed her, Keriya looked up at the dragon god. Her heart was overflowing with things she wanted to say, but all she could manage was, "Thank you, Shivnath."

Shivnath tilted her head. "Thank *you*, Keriya."

Keriya awoke to the kiss of a soft breeze upon her cheek. Rolling over, she pushed herself up on her elbows and gazed around, blinking against the brightness. She was alive again, back on the sandy beach! The sun had never felt so warm, the air had never been so fresh, and her world had never been so beautiful.

The joy of being alive was quashed at once by anxiety. Now she had to make good on her end of the bargain. She had to go to Allentria, find Necrovar and . . . what? Kill him? Shivnath had been vague on the details.

Thinking about it, she almost laughed. If she were the Elders, she'd lock herself up for being crazy. She must have passed out in the sea and washed ashore. Maybe it had all been a dream.

"Obviously it was a dream," she muttered, getting up and trudging toward a tidal pool. She knelt on a barnacle-speckled rock and leaned over to splash water onto her face.

Then she froze.

"My eyes!"

Her reflection floated on the surface of the pool, above the rocks and algae, but her eyes were no longer gray. They had turned a vibrant shade of purple. She tilted her head this way and that, clutching at her cheeks. The eyes flashed blood-red when they caught the light, making her look like a monster.

This would solidify the worst of the Aerians' suspicions. They would banish her. They might even kill her. Nobody had been accused of witchcraft in almost ten cycles, but she remembered the public execution of the last woman who'd been found guilty of consorting with evil spirits. Her screams still sometimes found their way into Keriya's nightmares.

Keriya desperately squeezed her eyes shut, then opened them again. They were still purple. The same shade of purple as Shivnath's slitted pupils.

It hadn't been a dream. Everything had been real. Her shaking hands strayed from her face to her chest. She placed them over her heart, as if trying to sense the magic that was locked away inside her. She couldn't feel it, but knowing it was there gave her courage.

She was going to become a hero. She was going to do as Shivnath had asked.

She would have to kill Necrovar.

CHAPTER FOUR

WITCH HUNT

"The eyes betray the soul."
~ Moorfainian Proverb

Roxanne Fleuridae gathered her dark, wavy hair into an elegant twist and secured it with a ribbon. She pulled on her finest green dress and leggings, which complemented her hazel eyes and hugged her slender form. Finally, she crushed some rose petals in a bowl and dabbed a bit of the paste on the creamy brown skin of her wrists. She was ready for the Ceremony of Names.

The ceremony began at moonrise, however, and it wasn't even sun-high yet. She had ample time to spare but was too nervous to sit around and wait. She needed a distraction.

Since her father was meeting with the other Elders, she was free to leave her hut. She walked through the village in a trancelike state and ended up on the grassy plateau where the Ceremony of Choice began.

She'd returned from the Felwood last night, but she hadn't received a sign. No dreams had come to her. No visions had gripped her. She didn't know what that meant, and it terrified her. People who didn't receive signs didn't have futures in Aeria.

She would have to lie. She'd make up a story to tell Erasmus. The Healer interpreted the signs the worthy children received and named them accordingly. Surely she could come up with something that would earn her a good trade. She'd hoped to be named a Hunter, but now she would settle on almost anything, so long as she didn't end up a Lower.

"Roxanne?"

She jumped and looked around. Sitting by the head of the forest footpath was a small, scrawny-looking boy with scruffy brown hair and an overlarge nose. His drab garments, almost the same shade as his fallow skin, were threadbare and poorly made.

"Oh!" she said. "Flint, isn't it?"

"Fletcher, actually." He offered a smile as he stood and approached her. "What are you doing all the way out here?"

"I can take a walk if I like," she snapped. "What about you? You're not allowed up here, either."

"I was waiting for Keriya. She'll automatically be named a Lower if she doesn't return before moonrise tonight."

Roxanne raised one of her finely sculpted eyebrows and stared down at him. She recognized him now—he was one of the Earengale boys. He got picked on almost as much as Nameless, for his magic was so weak he could barely use it.

"I wouldn't bother," Roxanne scoffed. "She's probably dead." Fletcher didn't respond, though it was clear the same thought had crossed his mind.

Roxanne started to head back to town since she didn't feel like talking. To her irritation, Fletcher followed, trotting after her like a little lost sheep.

"Where are you going?"

"Home," she said curtly, though home was the last place she wanted to be. She paused at the crest of the hill to let Fletcher go his own way. Instead he hovered by her side.

"What do you want?" she moaned.

"Nothing," he said, his dark eyes going wide. "I thought we were leaving."

"*I* was leaving," she clarified pointedly. If her father saw her consorting with the likes of Fletcher, she'd be in trouble. "So if you'll excuse me, I . . ."

She trailed off, and Fletcher scrunched up his nose in confusion. "What's wrong?"

Roxanne pointed over his shoulder. She couldn't believe it. There, limping out of the Felwood, was Keriya Nameless.

Fletcher gasped and ran toward his friend. Roxanne followed out of sheer curiosity. Truth be told, she was shocked the crippled girl had survived.

"You're alright," Fletcher cried.

Keriya's arms were spread wide to embrace Fletcher, but he slowed to a halt just before he reached her. Roxanne stopped when she was a few heights away from them, because even from that distance it was evident that Keriya was *not* alright.

"What happened to your eyes?" whispered Roxanne. She wasn't easily rattled, but she felt snakes of fear coiling in her gut as she stared at Keriya aghast.

"That's a bad omen if ever I saw one," said Fletcher.

"I know," said Keriya. It seemed to be an effort for her to keep her head up instead of dropping it in shame, or perhaps burying it in the sand. Those haunting, ethereal eyes flicked to Roxanne. "Why are you here?"

Without bothering to reply, Roxanne spun on her heel and walked away. This wasn't her business, and she didn't want to be anywhere near Keriya when the Elders saw her changed appearance.

She hurried downhill to the path that led to the village green, sifting through every story she knew about the evil forest spirits. She'd never believed them to be more than stories, but was starting to reconsider. Eyes didn't just change color like that, not unless witchcraft was involved.

She was so absorbed in her thoughts that she almost collided with Penelope Sanvire, who was strolling along the sandy trail that encircled Aeria and Lake Sanara.

"Watch where you're going," Penelope complained. Roxanne tried to push past her, but Penelope shifted her weight to block Roxanne's way. "Why were you up there?" she asked, nodding toward the sacred hilltop.

"I wasn't," Roxanne replied, a little too quickly.

A grin pulled at Penelope's pouty lips. "Wait until my father hears you were trespassing on ceremonial grounds."

"I wasn't trespassing!"

"I bet you were practicing magic again. You know it's forbidden outside of school until you're named, and I heard the Elders say they'd name you a Lower if you misbehaved one more time," said Penelope, idly twirling a finger through her hair.

"I wasn't using magic. Even if I was, you couldn't prove it."

As soon as the words were out of her mouth, Roxanne knew she'd made a mistake. Penelope began backing toward the plateau. "Of course I could! After all, you made such a mess up there. My father will be furious. And I can't even imagine how angry *your* father will be when he sees what you did."

Almost involuntarily, Roxanne's hands clenched into fists and she used her mind to reach for her magic, mentally embracing the soft, greenish glow of the power source within her. She'd fed a strand of energy out from her body and into the ground before she got her anger under control. If she actually did use magic, the Elders would punish her and Penelope would win. Her only hope was to put as much distance as possible between herself and that hilltop.

Reluctantly, Roxanne loosened her mental grip on the spell and felt the energy seep back into the depths of her consciousness. Penelope had almost reached the plateau, and whatever happened next wouldn't be pretty. Heedless of impropriety, Roxanne hiked up her skirt and ran.

She barely made it three heights before a resounding shriek echoed across the valley.

"Witch!"

Keriya didn't know how Penelope had discovered she was back, but it hardly mattered. Now more people were coming up to the ceremonial hill to find out who was screaming. As soon as they saw Keriya's eyes, they took up Penelope's cry.

"Witch! Witch!"

"What's all this racket?" Holden Sanvire blustered as he elbowed his way to the front of the rabble. His jaw dropped when he caught sight of Keriya. "You! Where did you come from?"

"The forest."

"Don't you take that tone with me," he said, glaring at her. Keriya glared right back until a horrified look crept across his face. "What did you do to your eyes?"

"I didn't do anything. Shivnath did this to me!"

The hilltop fell silent at her pronouncement.

"How dare you take Shivnath's name in vain," Sanvire spat.

"This isn't Shivnath's doing—this is a clear mark of evil," declared Elder Remaine, who'd joined the fray. "I always knew there was something wrong with her. I'll bet she caused our livestock to die during the last harvest. Remember the disease that spread through our sheep?"

Cries of agreement met his words and more people spoke up, blaming Keriya for everything from failed crops to stillborn children. Her heart skipped a few crucial beats when she heard someone call for her death.

She leaned toward Fletcher and breathed, "We need to leave." She attempted to nudge him toward the cover of the trees, but he edged away from her.

"Keriya, I don't think—"

"They're trying to escape," shrieked Penelope, tugging on her father's sleeve to get his attention. "Don't let them get away!"

"Run!" Keriya shouted. This time, Fletcher listened. The two of them pelted into the forest, chased by angry shouts and threats of violence.

They ran until they reached Erasmus' hut. Keriya burst through the back door and grabbed a satchel from a hook on the wall. She began stuffing it with everything that would fit: wool mittens, a hunk of half-eaten sheep cheese, a loaf of bread.

"What are you doing?" Fletcher asked timidly.

"Packing." She turned to him and he cowered away. It wasn't his usual cower either — he was genuinely frightened. A painful lump formed in Keriya's throat. "You really believe I'm a witch, don't you?"

Fletcher said nothing, though at least he had the grace to look ashamed.

"Fine," she said, mortified to find hot tears clouding her vision. She refused to cry. She wouldn't show weakness. "Fine, I am a witch. So you better get out of here!"

"Shivnath couldn't have changed your eyes." It sounded like Fletcher was trying to convince himself the dragon god wouldn't have done such a thing. Did he think Keriya would lie about that? Or did he just think Shivnath would never appear to someone like her?

"Even if she did, it wouldn't matter to you or anyone else. Now leave."

Fletcher crept toward the front door. Keriya watched him go, her arms folded and her face set in a scowl. He opened his mouth to say something, then seemed to think better of it. He slipped outside, and just like that, he was gone.

A wave of sorrow crashed upon Keriya, so heavy it almost brought her to her knees. Well, who needed him, anyway? Not her. Not if he was going to treat her like she was a witch! She'd become a hero and have a great life without him.

The front door opened and closed once more, and there was Erasmus. He studied her for a few silent moments, his sharp gaze taking in her awful eyes and half-packed satchel.

"You're leaving, I presume?"

Keriya could no longer pretend to be strong. The tears she'd been holding back burst forth. "I d-didn't think it would hurt so much," she sobbed. She wasn't sure if she was referring to the villagers' reactions, or just Fletcher's.

Erasmus said nothing; emotions weren't his strong suit. Keriya wished she could be more like him. Tears would do her no good.

The door burst open yet again and Fletcher darted back

inside, followed by Roxanne Fleuridae. Choking on a hiccup of surprise, Keriya hastily scrubbed the incriminating wetness from her cheeks.

"What's the meaning of this?" Erasmus asked Roxanne.

"Penelope told everyone we were possessed by evil spirits!" Her long, shiny hair had fallen out of its twist. It hung around her face, obscuring her features as she glowered at Keriya. "You go out there and tell them I was in the wrong place at the wrong time. Tell them I'm not associated with you!"

"The whole world is after us," Fletcher wheezed. "They're looking for you too, Keriya. I've never seen them like this. I think they mean to kill you."

Erasmus' expression hardened. "Keriya, you must go."

"What about us?" said Fletcher.

"What about you?" Keriya had meant to inject more icy venom into her question, but it came out sounding like a plea instead.

"Erasmus, I can't go back there," said Roxanne. "They're so crazy they'll believe anything right now. My father's with them, and . . . I don't think I'm safe anymore." She looked back at Keriya. "I need help."

The heartfelt request made Keriya's anger melt away. "You can come with me."

The instant she said it, Keriya felt as though a weight had been lifted from her shoulders. Fletcher wrinkled his nose doubtfully, but had no time to ask questions. The first sounds of an angry mob reached the hut. The villagers were approaching.

"Go," barked Erasmus, ushering them to the back door. As they stumbled out and started for the woods, Keriya glanced over her shoulder. The old Healer raised a solemn hand in farewell.

Whatever was to come, she was certain she would never see him again.

CHAPTER FIVE

INTO THE MOUNTAINS
"A journey across the world begins with a single step."
~ Elven Proverb

"This is all your fault!"

"*My* fault?" said Fletcher. "How is it my fault?"

"It's your fault for getting me tangled up in your mess," Roxanne retorted in an angry whisper. Fletcher decided to ignore her. If she was dead-set on blaming him for everything, he wasn't going to waste his breath arguing.

"Quiet," Keriya hissed. The three of them were hidden in a copse of briars, peering out at the green between the Felwood and the Aerians' huts.

"Why can't we stay in the forest?" Fletcher didn't like Keriya's plan of crossing Shivnath's mountains. Stepping foot in the dragon god's territory was a sin. Besides, they'd have a better chance of survival in the Felwood, even factoring in the evil spirits.

"Because no one will follow us into the mountains."

"There's a reason for that," Roxanne snapped. "We'll die if we go up there!"

"You're free to leave any time," Keriya snapped back. "Go on. Have fun explaining yourself to the Elders."

"Shh!" Fletcher held up a hand to silence the girls and pointed toward the green. Someone was emerging from behind a nearby hut. He squinted at the figure and let out a sigh of relief.

"Asher! Over here!" he whispered, poking his head out from the bushes and waving to his younger brother.

Asher turned, but did not approach. In fact, he started

backing away. It was only then that Fletcher noticed the heavy wooden club in his sibling's hand.

"I've found them," Asher yelled, brandishing his weapon. "I've found them! Elders, to me!"

Fletcher gaped at Asher, unable to believe what he was hearing. Answering shouts echoed across the valley.

"You better surrender before you bring any more shame on our family," said Asher.

"Why are you doing this?" Fletcher asked in a thin voice, the words a paltry reflection of the tumult he was feeling inside. "I'm your brother."

Asher's face clouded. "I don't have a brother anymore."

A dull roar filled Fletcher's ears and he swayed on the spot. If he looked at things objectively, he could understand why Asher would choose to denounce him. Handing him over to the Elders would spare the other Earengales from sharing in his punishment.

Understanding didn't take the pain away.

Fletcher was jolted back to reality when Keriya grabbed his hand and pulled him into the open. Asher tried to intercept them, but dropped his club and shrank away as soon as he caught sight of her red-violet gaze. Pressing her advantage, Keriya ran.

Fletcher allowed himself to be dragged off, feeling numb. He'd always been bullied, and his relatives had been in the lowest social caste since his father's death, but at least he'd had his family to rely on. Now he was alone, adrift in a river, slowly sinking. His only brother had disowned him.

The outcast children wove through clustered huts toward the Lowers' settlement, which lined the base of Shivnath's mountains. The slave quarters were separated from Aeria by a muddy ditch surrounded by huge, thorny bushes. There was a sorry excuse for a bridge—no more than a couple of rotting logs—that led to an ill-kempt path through the thicket. They leapt over it and raced down the overgrown trail.

Fletcher coughed and panted as he struggled to keep up.

The only thing that kept his legs pumping was a deep-rooted fear of what would happen if he slowed down and the girls left him behind.

They came to a halt when they emerged from the bushes onto a muddy, weed-ridden plain. Decrepit huts were scattered across the open land. Some sagged against each other, each preventing the other from falling down. Rag-clothed people with sunken eyes milled about, all of them filthy. Fletcher had never been here before. Lowers were slaves, yes, but he couldn't believe they were forced to live this way.

"That's where we have to go," said Keriya, pointing to the only passable section of the mountain cliffs. About thirty heights up, dirt turned to gravel, grass turned to rock, and trees became gnarled and twisted roots, clinging to the ground in whatever way they could manage. Fletcher craned his neck back to scan the soaring peaks that stretched as far as the eye could see. The tops of Shivnath's mountains were lost in cloud before they even began to taper to a point.

"I don't like this," said Roxanne. "Leaving now means leaving forever. It's self-banishment. Going up there . . . it's mad."

"You think your chances are any better here?" asked Keriya.

"They're better than yours!"

Keriya's face twitched in anger. She shot a questioning glance at Fletcher, as if to ask if he was backing out, too.

He didn't know. His chances of survival were marginally better than hers, though that wasn't saying much — but it was too late to go back. Behind them, a mass of angry people flooded into the settlement. The crowd was led by a livid Elder Fleuridae.

Roxanne blanched at the sight of her father and fled before him. Fletcher tore after her on instinct. They passed the last of the Lowers' huts and entered Shivnath's domain. He was in forbidden territory now. He began to wonder if he'd have a private execution or if it would be made into a public affair, complete with festivities and a feast.

Enraged shouts carried up to them, but as Keriya had

predicted, their pursuers stopped before setting foot on the slope. Ahead, Fletcher could see the abrupt shift from dirt to rock. He was nearly there.

Crash!

He barely managed to fling himself out of the way as a large boulder careened toward him. The villagers had resorted to using magic to stop them. Fletcher scrambled up and kept running, certain his doom was upon him.

"Can't you do something?" he asked Roxanne, gasping for breath. "Use your magic!"

"I'm already doing everything I can," she said, her face shining with sweat. Fletcher squinted at her, as if hoping to see a spell. It was no good, of course—people with strong magic could sometimes see the strands of energy that created spells, but Fletcher had trouble performing even the simplest of magical feats.

Another rock tumbled across his path. It might have crushed him had Roxanne not diverted the boulder with a graceful gesture, forcing it to bounce away into the trees.

"You could consider helping, you know," she said through gritted teeth.

"I'm not strong enough. Besides, my brother's down there!"

"Your idiot brother's probably the one who threw the rock at you in the first place. Do it if you want to live!"

A lifetime of strict discipline and punishment had cowed Fletcher. Children were forbidden from using their powers outside of their lessons, and to commit violence with magic was a crime punishable by death. No matter the danger he was in, he couldn't strike against them—not even against Asher, who had so easily betrayed him.

Roxanne cried out and fell. Someone had conjured vines from the ground and twisted them around her ankles to restrain her.

There were two kinds of magic: manipulation and creation. Manipulation was the easier of the two, since it made use of already-existing materials. Creation required much more power—and Fletcher was certain there were no vines living naturally beneath the boulders. Whoever had done this was dangerous.

"Roxanne! So help me Shivnath, if you don't come back down here, I'll name you a Lower myself!"

It was Elder Fleuridae. Most of the Aerians were hesitant about pursuing them into the mountains, but not him. Roxanne struggled against his vines like a moth in a spider's web as he clambered toward her.

"Do not disobey me," he screamed. "You will do as I command!"

Tears formed in her lovely eyes. "Not anymore," she whispered, and the vines snapped, falling away from her in shreds. She pushed herself to her feet and made a sweeping gesture in the air. More boulders crashed down around them and the men below scattered, trying to escape the avalanche she had caused.

Elder Fleuridae was strong, but it appeared Roxanne was stronger. Amid the storm of rocks and dust, Fletcher caught a glimpse of him attempting to stop the earthen deluge. He held fast against Roxanne's spell for a moment, arms outstretched and face red with the strain of rerouting the tumbling stones; but ultimately he, like the rest of the Aerians, fled before the force of nature his daughter had conjured.

Shying away from a rock that tumbled too close for comfort, Fletcher limped onwards, crossing from gravelly dirt and pebbles onto hard granite. Keriya, who had been up ahead, ran back to help him. She led him to a small opening in the mountainside, waving Roxanne over. Together, the three of them crawled to the back of the small cave and huddled in a corner.

They hid until the last of the tremors stopped and the angry voices died away. Fletcher rocked back and forth rhythmically. He tormented himself by dwelling on Asher's final words to him, repeating them over and over in his head.

When the light began to fade, Keriya and Roxanne left the

cave. Fletcher, who didn't want to be alone, plucked up the strength to follow.

"All clear," whispered Keriya, scanning the deserted slope and the Lowers' settlement, which was as dark and still as a grave. "Let's go."

"Go where?" said Roxanne.

"We should keep climbing. The villagers might decide they hate us enough to follow us into the mountains. And in my case, they've always managed to dredge up a little extra hatred."

"You missed my point," said Roxanne. "There's nowhere to go. Shivnath doesn't want us up here."

"Yes she does!"

"You think you know what Shivnath wants? You're as crazy as everyone says!" Roxanne whirled downhill, then stopped. Fletcher knew she was thinking of what she'd done to her father. There was no going back after that.

"Helkryvt take it all," she cursed, kicking a stone in frustration.

"Our only hope is to leave," said Keriya. "Once we're over the mountains —"

"There is nothing beyond the mountains," interrupted Roxanne. "It's a wasteland and we're all going to die!"

"Are you a Hunter or aren't you, Roxanne?" said Fletcher, speaking for the first time since they'd entered the cave. "I think we can survive if we try."

He didn't really think that. He *hoped* it, because moving on was better than waiting for the Elders to get them. He hoped there was something on the other side of the mountains, because the alternative was frightening and grim.

"I'm not a Hunter because I haven't been named yet," said Roxanne. "How do you even know about that?"

Fletcher shrugged. "I pay attention. I know lots of things. You want to be the first female Hunter. You think Cole Ballebrus is good-looking. You've always dreamed of being free of your father."

He half expected her to get angry and yell at him, but she

didn't.

"Free of my father," she repeated softly.

Wind whistled through the peaks and raced down the slope. Fletcher wrapped his thin arms around himself. His warm-weather clothes did little to ward off the chill of the impending night.

Finally, Roxanne voiced aloud what Fletcher feared most: "What if we don't make it?"

"Would you rather go back?" said Keriya. Fletcher closed his eyes, unwilling to think about either of his options. "We can sleep here tonight, but we need to leave at dawn."

He nodded. His shock was wearing off and soon he would vomit, scream, possibly even cry. But everything would turn out alright in the end. They would survive if they stuck together.

By their third sun of climbing, he was not so optimistic.

Fletcher estimated that they'd ascended at least ten thousand hands from Aeria. The air was thinner up here, and colder. It hurt his lungs and nose when he drew breath. He felt like he was always on the verge of being sick.

He lurched over the edge of a large rock and fell flat on his stomach. "I hate this," he whined to the girls, who were waiting for him.

Keriya patted his shoulder reassuringly as she helped him stand. "It's not that bad. We're nearly there, see?" She pointed directly up at the summit, which was wrapped in a swath of cloud.

"Are you joking?" said Roxanne. "Do you think any part of this situation is funny?"

"I'm just trying to lighten the mood," Keriya retorted.

"Well, stop it."

"Give her a break, Roxanne," said Fletcher. He didn't think he could stand listening to them argue again.

Keriya flashed Fletcher a thin smile. He tried to smile back, but as soon as he met her gaze, now so foreign and frightening, he had to look away.

They stopped when it grew too dark to continue and took turns drinking from a trickle of glacial runoff. Roxanne put her hand over a patch of gravelly dirt, and green buds magically sprouted beneath her fingertips. She completed her spell and yanked on the sprouts, producing three grubby carrots.

"Is this it?" Keriya asked, as Roxanne handed her one.

"I'm sorry, are these not good enough? Let me use the last of my energy growing an apple tree for the two of you. And no," Roxanne added, noticing the look of longing that crossed Fletcher's face, "I can't do that. A carrot will grow in three moons on its own—it's a relatively low-energy spell. The amount of energy I'd have to use to grow a tree would kill me right now. You ought to know at least that much about magic."

Fletcher's cheeks grew hot. He *hadn't* known that. Using magic was an innate ability, like breathing, but using it well was a precise and exacting science. His schoolteachers had never taught him anything beyond the most basic manipulation spells, like moving pebbles back and forth. Even Keriya knew more than he did, for she studied magic obsessively.

The reminder of his shortcomings would have upset him at any other time, but by this point he was too exhausted to care. Besides, Roxanne was right. They ought to be grateful for what she was offering.

As they settled down, Roxanne's mood worsened and she complained of a headache. In fact, she complained about a lot of things.

"I think I can see where we stayed last night," she groused. "We've hardly moved."

"I wish I had different magic," Fletcher commented absently, staring off into space. "Maybe some kind of powers that could let me make a fire."

"There's no such thing as fire-magic," said Roxanne. "And a fat lot of good that kind of talk will do you."

"Don't take it out on us if you're feeling sorry for yourself," said Keriya.

"Oh, I haven't even begun to feel sorry for myself. Don't get me started on what a bad decision this was, because I could go on all night."

Another argument was imminent, and Fletcher didn't have the strength to mediate between them anymore. He stuffed his fingers in his ears, trying to blot out their voices.

"If it was such a huge mistake, why did you come?"

"My father would have killed me if I'd gone back. There was no choice!"

"There is always a choice," Keriya countered authoritatively, crossing her arms and sticking her nose in the air. "Go back now if you're so unhappy."

"Maybe I will!" And with that, Roxanne stood and stormed off.

"Great," said Fletcher. "You couldn't be nice; you had to drive her away. Now we'll die up here! She's the only one of us who can use magic properly."

"Heroes don't need help. I'll get us over the mountains by myself."

"Keriya, stop! There's nothing out there. We're alone. We left our home, our families . . ." He trailed off, breathing heavily, suffocated by hopelessness. Another panic attack. This would be his fourth since leaving. "We can never go back. We'll never see them again."

"Why are you upset? You didn't even like your family."

"But I loved them," he cried, shocked that she could be so insensitive. Keriya stared at him blankly, her awful eyes catching reflections of phantom lights. She just didn't understand what being part of a family meant.

"I'm sorry," she said.

Fletcher could tell by her tone that she didn't mean it.

CHAPTER SIX

ARGOS MOOR

"Come not between the dragon and her wrath."
~ *Rheenaraion Proverb*

Roxanne stomped through a patch of loose pebbles. *Stupid Keriya Nameless,* she fumed to herself. *What choice did she think I had?*

She'd had to choose between climbing to her almost certain death or staying in Aeria with a mob of raving villagers and her father—some great choice that was. Though it *had* been a choice. She had gone into the mountains willingly. That said something.

Look on the bright side, Roxanne thought, sitting on a rock and massaging her temples to ease the headache that had been plaguing her. *He can't hurt me anymore.* Running from her father was the first choice she'd ever made alone. Whether it had been right or wrong didn't matter; it had been hers.

That revelation calmed her, and she decided she'd return to the campsite. Putting up with Keriya was better than braving the mountains on her own.

She forced herself to stand, and a wave of dizziness overtook her. "Get a grip," she told herself, swaying on the spot. This was just a side effect of the altitude and dehydration. It was a wonder she hadn't gotten sick sooner.

As Roxanne ventured back to camp, she lost her balance and fell to her knees. Her vision went black, and for the briefest of moments she imagined she was high in the air, circling the rugged peaks.

The image vanished as quickly as it had come, leaving her breathless and shivering. She stared down at her body, as if making sure she was herself. Fine time to start seeing things. Why couldn't that have happened during the Ceremony of Choice?

"It's okay. Just a hallucination," she whispered, though if she was sick enough to hallucinate, that was hardly comforting. Trying to shake the horrible, nagging idea that her vision had been real, she hurried back to Keriya and Fletcher.

"We should find cover," she said when she reached them.

"Why?" asked Fletcher. "What's wrong?"

"I thought I saw something out there." She gestured vaguely behind her while scanning the area for a place to hide.

"Something like what?" said Keriya.

"Does it matter?" barked Roxanne. "Everything in these mountains is dangerous. If it's not a wolfcat, it'll be a snow bear, or a wild boar, or —"

She was interrupted by a far-off grating screech. It was a sound every Aerian knew and feared.

"Or a drachvold," Fletcher finished, shrinking in upon himself. Roxanne's stomach twisted in a knot. The fear that her hallucination had been more than a mere hallucination resurfaced.

They scrambled beneath a rocky overhang just as the thud of the creature's wings reached them. With another wail, it emerged through the fog. It was massive, nearly three heights long including its barbed, reedlike tail. Powerful chest muscles flexed beneath its short neck and its hind legs were curled up against its round belly. Slitted nostrils flared at the end of its stubby snout, and its bulbous yellow eyes flashed as it scanned the slope.

It passed their overhang and, for one happy moment, Roxanne believed they were safe. Then it banked and spotted them.

With a bloodcurdling cry that revealed a thick, black tongue in a toothless mouth, it circled around. Its stomach convulsed, rippling grotesquely, and it spat a sickly green liquid down upon them. Roxanne leapt into the open as the rock above her began bubbling and boiling away, melted by the drachvold's stomach acid.

She mentally embraced the mine of power within her, pulling energy from her body and directing it into the mountainside.

"Stop," Fletcher cried as she manipulated a boulder into the air. "The rocks up here are too unstable!"

To illustrate his point, the drachvold dove and landed heavily in front of them, causing loose stones to shake and tumble downhill. Roxanne ignored him and prepared to attack, but Keriya beat her to it. The pale girl rushed the monster, forcing Roxanne to drop her spell. The boulder crashed back to the ground and she felt an uncomfortable pinch in her chest as she abruptly severed her connection to her magic.

Keriya hurled something at the drachvold. Was she throwing rocks? The drachvold hissed and began retching again, ready to strike.

"No!" Roxanne screamed. She squeezed her eyes shut and threw up her hands in a vain attempt to protect herself from the spray of deadly acid.

But it didn't come.

Daring to peek through her dark lashes, Roxanne saw that through some miracle, the drachvold seemed to have choked and was unable to spit at them. With its strongest weapon disabled, it couldn't attack. It snapped its toothless jaws in a show of aggression and leapt into the air with one mighty flap of its wings. Roxanne waited until it had vanished before rounding on Keriya.

"Are you crazy?" she demanded. "You could have gotten us killed!"

"I had to do something."

"I was taking care of it," Roxanne grated. "Throwing rocks wouldn't have done any good."

"Why not? That's basically all you do with your magic, isn't it?"

"Can you two please shut up?" said Fletcher. He was

trembling all over. "We need to keep going, because I don't want to be here when it comes back!"

In a huff, Fletcher started to climb again. Keriya set off after him and Roxanne trailed in the rear. Not even a word of thanks for warning them and saving their lives. Ingrates!

It wasn't long before a fierce wind picked up and snow started to fall. The conditions were too hazardous for climbing, but if they stopped before finding stable shelter, they'd freeze to death. As Roxanne braced herself against a rock to climb over a ledge, she slipped on a patch of black ice. With a scream, she slid back downhill and smacked into a boulder.

While the rock kept her from falling to her death, the impact felt like it had broken half the bones in her body. The cold sank its agonizing claws into her at once. The sweat that had formed on her brow turned to ice, making her feverish. Somewhere far away, she heard Keriya and Fletcher calling for her.

"Over here," she managed feebly. She waited—how long, she couldn't say—crying out every now and then until they found her.

They didn't look much better than she felt. Keriya's lips were blue and her face was so white that she practically blended into the snowstorm. Fletcher had a nasty gash on his brow. He was talking, but Roxanne couldn't understand his words. There was a ringing in her ears and everything was going dark.

She closed her eyes and knew no more.

Keriya gazed hopelessly at her companions. By now they'd both succumbed to the cold. She tried to shove Fletcher's body toward a rock to protect him from the storm, but she was too weak. Fighting off sobs of despair, she huddled next to him to keep him warm. She could do this. She *had* to, but she was too frozen to move, to think, to save him.

The cold dragged her into a frigid slumber without her even realizing, and part of her believed the dreams that ran through her mind were real. First the Aerians followed her into the mountains and burned her alive for being a witch. Then she was walking across a barren plain next to a dark-haired man with strange blue eyes — a Prince Charming that Keriya had invented for herself, just like the ones in her storybooks. Next she was lying naked and beaten on the edge of a cliff, and Shivnath was standing above her, telling her she'd failed.

That last image was disturbing enough to jolt Keriya awake. She blinked as her senses slowly returned, wondering if she wasn't still dreaming. A cluster of glowing mushrooms illuminated her surroundings, revealing that she was in a small and wonderfully warm cave.

A soft noise drew her attention to the far side of the grotto. There, a few hands away, Fletcher and Roxanne lay nestled on a lush blanket of emerald moss.

"Fletcher," she gasped. "Hey! Wake up!"

Despite her best efforts to rouse him, he didn't stir. He and Roxanne appeared healthy — the injuries they'd sustained while climbing the mountain had vanished — but they remained in a deep slumber, no matter how much Keriya yelled or how hard she shook them.

This was bad. She had to get them out of here — wherever *here* was. Keriya crawled across the cave toward a narrow egress and emerged into an enormous cavern peppered with ancient stalagmites and stalactites. And there, reclining on a granite ledge, was Shivnath.

"Leaving so soon?" Her voice, deep and feminine, hummed in Keriya's chest, and her eyes pulled Keriya into their endless depths.

"Um . . . hello," said Keriya. "So, where are we this time? Not dead, right?"

"This is Argos Moor, my home. You're alive, but only because I took it upon myself to save you. I nearly broke the binding laws doing so."

"Thanks," whispered Keriya. Shivnath disregarded the gratitude.

"Your friends will be fine by tomorrow, at which time I will place you on the western side of the mountain and you will continue your quest. Bringing along an entourage was not part of our agreement," she added.

"Sorry," Keriya mumbled. "It just sort of happened."

The two stared at each other, Shivnath statuesque, Keriya fidgeting. She had a thousand questions she wanted to ask.

"I was wondering," she began awkwardly. "How am I supposed to find Necrovar?"

"The easiest way is to go to the Rift. This is the place where the threads of the spell that separates his world from ours have been torn apart. The widest section of the Rift is located in the southern part of the Fironem, atop Mount Arax," Shivnath replied.

"Okay," said Keriya. "I assume I'll have to use your magic to kill him, but I've never used magic before, so . . . how do I *do* it?"

"This is already an encroachment of the rules that bind me, so I cannot answer your question in a way that will satisfy you. All I can tell you is that wielding magic is the most natural thing in the world."

Keriya scowled. She appreciated that Shivnath had restrictions on what she was allowed to reveal, but really, how hard would it be to offer a few pointers?

"Fine, just one more question," said Keriya, sensing the god's patience was running thin. "Why did you change the color of my eyes?"

"The magic I placed within you manifests itself in strange ways. Your eyes are simply an unfortunate side effect."

"Oh." That answer was disappointingly dull.

Shivnath rose to her feet. "I have business to attend to. I will provide food and water for you, so you needn't wander while I'm gone."

"What business?" Keriya asked, trailing in Shivnath's wake as the dragon plodded toward the white light shafting through the mouth of her cave.

"That is none of your concern." Shivnath spread her wings, and the chamber was washed in green as the glow filtered through the translucent skin stretching between her bat-like fingers. She leapt into the unknown and was swallowed by the mysterious brightness beyond.

Keriya followed, but the moment she crossed the cave's threshold, the warmth vanished. She staggered backwards as a blast of icy air slapped her and the world came sharply into focus. A blizzard was raging outside, but some manner of enchantment prevented it from entering the god's lair.

She darted back into the shelter of the cave. How long would she have to wait until Shivnath returned? What could she do in the meantime? Her hobbies in Aeria had consisted of reading, studying with Erasmus, and exploring—but Shivnath had basically forbidden her to explore.

"Although she probably won't be back for a while. I could just look. I wouldn't touch anything," she explained to a nearby stalagmite. The stalagmite said nothing to dissuade her, so she squared her shoulders and headed for a tunnel that led into the depths of—what had Shivnath called her mountain?—Argos Moor.

The winding passage split about twenty heights in. Keriya peered down the left fork and saw a cave with a rock basin rising out of the ground, from which shone a cold, silver light. Though she wanted to investigate, a warmer light from the right tunnel caught her eye.

This friendlier light drew her toward it, and she rounded a bend in the passageway to discover a cavern filled with mounds of sparkling things. She stooped beside a wooden chest overflowing with gleaming treasures and picked up a round item. It was heavy and oddly soft. She'd never seen anything like it.

Keriya spotted another chest that held an assortment of books, and she raced to it at once. Disappointment filled her when she saw the books were written in strange runes. She looked through them anyway, placing her hand on each one with delicate reverence, as if simply touching them would unveil their secrets. She was rewarded when she moved one heavy tome aside and saw familiar letters on a ragged clump of vellum pages, strung together by a thin cord.

She gingerly extracted the sorry excuse for a book and leafed through it. The handwritten runes were Aerian, but the text was in the ancient tongue. Erasmus had only taught Keriya the basics of the old language, for basics were all anyone knew of it, but one passage caught her eye:

> . . . called me 'Soulstar,' for she, above all others, understood the light inside me. I had no family name, nor a land of birth to mark me; even my given name, the only remnant of my lost past, seemed unsuited in a way I could not explain. But 'Soulstar' always sounded right when she spoke it to me, befit for the great hero I had become.

"Soulstar," she repeated to herself. It felt good to read. It calmed a part of her that had been snarled with anxiety ever since she'd gone into the Felwood for the Ceremony of Choice.

Nothing else jumped out at her until she reached the end of the book, where a poem had been scratched onto the last tattered page. Some of its vocabulary was beyond her, but the first few lines were fascinating:

> Flesh into sword, bone into blade,
> Magic and blood and legend are made.
> Eternity binds only those who are dead,
> But thence from this spell shall I rise once again.

The words echoed in Keriya's head as clearly as though someone had spoken them aloud. They thrummed in her brain, pulsing like a heartbeat. Whoever the author was, he had been powerful. Powerful enough to have woven a spell to bring himself back from the dead, if she had it right. Surely he was someone who'd rivaled Shivnath in terms of magical strength — no wonder she'd kept his book.

Keriya shivered and carefully returned the vellum tome to its resting place.

Looking around again, she spied an arrangement of smooth rocks half-hidden near the back of the cave. They surrounded the cracked remains of an eggshell, gray with age. Could this be Shivnath's nest?

Upon closer inspection, Keriya decided the nest was too small for the god. Perhaps it belonged to another dragon. But that couldn't be; weren't all the other dragons imprisoned?

"Yes. They were imprisoned in the Etherworld, along with Necrovar."

Keriya yelped and spun around. Shivnath loomed behind her, stone-faced but seemingly unsurprised to find Keriya there.

"You're back," Keriya stammered. "I'm sorry. I just wanted to know more about you. I had some questions."

"Such as?"

"Well, for instance . . . how come you weren't imprisoned, too?"

"Because I am the Allentrian guardian of earthmagic. I am not a creature of light, as the dragons are. When Necrovar was banished from Selaras, a magic equal and opposite to his had to be removed to preserve the balance. Thus, when the Shadow Lord's legions were imprisoned, so the dragons were, too."

For some reason, Keriya felt sadness tug at her heart. Was it for the dragons, who were trapped in a different world forever? Or was it for Shivnath, who was trapped in this world alone?

"Was there anything else you wanted to ask?" Shivnath prompted in an ominously pleasant voice.

Keriya was wise enough to shake her head. "No. I didn't mean . . . I'm sorry I snooped around."

"I expected nothing less," was the reply.

Keriya left the treasure cavern with as much humility as she could muster, but she couldn't resist looking back one last time before entering the tunnel that led to the mossy grotto.

Shivnath was no longer paying attention to her. She was staring down at the nest, her face half-bathed in shadow, a small, sad smile fading from her lips.

CHAPTER SEVEN

ALLENTRIA

"Derived from 'allentas', meaning land, and 'riaer', meaning perfect."
~ **Etymology of the Language of Power**

The next morning, Keriya found herself back outside. It seemed Shivnath had taken care of everything. The dragon god had deposited them on the western face of Argos Moor, and Keriya suspected she'd tampered with Fletcher and Roxanne's memories. Both had vague recollections of the snowstorm, but neither could quite say when it had happened. They didn't know how they'd gotten to the far side of the mountain, yet they didn't question the suspicious nature of their good fortune.

"I think it's altitude sickness," Fletcher said as they began their descent. "I heard it can cause memory loss."

"Mm," said Keriya, and left it at that.

It was slow going, for they were soon lost in a thick mist. Their path—such as it was—led through a narrow cave. They squeezed through in single-file, but when they emerged into the open once more, they were met with the edge of a cliff.

Roxanne let out a growl and kicked a stone off the precipice. It hurtled downwards, disturbing the eerie still of the fog.

"Where do we go from here?" asked Keriya. The drop-off stretched into the murky brume for as far as she could see. There was no clear way to continue.

"There's nowhere to go," said Roxanne. "It's just a great big wasteland!"

"Then what do we do?" whispered Fletcher. His question went unanswered, ringing in the silence and burrowing into Keriya's chest. Should she try to return to Aeria, or should she just hurl herself into the trench and be done with it?

She sank down and put her head in her hands. Some hero she was.

Night descended upon them. Roxanne paced paths into the rock until exhaustion claimed her and she collapsed onto a flat stone. Fletcher huddled in the shadows as far from the edge of the cliff as he could get. While they fell asleep, Keriya stayed up, staring into the fog.

"Show me the way, Shivnath," she murmured, lying back to gaze at the sky. The higher mists had thinned, allowing a few brave stars to peek through. A breeze meandered up the slope, sweeping the remaining clouds away.

But no hint of a sign was forthcoming.

Eventually the heavens faded from black to purple, then to gold as the sun rose behind the mountains. Keriya still didn't feel tired—she just felt empty. She rolled onto her side to look at her new nemesis, the chasm.

"Fletcher," she gasped, standing so quickly that she nearly tripped. "Fletch, get up!"

Fletcher groaned behind her, complaining of too little sleep. There was a sharp intake of breath and she heard him scramble to his feet. He joined her, gawking at the slope below. Through the fading fog, a meadow of flowers was visible at the foot of the mountain, extending into the rolling foothills of an emerald valley. To the left, a verdant forest crawled across the horizon. And to the right . . .

"Holy Shivnath," said Roxanne, sitting up and rubbing her eyes in disbelief.

"A village," Fletcher breathed. "There are people here!"

This was it. Allentria. It was real. Gazing down upon it, Keriya felt as though she were coming back to life all over again: the air was fresher, the sun was brighter, and the grass was greener than in Aeria. The world on this side of the mountains was a far better place to be.

The three of them laughed and screamed. Now that the fog had lifted, Keriya managed to spot a place where they could safely descend. They dashed along the lip of the cliff to a steep pass, and clambered down at a speed that wasn't safe at all. They careened toward the flower field, jumping from boulder to boulder in their haste to reach it. Finally they were out of those accursed stones.

"My magic feels so strong here," Roxanne exclaimed. Her cheeks flushed with newfound joy and she crouched amidst the blossoms to place her hands on the ground. A sapling burst forth beneath her fingers, growing rapidly.

"Stop! You'll use up all your energy," Fletcher gasped, but Roxanne had already created an apple tree as tall as herself, its limbs dotted with small, ripe fruits.

"I hardly felt a thing," she said, gazing at her creation in awe. She shook her head and gestured to the tree with a disbelieving grin.

The three of them converged upon the apples. The fruits were small and a little bland, but to Keriya they seemed like the best food she'd ever tasted. Chewing contentedly, she turned to take in the view of the countryside. The flowers, the vine-coated cliffs of Argos Moor, and—

She choked on a bite of apple and elbowed Fletcher in the ribs.

"What was that for?" he grumbled, massaging his side.

Keriya pointed. There, trundling along a dirt path just a few heights away from them, was a man. He sat at the prow of a covered wagon pulled by a large, spindly-legged animal.

Fletcher's eyes widened. He nudged Roxanne to get her attention, then glanced back at Keriya apprehensively. But Keriya had already taken her first step toward the Allentrian man.

"Hey! Over here," she cried. She began running toward him, beaming and waving her arms. The animal flattened its ears to its skull and let out a braying noise as she approached, rearing up and away from her.

"Whoa, Winni!" The man quieted the animal by pulling on strings attached to its mouth. He rounded on Keriya angrily.

"What the blood do you think you're doin'?" He had a frock

of wild, dark hair that hung down to his shoulders and one sharp, blue eye—the other was covered by a black patch tied around his head. The material of his clothes was like nothing they'd had in Aeria. He wore a long vest over a dirty white shirt, and his loose pants were bunched up over the turned-down tops of knee-high boots.

"Trying to attack honest, unsuspecting folks and rob them of their derlei?" His accent was odd, and his gruff, no-nonsense voice held a hint of command, as if he was used to being obeyed.

"Uh . . . no," said Keriya, as Fletcher and Roxanne ran up behind her.

"You lot scroungers, then? You're awful far from city traffic. Ain't able to beg for much all the way out here."

"No," Keriya repeated. "I was wondering . . ." But she hadn't been wondering anything. She had just wanted to speak to a real, live Allentrian.

Suddenly it hit her. "Maybe we could come with you? South, if you're going that way?"

"Hmph! Well, I'll give you a ride as long as you can pay. Where you headed?"

"South."

"Yeah, I got that," he said snidely. "What town?"

"Um," said Keriya, wracking her brain to remember what Shivnath had told her about finding Necrovar. "The Fironem?" She noticed Fletcher and Roxanne both cast suspicious looks in her direction.

"Hah! I ain't goin' that far. I can get you to Senteir for five silver derlei each. Reckon you can hitch a ride downstate from there with a trader or merchant or whatnot. They'll all be in town for the solstice festival, of course."

"Of course," said Keriya, though she'd hardly understood a word he said.

"So, you got names?" he asked, glaring around at them.

"Roxanne Fleuridae."

"I'm Fletcher Earengale. Pleased to meet you, Elder."

"Elder? Whaddya think I am, a bleedin' elf?" The man

turned his eye upon Keriya. "What about you?"

"Keriya Na—" She cut herself off. Here, she didn't have to be nameless. Nobody knew her past and she was free to create her own future. The words from Shivnath's book swam back to her, and she hesitated only a moment before issuing a firm response. "Keriya Soulstar."

Roxanne let out a rude snort and Fletcher scrunched his nose in a skeptical expression. Keriya's cheeks flushed, but she held her head high. 'Soulstar' sounded right to her, just like it had to the book's unknown author. Keriya Soulstar, Allentrian Hero.

"Soulstar? What the blood is that? You even from the Smarlands?" The man didn't wait for her to answer. "Look, I got places to be. You want a ride or not?"

"Yes," Keriya said hastily.

"Then we're in business. If you wanna go all the way to Senteir it'll be nine silver derlei each, a bargain if ever I heard one. I'm bendin' myself over backwards helping you, but I s'pose that's just the sort of fellow I am. C'mon, get in. Don't dawdle."

Fletcher squinted at Keriya as they approached the man. "What?" she whispered defensively.

He raised his hands and shook his head. "Nothing."

The Allentrian was busy chattering away in the background, but he cut himself off as Keriya clambered into the wagon. He stared at her, flipping up his eyepatch to reveal a second clear blue eye. Too late, she remembered the color of her own eyes. He cleared his throat and opened his mouth. She tensed, preparing for the worst.

"Forgot my manners," he said, extending a grubby hand covered by a fingerless glove. "The name's Skyriver. Cezon Skyriver."

Keriya stared at the proffered hand. Was this a strange Allentrian way of saying hello? It certainly didn't seem like a condemnation, which was what she'd been expecting. She held her own hand out, mimicking the way he held his. He huffed in exasperation.

"Never mind. Now, where'd you say you were from?"

"We're from Aeria," said Fletcher. Cezon let out a bark of laughter which he quickly turned into a cough.

"I see. Well, we'd best be off. That'll be fourteen silver derlei each." He patted the seat next to him, inviting them to join him. "So . . . Aeria, eh? What's it like over there?"

They told Cezon about the Elders, the customs and ceremonies, the dark spirits of the Felwood, the healing waters of Lake Sanara, and Shivnath's mountains. It was the mountains he was most interested in. According to Cezon, no one had crossed them in living memory.

That sun passed in a whirlwind of new sights. In answer to Keriya's incessant questions, Cezon irritably told them about Allentria—everything from the intricacies of the Imperial government to the geography of the Smarlands.

At night the moon shone bright and full. To Keriya's surprise, a second moon rose with it. In Aeria it had been hidden by the mountains because it hovered low on the western horizon. Cezon explained that the bigger satellite—the one they'd grown up with—was called the Oldmoon, and the smaller one was called the Bloodmoon because of its ghostly red hue.

The following day brought more wonders. Farmlands and forests rolled past, simple yet awe-inspiring. These trees weren't so different from the ones back home, but they were infinitely more beautiful because they were Allentrian trees.

The sun began to set again, drawing twilight behind it. Winni's hooves made a soft clip-clop sound on the hard-packed dirt road as she plodded west.

"Look!" Cezon's voice cracked through the peaceful silence. "I'll reckon you Aerians"—he said the word rather derisively, Keriya thought—"ain't never seen a proper Allentrian city before." They crested a hill and Cezon spread his hands before him. "This is Senteir."

A town sprawled across the valley below. It was smaller than Aeria, but what it lacked in size it made up for in grandeur. Colorful lights flickered in the windows of tall buildings silhouetted against the blazing sky. In Aeria, there was no such thing as building a room on top of another one. To the south, the sunset turned a shimmering lake into a pool of molten fire.

"We'll stay the night at The Olde Dragyn. Favorite inn of mine."

"What's in it?" Fletcher asked.

"No, an *inn*. Oh, don't play stupider than you look. I know you got inns and such where you're from." The three of them shook their heads blankly. Cezon growled in aggravation.

"Think they come from bloody Aeria," he muttered. "You won't have Allentrian money anyway, which is a dead sodding giveaway. I'll have to lend you some." By his tone, it was clear he would rather be melted by drachvold acid. Money was people's way of determining importance, and it was also their means of survival—and Cezon had gotten very upset when he realized the Aerians didn't have any. The villagers had always simply bartered for whatever they needed, or made things for themselves.

Cezon twitched Winni's reigns and she set off down the hill, clip-clopping toward Senteir. By the time they reached the town, Cezon had explained what an inn was.

"And you're to stay in the inn while we're here. Don't go out. Don't talk to anyone. And you," he snapped, pointing at Keriya, "don't look at anyone, neither."

Keriya bristled with indignation, but privately conceded that this was good advice.

"Here we are," he announced, pulling Winni to a stop in front of a modest building. It was marked by a wooden sign that sported a painted green dragon. Cezon hopped off the wagon and whistled sharply, and a boy in an overlarge tunic rushed out from a side alley.

"Put the wagon in the barn," said Cezon, flipping him a copper derlei coin. "And make sure Winni don't get stabled all sweaty and hungry-like."

"Yes, Sir Leafwhit," said the boy, bobbing his head and

pocketing the money. Cezon swept inside without a backward glance, and the Aerians hastened to follow him.

A swell of music hit Keriya's ears as she pushed the front door open. The inn was filled with people sitting around wooden tables, talking and laughing. In the corner, a man played a merry tune on a strange instrument.

Cezon walked toward a bar that stretched along the left side of the room. People sat before it on tall chairs and offered their mugs to serving girls for drinks. He waved, catching the eye of a rotund aproned fellow behind the counter.

"Sir Leafwhit," the man exclaimed, offering his hand. Cezon grasped it and shook up and down. Apparently, public physical contact wasn't illegal here. In fact, judging by the behavior of the inn patrons, it seemed to be celebrated. "The usual?"

"No, Master Treeskon. I got company this time. My cousins from Oseri, traveling to be apprenticed. We'll be needing two rooms."

"Make that three. I'm not sharing a room with him." Roxanne pointed at Fletcher. "Or you," she added, glaring at Cezon.

"You'll share a room and you'll be grateful you're gettin' that much," said Cezon.

"Don't you worry your pretty little head, miss. Three rooms it is, and they'll be the best that money can buy," Master Treeskon promised. Cezon groaned and gnashed his teeth, but Treeskon chose not to notice. "Names?" he inquired, opening a ledger beside him.

"This is Ava Cloudmeadow," Cezon said before anyone could speak, indicating Keriya. "And these are Armena and Joni Leafshield." He pointed to Roxanne and Fletcher.

"You'll find your rooms on the second floor, first three doors on your right," said Treeskon. "Enjoy your stay. Have a couple drinks!"

"I think not," Cezon said frostily. "They have no money. Come, children." He stalked across the bustling room, the Aerians trailing after him.

"Why'd you change our names?" said Keriya.

"Shh!" Cezon glanced around. No one was paying attention to them, but he lowered his voice conspiratorially. "Your names don't sound Allentrian, that's why. And if people find out you ain't from here, you'll be in a lot of trouble."

"Why?"

"Never you mind about that," he said, stopping at the foot of a wooden spiral staircase. "Now, I gotta meet someone, so go upstairs and stay out of sight." He didn't wait for them to answer before slipping under the stairwell into a darkened hallway.

The moment he was gone, Roxanne went to the nearest empty table. No sooner had she sat down than a serving girl appeared to speak to her.

"Hey, wait for me!" said Fletcher. "Come on, Keriya."

Keriya hesitated. Any of these people might see her eyes, and all of them had the potential to be her enemies. She shook her head and backed away. It was easy for Fletcher and Roxanne. They looked like everyone else.

Once upstairs, Keriya found her room with ease. It was small, but luxurious by Aerian standards. A four-poster bed complete with lacy curtains stood in one corner. In the opposite corner were a wooden chest of drawers and a washstand. Light from the town filtered through an open window, tingeing the room with a serene amber glow.

She sat rigidly on the bed for a while. Noises of merriment and the delicious scent of exotic foods drifted up to her, filling her with a longing she'd never known. She didn't want to be alone anymore. She wanted to be with the Allentrians.

Standing resolutely, Keriya marched back downstairs. The common room was even more crowded now, and she was surprised to see that Fletcher and Roxanne had been joined by two young men.

"Who are you?" she asked warily as she drew near the table.

"They're our new friends," Fletcher said in a slurred voice, looking up from a large mug filled with a frothy drink.

"Nice to meet you," said one man, holding his hand out to Keriya. Behind him, Roxanne mouthed the words '*take it.*' With a palpable awkwardness, Keriya reached out. He clasped her hand firmly in his own, smiling and shaking her whole arm.

Then his smile faded. He furrowed his brow and peered into her eyes. Though the flickering light of the candles and lanterns helped mask their unnatural color, Keriya fearfully dropped her gaze.

"This sounds like a good song," Roxanne said suddenly. She stood and twirled so her dress fanned out around her limber legs. "I feel like dancing!"

The men forgot all about Keriya and got up, heading to an open area where people were pairing off. As Roxanne passed by, Keriya hissed, "What are you doing? Cezon said not to talk to anyone."

"I don't care what Cezon said," Roxanne retorted. "Don't you get it? We're finally free to live our own lives. I don't have to listen to him — or you." She sashayed into the midst of the cavorting crowd, leaving Keriya gaping after her in dismay.

"Can you believe her?" Keriya grumbled, flinging herself down next to Fletcher and crossing her arms. Fletcher wasn't listening. He made a groaning noise as he finished the contents of his mug and toppled backward off his bench, unconscious.

CHAPTER EIGHT
CEZON'S SCHEME
"It is most unwise to deal with humans."
~ Draconic Proverb

Cezon sidled down the back corridor of The Olde Dragyn. Treeskon ran a respectable inn, but he was also a businessman and he knew where most business came from. That was why he'd built this handy space.

Cezon peeked into a chamber whose occupants had left their door ajar. Seven men were seated around a circular table, smoking tobacco-leaf and playing a game with dice. Gambling itself wasn't illegal, but the stakes they were wagering certainly were.

He reached the room he'd leased at the end of the hall and rapped twice on the heavy oak door, then once again, then three times fast. There was a moment of silence before a voice from within said, "Password?"

"What? There ain't no bloody password, you lagwit," growled Cezon.

"There is now."

"Since when?!"

"Since last night."

"Well, how am I s'posed to know it if I wasn't here when you made it up?" he demanded. "Open the door before I gut you like a codfish!"

"Iako, it's him," said another voice in a bass rumble.

"But if I open the door, he says he'll gut me like a —"

"Helkryvt's blood, how did you get to be so stupid?" Cezon hissed. "Let me in! There's things we need to discuss."

He heard the iron deadbolt slide back and the door creaked

inwards. Iako's thin, pointed face appeared, replete with scraggly black hair, almond-shaped blue eyes, and a pathetic excuse for a goatee.

"Outta my way," Cezon grumbled, kicking the door and shoving past his associate. "I hope the bogspectre sucks out whatever brains you got and leaves you in a ditch somewhere."

Iako relocked the door as Cezon directed his attention to the table, where his other business partner sat. Endred was a giant of a man, a hulking Fironian who stood a foot taller than Cezon and who positively towered over Iako. He had dark skin, a bald head, and enough muscles to make even the bravest of bar brawlers think twice before tangling with him.

"You're late," said Endred, his leather jerkin straining over his chest as he crossed his arms.

Cezon sat down and pulled a flask of mead toward him. "Got held up."

"Trouble with the Imperials?"

"Not yet. The hand-off went just fine. The wagon's in its usual spot and Deathly'll take care of it from there." Deathly was another one of their associates. They had never learned his real name, and frankly, Cezon didn't care what it was.

"So, what was the holdup?"

"I found some . . . imports on the Northroad," Cezon replied in a delicate voice, popping the cork off the flask and taking a large swig.

"How come the imports was all the way inland?" said Iako, pinching his face into a look of deep thought. Cezon sighed. Iako was a lost cause. Still, you always had to have at least one expendable man in your group. Someone to throw to the wolves if you found yourself in a bind.

"Because these imports are people," he explained, tipping back in his chair and propping his booted feet on the table.

"But then why—"

"It was code, Iako," said Endred. Cezon would never understand why Endred bothered to be patient with the Galantrian when he could snap the smaller man in half if he wanted. And he had never understood how Endred had landed in this line of work, either. He seemed too . . . *nice*, for lack of a better word.

"Found some migrants. No effin' idea how they managed to get past port security, 'cause they haven't two brains to rub together between the three of them. But the real kicker is they're royal."

"How do you know?" Endred inquired.

"They got weird accents. One of 'em called me Elder, all formal and respectful-like, so they're some sort of nobility for sure. And they didn't want people to know where they're from—they had some crackpot story about Aeria, of all places." Iako snickered, and this even coaxed a smile from Endred. "Yeah, they tried telling me about how they crossed Shivnath's Mountains. I says, 'How did you do that?' and they go, 'Oh, we don't remember!'"

"Probably heard enough legends about Aeria to think it actually exists," said Endred.

"Two of 'em gave me names that might be real. Didn't sound Smarlindian, and the surnames were all foreign. But the third one—this albino-looking bird—she comes up with some real nonsense. 'Keriya Soulstar,' she says, like she's all important."

"Stupid wench," Iako said sycophantically, grinning to reveal yellow teeth he'd sharpened to fine points.

"I ain't even told you the best part yet," Cezon said smugly. "She's got purple eyes."

"Blood and bones," whispered Endred. "You think she's from Moorfain?"

"Where else would she be from? Aeria?" Cezon snorted in contempt. "They was tryin' to get to the Fironem. Probably wanted to get to the Cinder Isle ports. Tryin' to get back home."

"You sure about this, Cezon?"

"Course I'm sure! I been sitting with her the past two days, having to put up with her questions. Can't keep her mouth shut to save her life."

"So you've got three Moorfainians," said Endred. "What're

you gonna do about it?"

"Sell 'em?" Iako suggested.

He'd said it because he was a moron. Slavery had been illegal in Allentria for ages. But even if they couldn't sell the children . . .

"You know," Cezon said slowly, "you might be onto something."

"Cezon," Endred began in a warning tone. Much to Cezon's annoyance, Endred insisted on having morals and a conscience.

"Oh, I wouldn't do that! But we're the only ones who know these twits are from Moorfain, right? That puts us in a good position. I bet the empress would want to get her hands on them."

"Actually, I bet she would," Endred agreed. "Just think about the political ramifications of that."

"What the blood is a ramification?" said Cezon. "You know what? I don't care. Point is, Aldelphia will pay to get ahold of 'em. And she will pay a lot. More than we've ever made before. More than we'd know what to do with!"

"Yeah!" Iako rubbed his hands together greedily.

"It'd be good if it worked," said Endred. "But them just being here is illegal. The government ain't gonna accept them with open arms. We need an excuse as to why they're here in the first place—a legal one. Or as legal as we can make it."

Cezon tapped his chin in thought. "Send a falcon to Miff. Have him draw up papers and a charter for a Syrionese commerce ship that they bought their way onto. It ain't that illegal in the grand scheme of things."

"Fine," said Endred, "but how are you going to get the Moorfainians to the empress?"

"I'll say I'm bringing 'em to Noryk for citizen registration so they don't get deported. Then we go to the palace, barter a hefty price and hand 'em over. Done."

"You'll need to forge papers for yourself—and us—so we can get paid."

"What, so the government can just tax whatever they give

us?" Cezon scoffed. "No thanks."

"Cezon, if you march into the Imperial Palace without any paperwork or planning, you won't even be able to introduce the Moorfainians before you get arrested."

Cezon growled and tipped further back in his chair, almost overbalancing. He waved his arms to set himself straight and the chair fell back on all fours with a clatter. Endred was right as usual, drat and blast him.

"Okay," he said at length. "Endred, send word and get Miff to start working on *our* papers, along with papers for the Moorfainians. Iako, I want you to go to Noryk ahead of us."

"Why I gotta do that for?"

"Because you already got legal papers, you half-brained clonch, and we need an inside man! You'll re-enlist with the Imperial Guard so you can push our files through and make sure we get in to see the proper people when the time comes."

"But what if they actually make me work? You know, fight and stuff?" said Iako.

"Have you seen yourself? They'd never put you on active duty. They'll probably have you do paperwork and whatnot."

"But I'm bad at paperwork. I en't even learned to read proper."

"Well, figure it out quick. Because we're headed for the greatest payday of our lives," Cezon declared triumphantly, taking another swig of mead. This was the break he'd been waiting for. It was the big haul, the mythical 'Last Job.' It was what men like him dreamed of.

What could possibly go wrong?

CHAPTER NINE

MAGIC AND MAYHEM

"Adventures are what you make of them."
~ Gavin Swiftwind, Ninth Age

"Up! Get up!" Roxanne was startled awake by a no-nonsense voice. Cezon banged open the door and strode to the windows, ripping open the curtains. Light poured onto the bed.

"You two've wasted half the day," he growled, storming back out of the room without looking at Roxanne or Keriya, who stirred on the far side of the mattress. "Go downstairs to settle your tab with Treeskon. I don't care if you have to wash dishes for the rest of the age, I ain't payin' for your party last night."

"Clodhopper," Roxanne muttered as the door slammed shut behind him. She loved being able to say things like that. The Allentrian swear words—most of which she had picked up from Cezon—were so colorful.

"It's almost sun-high," said Keriya, peering through the transparent wood, which Allentrians called 'glass,' that covered the windows of The Olde Dragyn.

"So? We've got nowhere to be." In fact, Roxanne was planning to set off on her own to forge a new life for herself. She wasn't sure where she'd go, but a lady of her fine upbringing and good looks couldn't do poorly, no matter what happened.

"Maybe *you* don't," Keriya said loftily as she crossed to the door and left the room.

Roxanne rolled her eyes. She was looking forward to putting some distance between herself and Keriya Nameless-Soulstar-whatever. The girl was a lunatic.

She went to the washstand to tidy up. Through the thin

walls, she heard Keriya knock on Fletcher's door.

"Fletch? You awake? You can't be that tired."

"Yes I can." Fletcher had no excuse for being lazy. He'd regained consciousness by the time they'd carried him to his room last night, but had then promptly fallen asleep.

Roxanne listened to their banter as Keriya coaxed him down to the common room. When she was sure they were gone, she slipped into the hall and headed for the back stairwell to avoid passing them — she didn't want any lengthy, insincere good-byes. Unfortunately, she ran right into Cezon.

"Where're you going?" he demanded, planting his fists on his hips.

"None of your business."

"You can't leave." Roxanne tried to shoulder past him but he blocked her. "Don't make me wield," he threatened.

"I don't know what that means," she retorted, "and I don't care."

Cezon's expression slid from anger to glee disturbingly quickly. "That's right. You lot ain't natural wielders, are you?" He raised a hand and a small mass of water formed above his outstretched palm. Roxanne's jaw fell open.

"How are you doing that?"

"I'm a water wielder. All I did was manipulate the water-threads in the air around us and concentrate 'em here."

"The what?" she breathed, transfixed by the graceful dance of the floating liquid.

"Threads, magicthreads. The molecules you manipulate to cast spells," he explained haughtily.

She couldn't believe it. There *were* other sorts of magic. Cezon could control water just as she could control earth.

"So you should really consider doing what I tell you," he concluded.

Roxanne was shaken, but not intimidated. She reached inside herself, embracing the power that slept there, reassured by its familiar warmth. Her source flared eagerly at her mental touch, stronger and brighter than ever it had been in Aeria.

"I'm done doing what people tell me," she said, wielding to gather up the ample dirt in the hall. She formed it into a clump and launched the compact sphere through Cezon's floating water, causing the liquid to splatter in his face. He flipped his eyepatch up to gape at her as she breezed past him, dusting off her hands.

Roxanne exited the inn and headed up the street toward a line of vendors hawking their wares. She paused to inspect a display of colored fabrics and picked up a scarf, Cezon and his watermagic already forgotten.

"A fine piece you've got there, miss," said the man behind the stand. He reminded Roxanne of a beetle with his bug eyes and wide mouth. "Would you like it?" He yanked it out of her grasp with thin, twitchy fingers and held it up to her shoulder. "It will go marvelously with your hair. You have such lovely hair. You must take it."

Roxanne couldn't see the harm in doing so, especially since he was so insistent. "Okay," she said, accepting it and turning away.

"What are you doing?" he shrieked, snatching the scarf back. "You can't just walk off like that, you thieving urchin. That's Erastatian silk!"

"You told me to take it," she replied, bewildered.

"Not without paying for it."

Ah, this was one of those things Cezon had spoken of. If she wanted the scarf, she'd have to trade money for it. "Sorry, I don't have any derlei," she said, and continued on her way.

Roxanne wandered for most of the afternoon looking for someone in need of a Hunter. In the first establishment she visited, the proprietor asked where she'd been apprenticed. Roxanne didn't know what that meant, so she lied and told him she'd been named and fully trained in Aeria.

The man laughed in her face and kicked her out.

After some more misadventures she ended up at a crossroads in the center of town. Five streets branched out from the lively cobblestone square. On one corner, people bustled in and out of a building guarded by a group of men in gray tunics.

This seemed like the sort of place Roxanne might find answers, so she hastened toward it. The gray-clad men eyed her as she ascended the flagstone steps, some with suspicion, some with appreciation.

A large desk was situated at the forefront of the entrance hall, and a brown-skinned guard sat behind it. Beside him lay a wolfish animal, its sharp eyes roving the crowd.

"Hello," Roxanne said when she reached him. "I'm Roxanne Fleuridae. Are you one of the Elders of Senteir?"

"Fleuridae. What a unique name." The scowl lines on his forehead deepened as he examined her. "I'm Major-General Lerofern of the Fourth Battalion of the Imperial Guard. I am stationed in Senteir only temporarily until my reassignment."

"Okay, well . . . I'm new to Allentria, and I'm looking for—"

"I'm sorry," Lerofern interrupted. "What do you mean when you say you're *new* to Allentria?"

"I mean I just got here," said Roxanne. The back of her neck began to prickle with unease.

"Where did you come from?"

"Aeria," she said, making a small gesture in the direction of Shivnath's Mountains.

Lerofern's face puckered in aggravation. "Is this your idea of a joke? Get out!" He flicked his hand at her and leaned over the desk to scribble something in a notebook.

Roxanne was taken aback by the man's abrupt shift in attitude. She had never been spoken to in such a way—her father had often screamed verbal abuse at her, but this man had just dismissed her like she was nothing. It was upsetting enough to cause a dull ache to surface behind her eyes.

"I'm serious," she said. "I don't know anyone here, and—"

Lerofern slapped his writing tool down and stood. "That kind of talk is awfully dangerous, and you picked the wrong day to pull a prank. So I'm going to count to five, and if you aren't out of my sight by then, I'm going to arrest you."

Time to go.

Roxanne didn't understand what had made him so angry, but she decided to back down. Lerofern was surrounded by swarms of guards, and hanging at each man's waist was a sharp weapon. Cezon had explained that these were called 'swords' and were mostly used for 'gutting bloody thieves who try to take your derlei.'

Go. Two-legger dangerous. Go!

The ache in her head intensified and Roxanne frowned. That thought, those words—they hadn't really . . . *belonged* to her. They'd come from somewhere else.

"One," Lerofern began, holding up a finger to count. "Two . . ."

Run now!

There they were again—someone else's thoughts in her head. A pressure in her left temple and some hitherto submerged instinct lured her gaze toward the wolf-creature. It was staring right at her and it tilted its snout toward the door.

"Three . . . four . . ."

Go!

Roxanne ran, heeding the advice of the tame wolf. Assuming it had actually spoken to her and she wasn't going insane. First the drachvold, now this?

Her headache faded once she got outside. She stopped at the bottom of the steps and took a calming breath to settle herself before setting off for The Olde Dragyn. It was late, she was clearly unwell, and she had nowhere else to go.

"Pst!" Roxanne jumped at the sharp hiss. She turned, peering down a narrow side street, and spotted Cezon lurking behind a waste barrel. He flapped his arm, gesturing for her to join him, but she wasn't in the mood to deal with his antics. She rolled her eyes and marched away.

Master Treeskon tried to greet her when she entered the inn, but she brushed him off and hurried upstairs. A figure emerged from the back stairwell just as she reached the second floor landing. It was Cezon again. He crossed the length of the corridor in two bounds and grabbed her arm.

A hundred ugly emotions reared up in Roxanne's chest—surprise, obviously, but more sinister things too, like fear, shame, even guilt.

"Let go," she grated, struggling against Cezon as he yanked open the door to her room. Keriya and Fletcher were inside, and Roxanne's fear subsided as soon as she saw them. Anger replaced it, surging through her like liquid fire.

"Take your filthy hands off me," she snapped, kicking at Cezon's shins. He yelped and let go of her, leaning down to massage the spot where her toe had collided with his leg.

"What are you doing?" Keriya asked Cezon.

"What am *I* doing? Do you know what your idiot friend did? She chatted up a bunch of Imperials! Waltzed right into their little hive."

"A bunch of what?"

"Imperial Guards," Cezon spat, sounding out each syllable as though he were talking to a group of toddlers. "Ugly gray getups, government employees—ring any bells?"

"I can talk to anyone I want," Roxanne said indignantly.

"Not if you want to stay in Allentria you can't. Imperials ain't like local soldiers. They're elite, Tier Seven wielders and higher, and they got jurisdiction throughout the whole empire. They make sure no one does nothing illegal, and they make sure no one from outside gets in."

"What's the problem?"

"Helkryvt's blood!" Cezon tossed his hands up in frustration. Roxanne dimly registered the interesting fact that the Allentrians must share some of the Aerians' theological beliefs, if Cezon was using the name of the Aerian god of evil. "They're the ones who keep foreigners out of our country. If they know you're here, it's only a matter of time before they find you and ship you back to where you came from. It's a tronkin' miracle they didn't arrest you on the spot!"

Lerofern had threatened to arrest Roxanne, but she hadn't known what that meant. Did he actually have the power to force her to go back to Aeria?

"We need to leave. Tonight. Now. Gotta get you to Noryk before you get yourselves deported. You!" Cezon pointed at Fletcher. "Go downstairs and tell Treeskon to hitch up Winni. Give him this to keep him from flapping his fat lips about it." He tossed Fletcher a gold derlei, which Fletcher caught clumsily. "And you!" He pointed at Keriya. "Find a bag to put over your head before we go!"

Keriya's face darkened and Roxanne let out a disbelieving groan. What would her plan be now? She didn't want to get deported — she would rather die than return to her father.

It sounded like she was going to be stuck with these lunatics a little while longer.

CHAPTER TEN

THE ROAD TO NORYK

"Contrition is meaningless without forgiveness."
~ Yalon Monkier, Second Age

Fletcher hurried down to the common room, clutching the gold coin Cezon had given him. The evening crowd was already trickling in, and Fletcher scanned the patrons for a few moments before he spotted Treeskon bustling around near the front of the bar.

"Excuse me," he gasped, running toward the innkeeper. "We'd like you to get Winni ready. Cezon needs to leave."

"So soon?" Treeskon raised a bushy eyebrow. "Is something wrong?"

Fletcher hesitated. There was definitely something wrong, but he didn't know what. He didn't know who the Imperial Guards were, nor did he understand why it was so important to stay away from them.

"Everything's fine," he lied. "Cezon said to give you this for your trouble." He offered the derlei to Treeskon, who let out a mirthless laugh.

"I'll bet he didn't say it that politely," the man growled, pocketing the coin. "Very well. I'll have the boys hitch her up. The wagon will be out front in a few minutes."

Treeskon stumped away and Fletcher left the inn. The sky was deepening from purple to slate gray. A warm breeze whispered through the streets, carrying the fresh scents of the meadowlands and lake. Sounds of music and laughter wafted toward him from the next street over.

An unexpected pang of sorrow shot through Fletcher. He'd only been here a day; why was he upset about leaving? Maybe it was just too soon after leaving the only home he'd ever known.

He was jolted from his thoughts by the telltale clip-clop of hooves. Winni trundled out of the inn's side alley, led by a servant boy who offered Fletcher the reins.

"Give my regards to Sir Leafwhit," he said before scuttling away again.

Fletcher was left standing there, holding Winni's reins at arms' length. She let out a whicker and stamped her hoof impatiently. He edged away from her.

More clip-clopping echoed along the street as a group of riders turned the corner up the road. The sight of them sent a chill down Fletcher's spine. Their horses were bigger than Winni, and outfitted with shiny metal plates across their chests. Fletcher screwed up his eyes to get a better view and his stomach dropped. All the men were garbed in gray robes.

"Hey, are we ready? Where's Cezon?"

Fletcher spun around to see Keriya and Roxanne emerging from the inn. Neither of them had noticed the riders. He dropped Winni's reins and leapt at Keriya.

"Quick, hide!" he squeaked. "Where's your bag?"

"My—what? Are you kidding? I'm not putting a bag over my head!"

Fletcher reopened the door and pushed Keriya back inside. He closed it not a moment too soon, for a sharp voice cracked through the air behind him.

"Here! Boy!"

The riders had drawn level with them. They halted their horses and gazed coldly at Fletcher and Roxanne. Fletcher noticed that Roxanne shrank away from them, retreating into the shadows of the doorframe.

"Can I help you?" Fletcher tried to sound as innocent as he could—though he still wasn't sure what his crime had been. Cezon had said the Imperial Guard kept foreigners out of Allentria, but why should that be a problem?

"It's a code violation to leave your animal unattended," said the lead rider, pointing at Winni.

"Sorry." Fletcher went over and hastily scooped up the reins.

"Are you leaving Senteir?" said another man. "It's quite late to be setting out. The nearest town is more than a day's journey by land. Where are your parents?"

Fletcher opened his mouth, but no sound came out. He looked at Roxanne for help, but she remained silent.

As if on cue, Cezon burst from the inn with a flourish. He'd traded his eyepatch for a bulky scarf, which he'd wrapped around the lower half of his face. Keriya was behind him, her unnatural hair and eyes hidden beneath the cowl of a traveling cloak.

"There you are, children! I've just settled up with Master Treeskon and — oh! Good evening, Officers. Is there a problem?"

"This boy left your horse unattended." The lead rider's voice was filled with suspicion.

"Tsk-tsk. I apologize. He's not the sharpest sword in the armory," Cezon chortled, sidling over to Fletcher and slinging an arm around his shoulders in a fatherly manner.

"Where are you headed at such a late hour?" the rider persisted.

"Been traveling down to Shudrash. My poor sister has fallen ill. We only stopped here for the day so I could restock our supplies, but we've got to be on our way. The children do so want to see their aunt," said Cezon.

The riders didn't look wholly convinced by Cezon's story, but their leader heeled his horse forward. "Keep a better watch on your wards," he warned Cezon.

Cezon waved after them, watching them until they rounded the far corner. Then he ripped off his scarf.

"Get in," he hissed. He grabbed Fletcher and Keriya and dragged them to the back of the wagon. "You too," he said, pointing at Roxanne. Though her hands curled into angry fists, she did as he commanded.

Fletcher clambered through the canvas flap and settled down on a pile of lumpy burlap sacks inside the wagon. He heard Cezon jump into the front seat and whistle to Winni.

"That was close," Roxanne said as the wagon lurched into motion. "At least they left without a fuss."

Fletcher nodded. The anxiety that had erupted in his gut ebbed away. The danger was past and Cezon was taking them somewhere they'd be safe. The only one who didn't seem relieved was Keriya. She sat rigidly on an empty crate, glaring at her feet.

"You okay?" Fletcher asked.

"No. You hid me. You wanted to keep them from seeing me."

"Well, yeah." Fletcher thought he'd been doing a good thing, but it was clear Keriya didn't agree.

"You're frightened of my eyes."

"What? No!" It wasn't that he was frightened of her eyes, exactly—he'd grown accustomed to their color and their weird aura of power. Now he was more frightened of how other people would react to her. He tried explaining this, but Keriya didn't want to hear it.

"You still think I'm a witch, don't you?"

"Quiet back there," Cezon snapped, banging on the wagon's wooden frame. "We're near the main gate."

Fuming, Fletcher leaned toward Keriya and lowered his voice. "If you remember, even when I did briefly think you might be a witch, I still stuck by you."

"I don't know why you bothered."

"I bothered because you're all I have left. Because family still means something to me."

"We're not family," she said softly, hugging her arms around her stomach, unable to meet his gaze.

"Not by blood," he argued, "but all I've ever tried to do is help. I warned you the villagers were coming. I followed you through the mountains and kept us together. When I hid you, I was only trying to protect you."

"Oh, for Shivnath's sake," Roxanne groaned, closing her eyes and massaging her temples.

"Will you three *shut up?*" Cezon squawked.

Fletcher turned away from the girls. Sure, he'd made some mistakes, but how could Keriya not see that he had her best interests at heart? He didn't have magic like Roxanne, and he didn't know this country like Cezon did. When problems arose, he had to muddle through and do the best he could with what he had.

"Guess my best isn't good enough," he murmured to himself.

They left the town without further incident, and spent the next few days trundling along a sandy path nestled between a fresh green forest and the river that flowed out of the Senteiri lake.

Fletcher made multiple attempts to speak with Keriya, but she was alternately pretending that their fight had never happened and ignoring him.

He tried talking to Roxanne next, but she was just as bad. When he struck up a conversation with her, she told him that her head hurt and she didn't want to hear his voice. With no one else to turn to, Fletcher settled on talking to Cezon.

"How long til we get to Noryk?" he asked, scooting closer to the Allentrian as the wagon rattled onwards.

"We've got a ways to go," grumbled Cezon, "and whining about it ain't gonna get us there any faster."

"Is it a big place?"

"Most impressive city you've ever seen. A hundred times bigger than Senteir."

"What will we do once we get there?" said Fletcher, leaning against the backboard and gazing up at the spotless sky.

"We'll start by fixin' it so you ain't arrested," said Cezon.

"I mean after that." Fletcher began imagining the city: friendly people, plenty of excitement, and ample opportunities, even for a group of unnamed Aerians.

"After that, with any luck you ain't gonna be my problem."

"After that, *some* of us have important things to do," Keriya announced from where she brooded in the back of the wagon.

Fletcher scowled. Part of him couldn't wait to get to Noryk, to find a new place to call home and get away from the hostility surrounding him. Another part of him feared reaching the city, because he didn't know what would happen there. Would Keriya and Roxanne want to go their separate ways?

Cezon noticed the change in his mood and smirked. "What's the story with her, eh?" He jerked his head toward Keriya.

"I don't know," Fletcher admitted in barely more than a whisper. "Something changed between us. And I'm not sure how to fix it."

"Women are all the same," said Cezon. "They're easy to deal with, but you gotta know how to handle 'em."

"Oh?" said Fletcher.

"Just tell her she was right and you're sorry. Don't matter if you know what you did, or even if you didn't do nothin' at all. They just like to think they win all the arguments."

"I already tried apologizing and it didn't work."

"Her loss. There's plenty other fish in the sea, if you catch my drift."

Fletcher didn't catch Cezon's drift, but his spirits lifted nonetheless.

When they stopped to make camp, Fletcher stuck close to Cezon and helped him prepare for the night. He brushed Winni, which Cezon seemed to appreciate, and started to organize the back of the wagon, which Cezon didn't like one bit.

"Out! Get out," said Cezon, grabbing Fletcher by the scruff of his shirt and yanking him away from a cluster of sealed wooden boxes. "Ain't anyone ever told you not to stick your nose where it don't belong?"

"I was just trying to—"

"Whatever it is, I don't care. Stop trying. Stop followin' me around. Go bother your little friends." He pointed at Keriya and Roxanne, who were sitting by the small fire he'd made in a sandy grove off the path.

Fletcher cast them a doubtful glance. Keriya was watching

him, and when he caught her eye she beckoned him over.

"Why are you talking to Cezon?" she hissed the moment Fletcher sat down on her mossy log.

"Because you aren't talking to me anymore," he returned angrily. "Why do you care, anyway?"

"Because you cannot trust anyone." With her inflection, it sounded like she was quoting somebody. "I don't like the way he looks at my eyes. I think he's up to something."

"Relax, Keriya. The whole world isn't out to get you."

Her pale cheeks flushed red in the firelight. "Right—it's only the Aerians and the Imperials and anyone else who might think I'm a witch."

She got up and stalked away. Fletcher half rose from his seat to follow her . . . then he sighed and sank back down, too tired to fight.

Cezon passed by and gave Fletcher a knowing look. He pointed at Keriya, then twirled his finger in a circle next to his ear.

With nothing else to do, Fletcher rose fully and began following Cezon again as he prepared their meager supper. It was only then that he realized he was clinging to the Allentrian because it eased some of the loneliness that had taken up residence in his heart.

And while Fletcher was glad he was forging a new friendship, he felt a twinge of regret when he thought of his crumbling friendship with Keriya.

CHAPTER ELEVEN

THE IMPERIAL CITY

"The man who does not dream will never be happy.
The man who dreams too far will never be content."
~ *Virix Temperflame, Seventh Age*

"C'mon, Winni. There's an old girl. C'mon, you stupid tronkin' donkey!"

"It's her left hind hoof," Roxanne grumbled from her seat on the wagon. Cezon glowered up at her before walking over to Winni's hind leg. He clucked and she lifted it obediently. Sure enough, he scraped out a sharp pebble that had gotten stuck in her shoe.

"How'd you know that?" Keriya whispered as Cezon clambered back into the cart.

"Lucky guess," said Roxanne, hunching down and crossing her arms.

They'd been traveling for almost a fortnight. During the trek, Roxanne had heard more and more voices and had suffered hallucinations similar to the one in the mountains. She no longer feared she was going crazy, but the truth of the matter — that she could speak to animals — wasn't much better.

You have great power, two-legger. Do not fear it.

Another voice inside her head. Only these voices weren't voices, they were images and colors and concepts that her brain somehow translated into human words and sounds.

Leave me alone, she thought dully.

"What's that?" Fletcher asked, interrupting Roxanne's silent conversation. He pointed to a shape shimmering through the humid haze.

"That'd be Noryk," said Cezon. "Not much longer, now."

Roxanne's surliness ebbed away the closer they got and

was slowly replaced by excitement. Beside her, Keriya and Fletcher were buoyant with anticipation. Noryk looked impressive, even from afar. It perched upon huge white cliffs and was surrounded by a stone wall, over which the tops of towers were just visible.

They left the country hills of the Smarlands and crossed a flat expanse of barren ground. Beyond, a river moat coiled around the base of the cliffs, glittering in the afternoon sun.

Cezon grudgingly paid a toll fee at a gatehouse before they headed across a soaring bridge, ascending toward a stone gate bordered by watchtowers. Roxanne's stomach fluttered with unease when she saw two armed Imperial Guards standing before it.

"State your name and business in Noryk," said the taller one.

"Andran Vierwind of Alakite, wishing to do some trade in the marketplace," Cezon lied easily, halting Winni and hopping off the wagon.

"Sign your names in the ledger and mark the day, month and year of your visit," the guard instructed, pointing to a thick book sitting atop a nearby stand.

Cezon motioned for the Aerians to follow him. They did so, slinking past the guards' stern gazes. He picked up a tool—a stylus, Roxanne thought it was called—and made a series of marks on a page. Then he offered it to Keriya.

"We can't sign in," she whispered to Cezon. "We don't use those runes."

"Oh, bloody bones of a—!"

"Is there a problem?" asked the second guard.

"No problem," Cezon said quickly. "My cousins are sore from the ride, so I'll have to write for them. That's fine, isn't it?"

"Are their hands sore?" the first guard drawled. "What, were they sitting on them?" His companion snickered. Cezon threw the Aerians a withering glare as he scribbled three lines of strange runes in the book.

"We'll need to check your wagon," the second guard stated in a bored voice, implying that he didn't particularly want to waste the energy doing so. Cezon picked up on this and brightened at once.

"Certainly, my good fellow. Will you have to look through each individual bag of fertilizer? I ain't been to Noryk for a while so don't know what protocol is anymore."

"Fertilizer?"

"The finest and most nutrient-filled combination of dung and mulch you'll ever come across, sir!" Cezon strode to the back of the wagon and hefted out a burlap sack that Roxanne knew was filled with nothing more than fruit rinds.

"Oh," said the tall one, looking at his companion. "Dung. And mulch. Well, that seems to be in order."

"Would you gentlemen be interested in buying some? I'd give you a discount."

"No, thank you," the guard replied hastily. "You're free to proceed."

A line of light burst through the gates as they swung inwards on well-oiled hinges, seemingly of their own accord. Cezon shooed the Aerians back onto the wagon and clucked to Winni, urging her forward.

"Welcome to Noryk," he said. "Greatest city in the world!"

Roxanne's heart swelled with awe as her eyes adjusted to the brightness. The cobblestone street stretching before them was broad enough for two lanes of traffic, separated by a raised strip of land from which sprouted exotic plants. People swarmed about in bizarre and vibrant styles of dress. It was a far cry from Aeria, where everyone had been forced to cover their arms, legs, and midriffs in plain garments.

They passed beneath a golden archway carved with arcane designs. Roxanne was shocked to see a sentence written in Aerian runes at the peak of the arch.

"*Keas seules endrat keas omnes,*" she murmured, reading the unfamiliar words aloud.

Keriya turned sharply to her. "What did you just say?"

"It's the city's slogan," said Cezon, who was in better spirits than Roxanne had ever seen him. "Means 'the light of one is the light of all'."

He glanced at the Aerians to find they were all staring at him. "Or some such similar nonsense," he finished gruffly, clearing his throat and twitching Winni's reins.

A mountain-range of buildings lined the thoroughfare, all of them built from a white material that glistened in the sunlight. Flags emblazoned with bright designs swirled in the breeze, strung between spectacular gold and crystal turrets.

"Just up there," said Cezon, "is the Imperial Palace."

Their view of the palace was blocked by a granite arch straddling the street. The road that ran beneath the archway was lined by more Imperial Guards. Fortunately, the soldiers gave them no trouble and they emerged into a wide courtyard. There, rising grandly toward the heavens, was the Imperial Palace.

Wide steps led to four entryways guarded by statues of magnificent creatures. The marble walls were peppered with elaborate tracery set between stained glass windows. Smaller statues clung to the corners of ramparts, spouting trails of water that thinned to a mist before ever reaching the ground. Towers topped by golden onion domes strafed the underside of the clouds that hung over the city.

"We're going to The Black Willow," Cezon said as Winni plodded along the edge of the courtyard. "Innkeeper's a friend of mine. Actually I can't stand him, but he owes me and he'll give me a room for cheap. Come to think of it, you can just work to earn your keep. Yeah, that'll be good."

Roxanne tuned Cezon out. She had better things to listen to, like the music of street performers or the songs of the birds that flew overhead, their feathers flashing in the evening sunlight. It was strange how quickly she'd come to love Allentria—a land that she knew nothing about, but which somehow felt like home.

True to his word, Cezon arranged with Grov, the innkeeper of The Black Willow, to let the Aerians stay for free if they worked for him. Thus Keriya, Fletcher, and Roxanne had spent most of their time in Noryk sequestered in a cramped, steamy kitchen, washing dishes.

Keriya hated it. She wanted to be out *there*, becoming the hero Shivnath had promised she would be. Instead she was stuck at the inn, hoping their papers would go through so they wouldn't get deported. Cezon had filled out numerous forms on their behalf and their information was now being processed, so all they could do was wait. And wash dishes.

The girls had retired to their quarters in the attic after a long morning of work. Roxanne lay on her cot, facing the wall. She might have been sleeping, or just ignoring Keriya—either way she was quiet, which was a blessing. She also hated being cooped up, a fact she wouldn't let Keriya forget.

Keriya was just about to nod off when the door to their room banged open.

"Up!" said Cezon, flapping his arms. "Your papers are ready. And make yourselves at least a little presentable, right? You look like a couple of bleedin' shifters."

"I thought that's what we were," Keriya muttered as he ducked out and vanished down the hall. They had learned that 'shifter' was a derogatory term for people who moved around, shifting alliances to different states or countries.

They collected Fletcher from his room, bid Grov a lukewarm farewell, and left the inn. Keriya smiled as the sun warmed her skin. Soon she would be free to continue her quest.

Cezon was waiting for them on the street. He'd disguised himself with a large feather hat and a bulky cloak, despite the fact it was the height of the second season, what the Allentrians called 'summer.'

Cezon whisked them through the city, herding them along like sheep. When they reached a bustling square, he ushered them into an alley beside a stately building. Keriya cast a suspicious scowl upon the muddy puddles and waste bins that riddled the dingy passageway.

Suddenly a man popped out from a recessed door a few hands away. He had a rat-like face, scraggly black hair, and a stringy, unkempt beard. He also wore a gray tunic, the uniform of the Imperial Guard.

"This is Officer Blackwater," said Cezon. "He's arranged everything for us."

"That's right. I'm an old pal of Cez—er, I mean . . . what name you usin' this time, Cezon?"

Cezon growled in frustration. "Just get us inside and keep your bleedin' mouth shut."

Blackwater nodded and waved them through the door. They entered a servants' hallway and ascended a rickety wooden staircase frosted with cobwebs.

"Took you long enough to get everything in order," Cezon grumbled.

"I got held up," said Blackwater.

"By what? What could possibly be more important than this?!"

"I been busy with the Guards. Got me a side job from Tanthflame himself—it'll be good money when it's done, Cezon. Real good—"

"Shh!" Cezon hissed as they reached a door at the top of the steps. "I don't care about whatever you got yourself into. Just tell me you fixed the paperwork."

"Course I did! That's why we're here, en't it?" Blackwater kicked open the door, revealing a bright marble atrium. He puffed out his chest and marched across the room toward a stone desk. Cezon glanced around furtively before shoving the Aerians out after him.

"We're here to meet the Manager of Homeland Affairs," Blackwater announced, hailing one of the desk workers.

"Do you have an appointment?" the woman asked without looking up from the paperwork strewn before her.

"Course I got an appointment. You think I'm stupid?"

"This'll explain things," Cezon said hastily, leaning over

and shoving a thick envelope under her nose. She flicked off the seal and scanned the notes within. Her expression of boredom vanished at once.

"Applicants sixteen-seventy-four, five, and six. Non-hostile, requiring immediate escort," she said to no one in particular. Moments later, a disembodied voice replied to her words:

"Admit them."

The woman pointed to a hallway that led out of the atrium. "Right this way, Officer."

"Ha!" Fletcher poked Roxanne in the shoulder as they followed Blackwater past the desk and down the short hall. "There *are* other kinds of magic."

"I knew that all the way back in Senteir," she retorted, brushing his hand aside.

They entered a smaller room lined with benches and potted plants. In the center of the chamber stood a silver-bearded man, who had to be the Manager of Homeland Affairs. His wintry blue gaze swept over Keriya's dirty clothes and unwashed hair and landed on her eyes. She fought the urge to cover her face.

"You are under arrest," he announced. Doors on either side of the room burst open and several Imperial Guards streamed in.

"What?!" A group of voices chorused a protest, Keriya's loudest of all. Cezon was supposed to have *prevented* this.

"Cezon?" Fletcher said in a shaky tone. He was looking at the Allentrian with a haunted expression. "What's happening?" He cringed away from the Imperials as they marched forward, but they passed the Aerians and went straight for Cezon and Blackwater.

"No, you can't do this to me!" cried Cezon, kicking and flailing as the guardsmen latched onto him. "I'm an Allentrian citizen! I have rights! *They're* the ones you want. They're effin' migrants! Iako, you half-witted trog, what the blood did you do?"

"I en't done nothin'!" Blackwater insisted. "I'm a member of the Imperial Guard, I am!"

"If you don't comply peaceably, we'll have to subdue you," one of the guards threatened. Blackwater went limp, forcing the men to drag him out the room. His pathetic whimpers and Cezon's angry shrieks faded as they were hauled off.

Keriya, Fletcher, and Roxanne were left standing, dumbfounded, in front of the Manager of Homeland Affairs. Anxiety simmered in Keriya's stomach as he turned his attention back to her.

"You are Keriya Soulstar?"

He knew her real name. That couldn't be good.

"No, my name is, uh . . ." But she'd forgotten the fake name Cezon had bestowed upon her.

"According to your letters of intent, you fled Moorfain due to their recent skirmishes with Jidaeln and are seeking refuge in our country?" he continued. Keriya made a noncommittal noise in her throat, mentally cursing Cezon for having gotten her into this mess.

"The Allentrian Empire is willing to accommodate you, but I'm afraid that the circumstances of your arrival are not traditional. Not legal, in fact. You crossed the Waters of Chardon on a ship captained by one Tarius Altian, is that correct?"

"I guess?"

"You guess," the man repeated, clearly unimpressed with her communication skills. "Were you aware that Master Altian's real name is Cezon Skyriver?"

"Oh, Cezon. Yes, we know him."

"Mm," the man said in a darker tone. "We have quite a record on Skyriver. We're going to have to take you into protective custody and —"

"What? Why?" Keriya demanded as more guards arrived to surround her. She had a brief flash of her last moments in Aeria, of the villagers closing in.

"Because," said the man, "the Empress of Allentria wishes to meet you."

CHAPTER TWELVE

THE NEW QUEST

"There is no such thing as coincidence."
~ *Jidaelni Proverb*

Flanked by five guardsmen, Keriya, Fletcher, and Roxanne followed a liveried servant through the halls of the Imperial Palace, heading toward their meeting with the empress.

Keriya's nerves were shot. Fletcher and Roxanne had been taught proper manners—how to curtsey and bow, how to address the Elders—but she had never learned such rubbish. Erasmus had taught her all about the animals in the Felwood and the medicinal properties of aloeferns, but nothing of how to conduct herself in high society.

They turned down a corridor lined with reflective glass on either wall. Keriya gazed at her endlessly repeating image and saw that she was a shameful mess. Her hair was frizzy and her dress still bore the grime of her journey across the Smarlands. She unsuccessfully tried to fix herself up.

A set of polished doors stood open ahead. The guards fanned out, taking stations on either side of the entrance, and the servant led the Aerians into the chamber.

Keriya had seen unimaginable splendor since coming to Allentria, but this room topped it all. Stained glass windows rested between carved pillars, each pane scattering rainbow light across the ivory floor. Before them, curved steps led to a semicircular dais where gauzy curtains framed a golden throne. Behind the ornate chair hung a tapestry depicting four creatures, one of whom was unmistakably meant to be Shivnath.

"Now announcing our sovereign majesty, her Imperial Highness, Premier of the Union of the States, Head of the

Council of Nine, Protector of the Threads, Leader of the First Free Nation, Lady Aldelphia Alderwood."

Keriya tore her gaze from Shivnath's embroidered eyes, not even half as dark as they should be, and watched as the empress stepped out onto the dais. Gray, arrow-straight hair reached halfway down her back, but she wasn't old. Her skin was silken brown and her patrician face was smooth, replete with a slim nose and long lashes framing eyes that were clouded and white.

Though Lady Aldelphia was blind, she walked unaided. Every step she took was full of an easy, graceful confidence. The servant sank to one knee. Taking their cues from him, Fletcher and Roxanne bowed. Keriya bent awkwardly, unable to look away from the woman. She wondered what it was like to be the most powerful person in the world, loved by her subjects, stunning and self-assured, and felt a pang of envy.

"Welcome," the empress said as she settled onto her throne. Her voice was soft and unassuming, yet it held the weight of a thousand winters. She nodded to the servant. A diamond circlet glinted upon her brow, catching a wild ray of light. "That will be all, Tevyn. Thank you."

Tevyn rose and bowed himself out of the room. The doors swung shut behind him with a thud that echoed in the silence, leaving the Aerians alone with the ruler of Allentria.

"Keriya Soulstar," she said, looking right at Keriya. "I've heard many things about you. Cezon Skyriver managed to convince a number of my employees that you were run-off Moorfainian royalty. Allentria is closed to trade and immigration is illegal, yet he maintained he had undeniable evidence. Since you stand before me now, it appears at least one of his claims held true." Her expression hardened. "He said that you have purple eyes."

Keriya nodded before she remembered the empress couldn't actually see. "I do."

"The color indicates you possess an ancient, arcane power," said Aldelphia. "A power no human has harnessed in ten ages."

Keriya squirmed, thinking of the power Shivnath had

woven into her soul. Should she tell the empress what had happened? That story hadn't gone over well in Aeria.

"The power is dangerous, and in the wrong hands, deadly," Aldelphia continued. "I want to know how you attained it."

"Um," Keriya said in a small voice, fiddling with the fraying ends of her sleeves. "It's kind of a long story."

"You misunderstand. I am fully aware that the only way to become a *rheenar* is by bonding with a dragon. Allentria's most powerful oracle recently had a foresight, a vision of a dragon escaping the Etherworld. So I don't need to know your story; I only need to know where that dragon is now."

Keriya stared up at the empress, her mouth hanging slightly ajar. Aldelphia clearly knew a lot about dragons—more than Keriya knew, in fact—and she seemed to think Keriya had inside information about the dragon who'd escaped imprisonment. Well, she wasn't wrong, but all Keriya knew about that dragon was that Necrovar intended to kill it.

And the Allentrians intend to use it as a weapon, she reminded herself. Unease began to bubble in her gut. She feared she knew where this conversation was heading.

"I don't know where the dragon is," she replied truthfully. "I don't even know what you're talking about. I'm not a *rheenar*—whatever that is—and I'm not sure what you mean by 'bonding'."

"On their own, dragons do not have emotions," Aldelphia explained. "But they are able to form bonds with mortals wherein the two share thoughts, feelings, sometimes even magic. It is through this bond that you gain power over them, for your power allows you to communicate with and control dragons."

Keriya thought about attempting to control a creature like Shivnath. She suppressed a nervous giggle.

"So I ask you again: where is the dragon?"

"And I tell you again, I don't know," said Keriya. Her words came out sounding much ruder than she had intended, and she hastily amended herself: "What I mean is that I didn't bond with anyone. I got this power directly from Shivnath."

The empress showed no hint of shock. After a moment of consideration, she nodded and steepled her fingers in thought. "I presume Shivnath gave you these powers for a reason?"

"Yes," Keriya admitted, shrinking away from that piercing, blind gaze.

"Then we must make use of them. Keriya Soulstar, you must find the last dragon for me."

Keriya sighed. There it was. "I can't really —"

Aldelphia spoke over her, burying her feeble protest. "Once we have it, we will harness its power and use it against our enemies. One specific enemy, in fact. A wielder who has been locked away for a ten-age."

"I'm sorry, Empress," said Fletcher, speaking for the first time, "but we're very confused." He indicated himself and Roxanne.

"Of course," she said, inclining her head. "The majority of my people do not recognize the signs for what they are, but Necrovar has widened the Rift enough to touch Selaras once more. He has sent shadowbeasts, his demonic minions, to—"

"Who's Necrovar?" Fletcher interrupted.

The empress speared him with a calculating glare. Keriya briefly wondered if there was some sort of magic that could give sight to the sightless.

"Necrovar's name has lived in infamy for the past seven thousand years. Kings and peasants the world over know of his crimes. I find it strange that you do not."

Fletcher shrugged in apology.

"Necrovar is pure, dark energy," Aldelphia said slowly. "It is a magic born of chaos and evil, but it has no power over man unless man chooses to *give* it power. Ten ages ago, one human offered himself as a vessel for Necrovar. When it gained a mortal soul, it gained the ability to wield magic. This meant humans no longer had to choose to be evil—for the first time, Necrovar could force them to do evil things.

"Ultimately, the warrior Valerion Equilumos went to the

gods and offered them his soul, giving them the means to defeat the Shadow. The gods wove a spell to destroy Necrovar, but the spell went awry. Instead they created the Etherworld, a parallel universe where Necrovar and his followers were imprisoned. Now he has returned to finish what he started. It was always going to come to this. He was — *is* — too powerful."

Keriya winced. It would have been nice to know a few of these details before setting off on a quest to kill Necrovar, a quest that seemed increasingly insurmountable.

"Keriya, you will summon the dragon and command it to fight for us in the impending war. For I can assure you, war is now inevitable."

War.

It was a more tangible, frightening concept coming from the empress. Even so, Keriya knew she had to speak against the plan.

"You want to know the real reason Shivnath gave me these powers? It's because she wants that dragon to stay safe. She wants me to fight Necrovar."

Aldelphia smiled and shook her head — definitely not the reaction Keriya had expected.

"You cannot fight Necrovar," she said with a note of resignation in her voice, "because only a dragon can kill him. So without a dragon, we will lose."

"Now announcing Prince Maxton Windharte of the Erastate, heir to the Sky Throne."

Max nodded to the herald and stepped into the chamber of the Council of Nine. The circular room overlooked the northern quadrant of Noryk. A round alabaster table gleamed at its center, where the Council members sat to discuss the most pressing problems of the empire. Only the rulers of the Allentrian wielding races were allowed to enter. Max, who was heir-apparent, had never been permitted to come here before.

"Be seated, Maxton."

"Your Majesty," he murmured, bowing to the empress. He slid into a seat at the table and his blue eyes swept over the other guests.

Taeleia Alenciae, the Council representative for the Delegation of Elves, was two chairs down from him on the right. To Max's left was a cleric, a Valaani priest judging by his red robes—that was strange. Beyond the priest sat old Master Rikoru, ward of the Imperial Library, which was even stranger. But the strangest guest by far was the white-haired peasant girl seated beside the empress, staring determinedly at her lap.

What in the world had brought this random assortment of people together?

"I apologize for calling upon you at such a late hour," said Lady Aldelphia, "but this is something that cannot wait to be addressed. I'm sure many of you have heard stories circulating throughout Noryk regarding Moorfainian migrants."

"Pardon, Empress," said the priest, "but I heard the visitors were not actually foreign."

"You heard correctly, Brother Azrin. This is Keriya Soulstar." She gestured to the peasant. "Keriya is not Moorfainian. She is a dragon speaker."

The girl—Keriya—finally looked up. Even from across the long table, the color of her eyes was evident. Max felt his stomach plummet toward the gilded floor. A dragon speaker? How was it even possible? His shock turned to fear, then slowly to excitement. This could change everything.

Rikoru gasped. Brother Azrin opened his mouth, then closed it and sank back in his chair. Taeleia placed both hands over her heart, her long ears quivering, her silvery eyes over-bright with emotion.

"Shivnath herself gave Keriya this power because Necrovar has broken free from the Etherworld." Max felt his jaw clench involuntarily; Aldelphia had never been one to mince words. "We had our suspicions, now we have our proof. The Rift is widening."

"But this is a good thing," said Brother Azrin. "Shivnath has sent us a savior in our time of need. And if the Rift widens, perhaps the dragons will return to Selaras."

"If they were the only ones returning, it *would* be good. But if the dragons return then Necrovar's forces must also return for the sake of the balance. We would resume the war where we left it ten ages ago. And ten ages ago, we were losing."

There was a heavy silence. Max glanced around the room, trying to gauge everyone's reactions.

"Yet the opposite holds true, for if darkness returns, so must light," the empress continued. "The balance has been preserved. One dragon has returned to Allentria, and Keriya will summon it for us."

"You mean to have the dragon fight Necrovar?" said Rikoru, taking the momentous announcement of the dragon in stride.

"I mean to have the dragon kill Necrovar," Aldelphia replied. "He will be weak and vulnerable from his time in the Etherworld. Where our ancestors failed, we will triumph. We can end this."

Max frowned. The conversation had suddenly taken a drastic turn for the worse.

"During the Great War, the dragons refused to aid the mortal races," said Taeleia. "Why should this one be any different?"

"If it refuses to help, it will be Keriya's job to force it to fight."

They were treating the girl as if she wasn't there. Keriya wilted, sinking down in her chair and closing her dreadful eyes. She looked so small and frightened—it was hard for Max to believe she held the power to decide the fate of the world.

"You think she can force the dragon's hand?" Azrin asked in a breathy voice.

"Prince Maxton?" said the empress, looking at him. "This is your area of expertise."

Max cleared his throat, wrenching his gaze away from Keriya. "That is one facet of her powers, yes."

"Forgive me, Empress," said Taeleia, "but this approach seems harsh and cruel. I have never seen you like this."

"You have never seen me with my country at war," she returned. "This is why I am not involving the Council. It is foolish to spend weeks deliberating over the best course of action and drawing up treaties. It will be equally foolish to waste our peoples' lives fighting a battle that cannot be won by mortal means."

Max glanced at the *rheenar* again. She was peeking up at him through her unruly bangs. He shuddered and looked away.

"It's been seven thousand years since the Imprisonment. We've come far in that time," stated Rikoru. "Our mages have discovered new and powerful ways to weave threads; our engineers have developed stronger weapons; we have technology our forefathers could never have dreamed of. Surely we stand a better chance if we fight, rather than leaving our fate in the hands of a child."

"Do not underestimate the Shadow," Taeleia cautioned. "If we fight, we may find ourselves outmatched."

"Then we ask for foreign aid," Rikoru retorted.

"We have estranged our former allies," said Aldelphia. "No one would deign to help us."

"But Necrovar is a threat to all of Selaras," Azrin protested. "Surely the other countries know that."

"Even if they were willing to help, how would we reach them to ask for it?" said Taeleia. "Allentrian ships are cursed, doomed to perish at sea before ever they reach their destinations."

Azrin shook his head. "Old wives' tales."

"The record stands with Lady Taeleia on this," said Aldelphia. "Foreign aid is out of the question. We will not send our ships to their certain demise, and I doubt we would receive any help even if they were to arrive safely. The dragon is our only hope, which brings us to the main reason I brought you here. Of everyone I trust, you are each the most knowledgeable in your respective fields."

Max repressed a sigh as he glanced around. Deep down, a small part of him wished the empress had placed her trust more carefully.

"I need your help," she told them. "Tonight, we are going to summon the dragon."

CHAPTER THIRTEEN

THE VALE ROOM

"Guard well the magic belonging to thee,
Lest you lose your grasp and set it free."
~ The Binding Laws, 15:8

"Excuse me, where are we going?" Fletcher asked, hurrying to keep up with Tevyn.

The stone-faced servant didn't respond.

"Hey," Roxanne said rudely. "We want to know what's going on."

"I'm showing you to your quarters," Tevyn said curtly. No mention of where Keriya had been swept off to. No explanation why Fletcher and Roxanne had been so abruptly dismissed from the throne room. It didn't seem like they were getting arrested, but it also didn't seem like they were being treated especially well.

"Your empress is making a big mistake," said Roxanne. "Keriya doesn't even have magic."

"We should be with her. We're her friends," Fletcher added.

Tevyn was unimpressed.

"And her assistants," said Roxanne. "She can't do magic without us."

Finally, Tevyn stopped. He turned to inspect the two of them. "I shall inquire as to whether Lady Soulstar has need of you. If it pleases my lord and lady to follow me?" He glided back past them in the direction they'd come from.

Fletcher glanced at Roxanne, who shrugged. Having no real choice, they hurried after Tevyn.

They snaked through crisscrossing corridors, passing other servants and the occasional Imperial Guard, until their hallway opened into a large room. The far wall was made of natural stone, rather than the creamy marble that comprised the rest of the palace. A modest wooden door stood at its center.

Tevyn pulled a key from his breast pocket, unlocked the door, and slipped inside. The door swung shut behind him and Fletcher jumped forward to catch it before he and Roxanne got locked out.

"Go," she whispered, pushing him through the entrance. The room within was three stories high and twice as wide. It was dry as a desert but as cold as a glacier, and filled with tall shelves stretching back as far as the eye could see. The shelves were stacked with countless books, and dimly illuminated by floating orbs that glowed with steady blue light. The orbs bobbed gently in the air, like bubbles anchored in a deep sea.

Tevyn walked down a wide aisle between the bookshelves. He stopped by a narrow table to confer with a tall, blonde-haired young man and a balding, wizened man who had two glass circles balanced on the edge of his nose.

"Fletcher?"

Fletcher perked up at the sound of his name and squinted through the sparse light. Keriya was sitting at the table, peeking out from behind the men. He opened his mouth to hail her, then paused. He was still reeling from the realization that Cezon had turned them over to the Allentrian government, and he wasn't sure he could handle any more nasty shocks. A hundred questions piled up behind his leaden tongue: *Is it true you're a dragon speaker? What do these people want with you? What's going to happen to us?*

"They cannot be here," said the old man, adjusting the glasses on his nose so he could scowl more accurately at Fletcher.

"Wait!" Keriya leapt up. She looked paler than usual, though that might have been due to the sickly light of the orbs. "Please let them stay."

The old man started to protest, but the younger one held out a hand to still him. "Peace, Master Rikoru. If she needs help, let them help."

"Fine," Rikoru grumbled. "On your own head be it. Tevyn, leave us. No more interruptions."

Tevyn bowed his way out of the room. Rikoru shuffled off into the stacks, muttering to himself as he disappeared in the dusty gloom. The young man gestured to Fletcher and Roxanne, indicating they were free to approach.

"Are you alright?" Fletcher asked when he reached Keriya.

"Yeah. You?"

"Oh, we're fantastic," said Roxanne. "How about you explain what's going on?"

Keriya glanced briefly at the young man. He inched away from the table, perhaps put off by the luminous gleam the orbs lent to her eyes.

"Okay, look," she whispered, leaning closer to Fletcher. "Back in Aeria, Shivnath appeared to me. She told me about Necrovar and she gave me some of her powers, but only because she wants me to *save* the dragon. She said I had to face Necrovar in its place. She said I was going to be a hero. Now the empress claims I can't kill Necrovar and she wants me to use Shivnath's powers to make the dragon fight, and I don't know what to do."

"So . . . what you said about Shivnath changing your eyes," Fletcher breathed, "that was true?"

"Yes," she snapped. "Why would I lie about something like that?"

"That's a great question," said Roxanne, her voice dripping with sarcasm. "It's a little suspicious, don't you think? You've always wanted magic and all of a sudden Shivnath conveniently gives you the power to save the world. I mean, why would she choose you, of all people?"

Surprisingly, there was no angry outburst from Keriya. Her face fell and she looked away.

"I don't know," she admitted.

Fletcher was having trouble sorting out his emotions. The anger that Keriya had led him away from Aeria for this madness was canceled out by shock, leaving him numb.

Master Rikoru cut the awkward moment short. He bustled over and carefully laid a rolled-up parchment before Keriya.

"This is one of the most valuable scrolls in the world." He opened the scroll, revealing rows of foreign runes. "It is a translation of *rheenaraion* wielding techniques originally recorded by Valerion Equilumos himself. It details how to weave the spell that will summon a dragon."

"Oh," said Keriya, staring down at the indecipherable writing with a pained expression.

"Prince Maxton, Master Rikoru?"

A new voice issued from the doorway. Fletcher turned to see a tall, lithe creature dressed in a fitted white tunic and leggings. She had silver eyes and ivory skin that shimmered like an opal. Long, pointed ears stuck out through waves of white-blonde hair that cascaded down past her shoulders.

"Brother Azrin has prepared the Vale Room," she said in a low voice. She held out a hand, extending clawed fingers too thin and long to look human. "Come, *Drachrheenar*."

Fletcher, Keriya, and Roxanne stared at the newcomer blankly.

"She's talking to you," said Rikoru, yanking Keriya to her feet.

"Right! Sorry." Keriya allowed herself to be marched over to the woman. Fletcher slunk after her, worried that at any moment someone would yell at him and cart him away.

"I'm holding you accountable if that scroll doesn't get back here safely, Maxton," Rikoru called out. Maxton smiled and nodded, and shut the door firmly behind him as they exited the book room.

The group followed the woman as she ghosted through the halls. This close, Fletcher saw that her opal skin wasn't skin at all — she was covered with thousands of tiny scales, like those of a woodland snake.

She led them deep into the palace. There were no windows here, and few lights. The artworks on the walls were replaced by unmarked doors with heavy bolts. Even Fletcher, who didn't know anything about anything, could tell this area was ancient—and dangerous.

They came to the end of a darkened corridor. Before them stood a stone archway that led to somewhere even darker. The woman walked through it, disappearing as she crossed the threshold. Keriya went next and vanished as well. Fletcher, who was right behind her, swallowed his reservations and stepped into the unknown. His vision went black. He grew feverish, feeling hot and cold all at once.

He didn't have time to panic, for one more step brought him into a round stone chamber with a domed ceiling. Twelve massive torches hung in golden brackets, casting harsh light across a floor of glossy tiles arranged in spiraling designs. Natural rock jutted up from the ground in the center of the room, forming a basin filled with gently swirling water. The rock formation was crusted with gemstones that sparkled with a violet tinge. For some reason, the structure made Fletcher's skin crawl.

The scaled woman led Keriya toward the basin. Fletcher started after her, but Maxton put out a hand to stop him.

"You'll want to stay back," he warned. "Follow me."

He showed Fletcher and Roxanne to a staircase sculpted into the curved wall and they ascended to a balcony that wrapped around the room. Lady Aldelphia was already there, standing across from them, blindly watching the proceedings below.

A dark-skinned man in red robes appeared and made his way toward Keriya. He offered her a golden chalice.

"Drink of the *alderevas* and be one with your power," he intoned, encouraging Keriya to take the cup. She sniffed at its contents and pulled a face. "In the name of our holy Guardians, Valaan the Pure, Zumarra the Merciful, Naero the Brave, and Shivnath the Mighty, we awaken the Vale Room and invoke its power."

Keriya reluctantly tipped her head back and sipped whatever was in the chalice. The man retrieved the cup and the scroll from her and pointed to the water.

"Step into the spring."

She stared dubiously at the liquid. "How deep is it?"

"Not deep," the woman assured her, taking her hand and helping her over the rocks and into the basin. "I will be nearby, should healing be necessary."

"Healing?" Fletcher asked, rounding on Maxton. "What are they doing to her? Is it dangerous?"

"Very," said Maxton, his lean face creased with worry.

The woman and the man retreated to the safety of the balcony. Then the empress raised her hands. A grating rumble met Fletcher's ears. He looked up to see that the ceiling had split down the middle. The two hemispheres were rotating open, revealing the cloudless sky. Night had fallen and the star-speckled heavens stretched above. The crescent Oldmoon flooded the torchlit chamber with cold light.

"Let the summoning begin," the empress declared.

All eyes turned to Keriya, who was huddled in upon herself in the water.

"You want me to just . . . call the dragon?"

"Yes," Aldelphia said simply. "Maxton, do you have any advice?"

"You must focus your intent." Maxton's voice was steady, but he looked almost as frightened as Keriya. His knuckles went white as he gripped the balcony's carved balustrade. "Wielding prowess stems from mental strength. You must want the dragon to come to you as much as you want to breathe."

Fletcher began to wonder exactly how dangerous this procedure was, and how dangerous the dragon would be once it arrived.

Keriya took a breath. She cleared her throat and tilted her head back to stare at the stars. "Dragon," she said loudly, "by order of, uh . . . of me, I guess, and of the Allentrian Empire, I—"

"You must speak in the draconic language." She was interrupted by Rikoru, who had emerged from somewhere behind Fletcher. The old man shuffled forward, leaning over the railing to shake a disapproving finger at Keriya. "Did you not read the scroll?"

"No matter what you think Shivnath may have wanted, only a dragon can save us now," said the empress.

"Don't be afraid," the opal-skinned woman added. "This chamber is strong. Use your magic."

Keriya looked down and mumbled something incoherent.

"Speak up, girl," said Rikoru, adjusting his glasses as if he thought that might help him hear.

"I don't have any magic!" Keriya's scream echoed in the chamber, rebounding over and over.

"Not of my own, anyway." Her voice was softer now, but in the silence that had descended, every word was clear as a bell. "I'm a cripple. Shivnath gave me some of her magic to fight Necrovar, but . . . I don't think I have the power to summon the dragon."

"Your eyes prove otherwise," Aldelphia said coldly.

"She's obviously lying," said Rikoru. "Bind her with the reliquary chains and she'll sing a different tune."

"Empress, you can't—" Max began, but Aldelphia had already raised one slender hand. She made a small gesture and two metallic chains whipped up from the depths of the spring, each tipped with a silver-white manacle. The manacles clamped around Keriya's wrists, locking her in place.

She cried out and started to struggle. "Let me go! You're hurting me!"

"What you're feeling is an effect of the platinum catalyst," said the empress, speaking over Keriya's yells. "The manacles are reliquaries that draw out your magic, just as a lodestone might draw iron filings. It will only hurt if you fight it."

"I don't—have—magic!" Keriya grated through clenched teeth. She sank to her knees in the spring, clutching at her chest.

"Stop it," Fletcher yelled as Keriya's face went sheet-white. "She's telling the truth!"

But the empress didn't stop. The manacles remained locked around Keriya's wrists and she doubled over in pain. Light began shimmering in the air around her. Bright flashes winked in and out of existence like sunlight playing across the surface of a stormy sea.

Fletcher didn't know what was going on from a magical standpoint, but he didn't have to understand it to see that it was killing the girl who he considered his only remaining family.

He started to run, meaning to go to the empress and use whatever force necessary to stop her from hurting Keriya. Maxton grabbed his arm before he could take more than three steps.

"Do not interfere," he hissed.

"Enough, empress." Shockingly, this came from Rikoru. He shook his head in disappointment. "If it hasn't worked by now, then something is wrong."

Aldelphia lowered her hand. The manacles sprang open with a soft clink and the chains retracted, snaking back into the water. Keriya let out a shuddering cry and slouched forward in relief.

"You're right; we should not have acted so rashly. It has been ten ages since the last *rheenar* lived, so we have no way of knowing if the Vale Room is safe for their kind. I'm sorry, Keriya."

Fletcher stifled a disbelieving laugh. Did Aldelphia think that was an adequate apology? It was obvious the procedure wasn't safe for Keriya the moment those chains had touched her skin.

The opal-scaled woman descended to ground level and gently pulled Keriya from the spring. She waved a hand back and forth over Keriya's chest, and with each pass a little more color returned to Keriya's cheeks.

"I've never seen such a phenomenon before," she commented, casting a meaningful look at Aldelphia.

"Now what do we do?" said Rikoru, irritable and snappish again. "The dragon is our only hope, but our only hope of summoning the dragon has failed." He gestured disparagingly at Keriya.

"Perhaps all is not lost," said Maxton, who had visibly

relaxed. "What if Keriya goes in search of the dragon? I would accompany her and teach her everything I know about the *rheenarae*."

"That is a time-consuming plan that does not guarantee results," said Rikoru.

"It's our best option," Maxton argued. "And right now, it's our only one."

Rikoru scowled at him. Then they both looked at the empress to make a decision.

"If you believe it can be done, Maxton—"

"I do."

"—then it shall be done. You will be outfitted with the fastest horses from the Imperial stables. A retinue of my personal guards will accompany you."

"Empress, I believe it best to keep the search party small," he said. "At the risk of overstepping my place, you don't know who you can trust."

"Very well; but take at least one more able-bodied fighter with you. Preferably a Tier Seven wielder or higher."

"I am too old for such a journey," said Rikoru.

"I'm afraid my duties to the church come first," said the dark-skinned man.

"What about us?" Fletcher asked, pointing to himself and Roxanne. If these people thought they were going to ship Keriya off on a dangerous quest alone with a bunch of equally dangerous strangers, they were dead wrong.

Aldelphia gave him an appraising look. "What can you offer?"

Fletcher pursed his lips. What *could* he offer? Did he think he could keep Keriya safe? He, a boy whose magic was so weak it was basically nonexistent?

"I can fight." Roxanne had finally spoken. Her expression was unreadable as she faced the empress. "And I'm good at it. Growing up, I had the most powerful magic out of everyone I knew. I taught myself the basics of being a Hunter, so I can track and forage, and cover my traces if need be. And as a Hunter, I'm sworn to protect those who need my services."

"Excellent." The empress gave her a business-like nod. "You will serve as an additional guard. What of you, Master Earengale?"

"I . . . I'm not sure," Fletcher admitted, realizing that he might have just dug himself into a hole he couldn't escape. "I don't have powerful magic. I can't speak to dragons and I can't fight."

He looked at Keriya again. She was silent, but her eyes, red-violet pools of fear, spoke volumes.

"I just know that I have to go," he said, feeling his resolve strengthen. He wouldn't abandon or betray her the way Asher had betrayed him. He didn't know how he could help on a journey such as this, but he couldn't let Keriya face whatever obstacles lay before her on her own.

The empress seemed to be sizing him up, and Fletcher resisted the urge to shrink away. It felt like she was staring right through him, passing judgement upon his very soul.

"It is decided," Aldelphia finally said. "The four of you will depart tomorrow at dawn."

CHAPTER FOURTEEN

THE PLAN

"To be different is a marker of greatness;
but if you do not embrace it, you will be neither different nor great."
~ **Ghokarian Equilumos, Second Age**

The Aerians returned to the throne room to prepare for their departure. Lady Aldelphia provided each of them with a satchel of provisions and signed, sealed letters detailing the nature of their mission. She delivered a few more speeches about Necrovar, but Keriya couldn't pay attention. Her mind was buzzing and her stomach was a tangled knot of shame and misery.

She didn't feel like she was destined for greatness anymore—she felt like a failure. Shivnath had told her not to trust anyone and she hadn't listened. Now she'd been roped into doing the exact opposite of what she was supposed to do.

Keriya dabbled with the idea of refusing the empress' demands. Then she remembered the threat of war, the promise that she would lose against Necrovar without the dragon, and the pain of the metal chains. When she looked at Aldelphia now, she was filled with the same cold, subtle dread she'd always felt when facing the Elders. She was too afraid to defy the Allentrian ruler.

She caught her reflection in one of the stained glass windows. Her eyes, two splotches of garish color in her otherwise achromatic appearance, glinted back at her.

"Why did Shivnath choose you?" she whispered as the empress and Prince Maxton talked over her head.

Her reflection offered no answers.

Eventually, Aldelphia instructed Tevyn to escort them to their rooms. He ushered them out and showed them to a set of spacious guest rooms in the east wing of the palace.

"Excuse me, Keriya."

Keriya turned just before she entered her quarters. Maxton had followed her.

"I was wondering if I might speak with you before you retire."

"What?" she said stupidly.

"I'd like the chance to explain what happened earlier. I know how frightening it must have been."

Keriya was keen to avoid talking to Fletcher and Roxanne about the day's events, but she didn't want to face the prince, either. This was a perfect opportunity to heed Shivnath's advice. She shouldn't go off on her own with someone who'd stood by and allowed the empress to torture her.

"I'll have you back to your room in a timely fashion," he added with a pearl-white smile.

She did want an explanation for what had happened in the Vale Room, and of all the Allentrians she'd met, Maxton seemed the most reasonable. It didn't hurt that he was also the most attractive person who had ever paid attention to her.

Despite her reservations, Keriya nodded. Without looking at Fletcher or Roxanne, she set off with Maxton, feeling awkward, dirty, common, and foolish. The prince was wearing a silver-threaded tunic that looked like it was worth more than her life and a priceless diamond amulet that caught and held the light of the chandeliers.

"How can I help you, Prince Maxton?" she managed.

"Call me Max," he said. She nodded, though she didn't think she had the courage to be so informal with him. "First, I'd like to apologize. The empress had no right to do what she did."

Keriya was too stunned to come up with a response. Abuse was something she'd grown used to in Aeria; apologies, on the other hand, had been rarer than dragons.

"You must understand the position we're in," he continued, placing a hand on the small of her back to guide her down a side hall. Her cheeks began to burn, and her heart filled with something halfway between fear and excitement. "Your appearance marks the beginning of a war that has been brewing for the past ten ages."

"My appearance? I think you mean Necrovar's return." She must have sounded terribly rude, but Maxton wasn't offended. In fact, he laughed.

"A fair point. But you are the spark that will start the fire; both the Shadow Lord and the empress need the dragon. You have the power to control it, which puts you in a powerful position."

Keriya's face fell. How could Maxton still think she was powerful after the Vale Room debacle?

As if he'd read her mind, he said, "I know you may not feel that way now, but it's true. I've studied the *rheenarae* for most of my life, and I can teach you summoning and command techniques."

Keriya rolled her eyes. Would none of these people listen? "Look, Prince Maxton—"

"Just Max. Try saying it. It isn't that difficult to pronounce." The blush that had crept across her cheeks spread to her ears and neck.

"Well, Max," she said to her feet, "Shivnath never said anything about finding or summoning or controlling the dragon. She wanted me to save it. That's why she gave me this power—to save the dragon by killing Necrovar."

Max didn't respond. When Keriya snuck a glance at him, she saw that he was frowning.

"You don't believe me, do you?"

The prince jolted himself from his thoughts and stopped walking. There was a whisper in the hallway, a sound like soft footsteps, but they were quite alone.

"I do believe you, Keriya," he told her. "I'm just not sure what to make of it."

"Oh." Keriya's stomach did an odd sort of flip-flop. Max actually believed her. "Why's that?"

"The idea that Shivnath would ask you to kill Necrovar

is . . ."

"Ridiculous?" she supplied in a bitter voice.

"Confusing," he finished with a small smile. "I'm sure there's more going on there than you realize."

"Don't I know it," she muttered.

"I think the best course of action is to find the dragon," Max said as he started to walk again. It was such an abrupt shift in the discussion it caused a shiver to run through Keriya.

"Why?" she asked, following him. Didn't that go against everything they'd just been talking about?

"You say Shivnath told you she wanted you to kill Necrovar. You can't do that without a dragon."

"But she—"

"Never explicitly told you *not* to find the dragon, did she?"

Keriya thought back on her conversations with Shivnath. The dragon god hadn't been explicit about anything, whether it was getting to the Fironem, wielding magic, or killing Necrovar.

"I suppose not," she conceded.

"There now." He beamed down at her. Looking into his sky-blue eyes, she couldn't help but smile back. "Doesn't it feel better to have a plan?"

"Yes." Perhaps this was all for the best. Before, she'd been floundering blindly without a clue as to how to complete Shivnath's quest; now she had direction and assistance. The visions of grandeur she had lost in the Vale Room bloomed brightly in her mind once more.

Max stopped again, and Keriya was surprised to discover they were standing in front of a familiar door. They'd done a full circuit of the east wing and had ended up back at her room.

"Back in a timely fashion, as promised," he said. "Get some rest. We've a long journey ahead of us. It will be an adventure fit for the storybooks."

Keriya was sure her cheeks were a flaming shade of red. She nodded. "Thanks. It was nice talking to you."

"Good night, Keriya. I'll return at dawn."

Keriya eased the door open and snuck into a common room

filled with comfy chaises. Fletcher was nowhere to be seen, but Roxanne was still up. She was gazing through a set of glass doors that led to a balcony, admiring the golden peaks of the cityscape that glittered in the distance.

"Hi," Keriya said tentatively. "So, about earlier — "

"Look," Roxanne interrupted, "I don't know what you're playing at. I think you're in trouble and I have no idea how you're going to get yourself out of this whole summoning-a-dragon business. I don't want to be involved in this, but every Hunter has to go on a journey to prove their skill before they earn their name, and this will be mine. So don't mess it up for me."

Having said her piece, she stalked to one of three doors that led to separate sleeping rooms and slammed it shut behind her.

The warm, tingly feeling from Keriya's time with Max evaporated, leaving a sour emptiness in its place. Keriya scowled after Roxanne as she headed to the second door. She yanked it open to find Fletcher was sitting on the edge of the bed, hands folded in his lap, as if he'd been waiting for her.

"Sorry," she said. "I didn't know you'd taken this room. I'll go."

"Wait." Fletcher stood up. "Can we talk?"

Keriya closed her eyes. She wasn't sure she was ready to talk. She didn't want to hear any more disbelief or accusations.

"You know," she said, "I wanted to talk back in Aeria."

"Could you let that go?" he asked in a tired voice. "How many times do I have to say I'm sorry?"

"I haven't heard you say sorry once."

"That's because you aren't listening," he cried. "I'm sorry you're angry, but you don't seem to realize that despite everything that happened, I stayed loyal to you. Besides, it's not exactly like you've apologized for anything."

"Me? What did I do?"

"Let's see — you made me leave Aeria under false pretenses, you got me roped into a dangerous quest — "

"You volunteered for the quest," she reminded him, crossing her arms.

"Yes, because I want to make sure you don't get killed!"

Keriya barely suppressed a laugh. Who was Fletcher kidding? He couldn't protect her.

"You had a rough time in Aeria," he continued. "But you know what? So did I. I was bullied, just like you. I was an outcast. People knew I was different and they hated me for it."

"Not as much as they hated me," she muttered to herself. She said it a little too loudly, and Fletcher heard her.

"This isn't a competition. I'm just trying to make a point. Bad things happen, but you can't let that turn you into a bad person."

When Keriya opened her mouth furiously, Fletcher held up a hand to stay her words. "I'm not saying you're a bad person, because I know you. I'm sorry your experiences have led you to believe that you can't trust anyone. But I wish you would trust me again."

The two of them stood in silence for a long moment. Keriya wasn't sure how to respond. She was still angry, but Fletcher had brought up some valid points.

"Fine," she said. "Let's just forget this ever happened, okay?"

"We can't really do that. Why don't we just agree to forgive each other?"

"Fine," she said again, more irritably this time. "I'm sorry. You're sorry. There, we're done."

Fletcher sighed in exasperation. "Good enough, I guess."

There was another pause as they stared at each other. Keriya felt like she should say something more, but she couldn't for the life of her come up with the right words.

Finally she said, "I'll let you get some sleep. The Allentrians want us to leave early tomorrow. So, uh . . . have a good night."

"Good night," he replied, as she retreated from his room and pulled the door shut behind her.

Keriya went to the third bedroom, which was identical to Fletcher's. She lay down on the soft mattress and stared at the ceiling, thinking.

They might have agreed to forgive and forget, but from what Fletcher had said, it was clear he wasn't going to forget everything that had happened since they'd left Aeria.

And as for Keriya . . . well, she had never been very good at forgiving.

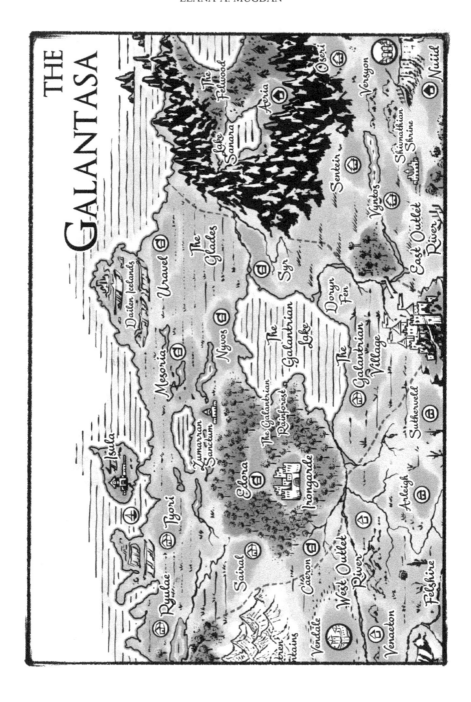

CHAPTER FIFTEEN

THE FIFTH COMPANION

"Your fate may be made or broken by your friends."
~ The Oracle, Second Age

The northern gates of Noryk creaked open. A warm wind slipped into the city from the plains beyond, carrying the fresh scent of morning dew and the promise of adventure. Keriya took a deep breath. She refused to be angry or upset, not at the dawn of a bright day like this one.

"Thank you, soldier," Max said to the guardsman who opened the gates for them. Then he turned to Keriya. "After you."

"Ready?" she asked, looking at Fletcher.

"Ready as I'll ever be," he said, though he didn't sound ready at all.

They passed through the gate and descended the stone bridge that led into the Galantasa, the northernmost kingdom of the Allentrian Empire. A hard-packed dirt road meandered through the wetlands, winding its way toward them through sapphire pools and tiny streams.

Keriya stopped when they reached level ground. "So . . . what now?"

Behind her, Roxanne slapped a hand to her forehead.

"That's up to you," said the prince. "You're the dragon speaker, so you're the only one who can sense the dragon."

"Ahh, there *is* a dragon," said a new, unfamiliar voice.

Keriya spun around. A lanky, dark-skinned boy with a shock of messy hair was sliding out from behind the tollhouse. He had a carefree spring in his step and his brown eyes gleamed with mischief as he nodded to Keriya.

At once, everyone was on guard. Max stepped in front of Keriya protectively and Roxanne raised her fists in a fighting stance. The newcomer didn't appear bothered.

"Sorry to interrupt. Effrax Emberwill, at your service."

"Nameless," Max growled. "What are you doing here?"

Nameless? Keriya narrowed her eyes and stared at the boy; did that epithet refer to the same thing in Allentria as it did in Aeria?

"I should think that's rather obvious," said Effrax, inspecting his fingernails as he advanced upon them. "I'm spying on you. I do have a nasty habit of that, you know."

"This time you've crossed the line. That dragon is an Imperial-level secret."

"Then poor show for chatting up your lady-friend last night where any fool could overhear you," Effrax quipped.

Keriya pursed her lips. He did have a point.

"Take another step and I'll be forced to hurt you," said Max.

"Oh, relax," Effrax said with a long-suffering sigh. "You think I'm going to blackmail you? I wouldn't do something like that. Well, I would — but not to you."

"Then why are you here?" Roxanne demanded.

"Because my state is in trouble," he said without looking at her. He was staring fixedly at Keriya. "And I'd like to strike a bargain with you."

"Sorry, we don't bargain with spies," said Roxanne. The ground rumbled and a thin wall of earth flew up between Effrax and the group, blocking his path.

Effrax took a step back. He finally turned his attention to Roxanne, peering at her over the top of the barrier.

"That was a warning," she told him.

Effrax chortled, still unruffled. "Oh, I like this one. She's got the fighting spirit of a tigress."

"You can leave on your own, or I can have you arrested," said Max.

"Wait," said Keriya. "I want to know why he's interested in the dragon." She glared at Effrax, who didn't flinch away from her eyes as people usually did.

"I mean no harm," he assured her. "My interests are as pure and self-serving as they come. The Fironem has been suffering for over a decade. Our crops are failing, our animals are sickening, our people are disappearing. So here's what I propose: I help you find the dragon, you use its power to help my state."

Max shook his head. "The dragon won't have time to—"

"To what, Maxton? To save a quarter of the Allentrian Empire?" Effrax tutted and sidestepped Roxanne's wall. "I'm disappointed by your shortsightedness. Besides, you might need someone with my talents on your journey. I'm a good spy, an even better shot with a longbow, and I can do this." He held out his hand and a tongue of fire flared above his palm, crackling with vibrancy.

Keriya stifled a gasp. *Fire magic.*

"It'll come in handy, Dragoneyes," said Effrax, noticing her admiration of the dancing flames. "Wouldn't you like to have the luxury of a nice, warm fire every night in this god-awful swamp?" He jerked his thumb over his shoulder, indicating the Galantasa.

"Even if we don't have you thrown in the dungeons for treason, you wouldn't be allowed to come with us," said Max. "Your prince will have need of your services, I'm sure."

"Zivan has twenty guards surrounding him day and night— he'll survive without me. Plus, it could be said that I'm doing much more good for the Fironem here, with you." Effrax turned back to Keriya. "We all want the same thing. You would be the savior of my people if you did this."

Something surfaced in Keriya's imagination at his words, a vision of her walking through a crowd of cheering people. Once she had thought of it, she found she couldn't let it go.

She debated with herself for a few long moments, then nodded. "Fine, you can come."

"Keriya, I must advise against this," said Max.

"It wouldn't hurt to have another person helping us look for the dragon, would it?" she argued.

Especially since I won't be able to summon it, added the tiny voice in her head.

Effrax smiled smugly at Max. "I suppose that settles it."

"No it doesn't," said Roxanne. "I don't want you to come, either."

Effrax pulled an insincere pout. "Come now, don't be like that. Is it because I wasn't frightened by your little show?" He patted her earthen wall. "Very impressive dirt wielding."

"It's because I was appointed by Lady Aldelphia as one of the guards on this mission," she returned. Keriya noticed that her hands were shaking, so tightly were her fists clenched. "And I don't trust you."

"I think he means well," Fletcher mumbled from Keriya's other side, scuffing his feet on the dusty road.

"You thought Cezon meant well, too," Roxanne snapped. "And look how that turned out for us."

"Cezon did mean well," Fletcher shot back. "He fed and housed us, he kept us safe, he brought us to Noryk, he just — "

"Just what? Accidentally turned us over to the Imperial Guards, the very people he claimed he was helping us hide from?" Roxanne snorted. "Yeah, he was really great."

"Ooh, had a disagreement with the Imperials, did we?" Effrax raised his eyebrows.

"Enough with the spying, Nameless," said Max.

"To be spying, that implies that I have to *secretly* collect information," said Effrax. "It's almost as if you four want me to know everything about you."

Max growled in frustration. "Get out of here. And if you tell anyone what you've overheard — "

"Not so fast," Effrax interrupted. "I count two votes to let me stay. But one of those votes was the Dragon Speaker's, which counts for at least three. The majority has spoken. I can come."

"Absolutely not," said Roxanne.

"Relax, Roxanne," said Keriya.

Roxanne rounded on her. "Why are you trusting someone

who's admitted he's a criminal? It's Cezon all over again!"

"'Criminal' is a bit harsh, coming from someone who's admitted she's on the run from the Imperials," Effrax put in blithely.

"For the record, I don't trust him." Keriya fixed Effrax with a calculating glare. "I'll help your state, but I'm not doing it because you asked me—I'm doing it because that's what any self-respecting hero would do. And the only reason I'm letting you come along is because you're more dangerous to us out there than you are here, where we can keep an eye on you."

Max considered this, and finally nodded his approval. Strangely, so did Effrax.

"If that's the case, you're wiser than you know," said Effrax, growing serious for a moment.

"Fine. Nameless, you're in. I expect you to pull your weight, and if we even so much as suspect you're up to something . . ." Max trailed off, leaving the threat unspoken.

"I wouldn't dream of acting up, Your Grace," said Effrax, offering Max a theatrical bow. Roxanne looked ready to chew knives, but she made no further complaints. The dirt wall receded into the road, leaving the path before them free and open.

Effrax turned to Keriya with an expression of polite interest. "Well Dragoneyes, what are your orders?"

Keriya supposed she could try calling the dragon, but she didn't want to flaunt her inadequacy again so soon after what had happened in the Vale Room.

Everyone was waiting for her. She squared her shoulders and straightened up. She had no idea what to do or where to go, but she knew one thing for certain: heroes weren't indecisive.

"We head north."

CHAPTER SIXTEEN

THE BARGAIN

"Wicked though the weasel be,
he kills the cockatrice for free."
~ Smarlindian Folk Saying

"You bloody tronkin' rotter! You fungus-brained son of a trollop!"

Cezon knew that berating Iako for the umpteenth time wouldn't do him any good, but it made him feel marginally better about things.

"It en't my fault," Iako insisted again, straining against the shackles that bound him to the wall of the Imperial dungeon. "I done everything you said. I gave the papers to all the right people—"

"Obviously you didn't, otherwise we wouldn't be locked up."

"Huh." This seemed to stump Iako. He stared off into the dreary haze of their jail cell and the two of them lapsed into silence.

Cezon resumed the only activity available to him, apart from screaming at Iako: planning his escape. Truth be told, he wasn't sure there was a way out. He and Iako had records bad enough to keep them locked up for life, but he was no fool. The Imperials didn't keep condemned prisoners alive for long.

He shifted his weight around on the dank stone floor, trying to find a comfortable position. His wrists were sore from straining against his manacles, and the iron collar around his neck was unbearable. There was a thin needle within the contraption that dug into his spine, delivering poison into his bloodstream to prevent him from wielding. Every time he moved his head, pain shot down his back and radiated across his body.

"I really effin' hate you, Iako. I really do. Before we die in here, I want to be sure you understand that."

"We en't gonna die. Endred'll save us when we don't come back with the reward money."

"When we don't come back, Endred will realize we've been captured and get as far from Noryk as he can. He don't want to get thrown in here with us. Same goes for Miff and the others."

"You think?"

"What would you do if you was them?"

"Oh. Yeah, that makes sense. Guess we are gonna die in here."

Cezon closed his eyes. So much hatred to dwell upon, so little time.

"You know who else I hate?" he grumbled. "Keriya bloody Soulstar. You're welcome for the Moorfainians, Aldelphia!" he yelled, his hoarse voice echoing throughout the dungeon. "And you're welcome, you dungbrain shifters, for bringin' your stupid arses to Noryk for free! You'd think that mighta been worth standing up for us and saying a few words in our defense, but no! Do a good deed out the kindness of your heart and this is what happens."

"Shut up in there." The guard on duty leaned into view and banged on the metal bars of the cell. Cezon quieted — not because the guard had said so, but because the poison had sapped him of all his energy. If he wanted to continue to hate everyone properly, he'd have to conserve what strength he had left.

A grating noise from far off indicated a door being unlocked. Cezon listened to the sound of booted footsteps approaching. Perhaps his screams had alerted one of the other guards, or perhaps it was simply time for someone to replenish the poison supply in their collars.

"You're relieved of your duty," said a deep voice from just outside the cell. Cezon squinted through the gloom and saw the guard salute and march off. That meant the newcomer was an officer — a high-ranking officer, given that the man hadn't asked any questions.

A cloaked figure stepped into view. He removed a key from a large ring on his sword belt and fitted it into the lock on the cell door. The door swung inwards, creaking ominously as the figure entered. He was short and stocky. A wicked scar snaked across the right side of his face and bald head. Though his light brown skin made him look Smarlindian, his eyes screamed of his fire wielder heritage: they were red, the color of angry flames.

"Gohrbryn Tanthflame," Cezon breathed, gaping at the Commander-General of the Imperial Guard. "Well, if you're here to kill us, you might as well get on with it."

"Capital punishment is forbidden under Article Three, Section 12A in the Laws of Allentria," Tanthflame said in a cold voice as he stopped before Cezon and Iako, glaring down at them with a practiced disdain.

"Hah! You ain't gonna keep wasting *evasdrin* on prisoners condemned for life. And that's what we are, right? So do your worst."

"Actually, that's what I came to speak to you about. The Allentrian judicial system is not in the practice of granting pardons to individuals such as yourselves, but for Officer Blackwater—and possibly even for you, Skyriver—I am willing to make an exception."

"Thankee kindly, Commander-General," Iako simpered, flashing a gap-toothed grin.

"Why are you interested in him?" Cezon demanded. "He's worthless!"

"You're in no position to ask questions. But since I may require your assistance as well, I'll indulge you." Tanthflame sneered, causing his scar to distort his countenance. "I'm working on a sensitive project, and I need men whose loyalty and silence can be bought for gold."

"I'm in," Iako said without hesitation. "You know I done good, Commander-General. En't I done a good job for you this past month?"

"You've done a passably mediocre job," Tanthflame said flatly. "I wouldn't be here at all, but for the fact that I don't have time to find new recruits who I can, for lack of a better word, trust."

"What's in it for me?" Cezon wanted to know.

"Your freedom, for starters," the guardsman growled. "And I'll throw in a handsome sum to ensure you do as you're told. In return, you will speak of this to no one. If you do, rest assured that I will find out about your insubordination and I will kill you, no matter what Article Three, Section 12A states."

"When you make us an offer like that, how can we refuse?" said Cezon.

"Lemme out and I'll do whatever," Iako groveled.

"Not so fast, Blackwater. Because of the nature of what I'm about to ask, I will first need you to enter into a contract with me."

Cezon and Iako glanced at one another. Cezon did his best to conceal a smirk. Sure. They'd sign Tanthflame's contracts if it made him happy.

"I will need to collect a vial of blood from each of you."

The smirk slipped from Cezon's face. Why did Tanthflame want blood? Perhaps he was a superstitious fool and thought blood contracts were meaningful in ways that written contracts were not. Cezon knew better. Any contract could be broken. In fact, breaking contracts was one of his specialties.

"Fine," he said. "Blood it is."

Without preamble, Tanthflame produced a dagger and a glass bottle from somewhere on his person. Cezon didn't even have time to cry out before the blade was drawn across his palm, splitting open his skin. Tanthflame flexed Cezon's hand and collected the blooming red liquid in the vial. When he'd gathered his fill, he corked it and stowed it away.

"And you, Blackwater?"

"I can't do it without givin' my blood?"

"Suck it up, Iako," Cezon grated, squeezing his hand against the pain of the wound.

Iako sighed and opened his palm in compliance. The Commander-General repeated the same motions upon him.

"And just like that, gentlemen, you've bought your freedom." Tanthflame produced another key and unlocked the manacles that held them captive. Cezon massaged his aching wrists, though he was more interested in getting rid of the poison collar.

"In good time," said Tanthflame, as if he'd guessed what Cezon was thinking. "First, let me explain the work you'll be doing. Four days ago, a young girl was brought to the Imperial Palace. The Manager of Homeland Affairs had been misled into believing she was a royal Moorfainian fugitive. Does that sound familiar?"

No. It couldn't be. Cezon couldn't believe that fate would lead him back to Keriya Soulstar.

"In actuality, this child possesses a power that has not been seen in a ten-age, a power that makes her incredibly valuable and dangerous. You two will be part of a group that will cover the Galantasa to track her."

"What sorts of powers she got?" Iako asked apprehensively.

"That is none of your concern," said Tanthflame. "You'll be working with officers who will give you details as necessary. There will come a time when she uses her powers, and at that time, it will be your job to capture her, along with anyone and any*thing* in her company. You will be paid for your services, but he who actually delivers her to me will be rewarded beyond his wildest dreams."

A reward beyond Cezon's wildest dreams? He didn't know about that. He could dream up some pretty wild rewards. Still, this sounded like a good mission overall. He'd have a chance to get back at Soulstar and he'd get some gold for his troubles. Maybe a lot of gold. Maybe more gold than he could imagine—didn't Tanthflame have access to the Imperial treasury? It was all Cezon could do not to salivate at the thought of the mountains of derlei that must be piled in that vault.

"And remember, if anything goes wrong—"

"You'll kill us, we get it." Cezon didn't need threatening, not for this.

"I find — especially when dealing with criminals — that a bit of extra incentive is usually necessary. Just to be clear, if you desert your mission, if you tell anyone what you're doing, if you mention my involvement . . ." Tanthflame leaned close to Cezon and his eyes narrowed to ruby slits. "Then your blood will be bound to a Master who is much less forgiving than I. You will burn as His slave for the rest of eternity if you betray Him, for He will take your soul."

Cezon cared not a whit for empty threats. He wasn't one to be intimidated, but even so, his blood — blood he'd just given to the loony trog before him — ran cold through his veins. The threat was so far-fetched that it almost seemed like it might be real. Cezon wasn't one for history either, but he knew his basic lore. In all of time, there had only been one who'd had the power to take someone's soul and bend the rules of the universe to his will . . . but Necrovar was gone, locked away in some parallel dimension.

Wasn't he?

"Understood, Commander-General," said Cezon, shoving himself to his feet. Tanthflame was shorter than he, and as he stared down at the man, everything seemed less serious. The prospect of liberation loomed before him and he knew that no matter what sort of garbage contract he'd gotten into, he'd find a way to wriggle out of it. He always did. "Officer Blackwater and I are at your service."

"You are," Tanthflame agreed. He produced one more key and used it to unlock Cezon's collar.

Cezon yanked the poison barb from his flesh and threw the accursed band into the far corner of the cell. Tanthflame freed Iako and strode to the door.

"You have one hour to get out of the dungeons while I create a distraction. You will report to the abandoned cathedral at the north end of Broad Street, where one of my officers will give each of you your specific assignments."

Then he was gone, his footsteps fading away down the long corridor beyond.

"We better get goin'," said Iako, tearing a scrap of fabric from his sleeve and wrapping it around his bleeding hand. "I'm glad yer workin' on this too, Cezon. Now, how you reckon we oughta get ourselves out of here? I'll be lettin' you take the lead, seeing as I en't got a clue where north is."

Cezon sighed. "Iako, I don't know if I say this enough . . . but I really, *really* hate you."

CHAPTER SEVENTEEN

THE SUMMONING

"He who tries not, succeeds not."
~ Zeherion Leatherwing

"So Dragoneyes, is today the big day?"

Keriya refrained from screaming at Effrax. Every time she tried — and failed — to summon the dragon, she felt more and more like it was an exercise in futility.

They'd first gone east along a trade route, then they'd cut back in a northwesterly direction. Now they were traveling on a dirt road through Doryn Fen, a sprawling marsh saturated with streams and ponds. Even with Max's lectures about 'intent' and 'thread weaving' and 'quantum-magical entanglement that would allow her to summon the dragon no matter where it was in the world,' Keriya feared they were doomed to wander Allentria forever, searching in vain.

"Can't you hear its voice in your head and figure out where it is?" Roxanne asked as she hopped over a puddle.

"No, it doesn't work that way." Though to be fair, Keriya didn't know how it worked at all.

"Maybe you're not trying hard enough."

"It's not easy, Roxanne. I'd like to see you do this."

"It would be my pleasure," said Roxanne. "I'd be better at it."

Keriya clenched her teeth and suffered the insult quietly. She didn't have the heart to defend herself. She shouldn't even be here. She should be heading in the opposite direction, toward Necrovar. That was what Shivnath wanted.

But you can't win, she reminded herself, as she did every time she thought of abandoning her search. *Only a dragon can kill Necrovar.*

She stopped thinking and kept walking.

That afternoon, they rested in a hilly area. Since they'd run out of provisions the night before, Max went to hunt for food, leaving the Aerians with Effrax. He conjured a fire by the side of the road and they all sat down to relax. At least, Fletcher and Roxanne relaxed; Keriya hunched on a driftwood log, stewing in her dark thoughts.

"Are you going to try again?" Fletcher asked.

"What's the point?" Roxanne muttered. "She can't do it."

That was the last straw. Keriya stood abruptly. "You want me to call the dragon? Fine. Hey, dragon!" she screamed to the empty fen. "Enough with the games. Time to come out!"

"Keriya—" Fletcher's placatory tone only made her angrier.

"Would you look at that," she said, cutting him off. "No dragon."

"Shouldn't you be calling him in his own language?" said Effrax.

"I'm sorry, are you an expert on dragons?"

"Not in the slightest. But seeing as everyone's made such a fuss about you being a dragon speaker, I figured you'd try to speak to the dragon in a way it would understand."

That was all fine and dandy, but she didn't know how to speak dragon. She was officially the worst dragon speaker ever.

Keriya suddenly found she couldn't face her companions any longer. She turned and fled into the fen, diving into a patch of tall reeds. She kicked a stunted bush out of her way and ended up tripping, falling flat on her face. With a growl of fury, she punched the muddy ground—only succeeding in making herself more dirty—and let out a string of swear words that would have made Cezon Skyriver proud.

"Stupid weeds, stupid fen, stupid dragon that I'll never find in a million ages!" She shoved herself up and headed toward a rocky, sawtoothed ridge. When she reached the crest she stared at the dreary storm clouds massing in the skies.

"What now, Shivnath?" she said, as if hoping the dragon god would miraculously appear to fix all her problems. "I'm sure you're not listening. I'm sure you're busy with more important things. I just wish you would answer me. I could use some help."

"Keriya?"

Keriya jumped, startled by the unexpected voice. Max was walking up from the far side of the ridge.

"I thought I heard you. What happened?" he asked, eyeing her mud-covered dress.

She felt her cheeks begin to burn. "I tripped."

"Ah. Then let's get back to the campsite before the storm hits. We can get you cleaned up."

"I don't mind the rain," she said quickly. "I think I need to be away from the others for a bit."

Max chuckled. "Fair enough. I'm not a fan of Nameless, either."

Part of Keriya—a very silly part, a part that made no sense to her—wanted to laugh alongside Max and agree with everything he said. Another part winced at the way he said 'Nameless.' It made her feel sorry for Effrax.

"Why do you call him that?"

"Because he has no formal claim to any title or lands in the Fironem," said Max. "He's King Embersnag's bastard son, so he's granted more clemency than he deserves, but Halixa Coalwill wasn't married to the king when Effrax was born—nor was she even nobility."

Keriya had generally found the Allentrians to be more enlightened than the Aerians, but it seemed everybody agreed on this issue: if you didn't have a proper family, you were unworthy of even a name.

"Well, it's not just him," she said, unwilling to dwell on the subject. "It's everything. I have no idea what I'm doing."

"Don't worry." Max put a hand on her shoulder. Her heart leapt, basking in the undeserved attention. "You're persistent, smart, brave—things will work out soon enough."

Keriya's cheeks were burning so badly that she was surprised her head hadn't ignited in flames. She didn't think anything he'd said was true, but if Max was suffering from the delusion that she was smart and brave, she wasn't going to argue.

"Would you like to take a walk?" he asked.

"The storm's about to hit."

"I thought you liked the rain," he said, grinning. Keriya was caught off guard. Was he flirting with her?

Who in their right mind would flirt with you? whispered the awful voice in her head. *No one.*

The voice was right, of course. Just to spite it, Keriya nodded. "Sure! Let's walk."

They set off together, watching the storm roll in. It often drizzled in the afternoons here, but the showers were mild. This one seemed to be working its way up to a monsoon. Fractured lightning skittered across the sky, followed by a distant growl of thunder.

"We've been so busy searching that we haven't had much time to talk. Why don't you tell me about yourself?" said Max.

"I'm not really that interesting," Keriya said as the first of the raindrops began to fall. "Apart from the whole dragon speaker thing."

"That's a pretty big thing. And your—" He stopped and stared down at her. "Your eyes."

"Yes, my eyes," she said heavily.

"No, it's . . . they're glowing."

"What?"

Max rummaged in his pack and pulled out a hand mirror. He held it out to her, revealing that her irises were emitting an eerie light. They shone so brightly that they lit up her pupils, turning them red and reflective. She squeezed her eyes shut and clapped her hands over her face, but even then she couldn't escape the horror—purple light painted the backs of her closed lids.

"What's happening to me?" she moaned.

"It's alright," said Max. "It's a side effect of your powers. Your eyes will glow when necromagic is wielded nearby."

"What's necromagic?"

"Exactly what it sounds like: magicthreads that have been poisoned by Necrovar's touch."

"That is definitely *not* alright," she said, aghast. She wheeled around, meaning to go warn the others, but Max reached out and grabbed her by the shoulders, pulling her back to him.

"Don't move," he breathed, leaning close enough for his lips to brush her ear.

She knew she should be asking questions — what was going on? What did he think he was doing? Why wasn't he letting her tell Fletcher and Roxanne about the necromagic? — but instead she whispered, "Okay."

They were in danger. She *knew* they were in danger. So why was she standing there like a moon-eyed fool? It was just that being close to Max felt strangely good. She felt calm and safe.

The calm feeling evaporated when Max shoved her sideways. She tumbled and fell into a shallow puddle.

"What was that for?!" she coughed, rolling over. As she rose, she spotted the problem. The anger drained out of her, leaving her limp and winded.

Max had drawn his shortsword and was facing off against a hideous animal. It had a vaguely feline body, with a broad chest and smaller hindquarters that ended in a barbed tail. Bullish horns stuck out behind its tufted ears and sloping brow, and its underbite proudly displayed gleaming, saliva-coated fangs. Every inch of it was a uniform shade of black, even the drool that swayed from its jaws in gooey strands.

"Shadowbeast . . ." The word floated up from deep within Keriya, though she still wasn't sure what a shadowbeast was. Lady Aldelphia had said they were Necrovar's demonic minions, and this monster seemed to fit that description pretty well.

The shadowbeast growled and launched itself at her, claws outstretched. Max wielded a current of air to intercept it, smacking it back to the ground. It howled in confusion, hissing and spitting.

Keriya cast around for something she could use to fight—a branch, a rock, anything—when a ghastly, rotted black hand clamped down on her wrist. Her gaze slowly traveled from the hand, up a skeletal, decaying arm, and landed on the face of a man whose skin, hair and eyes were all the inky, hopeless color of death.

A shadowman.

She tried to break free from him, but he tightened his grasp. With his free hand, he grabbed her other arm and squeezed so hard that it felt like her bones were about to snap.

"We've been looking for you," he said, blowing rancid breath into her face.

"Don't kill me," she whispered.

"We don't want to kill you." He pulled her close, as Max had done mere moments before, catching her in a suffocating embrace. "We need you."

"Let me go! Max," she cried, as her captor began dragging her away. "Help!"

Max was busy fending off three more dark monsters who'd joined the first. Though they appeared reluctant to attack the prince, perhaps fearing his magic, it was obvious that he was in trouble. A black fog was rising beneath them, flickering in the wind.

"Wield, Keriya!" he yelled.

"I can't!" He was fully aware of her disability, and she'd told him time and time again that all the power she had been given was locked away.

Or was it?

Shivnath had promised she would be able to wield when the moment was right, and if this didn't qualify as the right moment, nothing would. Keriya closed her eyes and focused her intent, wanting—no, *needing* to call the dragon, needing it like she needed air and water and sunlight. She imagined her voice as Shivnath's: all-powerful, commanding, a voice that was designed to be obeyed.

"Dragon, come to me! Help me!" An ancient, foreign language slipped from Keriya's mouth, a language filled with the same essence of power that had lived within every syllable the god had uttered. The shadowman's grip loosened as soon as she spoke. A spark of energy flared in her chest, and some long-submerged instinct told her that whatever she was doing, it was working.

For the first time, she was doing something right.

She elbowed her enemy and he released her. Finally able to breathe, she drew air into her lungs and shouted again, this time for the whole world to hear:

"Dragon, come to me!"

She wanted to open her eyes to see what was happening—especially since the glow reflecting off her lids was blinding her—but she couldn't. She was caught in the thrall of her spell. Whatever magic she had harnessed, it had taken control of her.

A rumble shook the earth. The wind and rain beat against her skin. Thunder boomed, but her concentration never wavered. She was no longer Keriya Soulstar: she was a singular, burning desire to summon the dragon. She was the universe, and the universe was on her side. It felt like every magicthread around her wanted this to happen.

Through the blur of power-lust and panic, part of her thought that if this was what it felt like to wield, then she wanted to feel this way forever.

Something hit her square on the forehead and she doubled over, opening her eyes at last. Hailstones were falling thick and fast. The black fog had grown so dense that it was impossible to see the shadowbeasts.

"Max," she cried. "Where are you?"

There was no response.

A sound echoed from above, and she squinted up to see a thunderhead seething and bubbling with lightning. Droplets of light spewed from the center of the cloud vortex, where a shape was silhouetted against the glow. Was it another shadowbeast?

Some new monster? The shape grew larger, drawing closer, landing in front of her.

Time churned to a halt. Keriya stood frozen for a moment, an age. She felt as though the world were falling away from her.

Then, with another rumble, the world actually *was* falling away. The ground caved beneath her feet, and she tumbled into a subterranean hollow with the creature.

It wasn't a long drop, but she landed hard. Her legs buckled and she slammed down on her side. She looked up to gauge how far she'd fallen, but all she could see was the black fog — it was sticking curious tendrils into the opening of the collapse as if searching for her. Or maybe it was searching for the dragon she had summoned.

He was hard to miss. He perched atop the pile of caved-in rubble, staring down upon her. It was too dark to see what he really looked like, but his eyes were ablaze with red-violet fire, their glow cutting sharply through the gloom.

It was like looking into a mirror, but this mirror was more telling than any reflecting glass Keriya had ever seen. His eye color was unsettling enough, but there was an aura that pervaded the irises, a sense of otherworldly-ness and danger. She understood now why people were so frightened when they looked at her.

"Who are you?" His voice was a calm tenor, dark and quiet, yet radiant with power and audible even over the howling wind. Keriya couldn't answer. She suddenly realized that this creature was not like Shivnath, and just as suddenly, she began to fear for her life.

The dragon glanced up at the fog seeping toward them. *"And who is wielding this darkmagic?"*

Keriya edged backward, scooting along the floor, feeling around behind her so she wouldn't have to look away from him. He noticed her movement and descended off the heap of debris to follow her.

"If you do not speak, human, you may force me to kill you."

"I don't know!"

Adrenaline pulsed through her, giving her the strength to get to her feet. She turned her back on the fog and the dragon, fleeing blindly into the open cave. She heard him running after her and sped up.

A wave of dizziness and nausea brought her crashing to her knees. She sprawled on the uneven ground. Stars winked across her scope of vision, then everything grew dark.

The dragon caught up to her. He lowered his head and opened his jaws. Keriya fought to stay awake, but her body was shutting down.

The last thing she saw was two spheres of purple, whose light remained engraved in her mind long after she surrendered to the oblivion of unconsciousness.

CHAPTER EIGHTEEN

DRAGON SPEAKER

"Though you may think you wish to disappear,
perhaps all you really want is to be found."
~ **Sagerius Fangheart, in the Age Before Ages**

A throbbing pain in her side woke Keriya. She opened her eyes and saw a carved rock ceiling, crumbling with age. To her right, an archway led to the outside world. The morning sun beat down upon stone ruins and toppled pillars that had been all but swallowed by vines.

She sat up slowly. How had she gotten here? Memories began to dribble back to her: the storm, the attack, the shadow-beasts, the cave-in . . . and the dragon.

Instantly she was on guard. She jumped up and backed toward a wall, gazing into the corners of the cave. It took only a moment to spot him, for even in shadow his bronze scales gleamed like the sides of a faceted gemstone. Though his eyes were no longer glowing, they shone with ghostly reflections of sunlight.

"Where are we?" she asked the dragon in his native language. Now that she had spoken it once, it was like a dam had broken. She had access to a pocket of her mind that had previously been sealed away—a pocket that held every word she needed to communicate with him.

"Selaras, fourth planet from the yellow star Esentia," he replied dispassionately. *"I cannot be more specific, for my people have been gone too long for me to identify this land with any degree of accuracy."*

Keriya blinked. That was hardly the sort of response she'd been expecting.

"If you are referring to where you are in relation to where you were

last, I brought you here. I determined that you were not a threat, and that it would behoove me to keep you alive to procure information from you. So I saved you from the darkmagic."

She wasn't sure how to react to that—nor to the dragon in general. He was smaller than she'd originally believed. From the tip of the sleek, reptilian head to the tail that swayed behind his lithe body, he was about the size of a small sheep. Overlarge wings stirred at his sides and floppy ears twitched behind the budding horns lining the back of his skull. It was clear that he was young.

Here in the light of day, it was hard for Keriya to remember why she'd been so terrified of him. She stretched out a hand in greeting, but he tensed as if to run away—or to attack. A set of translucent inner eyelids flickered up, briefly shrouding his purple gaze.

"My name is Keriya Soulstar."

"Keriya," he repeated.

"That's me. Do you have a name?"

"I am Thorion Sveltorious."

"It's nice to meet you, Thorion."

Thorion didn't reply; he just kept staring at her. Keriya began to fidget. She figured she should say something else. What did people usually talk about when getting to know one another?

"So . . . how'd you get here?"

"I dragged you through the tunnels until I found this place, which is safe and defensible."

"Yeah, I sort of figured that out. I meant, you know, here-here," she said ineloquently.

"I am here because you called me."

"No. Like . . . how did you first come to be here?"

"I understood the context of your question."

"Okay," she said, trying to stay patient. *"Here, as in Allentria. How did you get out of the Etherworld?"*

Thorion's eyes unfocused, glassing over as if he were staring at something far away.

"I cannot remember my escape. It was abrupt. First I was else-where, and that place was a slow death for the dragons. We were all together, but we were each of us alone. We were cut off from our magicsources, always drained of our powers."

Though he spoke in a bland, unaffected voice, something about his words sent shivers crawling down Keriya's back.

"Then I felt a great pull. There was pain all over my body, and I was brought to a place where the weight of eternity pressed upon me. And then I was in your world."

Keriya raised an eyebrow as the young dragon waxed poetic, feeling lost.

"The crossover from the parallel universe has left my sense of time and space distorted," Thorion continued. *"It may have taken milliseconds or millennia to re-enter Selaras – though it is improbable that it is the latter, seeing as I would have aged, either physically or relativistically."*

She was fluent in his language, but it was difficult to understand him. He was so detached and cold. No, not cold exactly . . .

"Emotionless," she muttered as he droned on. Lady Aldelphia had mentioned that dragons didn't have any emotions, but she hadn't mentioned how off-putting the lack of emotions would be.

"Therefore, I believe I was brought back to your universe in order to maintain the balance," Thorion concluded.

"Mm," she said. *"You know, I've heard a lot about the balance, but no one's explained why it's so important."*

"The balance is what keeps the magics of our world in check," he told her. *"In an isolated system, all magicthreads tend toward entropy."*

"What's entropy?"

"Entropy represents the unavailability of a thread's potential energy. The more entropy there is, the harder it is for wielders to use magic. If the buildup of potential energy reaches a critical point, it can cause a reaction capable of destroying our universe."

"I see," Keriya lied. She was sorry she'd bothered to ask.

Thorion's indifferent voice and complicated words were getting on her nerves.

"But balance prevents entropy and keeps threads in a wieldable state. The amount of darkmagic in the world must have been too great, so I was brought here to even the scales." He tilted his head toward her. *"Now it is my turn to ask questions. Can you free my family from the Etherworld?"*

"I'm not sure," she admitted.

"You called me. Surely you can call them, too?"

"I don't think I have that kind of power."

"Then it would appear that you are useless to me, and I saved your life for nothing." He moved toward the archway and spread his wings.

Keriya might have been offended, if not for the fact she was used to being told she was useless. That, and the fact that he'd delivered his biting words in the calmest of monotones.

"But I will try to help you," she added. He paused and glanced back at her. *"Our empress will help, too. All of Allentria will help, as long as you stay with me."*

The empress also wanted him to fight Necrovar, but Keriya suspected it was best to omit that information.

She held out her hand again, and Thorion drew near to inspect it. His nostrils flared as he breathed in her scent, tiny scales slipping seamlessly over one another to accommodate the subtle movements of his face.

"This offer of assistance sounds as though it could prove beneficial to me," he said. Relief washed over Keriya. That was as much of a pledge of cooperation as she was going to get. Now it was time to figure out her next step.

The first thing she wanted to do was find her friends. They had all agreed to return to Noryk if anyone got separated from the group—but she had no idea how to get to Noryk, lost as she was in the middle of the fen. There was also the added worry that if she brought Thorion to the Imperial City, she might anger Shivnath. But if she didn't, she would definitely anger Aldelphia.

"Why are you upset?" It was clear by the way Thorion said the word that he had no idea what 'upset' meant. He'd used it perfectly in the sentence, but the concept of feeling upset appeared unfathomable to him.

"I'm not sure what to do," she admitted. *"I'd like to get to Noryk, but —"*

"No need for uncertainty. We can go this way," said Thorion, indicating a tunnel behind him with a nod.

Keriya gazed dubiously into the dark, gaping maw of the tunnel. *"Why?"*

"The last time we were above ground, we were attacked," Thorion reasoned. *"The runes on the walls indicate that these are dwarf tunnels, which were extensive even in the age of the dragons and led to every major mortal metropolis, the most famous of which was Noryk. We should be able to find our way easily."* With that, he trotted toward the tunnel.

"Who exactly is leading this quest?" Keriya growled, though she offered no argument as she hurried after him. Now that she'd found the dragon, she wasn't going to let him out of her sight.

They descended into the tunnel, moving away from the sun. Fortunately, glowing lichens and mushrooms crowded the walls, providing just enough light for them to find their way.

The tunnel opened into a circular room that branched into four paths. A star had been etched into the center of the stone floor, each of its points angled toward a corresponding corridor. Runes and pictures marked the star points and — though the letters were undoubtedly Dwarvish — one of the tips pointed at a carving of Noryk. The distinctive onion domes of the palace made it unmistakable.

"This way." Keriya strode down the tunnel, her footsteps echoing in the vast emptiness. As she walked, her anxiety began to fade. Somehow, against all odds, she was finding her way. She had successfully summoned the dragon. She would reunite with her friends in Noryk. From there, it was only a matter of time before they defeated Necrovar.

"Actions fit for the great hero I have unwittingly become," she murmured, recalling the words from the book she'd found in Shivnath's lair.

The vision of walking through throngs of cheering people came to her again, except this time she was in the Imperial City, parading up and down Broad Street with Thorion at her side. It pushed her lingering worries about Shivnath to a far corner of her mind.

Something welled up against her heart and bubbled out of her, and she laughed aloud.

"*What are you doing?*" Thorion's voice cut short her moment of exuberance. She turned to find he was watching her like a hawk.

"*I was laughing.*"

"*Why?*"

"*I don't know. Because I feel like I'm on the right path.*"

Thorion tilted his head, his eyes roving across her face. She thought she saw something flicker deep within them.

"*Can you do it again?*"

"*It doesn't really work like that,*" she said with a wry smile. "*Hopefully it will come again soon enough.*"

But it didn't, for her happiness evaporated shortly thereafter. Without the sun, it was hard to tell how much time had passed. They walked for what felt like hours, and Keriya finally stopped when she found a small alcove where they could spend the night.

Her stomach grumbled as she lay down on the cold floor. She longed for a good, hot meal and found herself missing Effrax — or rather, his ability to make fires.

"*Do you have any provisions?*" asked Thorion, reacting and responding to her thoughts in much the same way Shivnath had. Keriya shook her head. "*I require sustenance.*"

"*Me too.*" She wished she'd considered the issue of food before agreeing to travel through the tunnels. "*I don't suppose there's anything around here we could eat?*"

"*I could eat you,*" he replied matter-of-factly.

"Why would you say that?"

"Because you are large and warm-blooded, so you would provide me with a satisfactory amount of nourishment; and because you are slow and weak, without the ability to defend yourself or do me harm if I were to attack you."

"No, I mean, why would you think it's okay to say that?" Keriya was appalled that the idea would even occur to him.

"It makes sense. But your usefulness alive currently outweighs your usefulness as a food source, so I won't eat you. I will forage, instead."

Thorion loped off into the darkness. Disturbed and feeling nothing like a hero anymore, Keriya scooted under a stone bench and curled into a defensive ball. Not that hiding under a bench would help if the dragon were to change his mind about turning her into his dinner.

Thorion returned with his stomach sagging. Presumably he had gorged himself on something she would rather not know about. Also, to her surprise, a dead rat was dangling from his jaws.

"For you," he said, dropping the rat in front of her.

"Oh! How nice." Keriya gave Thorion a smile. It wasn't much of a smile, but at least she tried.

After a moment he smiled back, his scaly lips twitching upwards at their corners. It was the only identifiable expression she had thus-far seen him make.

"Why'd you bring it?" she asked, figuring that his lack of emotions meant he couldn't be thoughtful, generous, or kind.

"Wise not to allow the guide who may help free my family from the Etherworld to starve to death," he said, settling down next to her and resting his head upon her ankles.

Regardless of this wisdom, Keriya did not eat the rat.

CHAPTER NINETEEN
WHAT WISDOM DICTATES

"The distance between bravery and stupidity
is measured by one's motives."
~ *Aldelphia Alderwood, Eleventh Age*

After an uncomfortable rest, Keriya and Thorion continued toward Noryk, following the dwarves' picture directions. She wondered where the dwarves actually were—why was this place abandoned? She'd only ever read about dwarves in her old books, but if she were a dwarf she would think this was an alright place to live. It was gloomy, yes, but the architecture was beautiful.

Keriya called a halt to their journey when they reached a large hall dotted with totem poles. She was tired, hungry, cold, and subsequently very grouchy. She couldn't bring herself to wander the tunnels anymore.

Thorion brought her another rat. She hid it—though he wasn't capable of being offended if she didn't eat his gift—and fell asleep almost as soon as she lay down.

Without the sun to wake her, she might have slept for days. Fatigue had seeped into her body, running bone-deep. She'd been away from the light too long, and she was in desperate need of food and fresh air.

"Keriya."

Keriya cracked her eyes open. Thorion stood over her, a little too close for comfort.

"What?"

"There is a water slug nearby. It is probable it will smell us and attack, so I will attempt to kill it preemptively. In the meantime, you should find somewhere safe to hide." With a flash of bronze scales, he turned and vanished into the darkness.

"Mm-kay," she mumbled to the floor before lapsing back into a light slumber.

<Keriya.>

"*What now?*" she groaned, rolling over and blinking blearily.

<The slug is in the tunnels north of the hall. It is heading toward you. Have you hidden yourself?>

She frowned. Thorion's voice had a flickering quality to it, reminding her of shafts of sunlight streaming through turbulent clouds. She could hear him as clearly as though he were standing right next to her, but he was nowhere in sight.

"*Not yet,*" she said, clambering to her feet. There were numerous hallways stretching away from the grand chamber where they'd stopped, one of which had a faint blue glow coming from it.

<Are you hidden? The slug is close.>

"*I'm getting there,*" she said, more loudly this time.

<Keriya?>

"*Alright, I'm going!*" she yelled as she began jogging away from the glow. In response, a gurgling roar reverberated throughout the chamber.

She glanced over her shoulder and saw the monster. It was enormous, fat enough to take up the entirety of the tunnel whence it oozed. A jelly-like substance, which was emitting the spectral blue light, encased it like a watery cocoon. The slug didn't have any discernible eyes, but it slithered straight for her and roared again, revealing a wide mouth with rows upon rows of sharp teeth.

Keriya now had a fairly good idea why the dwarves had abandoned these tunnels. She turned tail and bolted across the hall. She'd died once before, and she had no intention of going back to that horrible void any time soon.

But then, of course, she tripped.

The slug hissed and spat as it drew near. Keriya scrambled behind one of the totem poles, wishing with all her heart that she could use Shivnath's magic at will, wishing that she was as strong a wielder as Roxanne or Max, wishing that she wasn't so inadequate.

Another sound filled the air. It was thin and high-pitched, but fearsome nonetheless. She peeked around the pillar and saw Thorion soaring through the hall. He was making a terrible racket to attract the slug's attention. The creature reared up and snapped at the drackling, and he dodged its jaws gracefully.

Thorion couldn't be frightened, but upon seeing those blade-like teeth nearly slice him in half, Keriya was seized by an irrational urge to run out and protect him.

<Stay there,> he told her—except he wasn't moving his mouth. Was she imagining his voice? It certainly sounded real.

<You haven't learned to speak telepathically yet,> he surmised. The statement appeared in her mind, as though the words had been planted there as seeds and had bloomed without her consent. She finally understood that he was using magic to communicate with her. <Keep clear until I've neutralized the threat.>

While she appreciated that he was trying to keep her safe, she couldn't just sit by and do nothing while his life was in danger.

<I do not need your help.>

Yes, you do, she thought privately, wincing as he barely avoided the slug's fangs. A half-formed plan surfaced in her brain when she spotted a loose rock on the floor. She snatched it up and hurled herself out into the open.

"Hey!" she called, heaving the rock with all her might. It hit the slug's mucus coating, having no effect other than to bring the monster's attention back to her. It lunged down, mouth open wide, intending to swallow her whole.

It was over in the blink of an eye. One moment the slug was on a collision course with her frail, human body; the next, its head had slammed against one of the totem poles. Thorion had flown at the slug, smashing it into the stone column. He was now trapped in the blue mucus, burrowing through it to get at the creature's flesh.

The slug made a valiant effort to dislodge him, but the mucus that protected it also proved its undoing. The substance was so thick that it held Thorion in place despite the monster's desperate thrashing. Thorion burrowed until he reached its bumpy gray skin, then burrowed further.

The slug's death screams were heartrending, yet Keriya watched, transfixed with morbid fascination, as it was decapitated. It died when Thorion was halfway through its neck, but he finished the job and dug all the way through.

The creature's head thudded to the floor, splattering Keriya with its glowing sludge. She was surprised to find it was merely water held together in a viscid capacity, presumably by the slug's magic. With its wielder dead, the water began to melt back to a liquid state.

Keriya stood dripping in shock, watching as Thorion nosed through the slug's remains. He snuffled at the head and began chewing on the withering flesh.

"*Why did you do that?*" she asked. Putting his life in peril to save hers didn't make sense, even if he did view her as a useful guide.

Thorion looked up. He seemed at a loss, but when he finished his mouthful of slug he said, "*I was hungry. As I grow, I must eat. Water slug flesh both hydrates and nourishes.*"

Keriya gazed at the corpse in alarm, wondering how much food a growing dragon needed. Thorion took a few more bites, then licked his snout clean with his long tongue.

"*All done,*" he announced, and bounded into the shadows.

The incident put Keriya off tunnels. After some strategic wheedling, she convinced Thorion it would be wise to return to the surface world. Thus, on their third eve of travel, they emerged from a dwarf hole back into the fen.

The next morning, after a much-needed rest, they continued their trek south. Thorion was suddenly quite talkative.

"*What are these things you put on your back paws?*" he asked, sniffing at her sheepskin foot-coverings.

"*In Allentria, they're called shoes. We wear them to protect our feet."*

"They smell bad," he observed.

"Well, I've been walking for a long time," she retorted, glaring down at him.

He lowered his brow ridges in irritation, mirroring her expression. The sight made her giggle. Thorion didn't imitate her this time, but he watched with rapt attention. He looked away when her laughter faded, flattening his ears to his skull and narrowing his eyes.

Keriya narrowed her own eyes. She was no expert, but didn't expressions indicate emotion? She wasn't sure. Maybe she was reading too much into it.

They walked for another hour, Keriya answering every one of Thorion's questions to the best of her abilities.

"What magic do you wield?" he finally inquired.

"I don't." Why did everyone always have to bring that up? *"I have no magic of my own."*

"Magic is the energy that powers all life functions," said Thorion. *"If you are alive, you have magic."*

"I don't. Believe me."

"You must wield at least one of the base magics, because you are human. And you must have at least one of the arcane magics, because you can speak my language and communicate with me telepathically."

"Shivnath gave me some magic, but I can't wield it until . . ."

"Until what?"

"Nothing." She still hadn't told Thorion about Necrovar, and this wasn't the time to do so. *"How about you? What magic do you have?"*

"Lightmagic. But I am too young to wield it. Dragons reach magical maturity at around three centuries. Perhaps the same holds true for you — perhaps you must grow into your magic."

"I'm not going to live for three centuries," she said flatly.

"But you —"

"Let's stop talking about it," she interrupted, lengthening her stride. To her surprise, Thorion heeded her request. He quieted

down and sped up, matching her pace so he could trot beside her.

The next day, after a bit of aimless wandering, Thorion's ears perked up and his eyes went wide.

"*I hear human voices.*" He paused. "*They're calling your name.*"

"*Really?*" Hardly daring to believe her luck, Keriya stood on tiptoes, straining to see over the tops of the phragmites reeds. "*Where are they coming from?*"

"*West,*" said Thorion, and he turned east.

"*Come back! We've got to find them — those are my friends. Fletcher,*" she screamed, jumping up and down and waving her arms. "I'm here. I'm okay!"

"*You think they will help us?*" he asked.

"*I know they will!*"

Thorion didn't share her enthusiasm. In fact, he tensed up and bared his fangs. As far as emotionless creatures went, that was a pretty extreme reaction.

"*What's wrong?*"

"*You intend to join them, so I am preparing myself for what is statistically likely to be a detrimental encounter. Wisdom dictates that it is inadvisable to deal with humans,*" said Thorion. It sounded as though he was quoting someone, but the words stung all the same.

"*I'm a human. You're okay with me, aren't you? You trust me?*" She tried to sound offhand.

"*If trust is what it means to accept help from another creature based on the belief that he or she will be useful to me, then yes, I trust you.*"

"*If you trust me, come with me.*" She started walking westwards. "*There's no need to be frightened.*"

"*What is 'frightened'?*"

"*It's when . . .*" She stalled, realizing she had no idea how to describe fear to someone who had never experienced it before. "*Never mind. Just come. I promise I won't let anything detrimental happen to you. I'd never let anyone hurt you.*"

She was surprised by the vehemence in her voice, but perhaps that was what convinced Thorion. He leapt into the air and settled onto her back, digging his sharp talons into her shoulders. It was uncomfortable and unwieldy, but it filled Keriya with a certain sense of pride. Thorion *did* trust her.

In this manner he guided her through the fen. Thus, when she reached Fletcher, Roxanne, and Effrax, she greeted them with a dragon perched upon her neck.

CHAPTER TWENTY

PRIORITIES

"To receive the right answers,
you must learn to ask the right questions."
~ Skalda Leech, Twelfth Age

Roxanne gaped in wonderment. Clinging to Keriya's back was the most beautiful creature she had ever seen. It bore the same general shape as the Aerian effigies of Shivnath, but a wooden statue of a dragon was nothing compared to a living, breathing specimen.

So it had all been true. Keriya's powers, Shivnath and Necrovar, everything.

"By Valaan's feathers," said Effrax, putting a hand to his heart.

"This is Thorion," said Keriya, presenting the dragon. Given the fuss everyone had made about him, he was much smaller than Roxanne would have imagined. And younger.

For all that his presence was supposed to be some kind of miracle, Thorion was somewhat underwhelming.

"And this is the dragon we were sent to find?" Judging from his tone, Effrax shared the sentiment.

"I don't see any other dragons around here."

"My lady, I meant you no offense. Nor you, Lord Thorion," he said in more formal a tone than he'd ever used before. In a surprising gesture, he knelt to one knee to address the small beast. "The world has missed you for ten ages," he whispered. "Welcome home."

Thorion observed Effrax from his place on Keriya's shoulder, but made no reply. Was he also less intelligent than they'd thought he would be?

Then Keriya spoke to him using words Roxanne had never

heard before, words saturated with an almost tangible power. Her voice—which had become deeper and more resonant— pierced Roxanne, sending shivers down every nerve.

"*Endrat Effrax Nameless oth Fironemos. Sirat revenra teos Allentriis. Et trelas endrati Fletcher Earengale et Roxanne Fleuridae, vrelei e'es. Endral naler trelos thystra.*"

Thorion responded to this. He nodded and leapt nimbly to the ground.

"I am at your service," Effrax said as the dragon approached him. Keriya translated his words, speaking again in that fearsome language.

Thorion directed his attention to Fletcher next. Fletcher actually recoiled from his gaze, so the dragon passed over him and turned to Roxanne.

"Hello, little one," she said, crouching to be on his level and smiling. Slowly, and a little uncertainly, Thorion smiled back. She could tell he was only mirroring what he saw, for the smile did not touch his eyes.

"Where's Max?" Keriya asked.

"He never returned after the storm," said Effrax. "We thought he was with you."

"He's not," said Keriya. "What if something happened to him?"

"A little thunder and lightning won't do him any harm."

"It wasn't just that—we were attacked. What if he's in danger? What if he's hurt? We have to find him!"

"Whatever trouble you think Max is in, I guarantee he can get himself out of it," Effrax assured her. "You vowed you would bring Thorion to the Fironem. Now that we have him, it's time to put him to use."

That seemed to strike a nerve with Keriya. "What do you mean?"

"You'd have to be blind not to see that our empire is falling apart," he said. "Fironians are suffering the most, and the people in power aren't doing anything about it. But we can change that." His eyes grew hungry as he looked at Thorion.

"*You* can change it."

Keriya looked at Thorion too, her expression unreadable. "I think we should rest first. We can make a fire, maybe catch a fish—"

"Why delay?" asked Roxanne.

"Max might see the smoke and find us," said Keriya. "And it will give Thorion a chance to recover. We've been hiking for days. We got attacked by a water slug. We had to fight for our lives."

A water slug didn't sound like it was much of a bother, but Roxanne considered the possibility that this didn't have anything to do with Max or slugs. Maybe it had more to do with the fact Shivnath wanted the dragon kept safe . . . and now that they had him, the first thing they were going to do was force him into a war.

"Fine," she said. "Let's stay."

Effrax was averse to the idea of resting, but that made Roxanne argue for it more stubbornly. Anything he wanted, she had decided she was against. She disliked everything about him, from his flippant attitude to his tendency to give people annoying nicknames.

"We could ask Thorion what he thinks," Fletcher suggested in a small voice.

"Good idea." Keriya turned and spoke to Thorion. Though he made no visible response, she smiled. "He wants to rest another night."

Effrax scowled. "He didn't say anything."

"We were speaking telepathically," she retorted, poking the side of her head with her finger. "One of the perks of being a dragon speaker. It's more efficient."

They settled down in a clearing that was almost dry. Effrax was clearly irritated that he'd been overruled. He went out on the pretense of hunting for food, leaving the Aerians alone.

"Alright," Roxanne said once he was out of earshot. "What's the plan?"

"I've never been good at planning," Keriya mumbled.

Thorion had lain down beside her and was inspecting a beetle that had crawled onto his paw.

"What's to plan?" said Fletcher. "We don't have much of a choice. We have to bring Thorion to Lady Aldelphia."

"I'm starting to think that's not such a good idea," Keriya admitted.

"Why?"

"Because then Thorion will have to fight Necrovar, and that's not what's supposed to happen," said Keriya. "Shivnath wants *me* to fight him."

"Maybe you misunderstood Shivnath," said Roxanne. She hadn't said it to be mean, but Keriya shot her a nasty look before wheeling around and stomping out of the camp.

Fletcher got up and hurried after her with an exasperated sigh. Keriya's departure also got a reaction from Thorion. He twisted his long neck around to watch her receding form, silent and unblinking.

Dragon.

Roxanne frowned at the intrusion of an unwanted voice in her mind. *Who's there?* she asked silently. She was finding it easier to communicate with animals now. In fact, it was almost alarming how quickly she was mastering the art. Her head hardly ached anymore, but she'd be lying if she said the uninvited voices didn't bother her.

Dragon! The mental image she was picking up on was tinged with a strange, wavering feeling. Judging from the upwards angle of the picture, Roxanne was picking up the thoughts of the beetle on Thorion's claw. The wavering became clearer— she was sensing the movement of the insect's antennae that signified excitement. Great. Now she was talking to bugs.

Yes, she thought back dully. *How observant of you.*

The beetle sent her a few more antennae-images before it buzzed away. With it gone, Thorion laid his head on his forepaws and closed his eyes. He spread his wings, soaking up the heat of the sun to warm himself.

Struck by an idea, Roxanne got to her feet. He sensed her

movement and his eyes sprang back open as she tiptoed toward him.

Can you hear me? She sent the thought out as forcefully as she knew how, but Thorion didn't respond.

"Hello?" she whispered. "Can you understand me?"

"You can't speak to him, Tigress. He wouldn't understand you even if you were one of those rare wielders who can mindspeak — or rather, you wouldn't understand him."

Roxanne glared over her shoulder and saw Effrax stepping back into the clearing. "Were you spying on us?"

He didn't know about Keriya's assignment from Shivnath, and if he'd overheard them talking about Necrovar . . . well, she wasn't sure it mattered, but she didn't want Effrax knowing things like that.

"Just forgot my hunting knife," he said amicably, digging in his travel pack and producing a small blade.

"What did you mean?" she asked before she could stop herself. "About the mindspeaking?"

"Strong wielders, Tier Nine and higher, are able to wield the root of their power, lifemagic," he explained. "One aspect of lifemagic is the ability to manipulate your brainwaves to communicate telepathically with other living organisms. Powerful wielders have been known to develop the ability to speak with plants and animals."

Something must have changed on her face, because a sly smile spread across his.

"I knew there was something about you. You can speak to animals, is that it?"

Roxanne felt her hands clench into fists. "So what if I can? Are you going to blackmail me?"

"Ah-ah-ah! Never lay your cards on the table before you know your opponent's hand," he chided her. "I didn't actually know you were a mindspeaker until you gave yourself away. If I had wanted to blackmail you, you'd be in trouble."

"Thorion's an animal, isn't he? I should be able to talk to him."

"He's a dragon," Effrax corrected her. "He doesn't use lifemagic to communicate, he uses something else. I'm afraid you'll never have the power to speak to him the way you want to."

"Keriya can speak to him," Roxanne said moodily. She was surprised by how upset that made her. "And she's a cripple, she doesn't have any magic."

"Oh, Keriya has magic. She has a power greater and more dangerous than you or I will ever know."

Roxanne didn't care anymore. If the bottom line was that she couldn't speak to Thorion, then it didn't matter one way or another.

"How'd you like to come hunting with me?" Effrax offered. "That gift of yours will come in handy. I'll teach you how to string a longbow if you like."

"Go away." She didn't want to spend time with Effrax. She didn't want to go hunting and she didn't want to talk to bugs. She might have wanted to talk to dragons, but according to the Fironian, she couldn't.

"Your loss," he said, slipping into the reeds once more.

Roxanne sulked on her own until Keriya and Fletcher returned.

"I've thought things through," Keriya announced, "and I've decided to bring Thorion to Lady Aldelphia. Then we can figure out what to do about Necrovar together."

"Fine," said Roxanne. It had taken Keriya all that time to come up with that? What had Erasmus been filling her head with for the past fourteen years, wood shavings?

Thorion stretched, kneaded the soft earth with his claws, and trotted over to Keriya. She reached out to scratch him behind his ear. He closed his eyes and his brow ridges — which, Roxanne realized, had been drawn together in the faintest of frowns — finally relaxed.

And in that one gesture, Roxanne began to understand the real reason Keriya didn't want to bring Thorion to Noryk.

Fletcher had come to an unfortunate realization: he didn't like dragons.

When Thorion conversed with Keriya he seemed almost human, and Fletcher saw more human mannerisms in him with each passing day. When he hunted for fish or listened to the sounds of the fen, Fletcher saw a wild, deadly predator.

He wasn't sure which version of the drackling bothered him more.

"Kemraté a'eos, Thorion!" Up ahead, Keriya called out and Thorion bounded to her side. This was the phrase she used whenever Thorion strayed too far.

The fact that Fletcher was picking up snippets of their language didn't mean he appreciated it. Quite the opposite, in fact. It frightened him. It was as if a great power was trapped in those words, waiting to be set free — waiting for a slip of the tongue to break free, more like.

Fletcher shook his head. Now he was just being paranoid. Still, if Thorion was the only one who could defeat Necrovar, who knew what sorts of magic he had hidden away?

Maybe that was what was really bothering Fletcher. He was fine with getting rid of the most powerful evil force in the world, but he wasn't sure where his place would be when the time came to actually do the deed. The only thing he'd ever been good at was crafting, which was a pretty useless trade. He wouldn't be any help fighting the Shadow.

As he wallowed in self-pity, he found himself missing his family and wishing he was still on the other side of Shivnath's Mountains. But if he'd stayed, he would have been named a Lower for his sins. He would have been living in that hidden part of Aeria, far from Asher and his mother. They were probably celebrating his absence, since he'd never been much use to them.

Seems to be a common theme for me, doesn't it? he thought bitterly.

"Maevraté aelra seuler nostite." Keriya spoke once more. The dragon made a chirping noise and wove away through the reeds, his bronze scales blending in with his surroundings. She slowed down, waiting for Fletcher to catch up. He joined her somewhat reluctantly.

"How are you?" she asked.

"Fine, thanks." They were being oddly formal with each other. Keriya knew Fletcher didn't like Thorion, but Fletcher didn't know how to bridge the distance that had created between the two of them. "What about you?"

"Can't complain," she said, in a tone that suggested she would have loved to complain.

"Worrying about Necrovar?"

"Sort of." She began fidgeting with the ends of her sleeves. "I just feel . . . not good about bringing Thorion to Noryk. He shouldn't be fighting."

"Uh, yes he should," said Fletcher. "Unless you want the Shadow to take over the world and do all that bad stuff Lady Aldelphia talked about."

"I know he *should* fight, but I can't—I don't want to ask that of him. He's too young. And it's too dangerous. What if he gets hurt?"

"Would you put the life of one dragon above the lives of every single Allentrian?" Fletcher squinted at Keriya, trying to figure her out. It had been a lot easier to do that back in Aeria.

"Tell me, why would you choose them over Thorion? Give me one reason. What have they done for any of us? Think about Cezon and Blackwater, the Imperials, Lady Aldelphia, even Effrax." She indicated the Fironian, who was scouting the way up ahead. "Why should I force Thorion to fight on their behalf?"

Fletcher sighed. "It's easy for you to think they don't deserve your help, but this isn't just your quest anymore. We're all invested in this. It's my quest, too, and I care about doing the right thing. Because if I was back in Aeria or Noryk or wherever, and I knew there was someone out there who could save the world, I'd want them looking out for me."

"Thorion doesn't owe them anything."

For a moment, Fletcher was too stunned to respond.

"Wha—? You're unbelievable," he spluttered. "If that's how you feel, why bother with Shivnath's quest at all?"

She frowned. "Hold on. This isn't about me."

"You're right," he said, "it isn't about you. It's bigger than you, and I don't think you understand that. Shivnath said you were going to be a hero, so you've gotten this idea that you're going to fight Necrovar, and you're stuck on it for all the wrong reasons. I think you just want people to . . . I don't know, respect you or something."

"So? What does it matter who's saving them, or why it's done?"

"Clearly it doesn't matter to you, and I guess it doesn't even matter to them, as long as they get saved," Fletcher conceded in a dark voice. "But I think it matters to Thorion. If he's going to fight, he should understand why he's fighting."

"He shouldn't fight at all. He shouldn't be involved in this. That's my whole point," she declared, stalking away. Fletcher let her go. He had no interest in talking to her if she was going to be mulish and rude.

When they stopped to rest that night, Effrax was the only one in high spirits. He made a merry fire and performed some magic tricks.

"This is for you, Lord Thorion." He waved his hands, and a web of conjured flames spread from his fingertips to form a fiery dragon. "Your name shall live in legends long after the rest of us have turned to dust. You shall restore honor and glory to the Fironem. You will lead us into a new and better age."

Roxanne wore a stony expression—she refused to be impressed with anything Effrax did—and Keriya was lost in whatever thoughts were haunting her. Thorion, however, watched the firemagic in fascination. He lay with his head resting in Keriya's lap, but his wide eyes followed the burning dragon's every move as it flapped its wings and circled overhead.

When at last they doused the campfire, Fletcher had trouble falling asleep. And when his body did succumb to exhaustion, his sleep was shallow and fitful. He tossed and turned and woke twice from night terrors.

In one dream he was running from the Elders. They were telling him he'd brought shame upon his family, that Asher and his mother would suffer for what he'd done. Their shouts grew louder and louder, until Fletcher realized the shouts were real.

He roused himself and stared around with bleary eyes. The golden rays of dawn were creeping across the fen. Mist spiraled up from the damp ground. Waterbirds floated through the sky, singing to one another.

And Roxanne and Effrax were locked in battle with three Imperial Guards.

CHAPTER TWENTY-ONE

CAPTURED
"An ounce of blood is worth more than a pound of friendship."
~ **Moorfainian Proverb**

"Keriya, wake up!"

Keriya felt herself being jostled around and opened her eyes. Fletcher crouched next to her, shaking her shoulder. Through a patch of reeds, she saw Roxanne and Effrax wielding against three gray-clad Imperials.

"Shosu, get behind 'em," cried one of the guards. Keriya recognized as Officer Blackwater, the degenerate who'd been helping Cezon. Why was he here? Hadn't he gotten arrested?

"No names!" snapped the tallest of the three. His dark hair was tied back to reveal narrow blue eyes and a bitter mouth. Given how Blackwater flinched, it was clear he was the leader.

"What's going on?" whispered Keriya.

"I don't know," said Fletcher, pulling on her arm. "I woke up in the middle of this, Thorion is missing, and —"

"What?!" Panic flared within her. Thorion had probably — wisely — fled as soon as he'd perceived a threat.

Struck by inspiration, she worked on forming a word in her mind and broadcasting it outwards. Pain tickled the center of her brain as she attempted to reach him telepathically.

<*Thorion,*> she thought. <*Where are you?*>

At first she was sure it hadn't worked; then she felt a faint answer drift back to her. He was too far away to be able to hear clearly, but at least she knew he was safe. She wanted to say more, but her head was already throbbing with the effort of sending out just one thought.

"Let's find him," she whispered to Fletcher.

"What about them?" He nodded to Roxanne and Effrax. "They're fighting because you can't!"

His words ripped off a scab on a wound that had only just begun to heal. Keriya angrily opened her mouth, but a cry yanked her attention back to the fight before she could say anything.

Shosu and Blackwater had gained the upper hand against Roxanne. The burly guard bound her with water that he quickly wielded into ice, and the rat-faced man pulled a tiny dagger from his robes and plunged it deep into her side.

All of Roxanne's spells unraveled, and the earth she was wielding crumbled to pieces. Her eyes rolled into the back of her head as she collapsed among the reeds.

Keriya lay on the ground in silence. She and Roxanne hadn't been friends, but a heavy guilt crushed upon her, numbed by the blunt impact of shock.

Fletcher, his face ashen, stood on trembling legs. He ran forward and wielded a chunk of dirt at Blackwater. The guardsman dodged his misshapen missile and produced another dagger. He grabbed Fletcher and stabbed him in the chest. Fletcher only had time to give half a strangled cry before he slumped to the ground.

Keriya's heart stopped.

Fletcher had been her first and, for most of her life, only friend. They'd been kindred spirits, for the Aerians had been cruel to them both. They'd gone on adventures together, learned from Erasmus together, grown up together, yet she had been so mean to him these past few weeks. She'd been angry for reasons that hardly mattered now. She wanted to scream, but no sound came when she opened her mouth. Without magic, she couldn't even fight—all she could do was sit in the mud, struggling to breathe, trying to hold onto her sanity. She could do nothing to avenge his death.

Nothing.

But then someone did scream. A tortured howl filled the air, a howl that embodied the maelstrom of anguish within her. Keriya managed to wrench her gaze from Fletcher's body to see whence it came. The sight that met her eyes was, in a way, even more terrible to behold.

Thorion was galloping toward the guards, wings outstretched so that he did not so much run as glide across the ground. Fury was etched onto his face, distorting his features into a mask of hatred.

He slammed into Shosu, who was knocked off his feet from the force of the impact, then went for Blackwater. Blackwater shrieked and wielded a steaming jet of water that hit Thorion head-on. The drackling growled and vanished back into the marsh vegetation.

His brief appearance distracted Effrax, who looked to see what had become of the dragon.

"Effrax, watch out!" Keriya cried as the tall officer raised his hand against the Fironian, brandishing another dagger.

Thorion re-emerged with a bloodcurdling cry. He burst from a clump of reeds, talons outstretched, lunging for the officer's throat. The man raised his arms to shield himself, dagger in hand. Thorion collided with him and they both went down, tumbling head over tail into an algae-infested pool. They landed with a splash, and then everything was still.

"Oy—Doru, you alright?" Blackwater asked.

Keriya looked back to him and saw that Effrax was sagging in his arms, a dagger lodged in his neck. Her whole body went cold. She was alone.

Blackwater dumped Effrax on the ground and approached the tangle of limbs that was Thorion and Doru. He kicked at them, but neither one moved.

"Thorion!" Keriya surged to her feet and staggered toward the drackling. She saw movement, and a small trickle of relief broke through the glacier of despair growing inside her.

But it was not Thorion who stirred. Doru groaned and shoved the dragon off him. Keriya froze in her tracks, watching as the bronze-scaled body slid into the water. Doru stood on shaky legs, his uniform stained black and slime-green from the mud and algae.

"We got him," he gasped.

"Can't hardly believe it," said Blackwater, kicking at Thorion again.

"Don't touch him," Keriya spat, her voice cracking. Doru looked up sharply.

"Why haven't you dealt with her?" he demanded of Blackwater. Blackwater remembered himself with a jump and pulled another dagger from his robes. Somewhere in the back of her head, Keriya wondered how such a tiny blade could be so deadly.

"Won't hurt a bit, wench," he said, advancing upon her.

Keriya stooped and grabbed a rock next to her foot. She hurled it at Blackwater, more out of anger than self-defense. It caught him in the thigh and he yelped in pain.

"Ow! Whatsa matter with you, you tronkin' blood-burned shifter?"

"You killed my friends!" She was teetering on the edge of a dark abyss, half-blinded by rage and sorrow.

"They're not dead," Doru wheezed. "We couldn't kill a dragon even if we tried."

"What?" Keriya squinted at Thorion and saw his chest slowly rise and fall. She glanced around — first to Fletcher, then to Roxanne and Effrax — and noticed faint signs of life in each of them.

"Thank you, Shivnath," she whispered, covering her face with shaking hands.

Doru produced another dagger from an inside pocket of his robe. "Darts dipped in *evasdrin* poison. If this gets in your blood, you can't use your magic. It's powerful enough to knock you out like that." He snapped his fingers in emphasis.

Before she could respond, heavy hands latched onto her from behind. Shosu had regained consciousness and snuck up on her. Keriya kicked and screamed, but her struggles were useless.

"Wait — don't waste that on me," she said, squirming away

from Blackwater and his *evasdrin* dart. "It's for people with magic, right? I don't have magic. Why do you think I haven't wielded against you?"

This question stumped Blackwater. He paused, tapping his chin. Now that she'd said it aloud, it stumped Keriya, too. This seemed like a moment when Shivnath's powers would be useful, but no energy filled her as it had when she'd called Thorion. She remained an empty husk.

"Everyone has magic," Doru scoffed. "I know what you are, *rheenar*. Your kind almost destroyed the world once, and I will die before I see you ruin Selaras again."

He nodded to Blackwater, who drove the dart deep into her shoulder. Keriya screamed. A burning sensation rippled outwards from the dart's tip, followed by an icy numbness. Her heart was on fire. It was beating too slowly, and every beat was more agonizing than the last. She was falling . . .

falling . . .

falling . . .

A cold drizzle brought Keriya back to consciousness. She dazedly looked around to find she'd been tossed onto the bed of a small wooden cart. Her wrists were tied behind her back with a coarse rope. Her whole body ached and there was a particularly sharp pain in her upper arm. She winced and looked at the dart—it had torn a hole in her dress, and her skin was green and swollen around the wound.

"Look who's up." Shosu leaned into view, leering down at her. A sluggish surge of anger swept through Keriya. She kicked at him and missed.

"If you're well enough to kick, you're well enough to walk." Doru appeared next to his subordinate. He took Keriya by her uninjured arm and hoisted her off the cart.

Half-delirious, Keriya allowed him to wrap another length of rope around her midriff, tying her to Fletcher, Roxanne, and Effrax. Their wrists were bound and their ankles were tied loosely to prevent them from running. The rope that connected them kept them uncomfortably close, so none of them had any freedom of movement.

"Come on," Doru growled. He grabbed the end of the rope and tugged them along like they were animals on a leash. As the caravan set off again, Keriya noticed Thorion. He lay on the cart, riddled with darts, his front and back legs lashed together, his mouth clamped shut with a rusty iron muzzle. With a wordless sound of distress, she strained to get closer to him.

"Don't you dare!" Doru's voice sliced through the air and a razor-thin tendril of water cracked across Keriya's cheek. "No one touches the dragon."

"You alright?" Effrax whispered as she stumbled, reeling from the sting of the attack.

"Never better," she muttered. "What about Thorion?"

"I don't know. Prolonged exposure to *evasdrin* can cut you off from your source forever."

"No talking, either!" Doru passed the lead line to Iako, who was pulling the cart along a dirt path that cut through the fen. Then he backtracked and fell into step beside Keriya.

"If you try anything, if you hurt my men, you'll regret it," he threatened. She glared at him and was pleased to see him draw back from her gaze. "There are a lot of people looking for you, and not all of them would be as hospitable as I've been."

"If you know who I am, why are you doing this? Empress Aldelphia wants Thorion to fight Necrovar."

Doru gave her a sad, knowing smile. "Ah. Well, you're making the assumption that we're on your side."

Keriya stared at him in disbelief. "You're working for the Shadow? Why would you do that? He's evil!"

Doru laughed. "What do you know of evil? The dragons have been painted as benevolent guardians for a ten-age, but they wielded a terrible magic that would have destroyed us all.

Necrovar isn't evil—he's trying to save the world."

"You're a traitor!"

"What has the empire done for me?" the guardsman shot back. "No one sent aid when the bogspectre attacked my town. No one cared when the crops failed in the north and people starved over the winter. I don't owe the empire anything—they betrayed *us*. I need no more reason to support a new Master."

Doru stalked away, but his words lingered with Keriya.

I said the same thing to Fletcher, she thought. *Am I really so awful? Am I any different from Doru? Are we the same, just fighting on opposite sides?* Then an even worse thought surfaced from a dark part of her drugged mind: *Which side is the right one?*

"There's more to your quest than you let on, Dragoneyes," Effrax whispered, glancing back at her. "How long have you known about Necrovar?"

"Long enough to know I shouldn't tell every spy who blackmails his way into our group exactly what I know. How long have *you* known?" she asked, realizing that perhaps there was more to Effrax than he'd let on, too.

"Long enough to know I needed that dragon to save my state," was the heavy reply.

The Imperials led them until they couldn't walk anymore, then set up camp. Doru seemed convinced that Keriya was capable of unspeakable acts of horror, so to be sure she couldn't escape, he tightened her bonds and gave them all water laced with more *evasdrin*.

When Roxanne refused the water, he produced another dart. "Don't make me use this," he said. She obstinately stuck her nose in the air and the hard lines of his face deepened. "I don't know how you got involved in this, but I don't want to hurt you—no more innocent blood needs to be spilled."

"What about Thorion?" Keriya demanded. "He's innocent!"

"He's a weapon," Doru spat, pointing at the dragon's prone form. "Why do you think your empress wants him? To use against anyone who opposes her."

Keriya was about to argue that Aldelphia wanted to use

Thorion against Necrovar, then realized this only strengthened Doru's point. What did she really know about Allentria, or the government, or the Shadow, or the history of the world outside Aeria? The empress had been all too happy to torture Keriya to get what she wanted; that didn't exactly speak volumes for her morality.

She shook her head to clear it of such thoughts. She didn't need to know anything beyond what Shivnath had told her. Shivnath was against Necrovar, which meant Keriya was, too.

"Our country is dying," Doru continued. "And if you deliver that dragon to the empire, *rheenar*, I promise things will get worse. There is a dark future awaiting us if this weapon falls into the wrong hands. I'm fighting to prevent that from happening."

"Then we will fight you every step of the way," Roxanne declared. Doru sighed. Slowly, perhaps even reluctantly, he stuck her with the *evasdrin* dart. She convulsed in pain before going limp, her head rolling onto Fletcher's shoulder.

Keriya glared after Doru as he went to the cart and pulled items out of his personal bag: a dagger, an oval mirror wrapped partly in cloth, and a handful of darts. He waved the darts menacingly at Keriya before retiring to his tent.

She decided she hated him. And she refused to be swayed by any of his arguments. He had hurt Thorion, so he was evil. End of story.

They made slow progress the next day. The second dose of poison had made the prisoners particularly lethargic.

"Once Doru runs out of poison, we can escape," Keriya assured herself in an inaudible whisper as she limped onwards.

They'll still have the magical advantage, said a contradictory voice in her head.

"But we have Thorion," she countered.

That's true. She smiled as she imagined Thorion doing to Doru, Shosu, and Blackwater what he had done to the water slug.

<Keriya?>

Keriya stumbled over her feet as a voice bloomed in her mind.

<Thorion!> She stumbled over her thoughts, as well. The poison made it hard for her to concentrate. Words kept slipping away from her before she could send them out to him — though that could be because she'd only just begun using telepathy. *<Are you alright?>*

In response, she received a deluge of confusion and pain.

<Why?> he finally managed.

<Why what?> she thought, and he sent her a feeling she was all too familiar with. *<You're frightened.>*

Thorion stirred on the cart. Keriya nudged Fletcher, who was toiling along in front of her.

"Look." She nodded at Thorion. "He's getting better. We'll be free soon."

But after another grueling day of travel, there was still no hope of salvation. Shosu stuck two more darts into Thorion's side, which plunged the drackling into a stupor. This time, Keriya could still feel the faint clamor of his semi-conscious mind. In an effort to keep him calm, she sent him a constant stream of thoughts. This not only forced her to sharpen her telepathic skills, it lessened the negative effects of the *evasdrin*.

<You know what will happen as soon as we're free? We're going to go far away, somewhere you'll be safe, and you're going to live happily ever after. Doesn't that sound nice?>

<What is 'happily'?>

<The opposite of this,> she quipped. But when Thorion pressed her, she found it just as difficult to describe happiness as it had been to describe fear.

To illustrate the emotion, Keriya sent him memories of the times she'd been happy. She sent the memory of her first view of Allentria. She sent the memory of when the Elders had told her she was allowed to participate in the Ceremony of Choice, though she neglected to share what happened after that. She sent the memory of when she had met him.

Keriya became more familiar with Thorion's mind as she continued their non-stop mental conversation. She began to pick up fragments of information from his brain—not things he shared with her, but things that were simply there, landmarks in the labyrinth of his consciousness. He was the only dragon to have been born in the Etherworld in over a thousand years; his grandsire had been murdered in the Great War, when Necrovar had first risen to power; he feared these new emotions, but he liked the comforting feel of Keriya's mind. He was entertained by her happily-ever-after stories. He was pleased with the image of eating Doru, Shosu, and Blackwater.

Oops. She had tried her hardest not to let him see that particular vision.

<*Don't actually kill them when we get out of this,*> she cautioned.

<*Why?*>

Why, indeed? Killing the Imperials was almost definitely a bad idea, but Keriya couldn't come up with any reasons why Thorion shouldn't rip them to shreds the moment he awoke.

The next day, they left the fen. Doru led them up a hill and through a small gorge. When they came to the mouth of the ravine, they were met with a spectacular sight: an impossibly immense waterfall stretched across the horizon, cascading from a high plateau. The sunset illuminated the spray from the falls, so the sky appeared as if it had been painted with rippling rainbows.

Blackwater set to work covering Thorion with a canvas tarp. Doru turned to his prisoners.

"We're heading into the Galantrian Village. You'll go without protest, or there will be dire consequences for him." He pointed to Thorion. "Understood?"

Bile rose in Keriya's throat. Yes, when Thorion woke up, he could kill Doru. She was fine with that.

They made their way to a road that led toward the town at the base of the waterfall-mesa. A group of travelers on horseback passed them by. The riders nodded respectfully to Doru, though they couldn't be bothered to spare Keriya a second glance. She was shocked at their disinterest until she remembered she looked like a common criminal being dragged to the stocks by Imperial soldiers.

By the time they reached the outskirts of the Village, the relentless din of the falls had become nothing more than white noise. Keriya figured there was magic involved in keeping the sound at a minimum, for the roaring lessened as they moved further into the bustling town.

She wished she could appreciate the exotic splendor around her. There were stone streets for horses and carts, and a network of crisscrossing waterways where boatmen poled long, thin vessels through giant lily pads, carrying goods and passengers alike. She viewed the beauty through a blurred haze, and she was sick with worry.

Doru marched them through a marketplace and led them over a bridge before leaving the hustle and bustle of the thoroughfare. They wound their way down streets which became increasingly dingy and narrow. This part of town was poorly lit. People garbed in dark clothing ghosted through side alleys, lurking in doorways to see who was watching before they disappeared into shops of the most ominous natures.

Finally Doru stopped before a large stone building. A black-robed figure appeared to greet him and the two conversed in low voices. Then Doru turned to his captives and smiled.

CHAPTER TWENTY-TWO

DARKSALM

"Blood of dragon, threads of the great,
Touched by Shadow, seals your fate."
~ Darksalm Incantation

Dread settled in the pit of Fletcher's stomach, making him feel sicker than the *evasdrin* had. He'd never been so scared in his life. When he'd fled Aeria, he had been driven by unthinking, instinctive panic that had disappeared as soon as he left his old home. This fear was slow and brutal. It haunted him even when he slept. All he'd been able to think about since he had been captured was whether he would get out of this alive.

More and more, he feared he wouldn't.

Doru pushed Fletcher through the front door of the building. He tripped over the threshold, dragging the others with him by the rope that bound them together.

Fletcher gazed around the entry foyer. To the right, a wooden staircase carpeted with moth-eaten fabric led to shadowed halls above. Before them stretched a long passage adorned with tapestries depicting savagery of ages past. Whoever had decorated this place had really nailed the 'imminent doom' motif.

Doru herded them up the stairs and into a room at the top landing. It was a large, windowless chamber lit by two brass firelamp stands. The only other furniture was a mahogany desk littered with trinkets and papers, and a chair behind it. Seated in the chair was an Imperial Guard whose torso was peppered with medals. Bands of color marked his sleeve, indicating his rank.

Two guards entered the room, carrying the tarp that contained Thorion. The man stood and walked out from behind the desk to meet them.

He wasn't tall, yet he was imposing. His head was devoid of hair save for his dark beard, which was meticulously trimmed to frame his mouth. Fletcher gasped when he noticed the man's eyes: they were a boiling scarlet, a color that rivaled Keriya's in terms of scariness. A jagged scar snaked across his right eye, stretching from forehead to jaw.

"Commander-General Tanthflame," they murmured in deference. They set the dragon on the wooden floor, and the man's face lit up as the body was unwrapped, revealing the bronze scales and bound limbs within.

"Finally," he breathed, moving to loom over the drackling.

"Get away from him," said Keriya.

Tanthflame looked up, as if he'd only just realized he had company. He approached them, his gaze traveling up Keriya's frame and resting on her face.

"Ah, the *rheenar* herself. Never have I met a person who had eyes more interesting than my own."

Keriya said nothing, but if looks could kill, Tanthflame would have been dead on the floor.

Tanthflame moved on, marching down the line of prisoners. Fletcher didn't want the guardsman to look at him, speak to him, or be anywhere in his personal space. Luckily Tanthflame passed over him and Roxanne and stopped in front of Effrax, whose head was bowed.

"What have we here?" he asked. "A Fironian, by the looks of it. You're far from home, boy."

Effrax looked up for the first time since entering the room, revealing his face.

"Effrax Nameless?" Tanthflame said in genuine surprise. Fletcher frowned — did these two know each other? "How do you come to be in such company?"

"Release us," Effrax commanded, ignoring Tanthflame's query, "by order of the Ember Clan. If you do, perhaps you'll be spared the worst of your punishment for the sins you've committed."

"Sins? Such melodrama. You, of all people, should be able to appreciate what I'm doing."

"Betraying and destroying our empire?"

"The empire has done a fine job of destroying itself," Tanthflame said with a negligent flick of his wrist. "All we have to do is give one little push, and Allentria will crumble and fall. And when it falls, we will be there to pick up the pieces."

"Who is 'we'? You and Necrovar?" Effrax growled.

Tanthflame graced him with a smile full of secrets. Then he turned to Doru. "Leave us."

Doru jumped to attention and brought a hand to his forehead, as if shielding his eyes from a bright light. The other guardsmen deferred to him as he led them out of the room — these soldiers certainly cared a great deal about rank and seniority. The hinges creaked as the door shut behind them, setting Fletcher's teeth on edge.

Tanthflame went to his desk and rummaged around in a drawer. He found what he sought and held it aloft so it sparkled in the firelight. It looked like another dart, except its midsection widened to form a hollow glass vial.

Slowly, the guardsman returned to Thorion. He knelt and placed a hand on the dragon's head gently, almost fearfully. Fletcher felt like he should try to stop whatever was happening, but he couldn't move. He couldn't speak, for he feared drawing Tanthflame's attention to him. He could only watch in panic-stricken silence.

"Don't," Keriya cried shrilly. "He's not the one you want — it's me. I was sent to kill Necrovar."

Tanthflame hesitated and looked up at her. He let loose a humorless laugh. "Who put that idea in your head?"

"Shivnath," Keriya said fiercely. "Allentrian guardian of earthmagic!"

"Oh yes," he replied, in a voice that surpassed condescension and sounded almost pitying. "Shivnath sent a little girl — a girl who, by all accounts, cannot wield any of the base magics — to kill the greatest mage who ever lived."

"That's right," she said, though the fierceness in her voice had been replaced with uncertainty. Fletcher felt uncertainty growing in him, too. Tanthflame made a good point. Why had Shivnath chosen Keriya to do anything? It seemed the dragon god would have done better to grant her powers to someone like Roxanne, who was naturally gifted.

Sensing he'd broken Keriya's spirit, Tanthflame busied himself with Thorion once more. He used the point of the dart to pierce the soft skin of the dragon's neck.

"Bloom of mandrake, snareroot thins, dust of salamander skins," Tanthflame intoned, "blood of dragon, threads of the great,"—he pulled on the end of the instrument and it elongated, drawing a dark, purplish liquid into its midsection—"touched by Shadow, seals your fate."

"They're making darksalm," Effrax gasped, his voice husky with disbelieving horror.

"What's darksalm?" whispered Fletcher. His question went unanswered.

Tanthflame stood with his liquid-filled dart. "Corporal Fireglaim?"

A figure unfolded from a shadowy corner. Tall and lean, he was garbed head to toe in black, and a veiled headscarf covered his face. Fletcher shrank away from the man. He hadn't even known anyone was there.

"We have what we need," said Tanthflame. "After you've given your soldiers their orders, send a messenger to the Galantrian Palace announcing my arrival. We'll want to have an alibi tonight."

"Yes, Commander-General." Corporal Fireglaim bowed. There was something strange about his movements. They were too fluid, almost inhuman. "What of the prisoners?"

Fletcher gulped. What *of* the prisoners?

"These aren't our prisoners, these are our guests—or should I say, our future allies." Tanthflame flashed a smile that didn't touch his blistering eyes. "Bring the dragon to The Waterfront and prepare the darksalm dispersion."

Fireglaim stooped over Thorion. He looped his arms around the dragon's frame as if to pick him up, but he didn't stand. He crouched there, in an awkward embrace; then the two of them began to dissolve into shadow, sinking into the floorboards.

"No!" Keriya tried to run to Thorion, who was melting into a pool of blackness. Moving with surprising agility, Tanthflame intercepted her, catching her around the neck and crushing her head in the crook of his arm. She struggled against his grasp. Her writhing movements pulled on the rope that connected her to Fletcher, yanking him around. He caught a glimpse of her face and felt as though someone had punched him in the gut. Her eyes were glowing.

"Do something," she implored him, choking out the words.

What did she expect him to do? He was no match against Tanthflame or Fireglaim. He should never have come on this quest! Look where he'd ended up: bound and poisoned with a possible death sentence hanging over his head. He would have been better off if he'd stayed in Aeria and lived out his days in the Lowers' settlement.

Roxanne sprang into action on Fletcher's other side. She lunged toward the drackling, as if intending to snatch him out of the midnight puddle. Effrax stumbled with her, and Fletcher felt his arms twist uncomfortably in opposite directions.

Corporal Fireglaim shot a dark spell at Roxanne. It passed through both her and Effrax without leaving any physical mark, but brought them crashing to their knees.

The sight of his friends collapsing ignited something in Fletcher. He had to help. He should assist Roxanne, or save Keriya, or hit Tanthflame, or —

A weight dragged on him from the left. The Commander-General had dropped Keriya's limp body, and Fletcher's blood ran cold. What was wrong with him? Why had he hesitated? His sole purpose in coming along had been to make sure Keriya didn't die, but every time his courage had been put to the test, he had failed miserably.

No more, he resolved. *I won't be afraid anymore. It's up to me now!*

But it was too late. Beyond Tanthflame, the tip of Thorion's snout turned to shadow, then disappeared altogether. As soon as he was gone, the black smear on the floor evaporated without a trace.

Tanthflame dusted off his hands, glaring at Roxanne and Effrax.

"That," he said, "was very stupid of you."

Thorion was vaguely aware of goings-on around him. He felt himself being dragged around. Sometimes he heard voices — usually loud or high-pitched, which he had come to associate with the emotions of anger and fear. More than once he gained enough control over his body to open his outer eyelids, but on those occasions his mind was unable to process his surroundings. All he could discern were blurry patches of light and dark.

At one point he felt something cold wrap around him, and purple light shone through his senseless state. That meant his eyes were glowing. The cold enveloped his body, then swallowed him whole.

When he re-emerged into warmth, the glow faded. Whatever necromagical spell had caused the reaction had been dropped or unraveled. The feverish effects of the *evasdrin* intensified. He lapsed back into true unconsciousness.

Later — how long, he couldn't say, for he had lost all sense of time — he awoke to a pain in the smallest finger of his left forepaw. The pain grew, spreading up his phalanx, into his arm, through his chest, past his wing joint and neck, until it reached his brain.

Finally his eyes snapped open and everything came into focus. He was in a dark room lit by smoldering coals in a metal basin hanging from the ceiling. The gray stone walls were slick with trickles of water draining from somewhere above. Thorion was lying on a cold slab of rock. He tried to get up, but couldn't move. Glancing left and right, he saw that he was muzzled and bound with iron shackles and chains.

With a whisper of booted footfalls, two human men came into view. On their heads, they wore metal contraptions inset with sheets of glass to cover their faces. White cloths hung down their torsos, covering their garments, and they each held metal instruments. One was a knife, the other was a mystery. Thorion tried to access his racial memories — thoughts and information that had been passed down from his ancestors — to identify the tool, but he found himself unable to connect with the dragons' hive-mind.

"It's awake." One man elbowed the other and pointed at Thorion.

"It's not moving," said his companion. "And it's clamped down pretty tight." He had a hooked nose that reminded Thorion of a hawk's beak, and his beady eyes were narrowed, possibly with apprehension. If Thorion had had the opportunity to be around more humans, he might have been able to identify their expressions more accurately.

"Yeah, well . . . let's hurry," said the first man, whose face was beading with sweat beneath his glass visor — that was a side effect of anxiety, wasn't it? "What else does Tanthflame want?"

"Blood's the most important thing," the hawk-nosed man replied. Thorion couldn't understand what they were saying, but their words were hurried and urgent. "We can harvest some of its parts, so long as we keep it alive and mostly in working order. Scales are safe, so are the claws."

"How about the teeth?" said the other. "Some stories say if you plant dragon teeth in the ground you can grow an army of warriors." That earned him a smack upside the head from the hawk-nosed man. "Ow! What'd you do that for?"

"Because you're an idiot. Now hold the claw so I can actually get at it this time."

With a scowl, the sweaty man stepped closer to Thorion,

raising his metal instrument. He pulled on the base of the tool and it hinged open at its middle, creating a space between the barbed ends. He bent and placed the ends on the tip of Thorion's littlest finger, the one that had pained him. The tool tightened around the pearly claw as the human squeezed the ends of the instrument together. Then he pulled.

Pain stabbed through Thorion's arm again. He could see that the base of his claw, where bone met flesh, was shredded and bloody. The hawk-nosed man raised his knife and began sawing at it.

Agony exploded in Thorion's mind. He tried to yank his paw away but the iron shackle around his wrist kept him firmly in place, bolted to the table. He wriggled his body but it did no good. Now that he was more alert, he could feel that his neck was shackled in two places. His hind legs and tail were clamped down and his wings were tethered.

"Almost there," the hawk-nosed man grunted. Thorion felt one of his tendons snap. He gave a violent lurch in response. He felt something in his belly now, a strange coldness accompanied by a stinging throb. It was more pervasive than nausea, for it was spreading to his heart and lungs, making his breath come in short, quick gasps. All his muscles tensed. Was there poison on the knife?

No . . . there was a word for this feeling. Keriya had told him in the fen.

Frightened.

A low growl worked its way up from the bottom of his throat. It rose in pitch until it was a shrill, piercing cry, a long note muffled by the iron locked around his snout. He shook his head back and forth, rattling the chains that held him in place.

"He's going mad," said the sweaty man, cringing away from Thorion's fettered thrashing.

"I'm nearly done. Just yank it out!"

There was a new pain now, a grating, twisting pain as the sweaty man gave a mighty wrench and the talon came loose. Blood spurted from Thorion's claw socket and spattered on the humans' white robes, sizzling with heat.

"Don't waste it!" the hawk-nosed man cried, stooping and grabbing a glass jar from under the table. He wedged it beneath the bleeding paw, collecting the draining fluid.

Another growl rose out of Thorion, and he suddenly wanted to rip through his iron binds and sink his fangs into the humans. He recalled the image Keriya had shared with him, the picture of Doru, Blackwater and Shosu torn to pieces, and realized he wanted the same fate to befall these two men. He wanted to see *them* bleed. He wanted to see them die.

Thorion drummed his fingers against the glass jar, jolting it from the hawk-nosed man's grasp. It fell to the floor and shattered.

"Gods damn it!" the human yelped. Thorion concentrated all his energy in his left arm. With an almighty tug, he broke free from the iron manacle. His movement toppled another glass jar, which had been standing outside of his view near the base of his neck. It rolled away, dribbling a thin trail of his precious blood along the table before falling and breaking. They had probably made a cut in the soft skin of his jawline to gather more.

He lashed out at the men with his free paw. They screamed and stumbled away.

"Go get some effin' *evasdrin*," cried the hawk-nosed man. They sprinted for a staircase in the far corner of the room, pushing each other in their haste to flee, and vanished through a door at the top of the steps.

Thorion let out a long breath from his nostrils and lowered his maimed hand. The men would come back. They would hurt him again. For as long as humans had existed, they had coveted power; and for as long as dragons had been the most powerful creatures in the world, humans had devised ways to take it from them.

The flesh-rats—awful, stinking, un-armored monsters that they were—had always been innovative and resilient. In terms of intelligence, brute strength and wielding force, they could never compete with dragons. Their power lay in their creativity.

They had imagined instruments of torture to make up for their lack of claws and fangs; they had cultivated poisons to tame superior wielders; they were so small, so foolish-looking, yet they had bent metal and stone to their will.

And now they had bent a dragon to their will, too. Thorion was overwhelmed by the realization that he was going to die, lost, alone and frightened. He squeezed his eyes shut. This . . . what was this?

Despair.

The enervating emotion seeped into his bones. His muscles relaxed and his heart grew heavy.

And then, for no apparent reason, a memory came to him. It was a memory of the water slug in the dwarf tunnels. Though defenseless, Keriya had felt the need to stand up to it. She had fought against all odds. She didn't know how *not* to fight.

He wasn't alone. Somewhere out there, Keriya was fighting for him. He knew it, he could feel it. So he gathered his wits, strained against his bindings, and cast his mind out to search for her.

CHAPTER TWENTY-THREE

THE RESCUE

"You are never as alone as you believe."
~ **Ishiro Vahari, Third Age**

<Keriya?>

From far away, Keriya heard someone calling her name.

<You're hurt. What did they do to you?>

Who's that? she wondered groggily.

<Thorion,> the voice replied to her private thought. Her attention sharpened. He was still alive!

<You're frightened,> he observed, examining her mind.

<No,> she insisted, though it was foolish to argue when he could see into her head.

<Calm,> thought Thorion, sending her some of the happy images she had given him: her first sight of Allentria; the handsome prince charming she had invented for herself; adventuring in the Felwood with Fletcher when they'd been young, when the worst problem in her life had been Penelope Sanvire.

<What about you?> she asked, feeling more alert. The mere touch of Thorion's mind was giving her strength. *<Are you okay?>*

<The poison is leaving my bloodstream, but there are men here who want to hurt me. I don't know why they're doing this,> he admitted, and she glimpsed emotional turmoil through a crack in his mental strength. *<I did nothing to them. I don't understand why I am being punished this way.>*

<It's my fault.> How she wished she'd had the courage to refuse Aldelphia's quest. She had done the exact opposite of what Shivnath had wanted: she had dragged Thorion into

mortal danger. *<They're working for Necrovar. He wants to kill you because you're the only one strong enough to kill him. Effrax said something about the guards making darksalm, and ->*

At the mention of darksalm, Thorion's thoughts became frenzied.

<What's wrong?>

<Darksalm is a substance – the main component of which is dragon blood – that burrows into your magicsource. It if it touches you, it will kill you slowly and your soul will belong to the Shadow when you die. You return to life as a shadowbeast, a mindless demon-slave for Necrovar.>

Keriya felt her own blood run cold. *<Thorion, you have to escape!>*

<Too much pain,> he complained. *<Too much poison, too many chains.>* A feeling of hopelessness leaked out of him.

<I'll save you,> Keriya promised. *<I'll make this right.>* Time for her to wake up. Time to be a hero.

She came-to, only to discover that she was tied up in a corner of Tanthflame's chambers. She was back-to-back with Roxanne and facing the wall, but by the sounds of things, there were guards on the far side of the room. Fletcher was bound next to her. His eyes brimmed with tears the moment he noticed she was awake.

"Keriya, I'm sorry. I wanted to help Thorion, but there was nothing I could do."

Keriya shook her head; this wasn't the time for apologies or arguments, for they had bigger worries. She hurriedly recounted what Thorion had told her about darksalm. Instead of whining or worrying about it, Fletcher was all business.

"Right. There's only one way out of the room, which is through that door. We're not tied too tightly." He began fiddling with the rope knotted around his wrists. "If I can get out, then we could – ow!"

"Stay still," someone said from across the room. Fletcher yelped as a whip of solidified air, wielded by one of the guards, lashed his face. Keriya expected him to cry, but he didn't. He clenched his jaw in determination.

'*I'll work on escaping,*' Fletcher mouthed at her.

"Even if we get free, we have to get past them," said Keriya, tilting her head to indicate the guards.

"They've been drinking," Effrax muttered from Keriya's other side. "We could wait until they're too inebriated to wield against us."

"You want to leave our fate to a chance like that?"

"That's it," growled one of the guards. Keriya felt the vibrations of his footfalls as he stumped toward them. "You wanna keep makin' noise? I'll give you somethin' to make noise about."

There was laughter in the background. The other men were getting up too, looking to share in the fun. Roxanne struggled against Keriya, and there was a grunt of pain that seemed to indicate the taller girl had kicked one of their captors. Keriya craned her neck around to see what was going on.

"Here's a feisty one," said a broad-shouldered Smarlindian, massaging his shin. "We like fighters, don't we lads?"

He unsheathed a blade from his belt. At first Keriya thought he meant to hurt Roxanne, but he merely cut the rope that bound them. It was replaced by an invisible current of air, confining Keriya, Fletcher, and Effrax once more.

"Let me go!" Roxanne's weight against Keriya vanished as the men pulled her up.

"Shut your pretty little mouth," said the Smarlindian, his voice now full of menace. "Or don't. We might have some use for it, eh?" His cohorts chuckled darkly.

Keriya found herself yelling, demanding that the guards leave Roxanne alone. She started kicking at the wooden wall behind her, but all that did was make her feet hurt.

Shivnath, help! she prayed. *Let me use your powers!*

Suddenly the wall splintered with a loud crack. Keriya froze mid-kick, gawping at the damage. Had *she* done that?

There was another cracking noise and Keriya flinched as the wall exploded inwards, showering her with debris. Wooden boards split apart and fractures fanned across the floorboards. The air-threads around her dissolved and she scrambled up.

Roxanne stood alone in the middle of the room, trembling with terror, or possibly rage. The guards lay at her feet, knocked unconscious by heavy pieces of the wall—the *evasdrin* had finally worn off.

Keriya stared around at the wreckage. There were earth-threads in dead wood, but Erasmus had always said it would take a very adept wielder to manipulate them. Maybe Roxanne was stronger than any of them had given her credit for.

Fletcher had actually managed to free himself from the rope that bound his hands behind his back. He leaned over and helped untie the cords around Keriya and Effrax's wrists.

"Right," said Effrax, standing and dusting himself off. "If we're all alive, let's find Thorion."

"What about the darksalm?" said Fletcher.

"They won't have it here," said Roxanne. "Didn't what's-his-eyes say something about the palace? They're going to do it at the palace."

"No," said Effrax. "Tanthflame just said he needed an alibi."

"They brought Thorion to the waterfront," Fletcher reminded them. "They're probably keeping him wherever the darksalm is. That means we'll be facing a ton of guards, and we won't be able to fight them all."

"Then what do you propose we do?" asked Effrax. Fletcher gazed around for inspiration, and his eyes fell on the black-robed men on the floor.

"I think I have an idea."

A short while later, Keriya and Roxanne were marched out of the old house with their hands tied behind their backs, escorted by two cloaked, hooded men. They were blocked by a group of Imperials standing watch at the front door.

"Those prisoners are supposed to stay here," said the foreman, drawing his sword.

"Stand down, soldier," said Roxanne's guard. "Commander-

General Tanthflame sent word to move these two and infect them with the darksalm."

Fortunately none of the soldiers recognized Effrax's voice, and the hooded cape he'd stolen from the Smarlindian hid his face well.

"Everything alright in there?" asked another guard. "We heard a disturbance."

"If everything wasn't alright, do you think we'd be moving them?" Effrax snapped.

"Weren't there four of them?" said the first man. "What happened to the others? The fire wielder and that smallish one?"

Keriya's guard made an insulted sound under his hood. Fletcher disliked anyone commenting on his height.

Effrax shrugged. "We left them. They're not as important as the *rheenar.*"

On cue, Keriya looked up so the Imperials could see her purple eyes. That did the trick. They stood aside, allowing Effrax and Fletcher to shepherd Keriya and Roxanne past.

As soon as they rounded the far corner of the street, the girls shucked off the ropes they'd held around their wrists and the four of them began to run.

"Which way is the waterfront?" Keriya panted.

Effrax's eyes lit up. "Wait—The Waterfront! I bet they're talking about the inn, not the actual lakeshore. Come on, it's on the border of the upper district."

He wheeled sharply and pelted down a twisty alleyway. As Keriya followed him through deserted corridors and across rickety bridges, she cast her mind out for Thorion in an attempt to pinpoint his location. He was still in considerable pain. The iron shackles around his legs burned his scales. Something was wrong with his left front paw.

<You're near,> he thought. Indeed, they rounded a corner and saw a decrepit inn sitting in a pool of flickering light cast by a lone street lamp. Its windows were shuttered, but the rotted wooden door, recessed in the wall to create handy shadows in which people could hide, was open. Perhaps this

was an attempt to be inviting, though Keriya thought she'd never seen a more uninviting building in her life.

"This is it," Effrax whispered, slowing to a walk.

"You come here voluntarily?" asked Fletcher.

"They serve the best rice ale in the empire. Plus, there's always a game of dice to be had, and it's easier to cheat if you're playing against drunkards."

"You're just a model citizen, aren't you?" muttered Roxanne.

Effrax indicated they should get back in character and wrapped the ropes back around the girls' wrists. As they approached, a thickset guard lumbered out of the inn to meet them. Small eyes glared out from beneath his heavy brows, and his face looked as if it had been poorly hewn from granite. Keriya had never seen a troll—she'd only read about them—but she decided this would be exactly what they looked like.

"We're bringing the Commander-General's prisoners to be kept with the dragon," Effrax said officiously. The troll curled back his lips, revealing gaps in his teeth, and nodded. Keriya hid a smile—Effrax had just ascertained that Thorion was hidden somewhere inside. They started forward, but the troll shifted his bulk to bar their way.

"Password," he grunted. For the first time, Effrax faltered. The troll noticed, and he did not look pleased.

Roxanne tore herself from Effrax's grasp and wielded a patch of dirt and pebbles from the street into the troll's face. He bellowed and clawed at his eyes, staggering backward.

"This is what we wanted to avoid," Effrax grumbled as she threw down her ropes and stormed inside.

Three more Imperials were sitting in the common room. Roxanne gestured to a potted plant in the corner, a browning shrub that had been neglected for too long. At the touch of her magicthreads, it turned vibrant and sprang to life, growing outwards to restrain the men.

The guards rallied and began to counter-wield. Keriya dodged an errant water spell and almost bumped into the troll. His face, now covered in angry welts, was scrunched in fury.

He reached for her with hairy hands and she ran. She heard him knocking aside furniture in his pursuit, but he didn't wield against her. Perhaps trolls weren't able to use magic?

Maybe I'm part troll, she thought to herself, giggling in hysteria as she scrambled beneath a table for cover. Fletcher was hiding there. He grabbed the legs of a bar stool and hurled it at the troll with all his might. The troll tripped, his limbs flailing comically, and toppled to the ground.

"Go!" said Fletcher, flapping his hands at Keriya. They crawled out on the far side of the table, and stood just in time to see the last remaining guard hurl a throwing knife at Roxanne.

It burrowed into her side. She dropped her spells instantly, and the potted plant, which had been strangling one of the gray-robed men, grew still. Red seeped down the front of her green dress, flowering around the entry wound. The knife-thrower drew his sword and grabbed her.

"She dies if any of you move," he spat, pressing the edge of the blade against her throat.

Effrax slowly raised his hands, as if surrendering. Then he twitched his fingers and fires burst to life around the guard's wrists. The man cried out in shock and dropped both the sword and Roxanne.

She fell, and Effrax darted forward to catch her as he wielded against the guard. Now that he'd regained the use of his magic, the man didn't pose much of a challenge to him.

For a brief instant it seemed like they'd won—then burly arms encircled Keriya, picking her up from behind. It was the troll. He squeezed, slowly but surely crushing the life out of her.

Effrax shot fire at him, but the flames splashed up against an invisible barrier. Apparently the troll *could* wield, and had created an air shield. Keriya choked and kicked against his tree-trunk torso. She feared her body was only a moment away from breaking, and she reflected, for what seemed like the millionth time, that if she only had magic of her own, she could do anything. Escape from trolls. Save Thorion. Kill anyone who stood in her way, up to and including Necrovar himself.

There was a strange ringing in her ears and her vision dimmed. Just before darkness overtook her, something blindingly bright passed over her head, singeing her hair. An acrid scent burned her nostrils. The troll's arms loosened and he collapsed. Keriya fell with him, gasping. She rolled over and saw the right side of his face was charred and steaming, seared to the bone. He was dead, though by what sort of dreadful magic, she knew not.

She felt warm breath on her cheek and turned. Thorion was there. His eyes were wide and his pupils were dilated. His lips were fixed in a snarl. She noted, with a lurch of her stomach, that he was missing the smallest talon of his left paw and his scales were caked with purple blood.

"You saved me," she whispered.

"You came to save me. Now we are balanced." Comforted by the drackling's crisp straightforwardness, she reached up and put her arms around his neck.

"I found my lightmagic," he told her. *"I wielded for the first time. For you."*

The strangely tender moment was ruined by the renewed sounds of battle coming from the opposite end of the room. Effrax was fighting another guard, and there were sure to be more Imperials nearby.

Thorion puffed himself up and opened his mouth. From between his fangs there issued a savage, white-hot flash. When the afterglow faded from Keriya's eyes, she saw that the enemy wielder lay in a sizzling heap on the floor.

Without pause, Effrax hefted Roxanne up and made for the exit. "Let's go!"

"Wait," said Fletcher. "We've got to warn everyone."

"Everyone who? We're all here," Roxanne said through gritted teeth. She had pulled the knife from her abdomen and now had her palm pressed against the injury to stop the flow of blood.

"The villagers," said Fletcher. "We need to tell them about the darksalm. Who knows what Tanthflame will do with it?"

Roxanne's eyes widened and she groaned.

"You're not coming," Effrax told her. "You need to rest."

"Yeah, I'll go have a nice lie-down," she snapped. "Not like there are Imperials all over the place who'd be happy to kill me." She broke away from him and started again for the door.

"Wait." Now it was Keriya who spoke. "Think what would happen if the darksalm touches Thorion? We'd be putting the whole world at risk. We need to leave."

Roxanne snorted. "That's some great hero talk right there."

Keriya's face grew hot, but she let the taunt slide. "It's too dangerous. He can't stay here."

"Then send him away," Effrax told her. "We'll warn the Galantrians, but the sooner he leaves, the better."

Yes, that was the obvious answer, wasn't it? Then why did it seem so hard to do?

Keriya took a deep breath and knelt before the little dragon. *"Thorion, we're in a lot of trouble and you're not safe. I need you to fly away as quickly as possible, as far as you can go."* He nodded. Fear was shining on his face again. *"There's nothing to be afraid of. Just . . . just fly. And then you won't have to worry."*

"I will have to worry," he said slowly. Confusion stirred within her, though whether it was his or her own, she couldn't tell.

Shaking her head, she scooped Thorion into her arms and carried him outside. The others followed in silence. Keriya could feel their watchful gazes as she threw her ward into the air. He took to the skies, beating his wings to gain altitude.

<Be safe,> he thought to her. Then his glittering form was swallowed by the night, and he was gone.

CHAPTER TWENTY-FOUR

THE PRINCESS AND
THE PEASANT

"The Waters of Chardon may be dangerous,
but that is not sufficient reason to stay ashore."
~ **Galantrian Folk Saying**

Princess Sebaris Ishira Wavewould roamed the streets of the Galantrian Village. Her distinctive fish-gill nose was hidden by the drooping cowl of a nondescript cloak. She'd been doing this for most of her life, walking amongst the commoners like she was one of them. Her father had forbidden her from leaving the palace unescorted, but Seba preferred to mingle with the crowd on her own terms.

She crossed the white stone bridge that spanned one of the seven major waterways in town, enjoying the sounds of the evening. She nodded to a passing nobleman, brushing her short, cobalt-blue hair from her eyes. How she longed to pull off her hood and show her populace who she was. She didn't need them to bow and grovel, though there was certainly no harm in that. She just wanted to learn from them as a ruler, not an onlooker.

A heavy hand fell on her shoulder without warning. She reached under her cloak for the blue-gold dagger concealed in her silk belt sash and clutched at her hood, which had almost slipped off. Her nose, which marked her as a member of House Ishira, would give her identity away in a heartbeat.

"Care for a drink, miss?" said the man who'd apprehended her. His breath was rancid and Seba closed her slitted nostrils in disgust. She tugged herself from his grasp and walked away without a response. Luckily, he was too inebriated to realize who she was and too lazy to follow.

It wasn't proper for a princess to know the arts of fighting, but Seba had taken it upon herself to learn. At age ten, she had begun to sneak out of the palace to practice in the Village, and had sought training in the Water Tower.

The Tower had originally been created to monitor the flow of the East Outlet River through the floodgates, and was privately guarded by a family of warriors. Seba had learned from Isi, an old master of martial arts. He'd been blind, and had never known her true identity. He had passed away three years ago, and still she mourned him. She had never been his star pupil, but she had always been his favorite.

Lost in her memories, Seba strolled down a side street to examine some necklaces on display in front of a seedy shop. The merchant claimed they were made from genuine sapphire stones, but Seba knew better. She left the stand, sniffing disdainfully.

Someone touched her shoulder again. She went for her dagger, but her assailant seemed to have expected this, and he grabbed her wrist. She tried to back him into a nearby wall and stamp on his toes. He evaded her slippered foot and used her movement against her, causing her to stumble sideways so they slid into an alley together. Seba felt a pang of panic and opened her mouth to scream, but a gloved hand covered her face to muffle the cry. Thinking fast, she bit down on his fingers.

"Gods curse it, Seba!" a familiar voice hissed as the hand was yanked away. She blinked in surprise and turned.

"Maxton?" she exclaimed, planting her fists on her hips in indignation and narrowing her slanted blue eyes. "What in Zumarra's name do you think you're doing?"

"Why, protecting you. I figured you might need it, especially after that fool almost revealed your identity."

"I can protect myself, thank you very much."

"You certainly can," he agreed dryly, removing his glove to reveal a set of teeth marks on his palm. "But can you protect yourself from your father?"

"Excuse me? Are you threatening to tell on me?"

"I'm not threatening you, I'm warning you. Commander-General Tanthflame just announced himself in the palace, and you'll be called to sit in as heir to the Coral Throne any moment now."

Seba's jaw dropped and all the fight flowed out of her. She hadn't heard about this, otherwise she'd never have gone out!

"You need to get back before they find you missing," Max continued, motioning for her to pull her hood back up.

Seba nodded, and followed Max northwards at something close to a run. Over the bridge, up Main Street, toward the square where the ice orb ferried people to and from the palace. There was a small gathering waiting for the next shuttle.

As she drew near, she saw that it was not a line, but rather some sort of commotion in the street. The cause of the hold-up was a bunch of intoxicated peasants. Seba glared at the hooligans as she passed.

"Max, stop!" Seba veered off course and pushed her way to the front of the crowd. She recognized one of the trouble-makers—it was Effrax Nameless. She didn't know him like she knew Max, but he was always in attendance at state functions alongside Prince Zivan.

"Effrax? Why are you here? Where's . . ."

She paused as her gaze fell upon the peasants beside him. They were filthy and bloodied. One girl, who had white hair and a pallid complexion, looked like a walking ghost.

"The Village is in danger," Nameless told her without any sort of prelude or explanation.

"Come now," scoffed one of the crowd members. "Stop with this nonsense!"

Seba tugged her hood lower. It was Yosiro Lakeward, a city official who was always barging into the palace to bother her father about trivial matters.

"You don't understand," said the scrawny-looking boy. "There's darksalm around here!"

Seba would have dismissed the claim as the ravings of a

lunatic, had it not been for her most recent foresight. In her vision, she'd seen a dragon and a terrible darkness—and her father had taken it seriously enough to share with the empress herself.

Max joined Seba, then passed right by, heading for the peasants. "Darksalm? That's impossible." He took the pale girl's hand to steady her, and her face shone like the sun. Seba eyed the two of them beadily. Why the display of familiarity?

"Not as impossible as you think," said the taller girl, who held her hands to a wound in her side.

"Max, you have to believe us," said the pale one. "Tanth-flame has all the ingredients."

Seba's lips thinned in angry disbelief. Why was this girl on a first-name basis with Maxton Windharte?! He had been traveling on 'Official Imperial Business' for the past month and had arrived at the Galantrian palace a week ago, but where had he been? Who had he been with? The details of his mission had remained secret. He couldn't possibly have been working with these ruffians, could he?

"Tanthflame?" said Lakeward. "As in *Gohrbryn* Tanthflame? Preposterous! He is the Commander-General of the Imperial Guard."

"He also happens to be a traitor." Nameless turned to address the crowd, which had grown considerably since Seba had joined it. "We don't know how he intends to disperse the darksalm, but you aren't safe. You need to evacuate!"

"Nameless," Seba snapped, "you have no power to give orders here."

"We're not trying to give orders, we're trying to save lives," said the horrid, pasty peasant. Seba gasped and took a step back. The girl had purple eyes.

A fretful noblewoman turned to her husband. "Perhaps we should go?"

"You should," said Nameless. "Take the Imperial Highway south, toward Noryk."

Seba resented the fact that a Fironian was ordering her

subjects around and had half a mind to command him to be silent. But if he was right about this, then —

"Don't listen to that prisoner! He's wanted for treason!" A captain of the Imperial Guard, flanked by a platoon of soldiers, entered the square and marched straight for Nameless. The people parted ways for him, muttering about how they had nearly been deceived. Lakeward loudly boasted that he hadn't believed any of this rubbish.

"What's he done that has been deemed as treasonous?" Seba demanded in her best princess voice. With her hood up she looked like any random villager, and the guards ignored her.

The Fironian drew himself up to his full height. "You are impeding a member of the Ember Clan — "

Seba stifled a cry of shock as he was sent reeling from a fierce slap of air across his face.

"You are a member of no Clan, Effrax Nameless," said the captain. "You are not recognized as royalty by any state in the empire, and you have no sovereignty over us." The guardsmen closed in on the Fironian. One of them shoved Seba aside.

"Move along," he growled.

Seba wanted a proper explanation — and she wanted people to treat her with the respect she deserved — so again, she reached up to pull off her hood. Max stopped her. He shook his head and whispered, "Too risky."

"We're working for the empress and we have sealed letters to prove it. You can't arrest us," said the tall peasant girl.

"Of course we can. For starters, you're in the presence of a demon," said the captain, pointing at the girl with the lurid eyes.

"Demon, he says," gasped an austere gentleman, looking scandalized.

"They might be in league with the bogspectre," someone cried.

"One of them might *be* the bogspectre!" said someone else.

"None of us are criminals or demons," the small boy insisted. "We're telling the truth! Tanthflame is working for Necrovar, and he—"

"Slander," screamed the captain. "Malicious slander against our highest officer! You're all under arrest! Commander-General Tanthflame is at a state meeting as we speak; there is no way he could be embroiled in any sort of criminal activity."

Seba's stomach sank. She was too late. Her father must have discovered her missing by now. She covered her face with her hands, wondering how she would get herself out of this one.

It was unclear who struck first; one moment the guards were closing in on the peasants, and the next, the stones of the street heaved upwards, throwing the Imperials backward.

"Hostile wielding in a public space! Arrest them," the captain shrieked.

Nameless began wielding to keep the guardsmen at bay. Max was almost clipped by a wayward tongue of fire, and he leapt to join the fight, fool that he was.

Another Imperial advanced upon the purple-eyed girl, wielding a white-hot jet of flame. She dove behind a waste bin to avoid his attack, then kicked it over to hinder his progress while she turned tail and ran up the street. Coward. Why not just wield back?

"I command all of you to stop," Seba shouted, but her cries were lost in the din of the brawling crowd. She was sure things couldn't get any worse.

Then there was a thunderous boom.

The ground shook.

Seba jerked around and saw that an entire line of buildings had erupted in an explosion in the upper district. A mountain of debris catapulted into the air and a plume of dust billowed upwards, blanketing the sky. The shockwave from the blast hit them, nearly knocking her off her feet.

Seba's vision narrowed to one spot: she watched as the Water Tower, the invincible edifice, the place that had once been her refuge, shuddered. Smoke swirled around it, engulfing it, consuming it . . . then it collapsed in upon itself, telescoping down amidst spirals of furious flames.

Suddenly people were running, screaming, crying, trying to find loved ones, wanting to go back and save their houses, their furniture, their belongings.

Even through her haze of shock, Seba knew what she had to do. This was the scene from her foresight dream. It was all coming true. After a lifetime of waiting, she reached up with trembling hands and pulled off her cowl.

"Galantrians," she cried, "I am Princess Sebaris Ishira Wavewould. Head for the Imperial Highway, aid will come to you there!"

Miraculously, people listened to her. The anthill of frenzied motion turned into a purposeful wave of bodies surging toward the highway. She urged them on, shouting encouragement.

The upper district was now shrouded in fire. How had it spread so fast? The malevolent red flames were pierced with tongues of black, which banished the last of Seba's doubts about the darksalm. There were some upon whom the dark magic had already settled, and more still who'd been injured, who were fleeing the northern quadrant sporting charred flesh and gaping wounds.

"Don't go back," Seba screamed at one hysterical woman who pushed against the crowd.

"My husband—he's sick! Our house is in the upper district—"

"Then the palace guards will save him!" That was a lie. Seba was sure her father had sent a response team by now, but there would be no survivors. Even if there were, no one in the Galantasa, in all of Allentria, could save them from their fate.

She watched as the woman was swept away by the masses before assessing the destruction that surrounded her. There was only one weapon available to her that would be effective against the fire.

It was improper for a woman of her rank to use magic. She had only wielded three other times in her life, and on each occasion she'd lost control of her threads. The fact that her power was so dangerous and volatile usually prevented her from using it, but this was an emergency.

She raced up the street, heading for the nearest canal. When she reached it she closed her eyes, retreated within herself, and connected with her magicsource. The feeling was intoxicating. Magic was life. It was a drug. It filled her with freedom and fear.

Brimming with energy, she mentally directed some of her threads into the waterway. A wall of liquid flew upwards, responding to her very thoughts. People paused to stare. "Keep going!" she yelled, waving them on.

Sweat beaded on her brow as she focused — clear intent was crucial to any spell, and a lapse in concentration would undo all her hard work. Slowly, she manipulated the water so it hovered over the Village. When it was poised above the outer edge of the black-tinged blaze, Seba let it fall. The fire spat and stuttered where she doused it, then resumed its voracious appetite, devouring shops and houses alike.

"You there! Stop your wielding!"

Seba paid no attention to the shout, because it was impossible that anyone could be speaking to *her* like that. Then, for the third time that night, someone grabbed her shoulder. An Imperial Guard stood glowering behind her.

"Unhand me! I am Sebaris Ishi—"

"I don't give a drop of Helkryvt's blood who you are. You're interacting with that fire, and for that we must detain you," he said, tightening his hold on her.

Seba imagined that she looked like a fish: her mouth was opening and closing, but no sound was coming out. She was furious. She was incensed! She—was being arrested? Two more guards came over, attempting to shackle her.

Words failed her, so she took action. She whipped out her dagger and punched its blunt end into the stomach of the man who held her. He crumpled with a grunt and Seba whirled around, her blade flashing as she cut at the remaining two. One doubled over and cried out, holding a bleeding arm. The other leapt out of her reach and wielded against her.

It pained Seba to admit it, even in the recesses of her own

mind, but she was a bad wielder. Still, what she lacked in finesse she made up for in raw power. So when the man shot a torrent of water at her, she poured threads from her source and channeled them into the liquid, deflecting his spell.

"Attacking a member of the Imperial Guard is illegal," he cried.

"Attacking a member of one of the royal families of Allentria is a Class-A felony!" Seba countered, blocking another of his attacks. She couldn't keep this up; she'd exhaust her source at this rate, because she had no idea how much power was necessary to combat this imbecile.

There was a dull thud, and the man collapsed. Max stood behind him. He had saved her.

"Why are you still here?" she yelled over the roar of the inferno.

"I came back for Keriya."

"Who?"

"Keriya Soulstar, the girl with the purple eyes. Did you see which way she went?"

Fresh anger boiled in Seba's stomach. Had he really come back for that heathen peasant brat?

"I saw nothing," she lied, sniffing in contempt.

"Sebaris, we must find her!"

"Why? Why is she important to you?"

"She's a dragon speaker," he said. Seba knew Max well enough to know there was more to it than that.

He turned his back on her and ran toward the fire, with nothing more than an air shield to ward off the tainted ash spiraling in the burning breeze. With a growl of frustration, Seba started after him.

"Princess!"

She stopped at once. The anger in her stomach turned to ice. Dreading what was coming, she turned to see the captain of her father's servicemen, Inido Rainsword, approaching with a group of his men.

She was in big trouble.

CHAPTER TWENTY-FIVE

THE DRAGON AND
THE DARKNESS

"Eternity binds only those who are dead."
~ Valerion Equilumos, Second Age

Roxanne could feel herself unraveling. In Aeria, it had been taught that one shouldn't wield while bleeding. She'd been inclined to think that this, like everything else she'd learned in that stagnant waste pit, was nonsense. Now she knew better.

With her mind's eye, she gazed upon her magicsource. It still emitted a healthy glow, but when she pulled threads away from her core, she *felt* it. That had never happened before. And more blood oozed from her wound every time she wielded.

She needed help, but Effrax had run off after some Imperials and Keriya had fled. Fletcher had actually stayed to fight, but he was making things worse. Where had the cowardly, whiny Fletcher gone? This new Fletcher, the one who was trying too hard to be brave, was just causing problems.

"Surrender now!" said a voice Roxanne knew all too well. Balling her hands into white-knuckled fists, she looked around to see Doru pointing his sword at her.

If she hadn't been so exhausted—and if blood hadn't been pouring from her side—she might have tried to kill him. The best she could do was to get rid of him as quickly as possible. She was too badly injured to even think about creation magic, so that left her with manipulation.

Roxanne threaded energy into the earth beneath the cobbles of the street. A pillar of dirt rose behind Doru and smacked into him. He collapsed beneath its weight and did not get up again.

After that, it was easy to dispense with the Imperial who was attacking Fletcher.

"Thanks," Fletcher wheezed as Roxanne limped over to him. He was on the verge of tears. Fine time to start being wimpy again. He'd hardly been scratched, and she was the one who'd done all the work. "Where's Keriya?"

"Haven't a bloody clue. She ran away."

"To find Thorion, do you think?"

"No, to run away."

"Come on, Roxanne, that's not fair," he said. "She doesn't have any magic."

"So? You barely have any magic, and you stuck around like the halfwit you are," she retorted.

"I . . . I was just trying to help."

Roxanne ignored him. All she wanted was to lie down and forget the horrific events of the evening. The sight of the Village burning had affected her deeply, and her experience with those guards . . . she wanted to block that out forever. It reminded her too much of what she had suffered at her father's hands.

Painful memories swelled within her, and Roxanne felt herself beginning to unravel in quite a different way. She sought for a distraction, but her mind refused to leave the room in the dark house. Tanthflame's words came back to her, haunting her: *All we have to do is give one little push, and Allentria will crumble and fall.*

Everything she knew about government and politics could fit in a thimble, but even so, Roxanne understood that what had happened tonight had changed the world.

Necrovar's forces had pushed, and she only had to look around to see things crumbling.

Keriya had intended to circle around and rejoin her friends, but the Imperial who'd first attacked her had followed her, preventing her from doubling back. She'd almost lost him at one point, but then the explosion had hit, and it had completely disoriented her. Now she was lost, running through empty streets with an angry fire wielder hot on her heels.

A flurry of flames erupted from his fingertips, and she ducked down an alley to avoid being burnt to a crisp. Ahead, a doorway hung open on broken hinges, leading to a deserted home whose inhabitants had fled the darksalm. She crashed through it and crawled to a corner, holding her breath until the guardsman had run past her hiding spot.

Once he was gone, she found the front door and exited onto a different street. The fire greedily consumed the Village in the northeast, but there was destruction here, too. Shops with shattered windows and broken doors, debris from the explosion, and . . .

Keriya's stomach turned over. There were bodies strewn across the thoroughfare next to the canal. One unlucky man who'd suffered severe burns lay motionless at the edge of a wooden quay. A smaller body lay beyond him, broken and bloody.

This is war, Keriya thought, staring at the tiny corpse. Shivnath's descriptions and Aldelphia's warnings paled in comparison to living it, experiencing it first-hand. Her eyes stung with tears and she turned away, closing them against the awful sight. She was rewarded with a purple glow beneath her closed lids.

"No," she whispered, her heart sinking.

"We meet again, *Drachrheenar*."

Her eyes sprang open again. A reedy figure was melting out of the shadows from the building next door. It was Corporal Fireglaim — the man who had taken Thorion.

"You hurt my dragon," she said slowly. "I should kill you for that."

Fireglaim laughed. "You couldn't so much as scratch me." He pulled off his mask, revealing his face for the first time. His flesh was blacker than pitch, as were his teeth, his tongue, even his eyes.

Keriya stooped to grab a piece of rubble and hurled it at Fireglaim with all her might. Throwing rocks: her only form of defense. Pathetic.

The rock would have struck him had he not turned into a wisp of darkness and vanished a moment before it hit. She looked around wildly to see where he had gone, and spotted two more figures materializing out of thin air.

These were foes she stood no chance against, yet Keriya remained resolutely in place as Fireglaim reconstituted himself from the shadows behind her. If this was war, then she would have to fight.

With a burst of dusky sparks, Fireglaim created a black mist and wielded it against Keriya. There was nothing she could do to counter it. The spell snaked around her arms and worked its way up to her face, seeping into her skin. Her bones weakened and she sank to the ground.

The necromagic enveloped her, sapping her of her energy. The rumble of the fire vanished and her vision faded. For a moment, Keriya was sure she had died — this emptiness was so similar to the place where she had met Shivnath. Even if she were still alive, it wouldn't matter. She had stupidly run off on her own. No one knew where she was. No one was going to save her.

Worlds away, she felt sinewy arms hefting her body up. Captured again — this time with no hope of escape.

Through the shroud of darkness and the fog of fear, a selfish, cowardly idea came to her. With the last of her strength, she opened her mind and concentrated on a thought.

<Thorion, I need your help!> She called for the drackling, though she knew he wouldn't come. Flying into the middle of the darksalm fire to fight three of Necrovar's demonic slaves wasn't exactly wise.

She waited for a minute . . . an hour . . . an age. Nothing happened, and she found she was relieved that he hadn't heeded her call. At least one of them would survive.

The arms relinquished their hold on her and she fell. Her body collided with the hard stones of the street, jolting some life into her. The dark spell around her seeped away. Her vision began to return and she blinked, squinting at a blur of violent motion in front of her.

It was Thorion! He was locked in battle with Fireglaim, the glow of his eyes diluted by his second set of membranous, protective lids. He kicked at the shadowman's chest with his back legs, causing Fireglaim to shriek and flail around. The drackling saw an opening and struck, biting down on Fireglaim's neck. The demon let out a strangled cry as he died, and his corpse turned to dust.

At once, the other men wielded defensive shadows around themselves. Thorion paid their magic no mind. He launched himself at the closer of the two, shattering the veil of darkness. The man hardly had time to react before the dragon's jaws were around his throat.

The last remaining shadowman crouched as his comrade died beneath Thorion's fangs, readying a concentrated spell of necromagic.

"*Watch out,*" Keriya croaked. Thorion sprang into the air, leaving the crumbling body he had just decimated. He beat his wings and circled around for another attack. The shadowman completed his spell and black lightning exploded from the palm of his hand.

The bolt struck Thorion square in the chest. He let out a screech that tore at Keriya's heart, but he valiantly weathered the lightning. He puffed himself up and a beam of pure energy blasted from his jaws. The shadowman burst into a million black granules the instant it hit him.

Thorion landed next to Keriya, the glow from his eyes fading now that the necro-wielders were dead. "*Are you hurt?*"

"*Not really.*" Her voice was faint, but she managed to conjure up a smile for him. "*You saved me again. Why?*"

Thorion opened his mouth to reply. Keriya could sense his confusion—confusion about why he'd acted so unwisely in the face of danger, confusion about the emotions clouding his mind, and confusion about the sensation of feeling confused.

"*Why?*" he asked her right back.

"*Why what?*"

"*Why . . . this?*" Thorion motioned to his chest with his right forepaw. "*This feeling.*"

"Oh. Worry?"

"*I already know what worry feels like,*" he said, shaking his head.

"*Relief? Happiness that we survived?*"

"*No,*" he growled, a crease forming between his brow ridges. Unable to articulate, he turned to gestures again. He put one claw to his chest, then reached out and placed that same claw over Keriya's heart.

She couldn't explain what he was feeling even if she had been able to, because the fire was upon them. The building next to them flared up. There must have been something combustible within, for its glass windows blew out, shattering on the street, and a plume of black-stained fire billowed toward them. Thorion leapt at Keriya and spread his wings, shielding her from the shower of ash, sparks, and detritus that rained down upon them.

Horror seized her. Thorion . . . touched by the darksalm?

"*I'm fine,*" he said, sensing her thoughts. "*But we must go.*" He backed off, and with his aid she got to her feet.

"Keriya!"

Keriya stopped, swaying on the spot. She was sure she'd heard someone calling for her. She strained to listen over the rumble of the fire.

"Keriya, where are you?"

"Max?" she called back weakly. "Max, I'm here!"

She squinted around, and her heart leapt when she saw the prince emerging through the haze. Max sprinted toward her, but slowed when he was about four heights away.

"It can't be," he breathed, sinking to his knees as he gaped at Thorion. He held out a hand, almost as if sensing the drackling's power. Thorion pressed against Keriya's legs and a growl wormed its way out of his throat.

<It's alright,> she assured him. <He's just excited. Maybe even a little scared of you.>

A crackle from the burning building startled Max out of his reverie, and he stood. Thorion tensed at his sudden movement.

"Is it safe to approach?" asked Max, warily watching the drackling.

"Of course it's safe." Keriya hobbled to Max's side, and he put an arm around her shoulders as he led her away from the fire. Thorion danced underfoot, leaning against her whenever she looked to be in danger of toppling over. When Max didn't move quickly enough for the dragon's liking, he nipped at the prince's heels.

"Alright, alright," Max said, recoiling from the snap of pearly teeth.

"*Be nice,*" she told Thorion, shaking a finger at him. He scowled at her, emulating her expression.

"You've bonded." Max's voice had a fearful edge which made Keriya feel worried and self-conscious. "That . . . is very dangerous."

"Why?"

"Because if you teach him to frown, he will frown. If you teach him to smile, he will smile. If you teach him to hate, he will hate. Do you see how that can be problematic?"

"Yes," said Keriya, but she didn't really. If she'd been more alert she might have been able to wrap her mind around it, but all she wanted to do was lean against Max's shoulder and rest.

"I didn't get a chance to ask what happened to you after we got separated," she added.

"I managed to fend off the shadowbeasts, but I couldn't see anything through the fog, so I took shelter. By the time the storm had passed, you'd vanished. I was alone, with no idea where anyone was, so I figured my best option was to head to civilization."

"I'm sorry," she whispered.

"You have nothing to be sorry for. Because of you, we have him," he said, indicating Thorion. He looked down at her and his expression softened. "I'm glad you're okay, Keriya."

"I am, too," she mumbled, earning a chuckle from Max. His face was dirt-stained and his hair was windswept, but even in the sickly light of the fire he was radiant. His clothes still managed to look well-kept, and his diamond amulet glinted pristinely.

Keriya was too busy admiring him to pay attention to where she was putting her feet, and she tripped, falling to her knees. Thorion let out a warble of concern.

Max knelt and gently gathered her into his arms. Keriya was reminded of the stories in her books where handsome princes carried their princesses off into the sunset. She was no princess, and their sunset was actually a necromagical inferno that had murdered hundreds of innocents and destroyed half a town . . . but nothing in life was perfect.

"Where are we going?" she asked, as they passed the road that led to the square where she had left Fletcher and Roxanne.

"Somewhere safe."

He held her closer, and the rest of her questions flew out of her head. Somehow, in spite of everything, this was better than all the happily-ever-afters she'd dreamed of.

CHAPTER TWENTY-SIX

DESERTION

"I have a very optimistic outlook on death,
mostly because of my excessively pessimistic outlook on life."
~ Relwin Anathar, Fourth Age

Cezon had gotten himself mixed up with a dangerous crowd, and for someone of his profession, that was saying something.

Until this point, he hadn't really believed Necrovar had returned. It was just too farfetched, too impossible, too frightening. Some even said the Shadow had never existed in the first place, that it was no more than a bedtime story used to scare young children into behaving.

Well, that bedtime story had become too real for Cezon's liking. Shadowbeasts were popping up left and right, there was darksalm everywhere, and he couldn't hide from the truth anymore. Necrovar was back.

And Cezon had given his blood to a man who served him.

He watched with mounting dismay as the Galantrian Village burned. The fire was growing brighter and darker at the same time. Black flames licked at the ceiling of smoke that shrouded the town.

"Skyriver!"

He turned to Wyster Raithcloud, his commanding officer. Raithcloud was a big brute of a man with a golden beard and tiny, mean eyes. He was aggressive and vulgar, and Cezon might have liked him quite well under different circumstances.

"That was an order, now get to it!"

"I wasn't listening," said Cezon. He was distracted. His brain wouldn't stop replaying the image of the Water Tower collapsing.

Raithcloud grabbed a fistful of Cezon's shirt, pulling him close. "I don't like your attitude," he growled.

"Well, I don't like your dress," Cezon retorted, shoving Raithcloud's meaty hand away. "You don't need to yell no more. I'm going!"

"Reconnaissance with the Commander-General on the Eastern Footpath in half an hour. Don't be late."

"Yes sir, Captain Raithcloud, sir." Cezon offered the man an insincere salute and backed into an alley. As soon as he was out of Raithcloud's sight, he bolted.

He had no intention of carrying out his commanding officer's orders—whatever they had been—and he had no intention of meeting Tanthflame on the Footpath. It was time to leave this business far behind.

The Village was teeming with people: King Wavewalker's servicemen, civilians fleeing the darksalm, the occasional moving shadow, and bands of Imperials. Cezon wasn't sure whether he was more frightened of the shadowbeasts or the soldiers, so he avoided both with equal care. It wasn't difficult for him to hide. If he hadn't been so excellent at sneaking around and not getting caught doing bad things, he'd have been long since dead.

"Cezon? That you?"

Cezon, who had been busy commending himself on his sneaking skills, hadn't noticed Iako sneaking up behind him.

"You," Cezon hissed. "This is your fault!" He would have hit the rat-faced Galantrian if Iako hadn't sunk into a sniveling crouch.

"I don't want no more part of this! Effin' darksalm all over the everywhere tryin' to get me murdered, they blowed up the bleedin' dragon and I en't even seen my share of bringin' it here—this en't what I signed up for!" Iako clawed at Cezon, shaking with sobs.

"Shut up and pull yourself together!" Cezon yanked the smaller man to his feet and gave him a good shake to rattle his undersized brain into place. "What's this about a dragon?"

"The dragon," Iako wailed. "En't you been payin' attention to your commandin' officers?"

Cezon hadn't been paying attention to much of anything for the past month—he had been too busy thinking about what he would do with his reward gold. He'd heard whispers of the dragon, but he had roundly ignored them. It was crazy talk; everyone knew the dragons were gone forever. He hadn't believed in that dragon any more than he had in Necrovar's return.

How wrong he'd been about everything.

"I'm the one what brung it here, and now they done it in without payin' me proper—"

"Hang on," he said, cutting off Iako's blabbering. "I thought they wanted that albino Moorfain witch. That's who they was paying us to find."

"She en't Moorfainian, she's a dragon speaker," said Iako, leaning close and whispering the last words fearfully. "That's what them purple eyes is about. They only wanted her so she could call the dragon out for them, see? They was after him all along. Tanthflame knowed about the dragon long afore the empress did."

Cezon gaped at Iako. "How in Naero's name do you know all of this?"

"Cause I'm a good listener."

"What? You're an awful listener!" Cezon shoved Iako so hard that he stumbled into the bamboo wall of the building behind him. "And so help me, if we don't get out of this town alive, I will kill you."

"I was ordered to do recomeuppance with Tanthflame on the Eastern Footpath," said Iako.

"So was I. That's why we're headed west." Cezon grabbed Iako's arm and dragged him away from the flickering glare of the darksalm. "Need to get out while we got the chance."

When they reached the corner, Cezon looked both ways to make sure the coast was clear. It wasn't. A young man— noble, by the cut and fabric of his clothes—trudged toward them, carrying . . .

"Bloody bones of a bastard," Cezon breathed, dropping down behind a wooden crate and pulling Iako with him. It was Keriya Soulstar, the clonch who'd started all of this.

And there, beside her, was a dragon.

Cezon, of course, had never seen a dragon before—but there were a million books about them. There were statues and tapestries galore. Every country had tales of Valerion Equilumos, knew stories about the Dragon Empress, told legends of Keleth Stellarion. Why, people half a world away even knew about Shivnath. Anyone anywhere would know a dragon if they saw one.

Yet the first thing Cezon said was, "What is that?" Each of its scales was a shiny treasure; its claws were slivers of ivory; its eyes were amethyst gems. It was the most beautiful thing he had ever seen.

"That's it," said Iako, tugging excitedly on Cezon's sleeve. "The dragon! It en't dead! We can still get the reward from Tanthflame!"

Those words penetrated Cezon's fog of admiration, sank through the layers of awe and fear, and activated the deepest and most primal part of his brain, a part that only ever thought of one thing: money.

This was perfect! The gods of Allentria were smiling down on Cezon today, because they had once again thrown Keriya Soulstar at his feet. She was headed his way, and from the looks of her, she wasn't in any state to put up a fight. He would capture her and the dragon both. He would bring them to Tanthflame and receive a reward beyond his wildest dreams!

A street urchin dashed out from a nearby road and ran toward Keriya. Cezon recognized him as one of the miserable Moorfainian brats. What was his name? Flemming, or something equally stupid. No, Fletcher! That was it.

"Thank Shivnath you're safe," he panted when he reached Keriya. "I've been looking everywhere for you. Roxanne's injury is getting worse, we need to—"

"Roxanne will be fine," the nobleman interjected. "There are healers in the Village who can tend to her. Right now our top priority should be getting Keriya and Thorion out of here."

"We owe Roxanne our lives," said Fletcher. "You can't just run away while she's out there fighting for you!"

"Get ready," Cezon whispered to Iako as Keriya squirmed out of the lordling's grasp. He would ambush them while they were wrapped up in their argument. Keriya and Fletcher hadn't ever wielded anything—proving they *were* Moorfainian—and the nobleman didn't look like he would be worth much in a fight. Cezon could take them all blindfolded.

"*Endrey naler elos sanara.*"

Everything seemed to glow and shiver for a moment, and Cezon went weak in the knees. The dragon had spoken, and the sounds it made were enough to freeze a man's heart.

Keriya spoke back in the same language. It transformed her from a lowly guttersnipe into the embodiment of power.

"Thorion says he can heal her," she announced in Allentrian.

"Oy, Cezon," said Iako, as Keriya, Fletcher and the nobleman began to argue again. "We gonna get 'em, or what?"

Cezon didn't respond. He suddenly knew there was no way he could best that creature in a fight. The dragon could probably kill him with a look, maybe even with a word from that fanged mouth.

In the end, Keriya and the dragon went with Fletcher, and the nobleman trailed in their wake. Cezon followed them, for no reason other than the magnetic pull he felt toward the beast. Iako also followed, for no reason other than that he was an idiot.

Cezon snuck after Keriya, skulking behind piles of rubble scattered about the ruined town, until she came to the ice shuttle square. He slipped into an abandoned store and peered through a broken window.

There was quite a commotion outside. Galantrian servicemen were swarming everywhere, barking orders, but the clamor died as soon as people noticed the dragon. Silence coiled around the occupants of the courtyard, constricting them like a snake.

A girl with short blue hair pushed her way through the ranks of stupefied servicemen. Cezon knew just enough about his home state to know that her nose marked her as part of the royal family.

"Time to leave," he said, turning to Iako. But Iako wasn't there.

That was no big loss. If Iako wanted to crawl back to Tanthflame, let him. Cezon was going to find the fastest route out of town and run as far as he could. He was going somewhere no shadowbeast would ever find him, somewhere no darksalm could ever touch him.

In the square, the royal girl let out a cry. She knelt, pressed her palms together beneath her chin, and bowed to Thorion. All of her soldiers emulated her.

"Um," Keriya said into the stillness, as Cezon stole away to the west. "Hello. This is Thorion. He's a dragon."

CHAPTER TWENTY-SEVEN
THE PALACE IN THE LAKE

"Watch closely your enemies."
~ Andrich Karvichr Dreiss, Tenth Age

Even Seba, who'd foreseen his arrival, could hardly believe the dragon was real. He was a nova eclipsing everything around him. People crowded close, straining to touch, crying, praising Zumarra. A group of her father's servicemen had formed a protective circle around him to keep the rabble at arms' length.

The purple-eyed girl, Keriya Soulstar, stood next to him with Max and the peasant boy. They were joined by Effrax Nameless and the wounded girl, who were admitted past the soldiers only because Soulstar insisted upon it. She spoke to the dragon and he pressed his snout to the tall peasant's injury. Then she turned to Max, who put his arm around her shoulders.

A wave of jealousy crashed upon Seba. She gathered her composure and strode across the square to give Max a piece of her mind.

Rainsword beat her to it.

"Prince Maxton, King Wavewalker has requested an audience with you," he said. His expression, usually as sharp as the tempered steel of a fighting blade, faded to one of apprehension as he glanced at the dragon. "He also requests that the dragon be brought before him. Immediately."

Max started to reply, but the *rheenar* cut him off.

"Could we meet with him some other time?"

Seba was doing the fish routine with her mouth again, opening and closing it without noise. Who did this farm girl think she was? While it was true that audiences were always 'requested' in polite society, it was also understood that requests were commands when coming from any noble ranking higher than a vaecount.

The servicemen shifted their stances. Before, they had been keeping the crowd away from the dragon; now it was evident they were keeping the dragon locked within their loose circle.

"The king has summoned you. You have to go," Effrax muttered to Soulstar. What kind of a name was *Soulstar*, anyway? A stupid, made-up one, that's what.

"Where are we going?"

"You'll meet with my father in the palace," said Seba, stepping forward to confront the peasant.

"I'm worried about Thorion's safety." Seba was struck by how brazen this low-life was, how she dared speak with such disrespect in front of her betters. "What happened to Tanth-flame?" she asked, training her red-violet gaze upon Seba. "Did you let him go, even after we told you he was working for Necrovar?"

That was the last straw.

"You shall not speak to the princess of the Galantasa in that tone!" Seba shrilled.

"The Commander-General quitted the palace with us after the explosion," said Rainsword, speaking over Seba's outburst. "He and his officers haven't been seen since we arrived in the Village. Any formal accusation against him will have to be made in a court of law before a witness."

"Captain Rainsword, we will stand before the king," said Max, forestalling Soulstar's next words.

Rainsword went to the ice shuttle and laid a hand upon it. A hole magically irised open, widening across the crystalline surface of the orb until it was large enough for a person to step through.

"Princess Sebaris, you first, along with Prince Maxton, Lord Nameless and the dragon."

"No."

There were a few stifled gasps as everyone turned to stare at

Keriya Soulstar.

"I command the dragon to come with us," said Seba. She had hoped to sound imperious, but her voice came out high-pitched and petulant.

"Where Thorion goes, I go."

"Peasants do not share space with royalty," Seba said with a dismissive sniff. "You can wait for the next shuttle."

"Then Thorion can wait with me."

"Princess, arguing will only waste more time," Rainsword whispered before Seba could make an angry retort. "And the king hates to have his time wasted."

Seba pursed her lips. She didn't want to back down—especially not in front of a crowd that was listening to their exchange with bated breath—but keeping her father waiting for something as important as this was a bad idea. She nodded stiffly, unable to believe she had lost.

She entered the orb with Max and Nameless. The shuttle's opening frosted over seamlessly and they sank into the water, speeding off into the basin of the Galantrian Lake.

"Congratulations," Roxanne muttered to Keriya. "I'm pretty sure the princess hates you. And tell Thorion I'm grateful for his help. My side is fine by the way, thanks for asking."

Keriya rolled her eyes, flicked an imaginary speck of dust off her sleeve, and did her best to block out the rest of the world.

"Why are you upset?" asked Thorion.

"I just feel like going to the palace is a bad idea."

It wasn't long before the shuttle reappeared with a splash. Rainsword touched the glistening orb and the opening widened once more.

"Lord Dragon," he said, bowing to Thorion and inviting him to enter. The drackling clambered inside, followed by Keriya, Fletcher, Roxanne, and Rainsword himself. With a faint, icy crackle the opening closed, and the orb plunged back into the water.

The pool in the square connected to an underground waterway. Phosphorescent sea sponges grew on its rocky sides, illuminating the passage as they sped north toward the lake.

Suddenly the ever-present background rumble of the falls became deafening, and the inky water turned to milky froth. Keriya braced herself as the shuttle passed through the turbulence of the waterfall. The noise faded as quickly as it had come and darkness pressed upon them once again.

The momentum of the ice shuttle changed. Keriya's ears popped as they ascended toward a pinpoint of light. The light grew brighter and brighter until they emerged into a round room made of polished white stone. They had arrived in the palace.

A servant in silver and blue robes awaited them. He fell to his knees when he saw Thorion, pressing his hands together and making breathless, incoherent noises.

"Useless," Rainsword muttered, scowling at the servant as he marched the Aerians into the hall beyond.

They were met by five more soldiers who escorted them down an open-air gallery. Through the archways to the left, Keriya saw a vast garden lit by dimly glowing starblossoms. Beyond the garden a glassy sheen stretched up and curved overhead. They were underwater, in another ice bubble of gigantic proportions.

Not so very long ago, she would have marveled at the magic that could make such a wondrous thing possible. Now she felt as though she were in a prison.

The gallery connected to the central palace, and after a few more twists and turns the group stopped before a set of doors made of pale blue wood. Rainsword tugged them open and admitted the Aerians into a marble chamber.

Flags bearing the state emblem — a winding blue serpent on a silver background — hung from the high walls. A long carpet ran down the center of the room, ending at a set of stairs that led to a dais. Four thrones graced the platform, each molded from sparkling golden corals and set with plush fabric.

On the middle thrones sat the king and queen. Fletcher and Roxanne bowed, and Keriya curtseyed clumsily. Thorion stared at the Galantrian rulers, stoic and unblinking.

King Wavewalker stared back at Thorion. He didn't show shock or fear, nor did he show awe or reverence. In fact, he could rival the dragon for lack of emotion. Only his azure eyes betrayed his inner turmoil. They were alight with something fierce and wild.

"Lord Dragon," he said at last, his voice echoing in the wide room. "The legends do not do you justice. Come forward."

"He wants you to go to him," Keriya translated.

"Come with me?" said Thorion. She nodded, and together they approached. Wavewalker stood and descended to meet them. His black hair was touched with gray at his temples. He had a short beard that tapered to a neat point on his chin and the same distorted fish-gill nose as his daughter.

"And you are his *rheenar*," he said to Keriya. He looked her up and down with the air of a vulture deciding whether to feed on a diseased carcass. "You are no more than a child."

Keriya knew the king hadn't meant it as an insult. It was true, after all. She wasn't yet fifteen, and even by Aerian standards she wouldn't have been considered an adult — but the barely concealed disparagement in his voice made her angry.

"Your coming was foretold, Lord Dragon, and the Galantasa gives thanks that you have returned to us after ten ages," said Wavewalker. "We shall honor you as you were meant to be honored. You are a miracle, a gift from Zumarra and all the guardians of Allentria."

"Thank you," said Keriya, when it became apparent he was waiting for a response.

"Yet your arrival is overshadowed by darkness. A terrible crime was committed against my state tonight. I have sent word to Empress Aldelphia, requesting an emergency meeting of the Council of Nine. I must travel to Noryk, so I will not be here to oversee the rebuilding of the Galantrian Village. You are to remain in my place," he said, directing his scrutiny toward Keriya once more. "And if our enemies should strike again, you shall command your dragon to strike back with all his power."

Keriya suppressed a shudder. Thorion's existence had been made known to these people less than two hours ago, and already they were trying to use him to their own advantage.

But I did the same thing, she realized with a jolt of guilt. *I tried to use him, too. That's why we're in this mess. I thought I could just bring him to Noryk or the Fironem and be a hero without any consequences.*

"Your Grace," she began, "I can't command Thorion to do anything. I can convey your request, but whether he decides to fight is his choice, not mine."

"That," rumbled Wavewalker, "is where you are mistaken."

There was a gaping pause that seemed to last an age.

"What?" said Keriya.

"The darksalm is proof that ancient magics and powerful enemies are once again upon us. The Council will draw up arms treaties and the states will increase their militias, but swords and soldiers will not save Allentria in this war. Lord Thorion must be the one to fight."

"I promise I will help you however I can," she replied, "but I'd like to keep Thorion out of—"

"Are you arguing with me?" Wavewalker's tone made Keriya snap her mouth shut. He wasn't angry, he was disdainful. In that moment, she knew there was nothing she could say to sway him. She became acutely aware of Rainsword's soldiers, who had taken positions along the sides of the throne room.

We're trapped.

In the time it took to draw a breath, a hundred ideas chased each other through Keriya's head: she should run, she should fight, she should ask Thorion to blast the condescending smile off Wavewalker's face—

She felt, rather than heard, a growl coming from the dragon, and put a hand on his neck to calm him. Those were all horrible thoughts, but the fact that she'd had to think them meant she needed to get away from the king.

"No," she said. "I'd never argue with you. I was just thinking that if you want us to fight, you should let us fight. Why don't you let us go battle those powerful enemies you speak of?"

She gave herself a mental pat on the back for coming up with such a good excuse to leave.

"There is little need to traverse the empire looking for a battle. Not when the first blow has already been dealt against the Galantasa," the king returned, his voice like silk scarves concealing knives.

Keriya frowned. He made it sound like he wanted her to fight for him, and him alone.

"It is late," he went on. "We will discuss plans for reconstruction and decontamination tomorrow before I depart. You will be provided quarters in the palace, and you will ensure the safety of its inhabitants. Captain Rainsword will show you to your rooms and my servants will tend to your needs."

Keriya didn't have time to protest—not that protestations would matter—before Rainsword and his men surrounded her. They ushered Keriya and Thorion out of the throne room, sweeping Fletcher and Roxanne up in the process.

Just before the great doors swung shut, Keriya heard the king say, "Send in my daughter."

Something in his tone made her smile.

"You disobeyed every order, every rule I set for you, Sebaris!"

Seba knelt before the steps of the throne dais, her head bowed in shame.

"You have brought dishonor upon House Ishira. Have you aught to say for yourself?"

"No, Sire," she murmured to the carpet.

"What possessed you?" His voice changed, and Seba knew he was addressing her as father to daughter now, not as king to heir. "In a few years, you will sit on the Coral Throne. It seems far off, but it is not, and it is apparent that you have yet to learn proper behavior for a princess."

Yes, but what of being a ruler? she thought bitterly.

That didn't matter, for Seba was not to be a ruler. She was merely to be a princess, and one day, a queen—a figurehead who would be seen and never heard. She was to sit by her husband's side and bear him children, and ultimately she would die and be forgotten, having never done anything substantive in her life.

"You risked too much tonight. We need your foresight abilities, but you refuse to take your gift seriously. You prance about unattended, when at any moment the power could take you."

"You know it doesn't work like that—"

"Hold your tongue," he bellowed. "On top of everything else, I hear that you wielded. Magic isn't fit for a lady of your rank, so again you shame your House, because again you cast aside your heritage and your duties as if they mean nothing to you!"

"I couldn't have avoided this," she argued. "It was in my last vision. I saw the dragon and the darkness. I saw myself saving the Village."

"And a fine lot of good that vision did us," he said, pacing in agitation. "The town lies in ruin."

Seba winced. She might not have saved the buildings, but she knew for a fact she'd saved hundreds of lives by ordering her people to evacuate.

"It is time you learned to read your visions properly. If you had understood your foresight, we might have been able to avert this catastrophe."

This was how it always was. Something in the Galantasa goes wrong? Blame Seba, who didn't interpret her foresight dreams correctly, because if she had, none of this would have happened.

"You are to stay inside from this day forth, and you will have a guard stationed with you at all times for your personal safety. Your lessons for your gift and for your royal duties will be doubled. We can't risk losing you, Seba," he added softly. "You're all my House has left."

The note of finality in his voice told Seba it was over. She rose slowly, biting her lower lip hard to keep it from trembling. She bowed to her father and nodded to her mother, whose dark blue eyes swam with concern. But she was a good queen, a silent queen who knew her place, and she said nothing.

Seba, also silent now, left the throne room and was greeted by two soldiers.

Her new permanent bodyguards.

CHAPTER TWENTY-EIGHT

SHIVNATH'S CHOSEN

"There will come a point, sooner than any of us would like to think,
when we each must decide where our loyalties lie."
~ **Viran Kvlaudium, Twelfth Age**

Keriya stood behind Thorion, pretending to be useful as
Rainsword and his men toiled on the shores of the East Outlet.
The soldiers systematically wielded water through a series of
silver nets that had been erected along the banks of the river.
The nets were designed to detect impurities, the intention being
to find any remaining trace of darksalm.

The threads in the darksalm were no longer volatile, so
they couldn't infect anyone by mere touch, but they were still
dangerous. The last fortnight had been spent extracting the
deadly substance from the ruins of the town and sealing it in
stone containers for deportation.

Thorion was overseeing the process—rather, he'd been
forced to oversee it. Though no one in the Galantrian government had explicitly stated that he and Keriya were prisoners,
she was no fool. Even Roxanne and Fletcher were watched and
guarded, and occasionally made to work.

Their shift ended at sunset and a detail of soldiers appeared
to bring Thorion back to the palace. An ache surfaced between
Keriya's eyes as she slouched off toward the coralstone square
where the ice shuttle awaited them. She longed for a moment of
peace, for her quiet chamber and soft bed.

However, there was no peace to be found. The palace was in
an uproar when they arrived. Servants and soldiers alike raced
hither and thither along the corridors.

"What's happening?" Thorion asked, locking eyes with a
servant boy who threw himself into a bow so forcefully that he

tripped over his own feet and almost fell.

"*I don't know,*" said Keriya. "*Probably nothing good.*" They rounded a corner and nearly collided with Max, who was hurrying down the hallway.

"Keriya! Thank Shivnath you're still here," Fletcher cried. He, Roxanne, and Effrax were following a few paces behind the prince.

One of Keriya's guards held out a hand to block her from joining her companions. "You're not to speak to anyone," he barked. "You're to return to your chambers."

"Stand down, soldier," said Max. "We have business with the Dragon Speaker."

"We thought they might have taken you away already," Fletcher added. Keriya stared at him blankly.

"Come now, Dragoneyes, no need to play dumb," Effrax said, noticing her expression. "You know I've a knack for overhearing things I shouldn't."

"What are you talking about?" she asked. The ache in her head intensified.

"You really don't know?" said Max.

"King Wavewalker returned from Noryk this morning," said Fletcher, his voice low and urgent. "The Council of Nine signed a writ, conscripting Thorion into active wartime service—"

"Speaking openly of Imperial business can be considered treason," the same guard interrupted.

"I told you to stand down," Max rejoined, his voice like a dagger. "Imperial business is my business. They may speak while I am present."

Keriya closed her eyes in defeat. Shivnath had wanted her to face Necrovar alone; the rest of Allentria wanted to wage war against him. Shivnath had wanted Thorion to be kept safe; Lady Aldelphia wanted him to fight. Shivnath hadn't explained anything satisfactorily; neither had anyone else.

<*Keriya?*> Thorion's thought patterns were distraught. <*Why are you frightened?*>

<*I'm not,*> she lied. Although, maybe it wasn't a lie—she wasn't frightened anymore, she was angry. She was fed up with everyone wanting Thorion to fight their battles for them.

So much for there always being a choice.

". . . and if that's true, why did they also sign a military treaty?" Max was arguing with Effrax. "They wouldn't bother with their armies if they thought it was going to end with Keriya and Thorion."

That was just a nicer way of saying they didn't believe in Keriya and Thorion, which meant they were knowingly and shamelessly sending her drackling to his death.

<*Keriya, please. I don't understand what's happening.*> Thorion bumped his head against her hip plaintively, begging for her attention. <*I am . . . very upset.*>

<*I don't want you to worry,*> she thought. <*Let me handle this.*> But she had no idea what to do.

"*Rheenar*, may we fetch anything for the Lord Dragon?" Keriya was jolted out of her telepathic conversation by two simpering servants who'd crept up behind her. One gawked at Thorion while the other tried to press a warm washcloth to her neck. It was a Galantrian custom that was supposed to soothe one's nerves. The gesture only infuriated her further, and she shied away from the servant's wandering hands.

"You're to be taken to Noryk," said Max, turning to Keriya. "Now that it's come to this, we must each decide what we will do."

"You act like it's a tough decision," said Effrax. "There's only one option: destroy Necrovar at any cost."

"It cost you the dragons last time," Keriya growled. "The Etherworld was meant for him, but the dragons got imprisoned for the sake of your precious balance. So no, *not* at any cost."

She needed to get away from these people, the soldiers who acted as her jailers and the servants who flitted around like flies asking if there was anything they could do for the great Lord Dragon. If they loved him so much, why were they all so eager to send him to his doom?

Everyone was arguing again. Effrax said something and Roxanne yelled at him. Fletcher tried to mediate between them and Max told him not to speak about things he didn't understand. Why was no one talking to Keriya? Better still, why was no one asking for Thorion's opinion? He was the lynchpin, the keystone, the one upon whom everything depended! A painful throb pulsed through her skull.

Another servant popped up in front of her, a groveling man who bowed and said something about preparing Thorion's supper, as if there wasn't a war brewing right under his stupid, oblivious nose.

"Just leave me alone," she cried over the clamor. Thorion lashed out as well, opening his mouth and spitting a thin beam of light at the servant.

The spell missed the man by a hair's breadth and hit the wall behind him, searing a scorched circle into the marble. The servant fell back, terrified. Everyone else froze.

Thorion didn't seem to realize what had just happened. In truth, none of the others probably understood, either. But Keriya knew.

She dropped to her knees before the drackling and took his bronze head in her hands. In his eyes, she saw all of her own ugly emotions glaring back at her accusingly. She was without magic, weapon, or political clout to do anything about her rage, but Thorion was her polar opposite. He could take out his anger — *My anger*, she amended herself — on anyone, at any time.

This was the phenomenon the Allentrians spoke of. She *could* control her dragon. She could pour her feelings into him and manipulate him, just like Wavewalker and Aldelphia wanted.

She looked up at the servant.

"I'm sorry," she stammered. She reached out to him and he shrank away.

"Leave us," Max instructed the remaining servants and the soldiers. While the palace staff withdrew at once, the servicemen were hesitant about abandoning Keriya. "That's an order."

Reluctantly, the men saluted and exited the hall.

"What was that?" Fletcher asked. "Is Thorion okay?"

"He's fine," said Keriya, petting the dragon's head in an effort to calm him. Then she stopped and focused on calming herself, instead. "I think he just needs to be alone for a while."

Roxanne gave Thorion a searching glance before she left for her chambers. Effrax vanished without a word. Max and Fletcher didn't move.

"There's nothing you can do," Keriya told them in a low voice. "Please leave."

Fletcher saw that she meant it. Slowly, he and Max retreated down the hall. When they were out of sight, Keriya let out a long breath. She found a nearby alcove for some privacy and slumped against the wall, sliding down until she was crumpled on the floor. Thorion crouched next to her. He sent her a feeling of confusion, and she telepathically recounted what she had just learned.

<Shivnath didn't tell me how to deal with any of this.>

<Shivnath is forbidden from interacting with mortals.>

"Then how do you explain what she did to me?" she demanded aloud, too upset to mindspeak. Thorion shook his head, at a loss.

They sat there for a long time. Keriya heard soldiers passing in the hallway and shrank into a corner, praying no one would find her. Eventually it grew quiet. Only then did she dare to speak again.

"Is it true that only a dragon can kill Necrovar?"

Thorion didn't answer, but his silence spoke volumes.

"I don't understand. Shivnath told me to do it. She wanted you to stay safe."

"Perhaps it wasn't so much that she wanted me safe; perhaps it was more about who she wanted me kept safe from," he suggested, his tone unreadable.

"What do you mean?" she asked, though a dark suspicion

stirred in her gut. Bonding with Thorion couldn't be more dangerous than sending him to fight Necrovar . . . could it?

Again, Thorion didn't answer. Fear was on his face, and Keriya felt ashamed of herself for having put it there.

Maybe that's why Shivnath chose you, whispered the voice in her head. Maybe Keriya had been meant to be a shepherd, to gain Thorion's trust and manipulate him into fighting—though that was less like being a shepherd and more like being an executioner.

"*I don't know what to do*," she murmured.

"*Do what you think is right*," Thorion said simply, rotating his wing joints in a shrug.

"*Then . . . I think you should leave. You could go back to the Smarlands. I bet Shivnath would take care of you.*"

"*Shivnath is also forbidden from interacting with me.*" An unusual anger tainted his tone.

"*Maybe you could head west, instead?*"

"*I could find refuge in the rainforest, if it still exists in this age. But if I leave, what will you tell everyone?*"

"*The truth*," she said. He raised a skeptical brow ridge. "*Okay, bad idea. Maybe I'll tell them you joined forces with Necrovar. That'll throw them off.*"

They shared a chuckle—perhaps their last, Keriya thought sadly—then they left the alcove.

She hadn't realized how late it was. The hubbub had died down and the palace was all but deserted. For that, she was supremely grateful.

She always got lost in the warren of corridors when left to her own devices, but they hadn't gone far from the shuttle room. She managed to find her way back to it with little fuss.

The orb hovered over the glassy pool of water, bobbing serenely in midair. She went to the frozen sphere and put a hand on its smooth surface. It didn't respond to her touch as it always did for Rainsword. Frowning, Keriya tried again in a randomly selected spot. Again, nothing.

"Helkryvt's blood," she swore. What was she doing wrong

this time? She put both hands on it, with no success. She tried kicking it, though she didn't think that would help. Thorion opened his mouth as if to blast it with light, but Keriya forbade it at once.

"You can't solve everything with violence and magic," she chided him.

"You always seem to think those things will work," he retorted.

That made her want to cry. Had she failed so miserably in mentoring him? Had she been unable to impart any good qualities whatsoever?

Thorion scrutinized the enigmatic bubble, then reared up on his hind legs and placed a paw upon the ice. The surface opened easily at his touch. One must need magic of one's own to activate it. As usual, Keriya didn't measure up to standards.

The drackling tilted his head at her. *"Are you sure?"*

She nodded. She would rather stand alone and defenseless against Necrovar than be the reason Thorion got killed. *"This isn't your fight, it's mine."*

Thorion leaned against her. She held him for a moment, staring at the ceiling and doing her utmost to stave off the tears she knew would come.

"Goodbye, Keriya." He pulled away and clambered into the shuttle. It resealed itself and sank into the tunnel.

Keriya watched it descend into the depths of the lake below. When it was no longer visible, she turned to go back to her room.

Fletcher and Roxanne were blocking her way.

"What have you done?" said Fletcher. It was pretty obvious what Keriya had done, he just couldn't figure out why she'd done it. Maybe Thorion had been summoned to the Village? Maybe he was feeling ill and needed some fresh air?

"Did you just send Thorion away?" Roxanne growled.

"Please say you didn't," Fletcher whispered.

Roxanne didn't wait for Keriya to respond. "What the blood is wrong with you?! We're all going to die without him!"

Keriya let out a peal of laughter. She sounded like she was on the verge of hysterics. "Everyone keeps saying that, but you forget that Shivnath chose me to face Necrovar."

"I'd say Shivnath made a mistake," said Roxanne.

There was a ringing silence. In that moment, Fletcher didn't know who he was more afraid of: Roxanne, with all her earthmagic, or Keriya, with the look that was slowly darkening her face.

"I'm doing what I should have done from the start," Keriya hissed through clenched teeth. "I'm doing what's best for Thorion."

"Really? Or are you doing what's best for yourself?"

"Yes, really. How could you even say that?"

"Because you're the most selfish person I know," said Roxanne. "You're so wrapped up in your own problems that you're oblivious to everything around you. We've been hunted, attacked, kidnapped, poisoned, and exposed to darksalm because of you, and you act like it's nothing."

Fletcher had never been the type to apportion blame, but he was somewhat inclined to agree with Roxanne. He'd sacrificed everything for this quest, and he'd never heard a word of thanks from Keriya.

"You want to kill Necrovar and save the world, but I know exactly why you're doing it," Roxanne continued. "It's got nothing to do with anyone but you."

Keriya took a deep, shuddering breath. Fletcher couldn't remember the last time he'd seen her so upset.

"You're right," she admitted. "I accepted the quest for selfish reasons. I never stopped to consider what I'd have to go through . . . or what I might put others through in order to complete the task Shivnath gave me.

"But it's not like that anymore. Now I'm trying to make things right. I won't force Thorion to fight in this war. I won't have his blood on my hands. So I sent him away. I did it to save him. It's probably the only heroic thing I've done in my life," she added softly.

Now Fletcher felt bad. Keriya was like a mother to that dragon, and wouldn't any good mother send her child as far from harm as she could? It might not have been the smartest choice—or the right one—but he could at least concede the act had not been entirely selfish.

"I have to ask," said Roxanne. "Did you think you would just wake up one morning and suddenly be a hero? Because it doesn't work like that. It's not something that's given to you by a god, or something you come upon by chance. Either you have what it takes or you don't."

Keriya closed her eyes. "I'm starting to believe I don't."

"Well, if that's your attitude, then you're right, and Shivnath *did* make a mistake," snapped Roxanne. She whirled around and stormed away.

Keriya tossed up her hands. "I can't win. No matter what I do, I'm wrong." She looked at Fletcher, but he said nothing. He didn't know if he *wanted* to say anything to her, not after what he'd just heard.

"Silent treatment, huh? Real mature, Fletcher. Do you think any of this has been easy for me? No, but everyone likes to sit there and judge, anyway."

"Oh, enough," said Fletcher. "You're not the only one who's had a hard life, Keriya."

She was shocked into silence. Though he regretted the harshness of his tone, he didn't regret his choice of words. If she planned to face Necrovar in Thorion's place, she'd have to grow up first.

"You need to earn respect. Once you do, maybe people will stop judging you."

"I earned the right to be respected when Shivnath gave me this quest. Who are you to talk? You haven't helped. You haven't done anything."

Keriya had crossed a line that Fletcher hadn't known he'd

drawn. She started to say something else, but he was done. He turned his back on her, ignoring her when she called out, breaking into a run when he heard her following.

He sprinted to his room and slammed his door shut on her apologies, locking it as his eyes and throat burned. From the start, he'd known he wasn't going to be much use on this quest. His sole purpose had been to give Keriya moral support.

But if that was how she felt about him, then he didn't want to be a part of the quest anymore.

CHAPTER TWENTY-NINE

THE BALL

"War and politics are the games of men."
~ Antigonus Leech, Twelfth Age

King Wavewalker requested an audience with Thorion the next morning. Keriya hadn't gotten any sleep after her fight with Fletcher and—even worse—she hadn't come up with a cover story to explain the dragon's absence.

She garnered surprised stares from the soldiers and herald who'd come to collect her when she exited her chambers alone. She chewed on her nails and fiddled with the frayed ends of her sleeves all the way to the throne room, dreading Wavewalker's reaction.

"What is this?" he demanded as soon as he saw her. "When I summon the beast, he is to be brought before me."

Keriya noted that Thorion had been demoted from 'Lord Dragon' to mere 'beast.'

"Well?" Wavewalker pressed when she remained silent. "Where is he?"

"He's . . ." Her mind raced as she tried to think of something clever. "Sick."

Miracle of miracles, the king bought the excuse. He grew concerned that Thorion might have been touched by darksalm, and it was all Keriya could do to assure him that wasn't the case.

"Thorion is cold-blooded, so he doesn't need to eat as much as we do," she said, which was the truth. "But he's been overeating, and when that happens, his body goes into a sort of hibernation state for a few days while his second stomach digests the excess food. It's a painful process." That was a complete lie.

"I see," said Wavewalker. He looked like he wanted to ask more questions.

"Why did Your Majesty request an audience with us?" she said quickly, trying to distract him.

It was nothing she hadn't expected: the Council of Nine had officially recognized Necrovar's return as a threat to the empire, Thorion was to fight the Shadow, and so on and so forth. Keriya listened with only half an ear, nodding at the appropriate times and murmuring assent.

"In three days' time we'll hold a ball to commemorate Lord Thorion's bravery as he embarks on his journey," Wavewalker concluded. "The following dawn, a contingent of Imperial Guards will escort the two of you back to Noryk."

It was unlikely that every single Imperial was secretly working for Necrovar, but even if they were loyal to the empire, it wouldn't matter. As soon as they discovered Keriya had sent Thorion away, they would string her up by her thumbs and gut her like a fish. And as for going to the ball . . . well, she'd rather be strung up by her thumbs.

She hid in her chambers for the next three days and refused all visitors, citing complications with Thorion's digestive system. She couldn't help but wonder what would happen when she was forced to emerge dragon-less for the ball.

When the third day dawned, she was at her wits' end. Thus, an unexpected knock on her door startled the breath right out of her. She cracked it open to reveal Roxanne and Effrax.

Roxanne wore a silk robe. Her hair was done up in fancy curls and she held a bundle of clothes. Effrax looked dashing in a wine-red tunic paired with black leggings and a cape.

"You haven't even started getting ready?" Roxanne tutted in irritation as she swept into the sitting room. Keriya wasn't sure how to react. She looked at the soldiers posted outside her door. One man met her eye and gave a little shrug.

"Do you know how many important people are expecting to meet a dragon tonight?" Roxanne said after Keriya shut the door. "Instead they'll get a peasant who hasn't brushed her hair in a decade."

"What?" Keriya's eyes darted to Effrax. "Of course they'll meet a—"

"I know what happened," Effrax interrupted. "When your friends went looking for you that night, I followed them. I overheard everything."

"The little nit tried to blackmail me," said Roxanne. "We ended up striking a bargain. He'll help us cover for Thorion at the ball, and in return, you find Thorion when we—"

"No," Keriya said flatly. "I'm not going to rope him into the war again."

"Perhaps you're unfamiliar with the punishment of disobeying the Council of Nine," said Effrax. "I'll spare you the gory details, but it isn't pretty. Besides, I'm not concerned about who ends up fighting Necrovar. All I want is for you to bring Thorion to the Fironem."

Keriya glared at Effrax. She trusted him about as far as she could throw him, and she doubted she could even lift him off the ground. "How can you possibly cover for a missing dragon?"

He raised his hands, palms facing outwards, and created a sphere of fire in midair. The fire grew, elongating into a distinguishable shape.

Effrax bent his fingers into claws and the fire intensified, growing white-hot and looking disturbingly solid. It was a dragon, like the one he'd created in the fen, but far more complex. He relaxed his hands and the fire fizzled out of existence. He was left with sweat on his brow and a smug smile on his lips.

"I can't keep that kind of wielding up for long, but I should be able to provide Thorion a dramatic entrance as he displays his lightmagic for all to see. I'll follow it with a hasty exit into the gardens when he becomes overwhelmed by the crowd."

It wasn't a good plan, but it was all they had.

"Fine," Keriya agreed grudgingly.

"Pleasure doing business," he said. "Now if you'll excuse me, I must be off to prepare for the show. Tigress. Dragoneyes." He nodded to each of them before leaving.

As soon as the door closed behind him, Roxanne seized Keriya and frogmarched her to the bathroom.

"You need to wash up. We can't have you looking like a vagabond tonight." She pointed at the porcelain tub in the corner and slammed the door in Keriya's face.

Keriya decided not to question what had just happened. It was true that she needed a bath, so she stripped down and turned on the tap. She wasn't sure if it was magic or science that made water run through the metal pipes in the palace, that heated and cooled the liquid with the twist of a knob one way or the other, but she suspected it was a bit of both. Either way, it was a vast improvement over Aeria, where she'd had to bathe with stale, freezing rainwater collected in buckets.

When she finished, she wrapped herself in a towel and went to her bedchamber. Roxanne had changed into a red gown that fit her like a glove. She stomped over and pushed something into Keriya's arms. "I got a few secondhand dresses from the servants. You can wear this one."

Keriya gazed down at the garment. It was purple.

"Hold on. Why are you doing this?"

"Because if you get arrested for treason, I'm probably going down with you," said Roxanne. When Keriya fixed her with an expectant glare, she sighed.

"I've been thinking about what happened, and I'm still angry. Based on what little I know of Necrovar, I'd say you made a terrible decision."

Keriya bristled. Was this supposed to make her feel better?

"But I was wrong to say you did it for selfish reasons. You were trying to protect Thorion. I can't imagine what it took to send him away." She paused, then slowly extended her hand in the Allentrian custom that signified understanding or kinship.

"I don't have to like a person to respect them. And what you did for Thorion . . . I respect that. You put his welfare before your own — before everyone's, really — but . . . well, we should all be so lucky to have someone like you." A haunted look passed over her face, clouding her beauty for a moment.

"Besides," she added, clearing her throat, "I'm a Hunter, sworn to protect those who need me. You're a mess, and you'll need all the help you can get if you plan on facing Necrovar."

Keriya eyed the proffered hand warily for a moment. Then she reached out and grasped it.

"Alright," said Roxanne, "you've wasted enough time. Put on your dress."

Keriya ducked into the bathroom and obliged. When she reappeared, she was frowning again. The dress was too big, and its swooping neckline and filmy sleeves were far too exposing.

"Not bad," said Roxanne.

"I hate it." Keriya held up her arms. "You can see all my scars."

"So?" Roxanne held out her own arms. Beneath her loose sleeves, dark, puckered patches of skin were visible.

"My father," she said in explanation, when Keriya's eyes widened in shock.

"I'm sorry," Keriya said softly.

Roxanne shrugged it off. "That's the past. Let's focus on tonight. Speaking of which, we *have* to do something with that hair."

"What?" Keriya never undid her hair from its ponytails, not even when she slept. It was impossible to manage, frizzy and unruly even at the best of times. "No! It's staying like this."

An hour later, when she descended the stairs that led to the ballroom, her hair hung loose down her back. Roxanne had styled it with dark magical items called 'curlers,' and now it spiraled around her face like wisps of mist.

A herald waited at the ballroom entrance to announce guests, just as Effrax had promised. He drew back the gauzy curtain that separated the stairwell from the vast chamber.

"Name?"

"Keriya Soulstar." Her stomach was a knot of anxiety. She prayed their plan would work. It seemed too simple and yet too complicated all at once.

"Lady Keriya Soulstar, the Dragon Speaker," he cried.

Keriya willed her feet to move, but they weren't going anywhere. Roxanne gave her a push, and she stumbled through the curtain onto the landing of a second, grander staircase.

A murmur swept through the room as she emerged. Crystal chandeliers illuminated a sea of upturned faces. Everyone was looking at her, waiting.

Long moments passed, but there was no evidence of a fake, fiery dragon anywhere. Had something gone wrong? Had Effrax betrayed her?

Across the room, brightness spilled through one of the high, open archways that led to the marble balcony. Even in the daytime it was always black as midnight in the underwater ice bubble. Keriya recognized her cue.

"And introducing the savior of Allentria, master of light-magic, Thorion Sveltorious," she cried as a blazing dragon glided into the room, trailing sparks from its wings. The crowd let out a collective gasp. People began cheering and applauding as the dragon gracefully spiraled toward the gold-inlaid ceiling.

Then it flickered. Keriya watched with mounting horror as Effrax's apparition sputtered, faded, and vanished altogether. The Fironian had overestimated his abilities. He hadn't been able to sustain the spell.

The silence was as vast and deep as an ocean. One by one, people looked back to her. She braced herself for cries of fury and words of condemnation, and was shocked when they let loose another cheer, greater and more enthusiastic than the first. Cries of "Long live the dragon!" and "Praise be to Zumarra!" rang out. They thought it was all part of the show.

Keriya nearly collapsed with relief. She hurried down the steps and slunk to the side of the ballroom to get out of the spotlight. Behind her, the herald announced Roxanne in between bouts of cheering. She flashed her winsome smile and waved to the crowd as if she herself were royalty, unfazed by their brush with disaster.

Keriya, however, was already done for the night. She lurked in a corner near the long buffet tables, hoping people would rather pay attention to the lavish feast and the artistic ice sculptures than her. Unfortunately, after that spectacle, everybody wanted to talk.

"Will the dragon return to the party, or is he resting before his journey to Noryk?"

"How does his magic work?"

"Is it true that he single-handedly killed twenty demons in the Village on the night of the attack?"

Just when Keriya feared she would have to start answering impossible questions, Roxanne appeared and took her by the elbow.

"Prince Maxton has requested an audience with the Dragon Speaker. Please excuse us," she said to the Galantrians.

"Thanks," Keriya whispered as they squeezed out of the knot of prying nobles.

"Don't thank me yet. Max really does want to talk to you."

Keriya groaned. She hadn't seen Max since Thorion had left. Would he, too, ask questions she couldn't answer?

Roxanne steered her toward their group. Effrax and Fletcher were there, but Keriya only had eyes for the Erastatian prince. He was wearing a white tunic garnished by a silver dress cape. His diamond amulet had been polished to a shine.

"You look lovely, Keriya," he said. A tingly sensation spread through her body, which for some reason made her forget how to talk. She looked around for assistance. Her gaze fell first on Fletcher, who was swimming in an overlarge set of borrowed robes. He ignored her, so she turned to Roxanne—but she just wiggled her eyebrows up and down suggestively.

"And Lord Thorion seems well," said Effrax. He looked rather the worse for wear, and it appeared his nose had been bleeding. "Will he join us or spend the night in the freedom of the gardens?"

"I'm sure he'll stay outside," said Keriya, playing along.

A lofty melody floated toward them as a group of musicians struck up a tune on the far side of the room.

"What do you think?" said Roxanne. "Want to try your hand at an Allentrian dance?"

"No," Keriya said emphatically, watching as couples began to pair off on the open ballroom floor.

"Does that mean you've never danced before?" Max asked.

"Um . . . well, I wasn't allowed to, growing up."

"Would you like me to teach you?"

Keriya opened her mouth to reply, but only a squeak came out. She couldn't decide whether this was the best thing that had ever happened to her, or the worst.

Max didn't wait for an answer; he simply led her out into the crowd. He held her right hand and placed her left on his shoulder. His other hand fell to her waist, and just like that, her cheeks were on fire.

"Follow my lead. This dance is easy," he assured her.

Keriya tried her best to keep up with him, but the so-called easy dance involved a lot of complicated foot movements.

"It's alright," he said whenever she trod on his toes. "You're doing fine."

She stumbled on the hem of her dress and knocked into him. "Sorry!"

"Try looking at me, rather than at your feet."

"How will I know where to step?"

"I'll guide you. Just relax."

Keriya raised her eyes and looked at Max. Something odd happened when she met his gaze—it was as if someone was weaving a spell upon her. Her surroundings faded away until all she could see was him.

"So," she said, breaking the silence. "Roxanne said you wanted to talk to me?"

"Yes. King Wavewalker brought news from my father when he came back from Noryk. I've been ordered to return to the

Erastate."

Her stomach plummeted and she missed a step. "Why?"

"Because the states are preparing for war, and I have duties elsewhere that I need to see to."

"Please don't leave me with the Imperials. Let me go with you!" She blurted it out before she could think about what she was saying, or how pathetic — and suspicious — it might sound.

"You know," he said slowly, "that's not a bad idea."

"Really?" A disbelieving smile grew upon her lips until she remembered Effrax's warning about disobeying the Council of Nine. "On second thought, I don't know if I could. I think I'd still have to go to Noryk, now they've signed that wartime writ."

"Of course you could," said Max. "In fact, I think this is better for everyone. I'll talk to Wavewalker and let him know what we're planning. That way he can handle the fallout with the Imperials when they find we've left without them."

"Oh," said Keriya. Max made it all sound so simple. "Will he listen to you?"

"I have more power in this state than you might guess," he said in a dry voice. "I'll work everything out."

"I trust you." She knew Max would protect her. He would fix everything.

"Now, I imagine we'll have to leave the palace early — and quietly. We should meet at — "

"Actually, can we talk about this later?" Keriya interrupted. "I know we don't have much time, it's just . . . this is supposed to be a party. And I've never been invited to a party before."

"Then I won't mention it again," he promised. "Instead I'll compliment your gown and praise the food, and ask you about people I dislike in the hopes of gathering useful information about them, as any self-respecting Allentrian lord would do."

"Is that what you guys really talk about?"

"Talking about the people one dislikes is a universal pastime."

Sometime during their conversation, the song had ended.

As soon as Keriya realized that, she dropped her hands and stepped away from Max. The odd feeling vanished and was replaced by a painful hollowness.

"What's wrong?" he asked.

Something inside her wanted to tell him how she felt. How *did* she feel? She wasn't certain, because she had never felt this way before.

"Nothing. I just need some air."

She hurried toward the nearest archway. If she could get away from all the noise, then she could hear herself think and try to make sense of her tangled emotions.

Keriya left the ordered chaos of the ballroom and emerged onto the balcony. She leaned her elbows on the balustrade and rested her head in her hands. She'd come so close to telling him . . . what? She barely knew Max. And anyway, what would be the point of telling him anything? He was a prince and she was a peasant, a runaway, a homeless, nameless child on a fool's errand.

The sound of footsteps told her that Max had followed. She supposed she should be flattered by his attention, but she was too drained to care.

"Don't worry about tomorrow, Keriya," he said, coming to stand by her side. "I'll collect you an hour before dawn. We'll leave before anyone can stop us."

And what will happen when you discover Thorion's gone? she wondered.

Her unease must have bled through to her face, because Max took one of her hands in a comforting manner. "You don't need to be strong all the time. You're only human."

"I'm sorry," she whispered, for that was all she could think to say.

"Don't ever apologize for what you are," he said with a small smile.

Do something, she told herself. *Say something! Now's the time to tell him. Do it right now —*

"Until tomorrow," he said, bringing her hand to his lips

and kissing it softly. Then he turned and went back into the ballroom, and Keriya's chance to say whatever she had wanted to say was gone.

CHAPTER THIRTY

THE FORESIGHT

"Knowledge is power, but ignorance is bliss."
~ Ghoori Proverb

Apart from the dragon's brief appearance, Seba's evening had been terrible.

She'd learned that Max had been ordered to return to the Erastate. That alone might not have been so upsetting, but he had known of this for days and hadn't bothered to tell her. On top of that, Keriya Soulstar had had the nerve to dance with him.

Seba was quickly growing to loathe that girl. She was in no way special — well, apart from the obvious. Her skin was too pale, her face too round. Her hair was wild and scruffy, and its abnormal color suggested a lack of proper nutrition. Her manner of speech was common and crass. She was a nobody. Okay, she could talk to dragons; so what? She was just a freak of nature.

It wasn't fair. Why was it that Princess Sebaris Wavewould, Eldest of House Ishira, Heir to the Coral Throne, was caged in an ice bubble with permanent bodyguards, destined to be never more than a figurehead, while that peasant was free to go off on grand adventures?

Seba wanted to stab things with her knives.

She spent the remainder of the party watching the other two tagalong peasants take advantage of their undeserved status. The scrawny boy had eaten more than half the food on the tables, and the tall girl had thrown herself at every good-looking nobleman she met. Why were they even here? They weren't *rheenarae*, so why was her father wasting his hospitality on them?

Seba now sat on her ornamental throne at the head of the ballroom, watching as the guests filed out. She leaned back upon her cushioned headrest, feeling ill. She should have recognized the warning signs, but she was so tired that she couldn't distinguish the foresight sleep from a normal wave of drowsiness. There was no time to prepare, as was usually the case. She closed her eyes for a moment . . .

And then she was in the dream.

The woman and the man walked down a pathway together. Both carried weapons; the woman bore a sword and the man clutched a longbow. A dragon soared through the mist to join them.

As soon as it landed, the dragon collapsed on the ground. It writhed in torment, powerless against whatever invisible power gripped it. The woman tried to help, but the man held her back from the flailing mass of talons.

They exchanged heated words. The woman sank to her knees. Tears drew clean tracks down her dirty cheeks. The man knelt before her and placed his hands on her shoulders. He spoke to her, lifted her chin, and gently kissed her.

He whispered in her ear.

The woman stood, and there was darkness in her eyes. She lifted the sword over her head and —

"Sebaris!"

Seba became vaguely aware that someone was shaking her, attempting to jolt her out of her sleep. She tried to open her eyes to escape the horrible images in her mind, but the foresight still had a hold of her.

"Get the healer!"

That was her father. She couldn't open her eyes yet, but she managed to speak.

"It's fine," she rasped.

"Bring water," the king commanded. Someone was still trying to shake her awake. They ought to know better. She would regain consciousness once the foresight relinquished her.

When she woke, the present appeared blurry to her eyes, which had grown accustomed to seeing the future. It was like blowing out all the candles in a room and waiting for one's vision to adjust to the dark. She was back in the mundanity of the here-and-now.

"I'm alright," she told her father, who was peering down at her. Behind him, her mother let out a cry of relief.

A cup of water finally appeared. Its contents, cool and refreshing, were tipped into Seba's mouth. She coughed as she gulped it down. Her breathing was labored, but that was only because she'd been so frightened by what she had seen. Perhaps she'd even been flailing like that dragon. That certainly would have caused a commotion.

"What happened?" her father asked. "Did you have a vision?" The surrounding servants drew near, awaiting her response.

Usually Seba had no problem speaking of her foresights, partly because they were often full of symbols that someone else had to interpret, and partly because she liked the attention. Even on the rare occasions when she saw full glimpses of the future, she never minded sharing. But the future had never been so clear, so scary, so directly connected to her.

"Can't . . . say here."

"Don't be ridiculous—"

"Sire, please," she cut him off, addressing him as king. "This I must tell you alone."

"Very well. We will retire to my study," he announced. A stretcher was brought in short order. She eased onto it and lay down, willing her head to stop spinning.

The king swept out of the ballroom, accompanied by the servants who bore Seba. They walked in silence until they came to the door of his private office.

"I can do it," she croaked, pushing the helping hands away and getting to her feet.

"Leave us," her father commanded, and the horde of

attendants evaporated. With them gone, Seba had to defer to the king's higher authority. She opened the door for him, following as he entered and closing it firmly behind her.

"What happened?" Her father began to pace, proving just how distressed he was. Seba was distressed too, but she tried to hide it. She sat in the plush chair before his icewood desk.

"I had a full vision this time."

"What did it reveal?"

"It was Max," she wailed. "He was with *her*, that wretched, ugly — father, he kissed her!"

"This is Maxton Windharte you're talking about?" She nodded, trying to catch enough breath between sobs to tell him the most important part. "Who was he with?"

"Keriya Soulstar."

"Impossible," the king said dismissively. "They're parting ways tomorrow. How far in the future did you see?"

He still needed to know the worst part of the vision, but now that Seba's brain was working properly again, she was beginning to formulate a plan. If she played her cards right, if she said just the right things at just the right times, then maybe . . .

She had to try it. She had nothing to lose.

"I know it was her," she hiccuped "I saw her bloody purple eyes."

"Do not swear, Sebaris," her father snapped. "What else was there? Where were they?"

"I'm trying to work out what everything meant," Seba said dramatically, holding her head and squinting. The images were so fresh and frightening that she could remember the foresight with utmost clarity, but her father might take more decisive action if he knew how distinct the dream had been.

"They certainly weren't in Noryk. They could have been somewhere in the Smarlands, I suppose. There was a canyon with striated stone spires. A black sky above. A glowing river below. A covering of moss on the ground, sprinkled with blood-red flowers." She shuddered as isolated flashes of her dream sprang back to her one by one, snippets that were irrelevant in the face of all she'd seen.

"There was a dragon with them. It was in pain. I think it was dying." Seba could still hear its cry echoing in her head. "Then Max and . . . and that *witch* started screaming at each other. I don't remember what they said." This was the truth. At that point, Seba had been too distracted by the dragon to listen to them. "But she was crying. And she had a sword."

"Was the sword a symbol? Did you recognize it from any of your studies? Does it represent something?"

"It was real. Max knelt before her and he . . ." Seba gestured uselessly with her hands, smacking them together, for she could not say the words again: *he kissed her.*

"Then he spoke." Seba had been listening to this. She wouldn't have missed it for the world. "He said, 'My feelings for you were never a lie, you saved the best part of me.' Then —"

"Cryptic words," her father interrupted. "It sounds like a symbol. It represents something else."

"It wasn't a symbol!" Seba took a breath; it was time to play her ace. "Father, I want to go to Noryk with Keriya Soulstar."

Her statement had exactly the sort of effect she'd expected. First he laughed. "Don't be ridiculous."

"I'm the only one who can stop this from happening!"

"That isn't true," he said, but there was doubt in his voice. Thank Zumarra for all those years of hazy visions. They had shaken her father, made him wary of what her dreams might mean.

"It is for this vision," she insisted.

"Sebaris, please." His voice was no longer harsh. Now he was reasoning with her, playing to her better senses. "Nothing is as important as you taking my place. Your brother cannot, *will not* be able to sit on the Coral Throne. His land-sickness set in early. He will be gone before he comes of age."

Seba mellowed, and for a moment she wasn't even sure she wanted to go. Her father sensed the weakness in her.

"Soon I will be gone, too. Then it will just be you. The future of House Ishira rests on your shoulders."

He thought he was going to win, but he still didn't know the severity of what she'd seen.

"I have to do this."

"And why is that?" he snapped. His other tactics hadn't worked, so now he would try to bully her. But Seba wasn't having any of it.

"She killed him! Keriya Soulstar took her sword and stabbed Max through his heart. He bled out on the ground. She murdered him, and I am the only one who can stop her."

That wasn't true, strictly speaking. Seba knew that someone else would be capable of preventing her foresight from coming to pass, but she was counting on her father's fear—and his lack of understanding of her power—to blind him to that possibility.

"This . . . yes. This must be prevented," he agreed, looking shaken. Before Seba had time for a triumphant smile to spread across her face, his demeanor hardened. "But you are not the one to do it."

"What? Father, I have the chance to do something great, not just for the Galantasa, but for the Erastate as well, for the whole empire."

"You can't protect Maxton any more than you can protect yourself. You won't survive in the outside world, especially now that our country teeters on the brink of war."

Seba was hardly about to point out that she'd been visiting the outside world for years, and no ill had ever befallen her until the night of the attack.

"You've done well in sharing your vision, but now it is out of your hands. I will deal with this."

The iron in his voice told her that any more arguments would be futile. Seba bit her lower lip, bowed her head, and left the room with as much grace as she could muster.

She slipped out and found Max standing there, his hand raised as if he'd been about to knock on the door.

"Max?" she breathed. Seeing him alive and whole brought back the vision of him bloodied and mangled, a sword sticking through his chest, his eyes growing black, dull and sightless. "What are you doing here?"

"I have to speak with the king," he said, taking in her haggard appearance. "Are you well?"

"I'm fine. Are *you* well?"

"Why wouldn't I be?" he asked with a bemused smile.

"No reason! You're just leaving tomorrow, and . . ." The words caught in her throat. Acting on impulse, she hugged him.

"Please be safe, wherever your travels take you," she whispered, pressing her face into the fine fabric of his tunic. Before he could say anything, she hurried away down the hall.

She rounded a corner and stopped to compose herself. It took her a few deep breaths and quite a bit of nervous pacing before she realized that her bodyguards, who'd been latched onto her like barnacles since her father had ordered it, hadn't returned after he'd dismissed them from the study. For the first time in what seemed like ages, she was alone.

Another plan began forming in her mind. A foolish plan. A dangerous plan. She'd have to get money, and she'd have to find that bogspectre-deterrent—she was sure it was just water and bad-smelling herbs, but it wouldn't hurt to bring it along. She would need her plainest, most durable clothes, some provisions, her knives . . .

"No," she murmured to herself. "It's crazy. I can't."

But the foresight swam before her eyes again, Max's broken body haunting her. Her resolve solidified.

She, too, was going on an adventure.

CHAPTER THIRTY-ONE

THE MONSTER

"If you live in the river,
you should make friends with the water serpent."
~ Galantrian Proverb

Thorion padded through a sea of bamboo, quiet as a beam of sunlight playing upon a cloud. A bed of water stippled by mangrove trees with rambling roots lay before him. He slid into the pool and glided through it, using his wings to propel himself to the other side, only the top of his head visible to the world.

He had gone west and had taken refuge in the rainforest. Here amidst the jungle trees, in the maze of rocky crevasses and vine-coated cliffs, he was safe from the humans.

Memories of humans had been passed down to him from his ancestors. All dragons were part of a collective consciousness, a network of united minds that made each individual's wisdom available to all the others. Though he was no longer connected to his kin, he retained the visions he'd received in his youth. From those shared memories, Thorion had known that to deal with humans meant *becoming* human. It meant gaining emotions and giving up his longevity and immunity to the base magics.

Yet when he'd met Keriya, he'd agreed to go with her. He'd thought he could work with her without falling prey to her emotions . . . but he had never imagined how tempting they would be. Now they just tortured him. Loneliness clung to him like lichen on a boulder, his sole companion in the vast rainforest.

And rainy it was. His travels had been hindered by torrential downpours. Thorion didn't like it; mud and mire got stuck between his claws and lodged under his scales, making him uncomfortable and unhappy.

He wished Keriya were with him. She would scratch behind his ears and clean his scales, and tell him happy stories filled with vibrant images and feelings.

As he plodded onwards, it began to drizzle. Thorion's head drooped low and he trudged over to a tree, huddling between its knotted roots to find shelter from the impending storm. He really ought to keep moving because there were shadowbeasts in the woods. They stalked the night, searching for something — probably for him.

The world slowly grew dark. The soft patter of the rain faded and was replaced by the sounds of the night. Tree frogs chirruped and crickets sang as the heavens cleared. The light of the Oldmoon floated down, dappling the forest in silvery light. With a sigh, Thorion got to his feet.

He'd barely gone three heights before he stopped again, catching a foul scent ahead. His racial memories told him he was smelling a dead carcass, but the way his gut writhed indicated there was something strange and unnatural about the odor.

Curiosity — something he'd eagerly picked up from Keriya — got the better of him. He headed toward the smell. As he crept closer, the sounds of the crickets and frogs vanished. The animals were avoiding this area.

When he peered through a thick curtain of vines into a clearing, he wasn't surprised to see a dead animal, but he was *very* surprised to find it standing and moving about. It was a jungle cat of some sort, though its skin was hanging off it in ribbons, exposing putrefied flesh and muscle underneath. The striped pelt was covered in festering sores of decay, and its nose, gums, and tongue had decomposed. Only its jet-black eyes were fully intact, glinting out of its skull.

It moved in a choppy manner, obsessively circling one of the shimmering pools of water that speckled the clearing. It looked as if it might fall to pieces at any moment.

The cat gave a horrible moan, then it actually *did* fall to pieces. Its legs buckled and it caved in upon itself in a heap. Thorion's stomach lurched at the sight.

The pile of flesh began percolating. Eyeballs rolled away from the skull, followed by a dark, viscous liquid. That liquid formed into a monster more wretched and intriguing than even the undead cat—this was the strangeness Thorion had sensed.

The boneless blob let out a few grating gasps. It lurched around, turning its attention to the body it had just vacated. It snuffled at the corpse for a while, then began to slurp up the fetid, atrophied mass.

Thorion had seen enough, and he backed away. Though he took care to retreat silently, the creature perked up. An oblong head and neck elongated from its body as it scoured the shadows at the edge of its clearing.

"Who goes there?" It spoke aloud, hissing something in Allentrian. Thorion was impressed that it had the capacity for speech. For something that looked so much like a pile of sludge, it was remarkably advanced.

As if it sensed his admiration, the creature whipped its slimy head around and locked gazes with him. Its lips curled into a snarl, revealing a toothless, tongueless hollow leading down to its gullet. It rose and began flying—no, not flying, more like gliding—toward him. Thorion was suddenly facing a hovering abomination that dripped darkness and breathed in death rattles. Dragon and monster regarded each other. Then the thing spoke again.

"Who are you?"

Thorion's eyes widened in astonishment. *"You know my language?"* he whispered, stepping through the vines and into the clearing. *"How?"*

"I know many things," it told him. *"All of them worthless."*

"This talent isn't worthless! My language has a power that stems from the First Magic, from when the Dragon Empress gave—"

"I know all this," spat the monster. *"And I care not. What I don't know is who you are or why you are here."* Its eyes flashed with

hostility. *"You've come to steal my treasure, haven't you? You all want it, but you shall never have it — it is mine!"*

"No," said Thorion, perplexed. *"I haven't come to steal anything."* His words soothed the monster's fury. Pressing his luck, he asked again, *"How is it that you speak my language? It isn't something one simply learns. There is magic involved."*

"I don't know. I knew many things, once. I spoke many languages, and they called me by many different names. Ages and ages and ages ago. I was many things."

Thorion tilted his head. The monster appeared quite unstable. *"Do you have a name I can call you?"*

"I have no name," it snarled. *"But the flesh-rats call me bogspectre. You may, too."*

"I'm Thorion."

With an air of sorrow the bogspectre gazed toward the pool the jungle cat had been circling. When it looked back at Thorion, it was as if it had never seen him before.

"Who are you? Why are you here?" It began speaking in Allentrian, and it was then that Thorion realized the creature was well and truly insane.

He made to leave, but the bogspectre interpreted his movement as a sign of aggression. It lashed out at him with a tendril that seemed to be a tail. He yelped in surprise, pinning his ears back and baring his fangs.

"Arrogant lightbeast! You've come to steal my treasure, haven't you? The Shadow Lord sent you, didn't he? I can smell his touch upon you!"

It struck again and Thorion dodged, but now he felt a stirring of fear in his chest.

"I'm not allied with Necrovar," he assured the monster. *"Are you?"*

"No," said the bogspectre. *"Never! He thinks he owns the world. He sends his demons out across the land to do his bidding. They have infiltrated my forest. They hunt for me, for my treasure, but they have not found my hiding place."* It gestured around the clearing, which, admittedly, was well-hidden by the vines and mammoth trees—well hidden, unless one was following the scent of death.

"*I don't think the demons are hunting for you,*" said Thorion. "*They want me.*"

The thing let out a chilling cackle. "*Oh, it was never you they wanted. It was me all along. You're just an extra treat. Listen.*" It raised its head and a gleam came into its eyes.

Thorion perked an ear up, though he didn't know what he was supposed to be listening for. Wind crept through the trees and an oryx called to her young from the next valley over.

"*The demons come. They want my treasure, but I shall never let them have it.*"

"*Be careful,*" Thorion whispered, as though he thought the shadowbeasts would overhear him. "*Necrovar's servants are dangerous. They won't hesitate to kill you.*"

"*They can't kill me. But they are closer tonight,*" the bogspectre observed in a casual tone. "*Perhaps they will find me. If they do, I will be powerless against them. Do you know how I kill my victims?*"

This was an unexpected turn in the conversation, one that Thorion wasn't sure he liked.

"*I shove their souls out and inhabit their empty bodies, and I rot their insides until they're dead.*" The bogspectre gestured vaguely toward the unfortunate cat.

Thorion decided it was time to leave. Maybe the bogspectre was in league with Necrovar, maybe it wasn't—but he didn't want to stick around to find out.

"*I usually go into villages and take humans,*" it was saying to no one in particular. "*I've had to make do with rainforest animals. I've had to stay here and guard my treasure. But a dragon? Yes, a dragon would be of good use to me.*"

"*Don't force me to hurt you,*" Thorion threatened, spreading his wings to give the impression that he was bigger. The bogspectre wasn't deterred. It lowered its head and stared into his eyes.

Thorion tried to run, but his feet were rooted to the spot. He couldn't turn away from the monster's deathly gaze. He tried to twist his neck, to close his eyes, but he had lost control of his body.

A burning feeling seeped through his veins. Something terrible was happening inside him. It felt like his soul was being suffocated. There was something squeezing in to absorb his light-threads.

He wanted to cry out, but he couldn't so much as whisper. He made a desperate mental lunge for his source and missed. His magic was out of reach; the creature was in his way, blocking him inside his own body.

Then he was suddenly himself again. For some reason, the bogspectre had let him go. Thorion stood shivering and gasping. He could feel his magic! He was once more the most powerful creature in the world.

His panic ebbed away and was replaced by fury. He puffed himself up and embraced his source. Without hesitation—or thought—he opened his jaws and blasted the bogspectre with light. It exploded in a shower of muck and guts.

"*Let that be a lesson,*" Thorion told the bogspectre's remains.

But—what was this? Little gloppy pieces of the monster's body were sliding across the ground toward one another, re-forming themselves to knit the vile creature back together.

"*How are you still here?*" said Thorion, awed in spite of himself. "*I killed you!*"

"*I cannot be killed,*" the bogspectre retorted. "*That was unwise, drackling. You've made a mortal enemy.*"

The bogspectre lashed its tail and shot toward him. Thorion leapt out of the way and spat a thinner but more concentrated light beam at the monster. His aim was poor and he missed. It gave the bogspectre the opportunity to vanish into thin air.

He stared around, unnerved. Could the bogspectre wield lightmagic? Was it using an illusion spell, bending photons around itself to make it invisible to the naked eye?

The bogspectre popped back into existence next to Thorion, but in its insanity it had already forgotten their fight. It hovered low and whispered to him in some guttural foreign language.

Though he couldn't understand the monster's words, he could hear what the problem was: shadowbeasts were approaching. His wielding had drawn them to the bogspectre's home.

"*Please help,*" the bogspectre gurgled, speaking again in the draconic tongue. "*I have no power against them and they cannot have my treasure. You mustn't let them find it!*"

Hesitant though he was to help the thing that had just attacked him, when Thorion looked into the creature's face, he saw genuine sadness and terror. Its eyes were the eyes of a sentient being who could feel pain and regret.

Thorion nodded reluctantly and the bogspectre sagged with relief, drooping and dribbling and even going so far as to touch him. It petted Thorion's back with one of its tendril-arms, and he made an effort not to withdraw in revulsion.

They stood side by side and awaited the arrival of Necrovar's minions. It wasn't long before a group of shadowbeasts galloped into the clearing. They were of varying species, though Thorion noted all of them were fast-moving carnivores who could cover much ground in little time. Perfect hunters.

The fight was over before it had even begun. Since he'd already revealed his presence, Thorion simply wielded against the demons. They burst into dust the instant his magic touched them.

Pleased with his work, he smiled and turned to his new companion.

"*Who are you?*" hissed the bogspectre, glaring at him.

Thorion sighed. "*I am Thorion Sveltorious, and before you ask, I wasn't sent by Necrovar and I'm not here to steal your treasure.*"

"*How do you know of my treasure?*" cried the bogspectre, squirming furiously in midair. "*How dare you speak of Necrovar in front of me? I can smell his touch upon you!*"

It was definitely time to go. Thorion felt he'd atoned for his aggression by helping the bogspectre in its time of need. He'd prevented the shadowbeasts from taking its treasure, and that was more than enough.

"*I'm leaving now,*" he announced. "*Your treasure is safe.*"

Thorion turned, only to find himself facing the bogspectre again. He tried to squeeze his eyes shut so he couldn't be hypnotized, but it was already too late. He was locked in place. All he could do was stare into the monster's hungry gaze as it clouded the light of his magic, burying his soul in darkness.

CHAPTER THIRTY-TWO

GOOD BUSINESS

"Losing one's way is only an opportunity to find a better way."
~ **Sandrine Althir, Fifth Age**

Cezon Skyriver swore as he stumbled over a clump of twisted vines. He lurched forward, sprawling on the damp ground of the rainforest. Hissing like a rabid raccoon, he scrambled to regain his footing and kept running.

He had been running since the darksalm explosion, even though he knew it wouldn't be pretty if Necrovar got ahold of his blood. He had to go back, if only to prevent whatever awful things were to happen if Tanthflame found out he'd deserted.

Unfortunately, he couldn't go back because he was hopelessly lost.

"Stupid Iako," he wheezed as he scrambled over a boulder. "This is all his fault, the blood-burned lagwit! If I ever get my hands on him, I'll wring his scraggy neck and feed his body to ducks in a pond, piece by little piece!"

Cezon was so preoccupied with hating Iako that he wasn't paying attention to his surroundings. He ripped aside a veil of hanging moss and strode into a clearing.

Then he froze.

The bogspectre, the most dangerous monster in all of Allentria, was hovering in the air not five heights from him. And standing before it was . . . *the dragon?*

No. Impossible! He was going mad, he was hallucinating, he was—oh no. No-no-no. The bogspectre moved, massing its liquid body around the dragon's head. It grew smaller and smaller, seeping into the dragon's eye sockets with a repulsive squelching sound.

Not even Cezon could dream up something so horrid.

The last little bit of the bogspectre snaked into the dragon's skull, turning the beast's eyes jet-black. It lifted one front paw and lowered it again. It stretched its wings and opened its mouth, baring sharp fangs. Then it let out a wail and collapsed, limp and lifeless.

The bogspectre oozed back out of the dragon's eyes and pooled in a gelatinous clump on the forest floor. Howling in anguish, it spewed sludge from the hole that served as its mouth, spattering the green moss with black vomit. Then it shuddered and disappeared.

Cezon was sure he was going crazy. No one had ever been dispossessed by the bogspectre—at least, no one he'd ever heard of. It just stayed in your body until you died.

He realized this would be an excellent moment to run, but now that the monster had gone, all that remained was the dragon. Maybe it was unconscious, maybe it was dead. Either way, Cezon stopped thinking about how much danger he was in, and started thinking about the lovely sheen of that bronze hide.

He sifted through every myth, legend, and old wives' tale he'd ever heard about dragons. Their scales were said to be so hard that not even a diamond could scratch them. Their bones supposedly made fantastic weapons because they were lightweight and porous, yet strong and durable. Eating the heart of a dragon was purported to heal any sickness in the world, and it had once been thought that drinking dragon blood could make you immortal.

Though he knew the bogspectre might return at any time, Cezon crept toward the dragon. He picked up a branch and prodded the body. No response. With a growing sense of glee, he drummed up the nerve to move closer. He crouched by the dragon's head and lifted one eyelid. The purple iris glimmered in the dim moonlight and the pupil contracted—the thing was still alive.

"Might be for the best," he murmured to himself. "If it was

dead, I couldn't bring it anywhere without it going bad, could I? This way it stays fresh."

He stood and circled it a couple of times, brainstorming. He didn't want to carry it through the whole jungle, so he'd have to make something to pull it on.

Cezon found two sturdy bamboo stalks and strung his blue vest between the shafts, securing it with his bootlaces. He rolled the dragon onto the sling, then grabbed the ends of the make-shift sled and began hauling.

Now that he was thinking straight again, he set his mind to finding a way back to civilization. He started paying attention to the growth of the lichens on the trees. It appeared he was heading in a southeast-ish direction. If he kept going that way, he would eventually reach the road to Noryk.

It would be difficult to bring the dragon into the Imperial City undetected, not to mention dangerous. He was a wanted man. Still, it would be worth the risk, for if he parted the dragon out and sold all its bits and pieces separately, he would end up richer than the empress.

He paused as a thought occurred to him. For the first time, he could imagine something more valuable to him than gold: a vial of blood.

"No." He shook his head and set off again, stomping through a patch of fleshy toadstools. "You'd barter the dragon to Tanthflame? What good will that do?"

All the legends said that only a dragon could defeat Necrovar. That was probably why Tanthflame wanted it—he was killing off the competition. Would Cezon doom the world, himself included, just to save his own neck in the short term? Was he so selfish that he would trade this creature for his blood?

He snorted. Of course he was.

"Besides, who's to say the legends are right?" he reasoned. "I'm sure someone else can take care of Necrovar when the time comes. Also, I'm sure I'll get some gold out of the deal."

That was all it took to convince himself that this was a fantastic idea, and he kept going.

He briefly wondered what Endred would say about his plan. Endred wouldn't approve, because Endred was too moral. That was why he was broke, while Cezon . . . well, Cezon was broke too, but soon he wouldn't be, and that was the point.

Only when he felt he'd gone far enough from the bog-spectre's clearing did he stop. He made camp in the hollow of a long-dead tree, keeping the dragon's body as close as he dared. Starblossoms cast a soft glow on his surroundings, and animals called to one another as they moved in the shadows just beyond Cezon's scope of vision. Though he didn't want to fall asleep, exhaustion overtook him.

He awoke the next morning and checked on the dragon. Still comatose. Good.

In the afternoon he came across one of the footpaths that led through the jungle. He could have followed it east, but this was a state road, not an Imperial one, which meant it was patrolled by Galantrian servicemen rather than Tanthflame's bunch of loons. He decided not to take it.

The next day, Cezon was in a foul mood. His vest was in tatters and he didn't know how much longer it would last. He'd been using his airmagic to lift the stretcher over rough terrain, but he was at the end of his strength and couldn't keep it up much longer.

Luck was on his side again. By noon he stumbled out onto the open brightness of the highway. There, not fifty paces to his left, was an Imperial watch house. He hid the dragon behind a spattering of large rocks before approaching the building.

"Oy! Anyone in there?" he shouted. No answer. This might be one of the empty houses, there for convenience to travelers. He tried the door and found it unlocked. Cackling, Cezon scuttled back to the rocks to get the sled, made sure the road was deserted, then dragged his cargo to the house.

The inside was barren. There were almost no fixings, so people like him wouldn't come in and loot everything of value. A straw-filled mattress lay in one corner. The opposite corner offered a chamber pot, a bucket, and a black-rimmed mirror that hung from the wall.

The mirror drew Cezon's eye. It was out of place; the frame was too fancy and the glass was weirdly distorted by a faint glow. Raithcloud had owned a pocket-sized version of this mirror, carrying it with him at all times. It had allowed him to speak with other Imperials and, more importantly, with Tanthflame himself.

Of course, Cezon had never paid attention to how Raithcloud had actually used the magic mirror. But if that idiot could do it, then it should be easy.

"Work," he said, stumping over to the glass. Nothing happened. "By order of the Shadow, I command you to work."

No dice.

"Show me Commander-General Tanthflame."

Nothing.

"I swear allegiance to Necrovar and to all who serve him, now show me who I want to talk to!"

The mirror refused to do so, and Cezon grew upset. He screamed some obscenities and wracked his brains for any clues that might help him.

"Think," he muttered. He recalled the last time Raithcloud had contacted Tanthflame, when the Commander-General had ordered them to report to the Galantrian Village. The only thing that stuck out in his mind was that Raithcloud had cut his hand and his blood had gotten all over the device.

No. That couldn't be it. Although . . . Tanthflame did seem to have an unhealthy obsession with blood, and Raithcloud's hands *had* been cut up all the time. Cezon had thought the man was just clumsy, but maybe he'd been bleeding himself to communicate with his friends.

"This better work," said Cezon, pulling out his pocketknife. With a wince, he drew its edge across his free hand, just as Tanthflame had done back in Noryk. Blood pooled in the cup of his palm, and he pressed it onto the reflecting surface, smearing crimson all over.

The blood shimmered on the mirror for a few moments

before it dissolved, seeping away and causing the glass to grow cloudy. Cezon was now gazing into a swirling vortex. He stewed in uneasy anticipation until a voice echoed out of the mirror.

"Report to me." The clouds beneath the glass cleared to reveal Gohrbryn Tanthflame. The Commander-General scowled, causing his distinctive scar to crinkle.

"Cezon Skyriver, is it not?"

"Ah . . . the very same, sir," said Cezon. "Surprised you remember me."

"I never forget a face, nor a pact such as ours."

"Yeah, about that pact. I'd like to get out of it, if you know what I mean."

"I'm afraid it doesn't have a termination clause. And I'm sure I don't need to remind you of the consequences that await a deserter or a traitor."

"I know, you give my blood to Necrovar, I get tortured for eternity," said Cezon, waving a hand. "I'd like to present a counter-offer: if you toss that vial in a fire, I'll give you what you want most."

"Which you think is what, exactly?" Tanthflame asked in a cold, irritated tone.

"The dragon." Cezon stood aside, revealing the limp body behind him. The general's red eyes went wide for a moment before narrowing to angry slivers. "Ain't this what you and your pal Necrovar are after?"

"Yes and no. But if you so desperately want to weasel your way out of our arrangement, you can kill it for me. Cut open its throat, and I'll pour your blood into the nearest gutter."

Cezon's heart sank. He didn't think he had the nerve to do such a thing. He might be a scoundrel, but this felt wrong even to him. Besides, he was pretty sure it would take more than a slit throat to kill a dragon—although its encounter with the bogspectre had left it little better than dead.

"Lemme see my blood first," said Cezon, hoping to buy more time. Tanthflame stepped out of view.

"Oy!" Cezon grabbed the mirror and rattled it. "Where'd you go?"

"Relax." Tanthflame reappeared, holding a small glass vial filled with dark liquid. "Here's your proof."

"That ain't proof. That could be anyone's blood. How do I know it's mine? How do I know you ain't given it to Necrovar already?"

"You would be well aware if Necrovar had your blood," the general growled. "As to the question of whether or not this is yours, I suppose I could add in some darksalm to prove it to you, but that would defeat the purpose."

"Alright, alright," said Cezon. "Just get rid of it and I'll kill the dragon."

"You kill the dragon first."

"That ain't fair!"

"Life isn't fair," Tanthflame retorted. "Do it."

Cezon looked over his shoulder again. What was his problem? The beast meant nothing to him. He couldn't believe he was hesitating. Maybe Endred was beginning to wear off on him — could it be that he was developing a conscience?

Cezon clutched his knife tightly, for his palm had become clammy. "Fine," he muttered, stalking over to the prone form on the floor. "Fine! You want me to kill the dragon?"

Bending down, he grasped one ivory horn with his free hand and pulled the reptilian head up, exposing the muted, lighter scales of the long throat. The dragon remained in its coma, helpless and defenseless

"Gods damn it." Unable to believe what he was doing, Cezon laid the head back upon the floor.

"I take it your blood isn't worth much to you, after all," Tanthflame taunted.

"Wait! How about I just give you the dragon so you can do what you like with it?" Cezon offered desperately.

"You're lucky that time is on your side. You will deliver the dragon to a contingent of my men at the outpost where the Northern Imperial Highway meets the Kingsroad. You have three days to reach it. If you don't . . ." Tanthflame raised the vial and shook it.

"Yes sir, Commander-General." Cezon didn't think he'd ever hated anyone as much as he hated Tanthflame. Though Keriya Soulstar and her friends came close. So did King Wavewalker. And that clodhopper Jigon, who'd cheated him in a game of cards that one time. And he really did hate Iako a lot. Also that city official who —

"You'd best be off. You don't want to miss your deadline," said Tanthflame, interrupting Cezon's thoughts. His reflection wavered as the surface of the mirror grew smoky and opaque. When the clouds cleared, Cezon was left staring at his own ashen face.

"No use delaying, I s'pose," he said, turning to the dragon once more. "Sorry, little fellow. Nothing personal. It's just good business."

CHAPTER THIRTY-THREE
ON THE RUN

"It is trust, rather than courage, that is the opposite of fear."
~ Calder Tryvash, Seventh Age

"Keriya, get up!"

Keriya was startled awake by a voice in her ear. It was dark, her hair hung loose around her, and she was wearing nothing more than a night shift. She was in her bedchamber and Max was standing over her.

"How'd you get in?" She was sure she'd locked her door after returning from the ball last night.

"I spoke to the king," he whispered, disregarding her question. "The conversation didn't go as planned. If you don't want to be carted away by the Imperials, we need to leave right now. Where's Thorion?" he added, scanning the empty room.

"No!" Keriya leapt from the bed, forgetting her state of undress. "I mean—you get Fletcher and Roxanne and tell them we're leaving. I'll deal with Thorion."

Things must have gone worse with Wavewalker than Max had let on, because he didn't argue. He nodded tersely and left.

"What am I going to do?" she moaned, ripping off the shift and changing into her old Aerian clothes. She wanted to tell Max the truth, but she feared how angry he would be. Maybe he'd never speak to her again. Maybe he'd hand her over to the Council of Nine for her treason.

He wouldn't do that. He kissed me, she reminded herself, as she grabbed her crumpled ribbons and tied her hair into her customary ponytails. *That must mean something.*

But she had to admit she didn't know that for sure. A kiss had been something intimate in Aeria; it was shared only between a husband and wife and was an unacceptable display of affection in public. In Allentria, it might mean anything. It might mean *nothing*.

Dashing to the sitting room, she grabbed the royal blue cloak the servants had given her. She ran the fabric between her fingertips, wondering whether or not she should steal it. She swung it around her shoulders and embraced its feel. It did seem like a useful thing to have.

It was dark when she slipped out into the hall. The guards who were usually stationed outside Keriya's door were nowhere to be seen, and she wondered what Max had done to get rid of them. Roxanne was already there, waiting with the prince.

"Where's Thorion?" Max asked again.

"Where's Fletcher?" Keriya countered.

"He said he wasn't coming," murmured Roxanne. Keriya snorted dismissively. She strode across the hall and, without stopping to consider the consequences, banged on Fletcher's door.

Max grabbed her arm. "You'll be heard!"

She wrenched herself from Max's grip and hit the door again. On her second knock, it swung inward.

Fletcher stood there, his face set in a cold expression she'd never seen on him before. Really, how long was he going to stay mad at her?

"We're leaving," she said.

"*You're* leaving," he corrected her. "I'm going to stay a few more days and get some provisions. Then I'm going back to Senteir."

Keriya heard the words, but somehow she couldn't fully process them. "You can't be serious."

"You said it yourself. I haven't done anything for this quest. I have no reason to stay."

She recoiled as though he'd slapped her. Was this what it all came down to? Had years of friendship been erased in the heat of one angry moment? She refused to accept that.

"What are you going to do in Senteir?" It was the only thing she could think to say. This was too sudden, too overwhelming, too painful.

"I still have the letter Lady Aldelphia gave me, which should be enough to prove I'm a legal citizen. I figured I'd go back to Master Treeskon and ask to earn my living with him until I find a place of my own."

He had this all planned out. How long had he been thinking of leaving?

"You can't," she whispered.

"Why? You think I won't be any use to him, either?"

"That's not it at all," she gasped, appalled. "It's just . . ." But she couldn't articulate all the things she was feeling. She wanted to yell at him, tell him he was abandoning her, betraying her — but she couldn't, because she knew this was her fault. She wanted to cry and beg him to stay, but the words were lodged in the back of her throat, trapped behind tears she would never allow herself to shed.

"I'm not sure this is the best idea," Roxanne told Fletcher. "You have no survival training and no Allentrian currency. How are you even going to get to Senteir?"

"I'll take the Imperial Highway, just like everyone else. I'd like to think I'm capable of walking on a road," he retorted with a scowl.

"A well-guarded road," Max added impatiently, not being helpful at all. "Keriya, we need to leave before it's too late. Where is Thorion?"

"He's already gone," she said in a hollow voice, staring at Fletcher. She was no longer worried about how furious Max would be, nor about what would happen if Wavewalker caught her trying to escape.

"Good — that was good thinking. Now let's go."

Still Keriya made no move to leave. For as long as she could remember, it had been her and Fletcher against the world. They'd found solace in each other when the rest of Aeria had scorned them. They'd been a team. He was the closest thing to family she'd ever had. She had assumed they would always be together . . . but perhaps that had been naïve.

Max tugged on Keriya's arm again. This time she allowed herself to be drawn away. She wanted to explain to Fletcher why he should come with her, but her throat was closing up and her lower lip was trembling, so speaking was no longer an option.

There was no more anger on Fletcher's face—only sadness. It was clear he wanted her to say something, but it was too late to fix the mess she'd made. Max pulled her around a corner, and just like that, Fletcher Earengale was gone from her life.

Time distorted for Keriya, who felt as though she were sinking in a sluggish river of mud. She barely registered where Max was taking her until they reached the ice shuttle. He laid a hand on it and the entrance irised open.

"Have room for one more?"

Max sucked a sharp breath between his teeth and closed his eyes. "Nameless, what are you doing here? How did you even find us?"

Effrax sidled into the room, shouldering a longbow and quiver. "You really need to stop chit-chatting about your top-secret plans in public," he drawled, giving Max a pointed look. "Besides, I struck a bargain with these lovely ladies and they've yet to hold up their end of it."

With a growl of frustration, Max scrubbed his hands over his face. "We don't have time to argue. Get in, and Naero help you if you slow us down or get us caught."

"Wouldn't dream of causing trouble, Your Grace."

A slim, rosy band was brightening the eastern sky by the time they arrived in the Village, muted by the plumes of mist billowing from the falls. Thankfully the streets were still empty, filled only with fingers of rising fog.

The four of them jogged westwards, away from the desolation of the darksalm, away from the palace, away from the rising sun. Even in her stupor, Keriya reflected again that Max's discussion with Wavewalker must have gone *very* poorly.

The world grew bright as they reached the lakeside path and left the village proper. Houses turned to rambling farms, and farms turned to rice paddies whose owners toiled in watery fields.

Though the countryside was quiet and deserted, Keriya couldn't shake the feeling that someone was following them. She kept glancing over her shoulder, partly fearing she'd see the king's soldiers, partly hoping she'd see Fletcher running after them, hurrying to catch up. But no matter how many times she looked back, the dirt road that stretched behind them remained empty.

"Where's Thorion?" Max questioned, finally breaking the silence.

"I told you. He's already gone."

Max stopped. He took Keriya by the arm and spun her to face him. For the first time since they'd met, she was reminded that he was a powerful political figure — and a potentially dangerous enemy.

"What do you mean by that?" he asked, his voice deadly soft.

"I was afraid for Thorion's safety. I was afraid he'd get pulled into a war he didn't belong in. So I told him to run." Keriya looked into Max's eyes, searching for some shred of understanding or forgiveness.

"Summon him," he said. "Call him back here."

"I think you need to calm down," said Roxanne. Max ignored her.

"Right now, Keriya."

"Thorion could be on the other side of Allentria," she protested, knowing how poor an excuse it was. "He won't hear me."

"It's not a matter of hearing," he said. "There's wielding involved."

"I can't," she whispered.

Max took her hand, cupping it in both of his. "Yes, you can. You have the power. You've done it before."

The problem wasn't that she didn't think she could summon Thorion—it was just the opposite. She feared she would reach the drackling and that he would return at her behest.

"In fact," Max continued, "it should be much easier this time, because you've bonded. The magicthreads of your soul are entangled with his, so you should each be able to sense where the other is, no matter the distance between you."

"Come on, Dragoneyes," said Effrax. "A lot of people are counting on you. We wouldn't want to disappoint them, would we?"

She shot him a glare. She hadn't forgotten their bargain. How could she?

"Just focus your intent and open your mind, and the magic will come to you," said Max.

The subtle hint of anger in his voice frightened Keriya, and her resolve slipped. She was ashamed of herself. Was she really going to call Thorion back into danger just because Max wanted her to? Was she that weak? Was she so easily swayed by a perfect smile and beautiful eyes?

"Shivnath wanted me to kill Necrovar," she said, returning to her age-old argument. It was the only defense she had, the one truth that gave her strength.

"Oh, Keriya." He shook his head as if disappointed by her obtuseness. "That isn't true because it simply isn't possible. You misunderstood Shivnath."

And finally, Keriya believed. She had been able to ignore Aldelphia and Wavewalker when they'd dismissed her claims, because they didn't understand. She'd even been able to ignore Roxanne, who had said such hurtful things only out of anger. But Max was calm. He was clever. He had devoted his life to studying the *rheenarae* and the dragons. There was no way he could be mistaken about something like this.

"Please," he said. "Do it for me."

She sagged beneath the weight of the crushing realization that she had been wrong. Then she closed her eyes and spoke in the draconic tongue.

"*Come to me, Thorion.*" The words lingered in the air before fading into the unknown. Without a dragon to speak to, the language felt alien. She could sense power in her words, but she didn't feel the stirring in her soul that had been there in the fen when she had first summoned him.

The group waited for a long time.

"Well?" said Effrax.

"No response. I'll try telepathically," she added quickly, glancing at Max.

<*Come to me, Thorion,*> she thought, broadcasting the message as far as she could. She cast her mind out to search for him, but all she found was a vast void of nothingness.

"Any luck?" said Max.

"I . . . I can't sense him."

"Try harder."

"I'm trying as hard as I can," she snapped. She and Thorion were bonded. Surely she should be able to feel *something*? The total lack of his presence frightened her. What if something had happened to him? What if the shadowbeasts had found him?

"Why did I send him away? What was I thinking?" she whispered. "What have I done?"

"Nothing we can't fix," Max assured her. "You're inexperienced, so it may be hard for you to sense him over longer distances. We'll keep moving, and you'll keep trying. Did the two of you discuss where he was going?"

"I—I don't . . . I said maybe he should go west, and he said something about a rainforest."

"Then that's where we'll start," said Effrax. "I guess we're doing this the old-fashioned way."

CHAPTER THIRTY-FOUR

BEST FRIENDS

"If you are not afraid, then you cannot be brave."
~ Darius Alderwood, Sixth Age

All in all, it was lucky Keriya had committed high treason by running away. Everyone was so caught up in looking for her and demanding warrants for her arrest that no one paid Fletcher any mind as he went about his business.

He spent the day gathering provisions. He headed to the kitchens, begged some food from the cooks, borrowed a coat that he had no intention of returning, and snagged a map from a helpful servant. After a decent night's sleep, he packed his things and slipped off to the ice shuttle. No use delaying his departure when Wavewalker's soldiers might decide to arrest him for being an accomplice to a traitor.

No one bothered him as he waited in line for the shuttle. People hardly looked at him as they passed him by—and why should they? He appeared to be a peasant, maybe even a servant. Just like Keriya, they had no use for him.

Don't think about her, he told himself. But of course, thinking about not thinking about her completely defeated the purpose.

When he arrived in the Village, he dug out his map of the Galantasa. While it was written in Allentrian script, it was drawn to scale. If he stayed on the Imperial Highway, he should have no trouble finding his way to Noryk, and from there to Senteir.

The highway was well guarded, as Max had promised, but it was guarded by the empire. That meant the watch houses stationed every league were occupied by Imperials. Traveling nobles were welcome to spend their nights in the houses, but

Fletcher didn't think he would be accommodated in the same fashion. Even if the guards offered him lodgings, he wasn't sure he would accept. What if one of them was in cahoots with Tanthflame? What if *all* of them were?

Fletcher grew paranoid and took to hiding in the roadside reeds whenever he heard an approaching patrol, figuring it was safer not to let the guardsmen see him. This worked well enough the first few times, but in the late afternoon a squad of three horsemen slowed to a walk abreast of where he'd hidden.

"You're telling me you didn't see someone on the road just now?" said a young man, scanning the fenlands. Fletcher sank lower in the brush. He hadn't really done anything wrong, but it would look bad if they found him lurking there.

"Even if there had been someone, what does it matter?" grumped a dark-skinned fellow.

"It matters because we can't have anyone overhearing our assignment!"

"The only reason someone would overhear us is because you trogs insist on talking about it," snapped the third man, who was tall and had a neatly trimmed beard. "Keep moving."

"Captain, it would only take a moment to—"

"That's an order! The Commander-General wants us to reach the crossroads by moonrise." The captain heeled his black stallion and the horse took off, cantering down the road. His subordinates followed.

Fletcher waited until the sounds of hoofbeats faded away. He'd seen the crossroads on his map—he'd been hoping to stop at the small town located there, but if Tanthflame's cronies were spending the night, he wanted nothing to do with it.

Since darkness was creeping up on him, he decided he would stay where he was. He ate the strips of cured fish he'd gotten from the kitchens and pulled the coat around himself for warmth. He tried to quiet his brain so he could get some rest, but it kept tormenting him with thoughts of Keriya, and the guards' conversation nagged at him.

He awoke the next morning, sore, damp, and cold. A

clammy fog rolled in as he plodded south. He scarfed down the last of the cured fish, but it did nothing to lessen his hunger.

Night had fallen again by the time the crossroads swam into view through the mist. What Fletcher had thought to be a town turned out to be little more than a cluster of guard buildings.

"Figures," he grumbled. He almost veered off the highway until he caught sight of three horses tethered to a post beside the house furthest from the path.

His brain told him to go into the fen and hide, but something in his gut urged him to investigate. Ignoring his better instincts, he approached, taking care to avoid the animals so he wouldn't spook them. An amber glow bled through the edges of the front door. Fletcher crept over and put his ear against it, listening to what was going on within.

". . . brought you the bloody thing, didn't I? Now you gotta hold up your end of the bargain!"

That voice—that was Cezon Skyriver! Fletcher quickly looked around and saw a patch of light on the far side of the building filtering from a small window. He gathered his courage and peeked through the corner of the glass.

Sure enough, there was Cezon. He was arguing with the three Imperials Fletcher had overheard on the road. And at his feet, on a piece of tattered fabric strung between two sticks, lay Thorion. Fletcher's heart stuttered and he choked on nothing at all.

"I thought the agreement was that you would kill the dragon," said the captain.

"Oh no," Fletcher moaned. What had Cezon gotten himself into?

"No, dolt, that's why I dragged it halfway across the Galantasa to you. Now gimme my blood and we can all leave happy."

Frenzy gripped Fletcher. He had to save Thorion, but his magicsource was too small to be of any use. He wouldn't survive a fight against elite soldiers.

"What's wrong with it?" asked the dark-skinned man,

nudging Thorion with the tip of his boot.

"Who cares?" Cezon blustered.

"Silence," said the captain, stilling his men before they could argue. "We will accept it as-is."

"You won't accept anything until I have my tronkin' blood!"

"Very well. Lieutenant Dustrock?"

Dustrock, the guard who'd been so keen to search for Fletcher, produced a vial from within his robes. He handed this to Cezon, who uncorked it and sniffed at its dark contents. Seeming satisfied, he tipped his head back and tossed the liquid into his mouth.

"Euch!" Dustrock pulled a disgusted face, watching as Cezon swiped a finger around the inside of the vial. "What is wrong with you?"

"Best way I know how to keep my blood safe from you rotters," Cezon explained, licking his finger clean. "Can't throw it away, cause you might still be able to get at it. Now we're square."

Cezon strode toward the door and reached for the handle. His hand, however, stopped short of the knob. He stood there for a second, fingers scrabbling in midair.

"You gonna let me out?" he asked, glaring back at the captain.

"I'm afraid I can't do that. Without your blood as collateral, there's nothing to stop you from revealing our secrets."

"Are you effin' serious? I ain't gonna tell anyone! Tanthflame gave me his word!"

"The Commander-General promised that if you brought us the dragon, you'd get your blood back. He didn't say anything about letting you live after you'd gotten it."

The captain made a sweeping movement with his hand, and a gust of air knocked Cezon against the wall. Fletcher winced, but Cezon sprang right back up and conjured a torrent of water. While the captain deflected his counterattack, Dustrock and the third man were caught full in the face. Cezon reached into a hidden pocket of his leggings and pulled something out.

He threw it on the floor and it caused a miniature explosion, filling the room with thick smoke.

It occurred to Fletcher that this might be his only chance to save Thorion. Though he had no semblance of a plan, he scampered to the door and tried to wrench it open. His hands, like Cezon's, slid past the handle. He couldn't feel any blockage in the air, but there was definitely some sort of magical shield around it. His hand ended up somewhere else every time he reached for the knob, and when he concentrated all his might on grabbing it, he met with a pressurized resistance that pushed back against him.

Groaning in frustration, Fletcher abandoned the door. He hefted up a nearby rock, dashed back to the window, and heaved it through the pane with all his might. It shattered, releasing smoke and screams into the night. Fletcher clambered in awkwardly, slicing his hands on the broken glass. He dropped to the floor, staying low to avoid the worst of the smoke as he crawled blindly toward where he hoped Thorion's body was.

A crackling noise entered the fray, and the room was filled with the red-orange glow of fire.

"Ouch!" Fletcher had crawled right into Thorion. He sat up and put his arms around the drackling. Thorion wasn't big, nor was he as heavy as he looked, but Fletcher knew he wouldn't be able to carry him. Even if he could, it would be impossible to get him out of the window.

"Wake up," he hissed, but Thorion didn't stir. Fletcher grabbed the poles of the sled and tugged the dragon toward the wall so they'd be out of the way. A wave of water—one of Cezon's spells, no doubt—washed across the floor, knocking into Fletcher. Spluttering and gasping, he gave one last yank and pulled Thorion to relative safety.

Fletcher stood up. He sought and found the door, and tried desperately to work the handle. No luck—whoever was wielding the shield spell was maintaining it with a vengeance. A discarded dagger lay nearby. Fletcher snatched it up and stabbed at the brass knob. The blade came closer than his hands had, but the shield held firm.

Cursing under his breath, Fletcher tucked the dagger into a pocket of his coat and crawled back to the dragon.

"Come on," he said, his voice cracking. He shook Thorion. "I need your help!"

A loud snap indicated the house was about one support beam away from collapsing. Fletcher put his head in his hands, trying to blot out the yells of the men and the howl of the flames.

Think, Fletcher. Think!

In Aeria, Erasmus had sometimes used smelling salts to awaken his patients, but this smoke smelled bad enough to wake the dead and Thorion hadn't so much as stirred. When Fletcher had been young, his mother had sometimes thrown water on his face to get him moving on cold mornings—but the dragon had just been doused by Cezon's magic and hadn't moved a muscle.

"Please, *please* wake up!" In his desperation, Fletcher leaned down and whispered into Thorion's ear, using the draconic phrase he'd picked up from Keriya: "*Kemraté a'eos, Thorion!*"

Thorion's eyelids fluttered open, revealing his brilliant purple irises. Fletcher cried out in relief and sent a silent prayer of gratitude to Shivnath. He got to his feet and motioned for the dragon to do the same. A spark of vitality kindled in Thorion as he pushed himself up on unsteady limbs.

"We're trapped." Fletcher led Thorion to the wooden door and banged on it with his fist. Thorion couldn't understand his words, but could clearly see they needed to escape. He glanced around the outpost, shielding his eyes against the smoke with his semi-transparent secondary lids. Then he opened his mouth and spat lightmagic at the door.

His spell broke through the shield and burned a hole in the wood. Fletcher kicked at the splintered boards, widening the hole just enough to squeeze through. He tumbled out into the cool night with Thorion close on his heels.

The horses were braying in terror and shying away from the burning house, but the appearance of the dragon sent them over the edge. The black stallion reared up, snapping the lead line that tethered them to the post, and the frightened beasts galloped into the fen.

An angry yell told Fletcher that their escape hadn't gone unnoticed. A lone figure grew visible through the smoke as it staggered toward the door.

It was Cezon. The two humans froze, staring at each other. Fletcher didn't know what to do. Cezon had betrayed him to the Imperials and he'd done something terrible to Thorion. Fletcher ought to take the dagger out of his pocket and stab the Allentrian. His hand stirred at his side, yearning to reach for the weapon.

But even in the face of mortal peril, he couldn't do it. He couldn't bring himself to strike against the man who, for one brief moment, had been his friend and confidante.

Cezon seized upon Fletcher's hesitation. He crashed through the hole in the door and grabbed Fletcher by the arm.

Stupid! Fletcher screamed at himself. He had endangered not only himself, but Thorion, too. Coming to his senses, he struggled against Cezon's grip and fumbled in his pocket for the blade.

"Stop it," Cezon snarled. He pulled Fletcher around the corner and shoved him away.

"What are you—"

"Run," said Cezon, pointing to the open fen. "And take him with you," he added, nodding to Thorion.

Fletcher stared at Cezon, unable to comprehend what was happening.

"Get out of here!" Cezon scuffed at Fletcher and flapped his arms at Thorion, who skittered away from his movements. "I can only hold 'em off for so long. Run!"

Fletcher raced toward the crossroads. He leapt over the low stone wall that lined the highway, slid down a gully, and landed in a mud puddle. Thorion jumped the wall gracefully and joined him. Behind him, he heard the Imperials shouting and Cezon swearing.

"He saved me," Fletcher said to himself. Someone cried in pain and he flinched. He almost stood up to go back and help Cezon, who was outnumbered and probably outmatched — but that would be foolish on countless levels.

Besides, Fletcher now had a drackling to care for. He couldn't risk Thorion's safety. They had to run.

He looked to the south. Noryk lay in that direction. Even if they kept off the highway and trekked through the fen, they could reach the city in a few days' time.

Then he looked north.

"Keriya," he said slowly, pointing back the way he had come. Thorion knew that word; he perked up and made a chirruping noise.

"I think I'd better get you back to her," said Fletcher.

A grave expression settled on the dragon's face and he said something in that haunting language of his. The air before him shimmered with the weight of his words. Fletcher had the impression that if Thorion used that language to command the universe to disappear, it would have no choice but to obey.

"Keriya," Thorion repeated. He looked meaningfully at Fletcher, then loped into the fen.

Fletcher sighed and, summoning the last of his strength, followed. He looked back only once, squinting at the outpost. The fire still burned brightly, but there was no movement outside the house . . . which meant that by now, Cezon was probably dead.

Thorion hadn't taken the time to get to know Fletcher before. He'd been so enthralled by Keriya and her emotions that he'd barely noticed her companions. However, since circumstances had forced them together, he made efforts to communicate with the Smarlindian boy.

Fletcher often spoke of Necrovar as a reminder that Keriya

was in danger. Thorion didn't need to be reminded—he had a brain. He was sure that Fletcher also asked how he'd been captured. In truth, Thorion couldn't recall. The last thing he remembered was his confrontation with the bogspectre. After that, it was one big blank until he'd awoken in that smoke-filled room.

Fletcher took to the habit of teaching Thorion the Allentrian language. The boy would point at random objects and offer their names, then he would look at Thorion, expecting him to repeat the words. Thorion rarely played along. While he'd inherited a healthy love of learning from Keriya, he didn't enjoy adjusting his palate to the odd, tawdry shapes of the human tongue.

"Water," Fletcher said on their third night of travel, pointing to a puddle and scooping some liquid into his hands.

"Water," Thorion parroted, his lips curling in a silent snarl around the ugly word. It was an annoying game, but if he had to learn Allentrian, he might as well start now.

They made good time, for Thorion set a breakneck pace, guided by an indescribable sixth sense. This, he supposed, was a result of his bond with Keriya. He wasn't sensing her telepathically, but he was drawn ever onwards like a moth to a light. He had no real way of knowing where she was, but he never once doubted his direction.

It would have been faster to fly, but he couldn't leave Fletcher behind. He was Keriya's best friend—so, through the additive property of their bond, that meant on some level he was Thorion's best friend, too.

They left the fenlands on their fourth day of travel. Unfortunately, they had to cross a river to do so. Fletcher whined and worried on the southern bank. He pointed at the river, then to himself, and made awkward motions with his arms while shaking his head.

Thorion took this to mean that Fletcher couldn't swim.

"Hold the spines on my back," he instructed, arcing his neck toward the boy. Fletcher didn't understand, and in the end

Thorion had to take his hand in his teeth — which Fletcher didn't like one bit — and twist around to put that hand on one of his pearly bone protrusions.

Fletcher's face went pale, but he nodded and pinched his nose shut with his free hand. The two of them waded into the shallows together, then Thorion shoved off, kicking against the current with his powerful legs, navigating with his tail and wings.

Fletcher's extra weight was unwieldy, but they had no trouble reaching the northern bank. The little human made quite a fuss considering he hadn't drowned and, in fact, hadn't even done any swimming.

"Thank you," he finally said, which Thorion knew was an Allentrian phrase of respect or gratitude.

"Yure . . . well-come," Thorion replied. Fletcher looked up at him, his eyes wide. "Yure welcome?" he said again, with less certainty.

"Yes," said Fletcher. "That's right!" He let out a disbelieving laugh and smiled, clapping his hands together.

Something swelled in Thorion's chest. It was a strange, fluttering sensation that spread from his heart and filled his lungs.

Happiness.

And slowly, deliberately, Thorion smiled back.

CHAPTER THIRTY-FIVE

INTO THE SHADOWS

"Do not fear the shadows, fear the monsters that hide in them."
~ **Syrionese Proverb**

Having procured everything she needed for her adventure, Seba slipped into the servants' hallway and clambered up into the air vents. She'd taken a big risk sneaking around to gather her provisions and wanted to do her utmost to stay out of sight now.

She crawled until she reached the corridor outside Keriya's room and sat, hardly daring to breathe, waiting for dawn to break.

Hours before dawn, however, Max arrived. Seba sat up, alert at once. He whispered to the guards on duty and pressed something into one man's hand—a bribe, perhaps? Seba put her ear to the thin wooden grate of the vent, but couldn't catch his words. The guards bowed and left.

Seba watched as Max dug the palace master key out of his pocket, unlocked the door, and entered. She was filled with an overwhelming fury and a desperate desire to see what he was doing—and to put a stop to it, whatever it was. She was tempted to kick out the grate and leap down into the hallway, but before she could, Max exited the room again.

Seba watched as he knocked on another door, soft but urgent. The tall peasant girl, Roxanne, opened up. After a few words, she vanished and hastily reappeared with a traveling cloak she had clearly stolen from one of the closets.

Keriya joined them next, exchanging a few more words with Max before stalking to a third door and banging on it. The noise startled a gasp out of Seba — but no one heard her, because

Keriya was practically yelling for her other peasant friend.

"We're leaving," she told him when he finally opened his door.

"*You're* leaving. I'm going to stay a few more days and get some provisions. Then I'm going back to Senteir."

Adrenaline jolted through Seba. If Max and Keriya were planning to sneak out of the palace, she would lose them while waiting for the ice shuttle.

As quickly and quietly as she could, she crawled off through the vent, hindered by her travel pack. There was only one other exit — the exit she always used to escape undetected — but it was in her father's chambers. It was a private shuttle, enchanted to respond only to the touch of those of the royal bloodline. It was easy enough to get to, but she'd never tried to use it while he was actually in his rooms.

The next chance she got, she dropped back down into the servants' hall and took off at a sprint, praying to Zumarra she wouldn't run into anyone. She reached her father's chambers and edged in through the hidden sliding panel that his attendants used to enter.

His living space was surprisingly modest — smaller than one would imagine for the king of the Galantasa, and furnished with simple icewood fixtures. The grand four-poster bed was the only mark of true luxury, bedecked with silver gauze hangings and outfitted with the finest silk sheets.

Her father turned beneath the covers, disturbing the soft, steady rhythm of her mother's breathing. For a moment, Seba was frozen with the fear that one of them would hear her. Only the thought of losing Max got her moving again. She inched toward a glass door at the far end of the room, its surface molded into patterns that warped the dim light of the chamber beyond. Grasping the handle with trembling hands, she eased the door open.

Inside was another icy sphere, identical to the main shuttle. It hovered over the entrance to the lake, sparkling in the light of a lone firelamp stand. Seba placed her hand on its surface.

A hole irised open and she jumped inside, bracing herself. The opening frosted over again and the bubble dropped.

A few minutes later, she arrived in a nondescript hovel at the edge of the Village trade district. She exited the rundown shack and tore east along the streets. The main shuttle square was just ahead and the orb itself was sinking back into its watery passage, returning to its home base in the palace. They must have only just arrived. She could still catch them.

Seba ran like she'd never run before, looking down every cross street and waterway, squinting in the pre-dawn gloom. She rounded a corner and spotted them: Max, Keriya, Roxanne, and Effrax Nameless were racing along ahead of her. There was no sign of Thorion. He must have flown up ahead to scout the way.

Seba followed at a more cautious pace thereafter, keeping her distance. Nameless was an expert tracker, and she didn't want to risk him spotting her. Why was he with them? And what were they doing, sneaking off like this? Seba didn't have the energy to guess at their reasons as she ducked from one hiding spot to another, but she was sure they were up to no good.

The sun had reached its zenith by the time Max and the others crossed the bamboo bridge over the West Outlet River. Seba skulked on the eastern banks. She expected them to turn left and head toward the Erastate, but they went straight for the rainforest instead. Right into one of the most dangerous places in Allentria.

"Helkryvt's blood," Seba groaned as she watched the green jungle mists swallow them whole. She'd come too far to go back, so she raced across the bridge and plunged into the trees after them.

That first night was awful. Seba had never been forced to sleep without the comfort of a thick mattress and silk sheets. Her traveling cloak served as a poor blanket, and her lumpy pack made for an even poorer pillow. Not that she *could* sleep — every sound made her jump. What if the bogspectre found her?

Or her father's soldiers?

Seba wasn't sure which would be worse.

The next day, she followed the group as closely as she dared. At night, she huddled in the shadows just beyond the reach of their campfire's light. Nameless would sometimes look toward her hiding spot when she shifted her weight or snapped a twig underfoot. Roxanne occasionally lifted her head and smelled the air, as if she were trying to catch Seba's scent. But neither one came looking for her, and she remained hidden.

By the fourth night, Seba began to calm down. She stopped worrying about being attacked by jungle creatures and started worrying about how she was going to survive this trip. She'd believed Keriya was going to Noryk, and had only packed so much food. She was already running low. The scent of the rabbit roasting on Nameless' fire made her mouth water.

Max was tending to the meat. He leaned over and spoke to Keriya, and she inched nearer to him, listening attentively.

"Keep away from him, you little nit," Seba growled. She clutched the hilt of her knife, though she knew there was no threat to Max's life just yet. They were nowhere near the dry, desolate mountains Seba had seen in her vision, nor did Keriya have a sword. Strangely, she didn't seem to have a dragon, either. Where was Thorion?

Too many questions and no answers. Seba glowered at Keriya, hating the pale brat more and more the longer she watched.

She shouldn't have gotten distracted. She should have been paying attention to her surroundings, rather than paying attention to the way Max's hand rested on Keriya's arm. She should have been listening to the sounds of the night, rather than trying to overhear their conversation. But she ignored it when everything went silent and she missed the faint, sickly-sweet smell of rotting flesh, so she didn't notice there was something behind her until it was too late.

Seba turned at the sound of a low hiss. She was met with a

horrifying vision of death.

"Flesh-rats in my forest," it breathed in a slow, rattling voice. "Thieving little monsters. You'll be sorry. All of you."

The bogspectre. This was Seba's worst nightmare come to life. Every Galantrian child was warned about the fiend and was taught what to do in this situation. Call for help; run fast and run far; don't look into its eyes.

Don't look into its eyes!

Seba made to squeeze her eyes shut and open her mouth to scream for Max. Better to be caught and returned to the palace than to fall prey to the bogspectre.

But it was already too late. She couldn't blink, couldn't open her mouth, couldn't move. The creature floated closer, its body oozing through the air like syrupy liquid. She couldn't do anything to defend herself as it pressed its moist skin against her face. She lost her vision as it spread over her eyes, blotting out all light.

Then there was pain. Terrible, searing pain. She would have been screaming if she'd had the use of her voice, but she was trapped, a prisoner in her own body. Her brain wanted her to cry and fight, but she was paralyzed. The pain sharpened to an unbearable point.

It vanished as quickly as it had come. Seba opened her eyes and twisted her head, examining her surroundings. She ran her hands along the length of her arms and through her hair. Who was she? Why was she here? Where *was* here?

Voices floated up from the campsite downhill, and the bogspectre remembered. It turned in its new body, narrowing its eyes. Yes. Flesh-rats. They reeked of Necrovar's magic. Evil mortal scum. They were here to steal the bogspectre's treasure for the Shadow Lord, and it couldn't allow that.

It wondered how best to strike against them. They were bedding down for the night and would be weak while they slept. Defenseless. Yes, perfect.

Three of the flesh-rats fell asleep, but the fourth sat against the trunk of a tree to keep watch. The bogspectre formed a cruel smile with its stolen human lips. It plotted its attack. Thirsted for their blood.

No! Don't hurt them!

It ignored the other voice in its head—its victims always went quiet eventually. This girl would be no different. As it considered how to murder its foes, the human's hands fell to her waist of their own accord, where they closed instinctively on the hilt of a throwing knife.

The bogspectre's smile widened. Too easy.

Take your hands off that!

"*Your* hands," it breathed aloud, correcting the stupid girl who was beating upon the walls of her mental prison, trying to break away from the bogspectre's control. It wouldn't do her any good. No one had ever escaped the bogspectre.

It stalked through the underbrush toward its new targets. It made no sound as it approached the sleeping bodies, for it had spent ages upon ages lurking amidst these trees and it knew the forest inside and out.

The guard would be the first to die. Sneak around behind her, slit her throat, slay the others without them ever knowing it was there. Good plan. Yes.

But the bogspectre, who had never once hesitated before a kill, froze when it caught sight of the guard's eyes. Purple. *Purple* eyes.

It stood motionless in the shadows, staring at the little human child. She sat there mumbling to herself, shredding the petals of a starblossom, unaware how close she was to her death.

The bogspectre watched her for some time. Strange things bubbled in the back of its mind . . . perhaps memories, perhaps only its imagination. It had seen purple eyes before, hadn't it? Recently, in fact—or perhaps ages ago. They meant something, didn't they? Yes. Something to do with . . . *something*. Something important. Something it couldn't recall.

Slowly, it released its grip on the hilt of the knife and backed away from the campsite.

Why?

"You want me to kill your friends?" it hissed, scratching at the side of its host's head with her own fingernails. But the question haunted the bogspectre. It was certain that those flesh-rats had been sent from Necrovar. It could practically smell the dark magic within them. Why, then? Why had it walked away?

"I don't know," it murmured aloud.

It settled down behind a flowering fern and sat until the sun rose, watching the purple-eyed girl. And when she and her pack of humans got up and continued their hike through the jungle, it followed.

CHAPTER THIRTY-SIX

DEMONS

"He who fights too long against demons becomes one himself."
~ **Cylion Stellarion, Second Age**

Roxanne crouched in a rocky grotto, stoking the fire with a dead branch. It was warm in the little cave, and fortunately, it was quiet. The mental voices of the countless jungle animals were almost enough to drive her mad. But none of them were speaking now, so she listened in on the voices of her human companions instead.

"Keriya, do you have a moment?" It was Max.

"I—I'm busy. Sorry." Keriya ripped apart the hanging vines that separated the cave from the outside world and darted inside.

"Lovers' quarrel?" Roxanne asked dryly. Keriya gave her an affronted look.

"It isn't like that! It's just . . . I don't want him to ask about Thorion again. And I don't want him to talk about—"

"About?" Roxanne raised a brow in interest, but Keriya was done talking. She clutched the edges of her cloak, pulled the fabric tight around herself, and shook her head.

They took turns keeping watch that night, as had become routine since they'd fled the palace. Whether they were on the lookout for Wavewalker's soldiers, Imperial Guards, or Necrovar himself, Roxanne didn't know. Maybe all three. They were in trouble with a lot of people, and she hadn't been able to shake the feeling that they were being followed.

They continued their route down a rambling game trail the next morning. Roxanne couldn't tell if Keriya was actually trying to find Thorion, or if she was just stringing Max and

Effrax along on a wild goose chase.

It was mid-afternoon by the time they broke for lunch beside a glittering stream. While the others removed their packs and cloaks to relax, Roxanne was on edge. Why was she so antsy? The stream trickled in its shallow bed, curling lazily past smooth stones. Verdant ferns crouched on the mossy banks, whispering in the breeze. It was peaceful and quiet.

Too quiet.

She studied the stream again. There were no fish, no insects, nothing. There was no life in the trees, either — no birds, nor any of the blue-winged butterflies that usually danced in the leaves. The animals were avoiding this part of the jungle.

"I think we should keep moving," she announced.

"We've only just stopped," said Max.

"We can rest, but not here. I don't think it's safe."

"The Tigress has a point," Effrax chimed in unexpectedly. "We're on the run, after all. It wouldn't do to have our enemies catch up with us."

So they kept moving, hiking into mountainous terrain. Everything seemed more ominous here — rocks jutted up like grasping fingers, sharp and wicked, and trees grew in stunted, tortured shapes.

Then a far-off scream reached Roxanne. It was the dying cry of an animal, the first mindvoice she'd heard all day. The mental picture was bright and vivid, a warning to all those who could hear: a herd of soulless abominations moved through the woods, heralds of destruction and death.

Roxanne whirled to face her companions. "We're in danger. Something's coming from the south."

"How do you know that?" said Max.

"Trust me," she growled, clenching her fists and reaching for her magic.

Max seemed frustrated with her, but Effrax drew his bow from its quiver and strung it without question. Roxanne edged closer to Keriya, who was unable to defend herself.

For a moment, all was still. Then a group of animals burst

into the clearing. She didn't recognize the three creatures with flat faces and barbed tails, nor could she identify the cat-like thing behind them, but she knew the wolves and the boar. Every one of them was as black as the night on a moonless eve, and their minds were empty and mute, as silent as a grave—shadowbeasts.

"Is this the best Necrovar can do?" Effrax asked, pulling an arrow taut against his bowstring and igniting its iron tip with flames. "He must be losing his touch."

With a grating shriek that set Roxanne's teeth on edge, two blackened drachvolds burst through the canopy of the trees, showering them with leaves and shattered branches.

"Ah—spoke too soon." Effrax loosed his arrow at the boar and burned one of the flat-faced creatures to dust before confronting the winged monstrosities.

Roxanne reached within herself, connecting to her magic in the blink of an eye. She mentally threaded strands of invisible energy from her source into a nearby vine, manipulating it so it strangled one of the wolves. The wolf stumbled and fell, and black froth bubbled at its mouth as it struggled to draw breath. Roxanne held onto her spell until the creature went still. She unclenched her fists, watching as its body crumbled away.

That was the first time she'd ever killed anything.

Sickness flooded her gut. She didn't know what was wrong. It had always been her dream to be a Hunter. She had no problem with violence. The thing had been a shadowbeast, for Shivnath's sake—it had belonged, body and soul, to Necrovar. It had deserved to die.

Trying to shake the guilt growing inside her, Roxanne turned her attention back to the battle. Max had wielded an air shield to protect them from the shadow-stained acid of the drachvolds; Effrax was fending off the injured boar and the cat; but the last flat-faced creature darted around him and made a beeline for Keriya, who was armed with nothing more than a rock and a broken tree branch.

Acting on instinct, Roxanne leapt forward and grabbed

the short, blunt horns on either side of its head to stop it. The shadowbeast skidded to a halt, staring at her. She was close enough to see every scar and bump on its leathery skin. It growled, revealing serrated teeth, and she pulled more magic from her source. She prepared a lethal spell . . . and found she couldn't wield it.

When she gazed into the shadowbeast's eyes, she saw something beyond its darkened soul. She saw an animal named Grouge. He had once been strong and noble, but death had come too early for him, so he had traded his magicsource in exchange for a second chance at life. He had no desire to kill, and he certainly didn't want to be killed, but that was why he was there. He was bait. He was meant to be a sacrifice, a distraction.

Shaken, Roxanne dropped her threads and let go of his horns. "Get out of here," she whispered over the tumult. Grouge didn't move.

"Run!" she screamed, kicking at him. He whimpered and galloped into the trees, ears flat against his skull, barbed tail curled between his legs.

She didn't have time to think about what she'd done. There were other shadowbeasts to be dealt with, and —

"Ahh!" She cried out as a snakelike cord of black water whipped out from behind a tree and slammed into her, knocking her to the ground. A few heights away, another tendril of shadowy liquid wrapped around Keriya. Two more phantoms revealed themselves, stepping out from the brush. They were human — or rather, shadowmen.

From what Roxanne had glimpsed in Grouge's head, she knew this pair was in command of the demons. They'd forced the shadowbeasts to fight and die, and they were plotting something terrible.

She wielded again, willing the vines on a nearby tree toward the shadowmen. The taller one created a shield of black ice that deflected her spell. Her vines withered when they touched it and crumbled to pieces of waste, just like the wolf she had murdered. With a chilling laugh, the man strode over to Keriya and grabbed her, encircling her neck with one strong arm.

Roxanne sprang back to her feet. She sank threads into the ground and found two stone missiles, drawing them up through the soft, mossy turf in the time it took her to draw a breath.

She launched them at the demons. The smaller shadow-man disintegrated as the first missile shot through his chest, but Keriya's assailant deflected the second sharp rock. Roxanne faltered, dropping her threads in shock. His face was lit by the purple glow of Keriya's eyes, and though his flesh had turned the color of age-old rot, she recognized him.

Doru.

He noted her expression and shot her a grim smile. "Oh yes. This is your fault," he hissed. "You left me to die in the Galantrian Village, but the Shadow Lord rewards his loyal servants."

She would have struck against him, except that she'd seen, in Grouge's thoughts, what Doru intended to do. He had a vial of darksalm and he was planning to infect Keriya. One wrong move on Roxanne's part and she might doom the girl to a fate worse than death. She would have to use all the skill and finesse she possessed.

But then Doru dropped Keriya. He screamed and staggered sideways as another figure, a human female, emerged from the jungle behind him. She had grabbed his head in both her hands and latched onto him with a tenacity Roxanne had only observed in predators holding onto prey.

Doru's shrieks filled the air as he struggled to break free. His desperate thrashing wrenched the woman around with him, and the cowl of her mottled cloak fell back from her face. A rabid snarl dripped from her mouth and her eyes were dark with mindless fury.

Roxanne was too stunned to move, or to offer any help. Their mysterious savior was . . . Princess Sebaris?

With a mighty tug, Doru wrenched himself from Sebaris'

clutches. His black skin was melting from his skull in thin strands where she'd touched him. He dematerialized, fading into darkness, though the echo of his tortured yells lingered.

Sebaris whirled to face Roxanne. Her eyes weren't dark with fury — they had actually changed color. Where before they had glittered like sapphires, now they were black like a shadow-beast's hide.

"There are more demons," Sebaris cried, turning tail and charging back into the trees. "If they get what they want, Necrovar will win!"

While Roxanne was too stunned to react, Effrax followed the Galantrian girl without hesitation, his bow at the ready.

"Stay here," he told Roxanne as he passed her.

"What—"

"Shadowbeasts aren't the only demons in this forest, Tigress," he warned. "Stay."

Roxanne didn't protest, and he disappeared into the jungle. She stared around dazedly, trying to work out what had just happened. The battle had ended while she'd been distracted with Doru. Max had finished off the last of the shadowbeasts. He was now kneeling by Keriya's side, pulling her into a sitting position.

"Are you alright?" he asked. She nodded, coughing. "Did necromagic touch you?"

"Obviously," said Roxanne. She was embarrassed to hear that her voice was an octave higher than usual. "It was Doru. He got turned into a shadowman. He was wielding against us. He was trying to infect Keriya with more darksalm, but . . ."

But a demonic Princess Sebaris had appeared out of nowhere at exactly the right moment to save Keriya and somehow defeat him with strange, toxic magic.

Roxanne wasn't sure how to articulate that.

Silence stretched between the three of them. In the stillness, every sound was amplified and distorted into the movement of a lurking shadowbeast. It was worse than the battle, in a way. Roxanne preferred enemies she could see over enemies hiding in the shadows.

Another piercing scream cut through the air. Roxanne didn't know Sebaris' voice well, but the shrillness of it suggested it was the Galantrian.

"We have to go help," she said feebly. She wasn't fond of the princess, but Sebaris had clearly landed herself in a heap of trouble—they couldn't just leave her to fend for herself in the demon-infested woods.

Keriya rose to her feet. She looked to Roxanne, who pointed in the exact direction whence the scream had come.

"Stick together," said Max. "And be careful."

They ran to her aid, hurtling across a rocky canyon, past a waterfall, up a muddy hill, through a skein of vines and into a clearing where stood three monsters.

Keriya nearly collided with Roxanne and Max, who had stopped short ahead of her. They were facing a glade where pools of water sparkled in a carpet of dark moss. Dead, stunted trees spotted the edges of the clearing, their branches contorted as if in pain, their bark worn smooth by the ages. Wisps of ghostly white vegetation hung from them, separating the glade from the forest like a shroud.

Effrax was already there, hidden behind one of the trees. He stared across the clearing at two shadowbeasts, massive animals that vaguely resembled humans in the structure of their face and arms.

Another figure stole along the edge of the clearing—Princess Sebaris. So, Keriya hadn't been hallucinating. It was her. What the blood was she doing here?

Sebaris glided to the edge of one of the pools. She drew a glittering dagger from her belt and hurled it at the smaller of the two shadowbeasts. The knife struck the creature square in the chest and it disintegrated.

Its companion rounded on Sebaris and charged her. She stood her ground, flexing her hands as if she intended to rip the animal apart with her bare fingers, but the shadowbeast was felled by an arrow before it reached her, tumbling to the earth and turning to dust.

Effrax stepped out from behind the knobbly tree. He fitted another arrow to his string as Sebaris turned to face him. He pulled the fletching back to his ear and loosed it. Keriya watched it fly straight and true, clean through Sebaris' left eye.

For one awful moment the princess stood there calmly, glaring at Effrax as if an iron-tipped projectile hadn't just burrowed itself in her head. In that moment, Keriya felt her stomach fall away from her body. The Galantrian's eyes had turned completely black.

A dark substance, much thicker than blood, oozed from Sebaris' wounded eye and ran down her cheek. She lifted a hand and yanked the arrow out, pulling the shiny black eyeball with it—but in the socket that should have been empty, another eye stared out at them, a normal ocean-blue eye.

Even as fear tightened its hold around her heart, Keriya found herself wondering what amazing magic was at work here.

With a sickly squelch, more darkness bubbled from Sebaris' right eye socket. It pulled away from her face and hung in the air. Behind the seething mass, her body collapsed.

The ooze coalesced into a floating, ghoulish creature. Its head curved neatly at the nose, but the back of its skull was ill-defined, dissolving into a pulsating spray. Its serpentine body percolated in a way that reminded Keriya of maggots writhing. It glared at Effrax with one black eye—its left socket was empty, dripping dark ichor.

"Flee while you can, bogspectre," said Effrax. "If you try to possess any more of us, you'll lose your other eye, and all your powers with it."

"The water-witch was begging for trouble, wandering my woods alone." Its grating voice was filled with hatred. "She was following you—plotting some evil against you, no doubt."

"Leave this place," said Effrax, drawing a third arrow from his quiver.

"Not this place. I'll never leave this place. I took her body to protect what the demons hunted, and their master will be furious when they do not bring it to him. I will be safe from his wrath, but you, pathetic mortals . . ." It let out a sound like flesh being ripped from bones, which might have been a laugh. "When he comes for you, nothing will save your souls!"

Grotesque though it was, Keriya found herself enraptured by the monster. It was dangerous, yes, but intelligent. It knew of Necrovar, and it seemed to hate him.

"Oh? What were you guarding that the shadowbeasts wanted so badly?" Effrax inquired as he slowly fitted the arrow's fletching to his bowstring.

The bogspectre ignored him. "I can feel his power, even from this distance, and I know what he wants," it babbled. "The Shadow Lord has taken everything from me. By his hand, I have been forced to live alone for ages, misunderstood, feared, hated—a shadow myself, of what I once was."

Though it was well masked by the chilling rasp, Keriya picked up on a note of sadness in the bogspectre's voice. She caught herself feeling sorry for it and quickly reminded herself that it was an enemy.

"Funny. I'd have put good money on you being one of Necrovar's thralls." Effrax's feet shifted into a defensive stance.

"Never," it spat. "He will never have my treasure! I will fight him! I am forced to fight him. I cannot do otherwise . . . I have no choice."

Those sorry words, that rueful tone—they tugged at Keriya, calling to something deep within her. Pity for the wretched monster swelled in her chest.

"He sends his minions to claim what is mine. But he shall not take it. It has been mine for a ten-age! You wish to take it from me, too, don't you? You will die before you steal my treasure, and when your bodies are rotting, I will feast upon your innards!"

It glided toward Effrax with a baleful hiss. Quick as a flash, he whipped up his bow and pulled the arrow back.

"No!" Keriya threw herself at Effrax, knocking his aim askew just as he released the bolt. The weapon whizzed through the air and sank harmlessly into the ground a few heights away.

Everyone froze, including the bogspectre. One by one, they all turned to stare at Keriya. Effrax opened his mouth in outrage, but it was the monster who spoke first.

"Foolish flesh-rat. It would have been better for all of you if he had killed me. Or tried to. Why save me?"

Keriya was asking herself the same question. She had acted on instinct, but now she realized how incredibly stupid she'd been. She pawed through layers of her psyche, searching for answers she didn't yet know how to find.

"I'm not sure," she admitted in barely more than a whisper.

Her answer calmed the bogspectre. Its eye swam with regret, only visible if one knew to look for it. Keriya noted that it wasn't pure black, as were the eyes of the shadowbeasts. There was another color buried underneath a film of darkness.

"I once knew others like you, long ago," it breathed, scrutinizing her. "What is your name?"

"Keriya Soulstar."

"Soulstar?" Its face buckled, as if its sludgy skin was trying to form a frown.

"That's me," she said weakly. She tried—and failed—to offer it a smile.

"You are a *rheenar*," it said, "but you reek of darkness and ancient magics. Are you allied with Necrovar?"

"No. I'm fighting Necrovar, just like you. I was sent by Shivnath, god and guardian of the Smarlands, to kill him." The automatic response tumbled out of her before she could stop it. It rang false against her ears now, but the bogspectre was intrigued.

"I . . . want to give you something," it said after a pause. It glided back to Sebaris' body. Keriya thought it meant to do something to the unconscious princess, but it passed over her and stopped by the pool next to which she'd collapsed.

It tipped its head back and let loose a bone-chilling roar. At once, the water began to slosh around, touched by its own private hurricane. A glow grew within its depths, becoming so bright that the brilliance forced Keriya to close her eyes. When the light died and she dared to peek through her lashes, the pool was calm and dark once more. But in the bogspectre's arms there now rested a muddy, algae-infested sword and scabbard.

The monster drifted back to Keriya. A mad gleam came into its eye, and she feared it would attack. Instead, it proffered the dripping blade to her. Figuring it would be rude not to do so, she accepted the sword. Muck oozed onto her from the bogspectre's body and she repressed the urge to gag.

"I believe this is what the demons are after," it told her. "It has a secret. Something to do with dragons. I don't remember the power of it—or perhaps I never knew—but if there is one who should have it, it is you."

"Why?" It was the only thing she could manage to say.

"Because you have to fight Necrovar. And this will help."

"Thank you," Keriya whispered, too softly for any but the bogspectre to hear.

"Do not let it fall into the wrong hands, Keriya Soulstar. It was a gift given to me long ago, and I now give it to you—not out of any love I have for your race, but in the hope that you may eventually save all races from the Shadow. And," it added as an afterthought, "to thank you for saving my life."

Then, without so much as a whisper, the bogspectre swirled and vanished.

CHAPTER THIRTY-SEVEN

THE SECRET OF THE SWORD

"The heart understands the things we do not."
~ *Keandre Anstellae, Eleventh Age*

Night fell as the group made camp on the outskirts of the bogspectre's clearing. It seemed like a defensible place—and they would certainly need to defend themselves if more shadowbeasts showed up.

They huddled in silence around Effrax's fire. Keriya fidgeted, knowing that sooner or later they'd have to discuss what had happened. When she could no longer stand the mounting tension, she took the initiative to speak.

"I know I owe everyone an explanation, but—"

"Do you have any idea what the bogspectre is capable of?" said Effrax, cutting her off. "Obviously not, otherwise you'd never have tried to save it. It's pure evil. It inhabits your body and takes over your soul. It controls your every movement. It feeds off you, slowly draining your magic until your source is completely used up."

"You die?" said Keriya.

Effrax let out an uncharacteristically cold laugh. "You don't die. Your *magic* dies. You're worse than dead—you are nothing."

Keriya flushed. Of course having no magic would seem like a fate worse than death to a wielder.

"After that, your body starts to decay. You watch yourself rot, feel yourself fester, but you can't do a bloody thing. *Then* you die." Effrax fixed her with a calculating glare. "The only reason you saved the bogspectre was to spite me, because you don't want to find Thorion. You don't want to hold up your end of the bargain."

"That isn't true!"

"Then please, indulge us: why did you do it?"

"I . . ." Felt sorry for the bogspectre? She didn't think that answer would go over too well. "I just figured it wasn't evil, since it was against Necrovar. So I saved it. What's the big deal? Nothing bad came of it, we're fine."

"Not all of us." Effrax nodded toward Sebaris' prone body. She hadn't woken from her comatose state since the bogspectre had left her.

"She needs a healer," said Max. "We should head for Irongarde. It's closer than the palace."

"Can you find your way?" asked Effrax.

"We'll head west until we reach the main footpath, and there are cairns marking the way from there. It should be simple."

Effrax shrugged. He waved a hand over the fire without another word, extinguishing it and plunging the camp into darkness.

"I guess I'll take first watch," Max said dryly.

Roxanne scooted closer to Keriya across the mossy ground. "For what it's worth," she mumbled, "I think you did the right thing."

"Really?"

"Yeah. You stood up for what you believed. You know, I didn't want to kill the shadowbeasts. They weren't our real enemies — Doru was forcing them to fight."

"More casualties of the war," Keriya murmured, thinking of the tiny body in the Galantrian Village, and the way the shadowbeasts exploded when they died.

Roxanne nodded. "I didn't try to save them, but now . . . I wish I'd done better by them."

"You let one of them go," said Keriya. Tentatively, unsure how well her words would be received, she added, "I think you did the best you could."

Roxanne considered this for a moment, then smiled. She gave Keriya a bracing pat on the shoulder before she went to shelter under the fronds of a large fern. Keriya stared after her in bemusement. The whole world, it seemed, had turned upside down.

Sighing and shaking her head, she lay down where she was by the warm embers of the fire. She tried to calm her overwrought mind, but she was plagued by the growing feeling that she *hadn't* done the right thing, regardless of Roxanne's kind words.

How she wished Fletcher were there. She would have given anything to talk to him. This was his area of expertise. He was the good one, the person who always did the ethical thing, the moral compass.

She needed a compass now more than ever. These days, she was feeling increasingly lost.

Without consciously realizing it, she reached out and placed a hand on the sword. She'd wrapped it in her cloak, partly because it was filthy, and partly to shield it from Effrax's disapproval. He wanted her to get rid of it, but she'd overridden his protests. In the off chance the shadowbeasts really were hunting for it, she needed to guard it.

However, it was a *very* off chance indeed. There was nothing special about the weapon as far as Keriya could tell, except that it might win first prize for the dirtiest piece of junk in Allentria. What could Necrovar possibly want with it?

Max's turn at watch ended and Effrax took his place. Keriya stayed motionless as they traded off so they wouldn't see she was awake. Eventually, the sound of snoring reached her ears. She sat up and saw Effrax slumped against a boulder, out cold. No one else was having trouble sleeping.

Keriya couldn't bear to be still anymore. She stood, taking care not to disturb Roxanne, who was closest to her. On a whim, she picked up the sword before creeping out of the camp.

She unwrapped her cloak as she walked, revealing the weapon. The sheath hung from a belt with an archaic buckle. She fitted the belt around her hips and, just for fun, grasped the sword's handle to pull it from the scabbard. It was so encrusted with grime that it took her several attempts before she managed to free the blade. It came loose, crumbling the dried build-up of muck around the hilt and showering the front of her dress with filth.

"Gross," she muttered, though she hefted the sword and gave it a few practice swings. It was too heavy for her and put a strain on her wrist.

"What's your secret, sword?" she asked, stabbing at an invisible enemy. "Why is Necrovar looking for you? If that's even true."

"Truth it is, dragon-child."

Keriya spun with a cry. There, hovering behind her, was the bogspectre. It tilted its head, fixing its one eye on her.

"Are you afraid?"

"No," she whispered. She wondered if it was there to reclaim its treasure, or if it had some other, darker purpose. If it intended to kill her, she deserved it—she'd been stupid enough to wander off on her own in the middle of the jungle, leaving the others without a guard on duty.

"Don't lie to me, flesh-rat," it sneered. "You'd be a fool not to be afraid. I'm sure you've grown up hearing the stories they tell about me. I'm sure you know what I'm capable of."

"Actually," she managed in a tiny voice, "I grew up in Aeria, and I didn't hear anything. But I've met you now, so . . . you know. I get the idea."

"Yet you saved me."

"I did." *But I'm not sure I should have.*

The bogspectre seemed to sense her unspoken words. "Saving a life is never a mistake," it told her.

Keriya wasn't even sure about that anymore. What if one day she decided she wanted to save Necrovar's life? What would happen then?

"When we are saved," it continued, though she was wrapped up in her misgivings and only halfway paying attention, "it will not be by a warrior or a wielder, or by someone who has done what thousands of people before her have done. We will be saved by someone who can look into the eyes of her enemy and see herself."

"I don't want to see myself in someone evil," she retorted, without a thought as to the consequences of being so rude. "No offense."

"Perhaps it isn't so much seeing yourself in someone evil," it mused. "Perhaps it is seeing someone evil and realizing he isn't evil at all."

Though it probably had a point, Keriya was certain that no self-respecting hero would have spared the soul-sucking bogspectre.

But she knew now that she was not a hero, and she was never going to be one.

The bogspectre hovered closer and she backed up, stumbling over a root and landing on the damp ground. It oozed through the air until it was only the sword's length away from her body.

"You remind me of someone," it said, its body undulating and twisting.

"Um . . . okay." The two of them stared at each other for a long time, and Keriya was surprised to discover that she actually wasn't afraid. The creature had given her a terrible shock when it had snuck up on her, but now that it was here, it wasn't so bad.

"So, why does Necrovar want the sword?" she asked.

"I knew, once. Something to do with dragons. And magic. The sword holds great magic."

"Really?" She sat up, her interest piqued.

"Perhaps." It lowered its head, and its eye flashed silver as it caught a stray beam of moonlight. "Necrovar is an enemy you *should* fear."

She wanted to boast that she wasn't afraid of the Shadow, but that was too great a falsehood for her to claim. "I know."

"Then you should also know to never lose that weapon. It was not given lightly."

"Maybe you should take it back," she said. The bogspectre's

face seethed and darkened. "I'll do my best to keep it safe from the shadowbeasts, but I don't think my best will be good enough."

"I wouldn't have given it to you if I thought you unworthy," it spat. Keriya let out a humorless chuckle and the monster growled.

"Do you mock me?"

"No, it's just funny. You're the only one who believes in me. I know what they all think. They see someone too young and inexperienced, someone easily controlled. A weak, worthless cripple with no magic." She didn't know why she was bothering to explain herself to the bogspectre. The words just kept pouring out of her.

"I want to fight Necrovar. I have to, in order to save—well, everyone, really. I want to show them they were wrong about me. But every time they tell me I can't do it, I grow more afraid that they're right."

"I believe it's time for you to decide who you are, Keriya Soulstar." She was surprised it had remembered her name. "Fear is a choice."

"Fear is *not* a choice. Who in their right mind would choose to be afraid?"

"You don't choose your fears, foolish human. You choose how to face them."

Keriya wasn't sure what to say to that.

A glassy, faraway look came across the bogspectre's face. It gazed around the trees idly, as if it had forgotten she was there. Then it announced, quite abruptly, "I was a dragon, once."

"You, ah . . . you possessed a dragon, did you?" If that were true, then the bogspectre really had lived for a ten-age, possibly longer.

"Yes," it said slowly. "I saw through his eyes and knew his thoughts as if they were my own."

"What happened to that dragon?"

The bogspectre's body grew still. "I killed him." There was a definite note of regret in its awful voice.

Then it shuddered and disappeared. Keriya blinked and stared around, but there was no trace of the monster. Had it even been there at all, or had it just been a dream?

"Fine dream to have," she grouched, standing and brushing herself off. She sheathed the weapon and headed back in the direction whence she'd come. Fortunately, she was able to retrace her footprints in the soft earth.

Keriya was finally tired by the time she reached the camp. She lay down and drew the cloak over herself like a blanket, the sword still buckled around her waist. Sleep wrapped her in its numbing embrace as soon as she closed her eyes.

Then a purple light blazed through the darkness, shattering her rest. Cold dread shot through her stomach and her eyes flew open. The first thing she saw was Doru. He grimaced as he leaned over her and wrapped his dead fingers around her neck.

Now that she was awake, she heard the sounds of a fight. Effrax was yelling. Roxanne was screaming. Keriya tried to call out to her companions, but Doru was squeezing her throat so tightly that no sound could escape.

"It's your turn," Doru hissed. The glow of her eyes illuminated his rictus of vengeance. "First your dragon. Now you."

Keriya's hands dropped to the sword's hilt. As soon as she grasped it, a tingling, pinching sensation flared in her chest. Doru let go of her, recoiling as if her skin had scalded him.

"What did you do?" he spat. Keriya had no idea what she'd done—she hadn't done anything except grab the sword.

Doru stood and made a sharp gesture. A jet of midnight-black water materialized before him, heading straight for her. She drew the ancient weapon on pure instinct, and something amazing happened: the blade repelled the liquid, dissipating the dark spell.

Both Keriya and Doru stared at the weapon in disbelief. The bogspectre had been right. The sword *did* have magic.

Doru let out a ragged howl and lunged at her. She pushed herself up and started to run—but she was always running, always calling for help, because she'd always been at a disadvantage. Now, for the first time, she found herself on even footing with her foe. Some power within the sword prevented Doru from wielding against her.

She stopped, pivoted, and struck at him. Her aim had been true, but he turned to shadow before the blade could connect with his chest. Keriya was quickly tiring of that trick. She wheeled around, seeking any clue that would tell her where he'd gone.

There was no sign of him, but her gaze fell upon Roxanne, who was battling four shadowmen at once. Roxanne, who — through some odd twist of fate — had become her friend.

Keriya tore across the clearing. She swung the sword, the weight of which nearly caused her to topple over, and slashed at a shadowman. He disintegrated the moment the blade sliced through his throat. One of the spells around Roxanne dissolved, freeing her to continue battling. Their eyes met briefly and the tall girl nodded her thanks.

"Soulstar!" A furious scream echoed through the forest and Keriya glared over her shoulder. Doru's form was just visible within the murky depths of the trees. Shadows wafted off him like hot steam. He raised a hand and pointed at Keriya.

"Your fight is with me, not my men," he yelled. "Let's settle this once and for all."

Keriya hesitated. She looked back at Roxanne.

"I've got this covered," Roxanne assured her, whirling around to confront another demon rising out of the darkness. "You take care of Doru."

CHAPTER THIRTY-EIGHT

THE GREATEST BATTLE

"Peace is ephemeral, war is eternal."
~ Tolbrayth Solarius, First Age

Thorion couldn't see his enemies, but the glow of his eyes gave their presence away.

"Careful," he whispered to Fletcher, who was struggling to keep up. The human nodded and made an effort to muffle his labored breathing.

Thorion thought he recognized this part of the jungle—hadn't he seen this mangrove swamp before? He squinted through the twilit trees to search for familiar landmarks. None popped out at him, but he noticed a shadow detach itself from the object that cast it. It skimmed across the surface of the swamp water and disappeared into the dark.

Fear. He was becoming fast acquainted with that emotion. His heart pounded, his stomach churned, his eyes dilated, straining to see his hidden foes.

He had long since cloaked his mind, for shadowbeasts were rampant in this part of the jungle and he didn't want any of the more powerful demons to sense him. The mindcloak meant Keriya couldn't sense or communicate with him either, but he kept it firmly in place. While he knew he was the equal of any ten shadowbeasts in a fight, he couldn't risk putting Fletcher in danger.

Even with his strongest sense disabled, his other senses served him well. He'd picked up Keriya's scent yesterday, so he knew they were gaining on her. He saw footprints in mud, broken branches, subtle signs that indicated she was close. He was always listening in the hopes he would hear her voice.

And suddenly, he did hear it.

He stopped so abruptly that Fletcher nearly tripped over his tail. He tilted his head, hoping he hadn't imagined it. Fletcher asked him something and he hissed, trying to emulate the noise humans made when they wished others to be silent. There, to the north — it was definitely Keriya. But something was wrong. She was screaming.

"Stay," he said, turning to Fletcher.

"Why? What's happening?"

Thorion didn't have time for questions. He butted his head into Fletcher's side, herding the boy toward the gnarled roots of a large tree.

"Stay," Thorion repeated, narrowing his eyes and flattening his ears to his skull to show he was serious. Fletcher nodded and shrank into the safety of the roots.

Satisfied that his companion was reasonably well hidden, Thorion took off. He galloped through the forest, scaling a cliff in two bounds. He heard other voices, shouts from Keriya's human friends, accompanied by the sounds of battle.

Thorion felt something rising within him and he opened his mouth. For the first time in his young life, he let loose a roar — not the yip of a pup nor the shrieks of a drackling, but a true dragon roar, a sound that had struck fear and reverence into the hearts of mortals in ages long past.

"*Leave them alone,*" he bellowed as he crashed through a tangle of vegetation and burst into a clearing.

Keriya was nowhere to be seen, but Effrax was there, fighting two shadowmen. A blue-haired girl lay on the ground, silent and unmoving — asleep, injured or dead, Thorion couldn't tell. He was distracted by Roxanne. She struggled against bonds of necro-threads, weakening in the grip of a tainted spell even as she wielded against three demons.

Thorion leapt at Roxanne's assailants. One of them tried to intercept him, but Thorion spat lightmagic at him and he disintegrated at once. Roxanne rallied and managed to wield an earthen spell that shot through the heart of a second shadowman, killing him on impact. Thorion landed beside her and turned neatly, baring his fangs at her last remaining attacker.

Strangely, the blackened wraith began to laugh. "Our Master has been waiting for you, dragon." He made a motion in the air with one hand, like he was clutching and holding onto something.

Thorion felt an unpleasant pressure within him, as if the man's hand had closed around his central organs. It wasn't a physical pain, but his legs weakened and he fell to the ground. He tried to wield, but the shadowman rotated his wrist, and Thorion's soul twisted out of reach.

Fear again, this time more powerful than anything he'd ever experienced. If this demon had dominion over his soul, that could only mean one thing: darksalm had touched him.

Thorion growled and choked. He tried to get up, to spring into the air and fly out of the shadowman's grasp, but the alien presence stopped him. It traveled through his veins, from the largest artery to the smallest capillary, until it filled his whole being.

His scales grew luminous, glowing red-hot. It was like there were a layer of fire trapped beneath his flesh rather than a layer of poison. His growling intensified to a wail of agony. Other emotions crowded in, mixing with the fear: confusion, anger, even shame — shame that he had doomed himself and the world with it. The darksalm would burrow deeper and deeper into his soul until it killed him, and his magic would belong to the Shadow.

"Stop!" Roxanne strained against the spell that bound her. She reached out for Thorion, but a tendril of necromagic yanked her arm back, pinning it to her side. The demon bent until his sneering visage was level with hers.

"The dragon and all who follow him will soon be dead." He whispered Allentrian words in her ear and her face grew ashen. "You'll be the first to go."

He splayed his fingers in the air and moved his hand toward

Thorion, who ceased his violent shaking. Smoke rolled off his scales as they cooled to their natural bronze color. What now? Was he being released?

No—he was being controlled. His legs moved against his will and he got to his feet. His head pivoted on his neck until he was facing Roxanne. He felt his mouth open, felt his tongue curl upwards.

"Thorion, no," she sobbed. "I don't know what they're doing to you, but whatever it is, you have to fight!"

He recognized that last word.

Fight.

Too late. The Shadow's touch reached his mind and forced him to drop his mindcloak. Instantly, the demon's control over him increased tenfold. He felt his brain reflect threads from his source, felt the catalytic conversion of those threads' potential energy into physical magic. He was puffing up in preparation to wield against Roxanne, to kill her. The fear mutated and became something else. Even in his panicked state, he sifted through everything he had learned from Keriya and narrowed in on the word to describe it: *hatred.*

He hated the shadowman controlling him. He hated Necrovar for starting this war. And he hated himself for allowing Necrovar to win it.

Time crawled to a standstill. He stared into Roxanne's tear-filled eyes. He heard the demon's laugh ringing in his ears. He smelled the rotten stench of burnt shadowbeasts. He felt needles in his soul as power churned inside him, and needles in his heart as despair set in.

Then he sensed something.

<Keriya.>

<Thorion?>

It was her. Keriya, who fought against all odds—and who gave him something to fight for.

So he dredged up the last of his strength and resisted the Shadow's influence, pressing back against the darkness that intoxicated him. Who would have guessed that his greatest battle would not be against men or demons, but deep within himself?

Time resumed its inexorable forward motion as Thorion wielded. He shot a beam of light at Roxanne. For a moment the clearing was awash in the searing glow of his power.

When it faded, Roxanne was sitting there, shaken but unharmed. She let out a weak laugh and put her hands to her chest, as if making sure she was truly still alive. His attack hadn't destroyed her, but rather the shadowy chains that had held her captive.

"*I am more powerful than you,*" he informed the shadowman. Then he spoke carefully in Allentrian: "Necrovar will never own me."

The demon's pitch-black eyes crackled with fury. He gestured again, more violently this time, and again Thorion felt his soul twist. He collapsed, writhing as intangible thorns dug into him from every angle.

His enemy gathered the surrounding shadows. With cruel precision, he molded them into a solid spear, aiming the point at Thorion's heart, and launched it forward.

A figure flew in from the periphery of Thorion's vision. It slammed into his side, knocking him out of the way just before the spell pierced his armored chest.

"Effrax?" whispered Thorion. The Fironian had saved him, but he'd caught the brunt of the demon's attack in doing so. The spear of solidified necromagic protruded from his left thigh. It began to melt, seeping into his leg.

Thorion stared at the human, thunderstruck. He'd paid little attention to Effrax before that moment, and most of the attention he *had* paid had been negative, for Keriya distrusted him.

Yet Effrax had just saved his life.

The shadowman was irked but undeterred. Now all his victims were helpless: Effrax lay maimed, Roxanne was spent, and Thorion's magic was beyond his reach.

"You'll meet your new Master soon, dragon." The demon

wielded blackened earth to bind each of them in place. Shadows seeped from his body, swallowing everything, blotting out the light of the moons and stars. Thorion could sense that this was the end. He was fading, fading away into nothingness—

Then the shadowman let out a noise of shock and dropped his threads. The iron soil around Thorion loosened into soft dirt, and at the same time the bonds on his soul relaxed. The shadowman's mouth opened in a noiseless scream as he died. His body crumbled to dust, revealing a scrawny boy behind him.

"Fletcher?" Roxanne gasped in disbelief. Fletcher Earengale was trembling all over, clutching the hilt of a shiny dagger, looking as if he were about to be sick.

Thorion stood shakily. He stared down at himself, then looked up at Fletcher, whose tan face was white with terror.

"I thought you might need some help," he whispered. "I know I've never been much help before, but . . ." He trailed off, looking anxious, and held out an apologetic hand to Thorion. Thorion was surprised to find that he understood every one of Fletcher's words.

"Thank you," Thorion said with a smile, bowing his head to the small human who had inadvertently just saved the world.

Then the smile faded from his lips. He sensed something terrible and foul, something far worse than anything they had yet encountered.

Keriya was in mortal danger.

CHAPTER THIRTY-NINE
NECROVAR'S SIDE

"No mortal's hand shall harm me, not by magic, sword, or knife;
Only the Blood can give me death, where once it gave me life."
~ **Necrovar's Prophecy, Second Age**

The sword sang as Keriya sliced at Doru. He dodged and wielded a razor-thin sheet of ice against her which nearly took off her head.

They cut back and forth at one another, she with her weapon, he with his magic. A strange energy blossomed inside her as the sword absorbed his attacks. Bolstered by the feeling of empowerment, she advanced on Doru, forcing him away from where her friends fought his shadowmen.

They battled their way toward a cliffside clearing that overlooked the sprawling rainforest. The Bloodmoon hovered low above the sea of treetops. Its red light mingled with the garish purple glow of her eyes, tingeing her surroundings with an eerie hue.

As she began to tire, Keriya mentally replaced Doru's face with the faces of everyone who had ever wronged her, from Penelope Sanvire to Gohrbryn Tanthflame. Her heart pumped with anger and she struck at him with renewed vigor, the force of her swing yanking her body around in a full spin.

Doru wove another spell, but lost control of his threads. At first Keriya thought it a fluke, a lapse in his concentration, but he tried once more and the same thing happened.

Panicked, he tried again, with just as little success. She watched him, the sword drooping in her exhausted arms. Could it be that the weapon was now blocking his wielding abilities, too?

Suddenly Doru went as still as an ice sculpture, his eyes

bulging out of his head. Then his body contorted into an impossible shape. Keriya drew back as she heard the crack of bones and the groan of straining tendons. Next he went limp, swaying on the spot like a puppet dangling from an invisible thread. If she had pushed him, he would have toppled right over—but she didn't dare draw near. Something was very wrong.

He twitched. Tension flowed back into his body. He straightened gracefully and turned to look at her.

"We meet at last, Keriya."

Keriya didn't know what had happened, but she was certain that the person standing before her was no longer Doru. She *thought* she knew who this new monster was, but there was no way it could be . . .

"Necrovar?" she whispered hoarsely.

"You recognize me." He smiled. "I like a woman with a modicum of sense."

"I . . . but—how?"

"Doru Maermist died in the Galantrian Village. He no longer exists; he is simply an extension of my power. I am all there is."

No, *no!* It was too soon, she wasn't ready. Keriya had been so busy worrying about Thorion that she'd hardly given any thought to what she would do when she faced the Shadow alone.

Necrovar made Doru's body step toward her. It was as if the mere presence of such power had transformed him, made him taller, more muscular, more intimidating, more deadly.

"Your awe is flattering," he said, addressing her thoughts as he circled her. "And the feelings are mutual. You've been the object of my fascination—and frustration—for quite some time. But actually seeing you . . . it's exhilarating."

"Why?" she croaked, reduced to single-syllable speech.

"Dear, naïve Keriya; your ignorance is delightful. Why? Because I've been waiting for this moment for seven thousand years." He stopped before her and reached out slowly, almost lovingly. He placed one of Doru's fingers on her cheek and traced it down her jawline. A cold thrill shot through her and she withered away from his touch.

"I was greatly wronged, you see." Suddenly his voice was sinister and angry. "Ten ages ago, I was unjustly banished to a parallel universe. You know it as the Etherworld. To me, it was hell. My followers were placed in a stasis, suspended in time, but I was conscious for my entire imprisonment. And I was tortured. The Etherworld feeds on energy, so the greater your power, the greater your suffering."

I need to kill him now, Keriya thought. *Get him while he's talking, wait til his back is turned, catch him off guard—*

"You can't catch me off guard. You are transparent and predictable—not just because you're human, but because you are you. I know everything about you." He waggled a finger at her, as a parent might when scolding a rambunctious child. "You cannot cheat the Shadow. And you cannot kill me."

"Yes I can. Shivnath chose me for this!"

She didn't care if it wasn't true. Just saying the words made her feel less alone, made her believe there might be a chance, however slim, that she would survive this.

Shivnath chose me. She gave me power. She brought me back from the dead to kill Necrovar. I just have to wait until the right moment and the magic will come! Though Keriya was wondering, with increasing desperation, when her magic would realize that the right moment was right *now*.

"Shivnath doesn't want to kill me," said Necrovar. "Shivnath wants balance. The balance was ruined long before my rise, and will remain in upheaval as long as humans are allowed to abuse and defile their powers. The world needs to be saved. And that's where you come into the picture, my dear."

"Yes," she insisted stubbornly, "to kill you."

"You are not listening to me," he growled as he began to pace back and forth. "I am not meant to be destroyed, I am meant to be the balance. The problem is that I am not, in fact, balanced— at least, not yet. I've gained enough strength to widen the Rift, to send my shadowbeasts out, but my body is still imprisoned.

In order to return to Selaras and ensure my eternal rule, I need a particular magic. Do you know which one?"

Given Necrovar's obsession with Thorion, she could make an educated guess. "Lightmagic?"

"Very good," he said, clapping slowly. Even through her panic, she was infuriated by his patronization. He leaned in close, as if the two of them were old friends.

"I'll tell you a secret," he breathed. "You are a peace offering, a bartering chip. Shivnath sent you to give me the magic I need."

"That's a lie!"

Shivnath would never have done that — not to me, not to Thorion. She wants to save Thorion. Shivnath is the ruler of all that is good and just, and the evil god Helkryvt is her worst enemy! Keriya repeated the line from her favorite book over and over in her head to remind herself that it was true.

A tick went off in Necrovar's borrowed face. "I'm evil, am I? You think so?"

"I know so."

"It says more about your character than mine if you believe that. Tell me, did Shivnath, who you so blindly adore and idolize, ever once describe me as evil? Did she ever explicitly command you to kill me?"

"Of course! She said . . ." But as Keriya went over all the conversations she'd had with Shivnath, she realized the dragon god had never actually said either of those things.

It couldn't be. It couldn't *possibly* be.

Keriya's knees buckled and she sank to the ground. She had lost control of her body and her brain was rebelling, trying to tell her that Shivnath had betrayed her.

Necrovar crouched and reached for her free hand. She was so in shock that she allowed him to take her pale fingers in his sable ones.

"You were a sacrifice," he told her gently. "Shivnath hoped I might take you, and give that damned dragon-child back his soul." Another painful frisson of fear shot through her. What did he mean by that? Was it possible that Thorion had been touched by darksalm?

"At first, I wasn't going to do it," he said. "I didn't want to win this war with unnecessary cruelty. Besides, your soul meant nothing to me—so instead, I decided to use you to call the one I wanted out of hiding."

Keriya's brows knitted in confusion. How had Necrovar used her? She'd called Thorion on her own . . . hadn't she?

"Then you wielded something you had no right to wield." He straightened and resumed his rhythmic pacing. "I will admit, up until that day in the fen, I'd thought you were no threat. But when I saw what you were capable of, I knew you were going to be a problem.

"My followers captured you, and I had them bring you to Gohrbryn Tanthflame. I'd planned our first meeting to be in the Village, but again you surprised me. You escaped. Not only that, you made Thorion wield, although dragons don't reach magical maturity until they've seen three hundred cycles and that pup is barely a centureling. That is a rare power, even among the *rheenarae*."

His words sparked an idea in her brain. "My power! If Shivnath wanted you to take me instead of Thorion, then do it! She gave me—"

"You think a dragon would *give* you magic? And not just any dragon, but Shivnath, god and ruler of them all?" A bitter chuckle escaped him. "No, Keriya, she gave you nothing."

"She asked for my help. She put magic in my soul."

"Do you mean this magical block?" Necrovar raised a hand and contracted Doru's fingers. Keriya gasped—it felt like someone had grabbed her heart and was trying to yank it from between her ribs. "It was supposed to prevent you from wielding."

No. Not true. Not possible.

"It hurts, doesn't it?" he whispered. "Never trust a dragon, my dear."

Keriya drew a shuddering breath. She was on the verge of

tears, but she had no tears to shed. She was empty. Lost.

Alone.

"You know, I admire you," he continued. "You've lived a hard life, yet you carry on with such determination. You are so desperate to prove your worth. In many ways, you remind me of myself when I was young. I understand how you suffer. And for your suffering, I am truly sorry."

He did sound sorry, but Keriya, who was trying to gather all the broken pieces of herself and put them back together, refused to listen. He was lying! He was trying to turn her against Shivnath in a pathetic attempt to save his own sorry neck.

"Still you stand by Shivnath, after everything she put you through. You are loyal to a fault. I admire that about you, too. You are quick to hate, but you wish only to love—and that love, once given, never goes away, does it? You can never just stop loving someone." A vacant look crossed the shadowman's face for a moment. Then the cruel glint came back into his eyes.

"I shall have to work to earn your trust. That's fine. I couldn't respect you if you were some harlot too easy to please." He shot her a roguish wink, and his charm somehow managed to shine through Doru's ghastly visage.

"You've been taught to hate me, but I will give you my side of the story. Once you have all the details, I'll let you choose for yourself what you believe. Does that sound fair?"

Keriya didn't respond. Necrovar began anyway.

"In an age before ages, when humans were just learning to wield, they began using their magic for evil—killing, destroying, taking and abusing powers that did not belong to them—and they ruined the delicate balance of nature. From that imbalance, I rose to power. I am the embodiment of dark energy. I grow stronger with every evil action humans take. The stronger I grow, the more evil humans become, and the more evil humans become, the more everyone suffers. Do you understand this concept?"

"Yes. It—you—are us. The evil is us."

"I hadn't meant it like that, but you aren't wrong," he

conceded. "I'm caught in a vicious cycle, for I also feel the repercussions of those evil actions, the pain and suffering they cause. So in fact, my only desire is to eradicate evil."

Keriya didn't believe that. Trust Necrovar? She would rather throw herself off the cliff, stab herself in the eye with an *evasdrin* dart, drink drachvold acid.

"When I bonded with my human host, I gained the ability to wield. I knew what I had to do with my newfound power. The world would only be saved if I ruled it. All who resisted would have to be struck down. The wicked would have to be punished. Those who were evil would have to die."

"If you gain strength from our evil," said Keriya, "wouldn't *you* die if you got what you wanted?"

"Unfortunately, evil can never truly be eradicated, it can only be contained. And I am the only one who can contain it."

"That's a paradox," she argued. "As long as you're around, evil won't be contained. Your whole plan is evil."

"I take responsibility for my choices. Everything I do is a necessary evil, if you'll excuse the pun." He favored her with a dry smile. "Your world doesn't have a future; without anyone to control them, humans will destroy it. Everything I do is to create a new future, a peaceful future—a better future."

"And murdering my dragon? Is that part of your better future?"

"I will forgive your stupidity," he said icily, "because there is no way you could know the truth. Dragons are not only evil by their nature, they are a threat to the balance. Their magic is a danger to us all, so they will be the first to go in my new world."

"I won't let you do that," she declared, sounding much braver than she felt.

"You think you can stop me? Not even the dragons could do that. The World Alliance couldn't stop me. Valerion Equilumos couldn't stop me. All the gods of Selaras couldn't stop me!" His voice had turned into a roar, and Keriya flinched away from his wrath.

"But," he went on, soft and alluring once more, "because I really do admire you, Keriya, I'll make you an offer. I want you to help me. Together, you and I can rule not only Selaras, but the universe. We will reshape destiny. We will balance the magics. And when we rule . . ." He knelt again and placed his hands on her shoulders.

". . . then no one will ever have to suffer as we have suffered."

Keriya stared into Necrovar's eyes. Why was he bothering to make this offer? Moreover, why was he bothering to make this offer to *her,* of all people? She wished it weren't so, but she felt flattered.

"Join me," he whispered, moving one hand from her shoulder to her chin, cupping it in his palm.

The fact that Keriya was even considering this made her question the core of her being. How could she, after all she'd been told about Necrovar, think of joining him?

But that had been his point, hadn't it? Why should she be swayed by the commands and opinions of people like Lady Aldelphia and King Wavewalker, who had already proven how dangerous they were? Necrovar's logic seemed sound, and he was open and sincere in a way that Shivnath had never been. Now that she'd heard his side of the story, she could make her own choice about who she believed.

Still, this was a pretty big choice. The fate of the world hinged upon the outcome.

I can't make this decision, said the voice inside her head. *I'm useless. I'm nobody.*

If I can keep others from suffering the kinds of things I suffered in Aeria, began another voice, *then it's my duty to join Necrovar. If I can prevent someone else's pain, I should.*

Why should I care about any of them? demanded a dark voice that swam up from the cavernous depths of her consciousness, a place she never dared to inspect too closely. *They've done nothing for me, and they mean nothing to me.*

He's lying! Don't trust him. Don't join him, pleaded a fourth voice.

He'll kill me if I don't. There's no choice, protested a fifth.

Then a different voice rang out above the cacophony in her head, a voice that was as familiar as her own:

<Keriya.>

<*Thorion?*> Had that been him, or had she imagined it? She listened, but there was no further communication. Still, the momentary connection with her dragon — even if it hadn't been real — had been enough to bring her to her senses.

There is always a choice.

Though Keriya had been torn asunder by Necrovar's exposition, she knew one thing for certain: he was a threat to Thorion, so she could never join him, no matter how golden his intentions.

"Well?" Necrovar crouched before her, waiting. He was no longer reading her thoughts. It seemed he was waiting for her to announce her decision.

Keriya drew a deep breath. Then she stood and backed away, hefting her sword.

"I see," he said, rising slowly. "Then I'm afraid I must kill you."

CHAPTER FORTY

THE SHADOW LORD

"Trying is more important than triumph."
~ Evran Mistforth, Ninth Age

"I had hoped you would see reason," said Necrovar. "I had hoped you would choose me."

Keriya said nothing. If she spoke to him, he would only draw her in again. She needed to keep her head clear.

"You are so young," he mused. "For all you've suffered, you know nothing of pain. I doubt you understand what you're facing. I doubt you've looked death in the eye and leveled with him."

"I've seen my share of death." She had stared death in the face in the Galantrian Village. She'd believed both Fletcher and Roxanne had died in the fen when Doru first attacked them. "In fact, I've died before."

Shut up, she screamed at herself. *Don't talk to him. Don't tell him anything!*

"Those were all escapable things. You could walk away from the men you saw murdered, men you never knew or cared about. You got your friends back mere moments after you thought you'd lost them. Even at the end of all things, it was not the end—Shivnath bent the rules of the universe and resurrected you. But death cannot be escaped. Death is final and infinite. Death is losing everything you have and everything you are."

That brought Keriya back to the void. Before Shivnath had returned her memories, she hadn't known who she was. She hadn't even known her own name. She had been nothing, and the memory of that nothingness still haunted her.

She understood death better than most.

"So I ask—are you sure this awful world is worth dying for?"

Maybe it wasn't, and Keriya was ashamed that a part of her felt that way. She would never be pure and kind like Fletcher, who saw the goodness in everyone; she would never be brave and strong like Roxanne, who feared nothing; she would never be powerful and wise like Thorion, who was revered and loved by everyone he met.

But they were all a part of this awful world. And if she had to die for something, it would be them.

Just thinking of Thorion made him seem close. She drew courage from his imagined presence and tried to prepare herself for a fight she couldn't hope to win. Necrovar shook his head, seeming disappointed. Then his eyes slid from her and fixed on something in the trees. His mouth widened in a feral grin.

A roar, deep and powerful, echoed through the jungle. The sound filled Keriya with hope. She turned her back on Necrovar to see Thorion burst out onto the mossy bluff, resplendent against a backdrop of emerald vines. He'd grown in the short time they'd been apart. Moonlight rippled across his scales, giving him a triumphant shine.

He ran to her side, and it was like a hollow place in her soul had been filled again.

<*You're here,*> she thought, not quite able to believe it. <*How? I didn't summon you.*>

<*I chose to come back,*> he replied, leaning his head against her shoulder.

"*Thorion Sveltorious.*" Necrovar's caustic hiss brought Keriya crashing back to reality. "*Welcome, friend.*"

He spoke the draconic language perfectly. Did that mean he was a *rheenar?* How could he be? Where would he have gotten that power?

Keriya glanced worriedly at Thorion, but the dragon's full attention was now on Necrovar. He narrowed his eyes and curled his lips in a snarl. "*I am no friend of yours.*"

"*Careful with that arrogant tone. I could kill you where you stand if I found you disagreeable.*"

"*I don't think so,*" said Keriya, surprising even herself. "*I think that's why you've been talking all this time instead of making good on your threats. You can't use your magic on us. Not while we have this.*" She waved the bogspectre's sword at him.

"*I could physically overpower the two of you, and I could rip the sword from your lifeless fingers if that's what you wanted,*" he returned. "*But it would be easier if we could conduct ourselves in a civil manner.*"

"*There is no being civil with you,*" said Thorion. Necrovar shrugged and began preparing a spell. Keriya felt fear clamoring to get in, but she shoved it aside. She was done being afraid.

Shivnath, she thought, *if you're listening, let me use your powers now. Whatever you wanted me for, I know you wanted Thorion to stay safe, but I will need a miracle to save him.*

Even as she prayed, Keriya felt a spectral warmth flicker to life within her. She smiled. Not everything Necrovar had said was true, and not everything Shivnath had told her was a lie.

Necrovar lashed out, and Keriya only just managed to deflect his spell. Despite her promise to be unafraid, fear started trickling in through her dam of resolve. Shivnath's magic wasn't ready yet. It was bubbling in the pit of her soul, ready to boil—she could sense it, she could almost see it, but still she couldn't wield it.

Thorion spat a beam of blinding light, hitting Doru's body in the heart. Shadowbeasts turned to dust and died when struck with a fatal blow, but Necrovar remained intact. He looked down in irritation as a small part of his chest crumbled away.

<*Why didn't it work?*> Keriya asked Thorion.

"*Nothing you do will work,*" said Necrovar. He shot toward Thorion with a shockwave of shadow, like an arrow fired from an invisible crossbow. He caught the dragon head-on and the two of them skidded backwards, slamming into the thick trunk of a tree.

Keriya started to run after them, but Thorion recovered and kicked off into the air before Necrovar could get a firm grip on him. He flew out over the valley, silhouetted against the Oldmoon, twirling like a leaf in the wind.

Necrovar wielded and launched himself into the night, hurtling at the drackling. They collided in midair. Thorion scratched and bit, but Necrovar's power seemed to provide Doru's body with an immunity to both magical and physical attacks. He ignored the talons slashing at his torso and wrapped his hand around Thorion's throat, just below his jaw.

With a powerful flap of his wings, Thorion wrenched himself from Necrovar's grasp and zoomed away again, diving for the jungle. Necrovar hovered in place, watching, waiting.

Thorion caught a warm updraft and soared back for another attack. He wielded a second beam of light at Necrovar, who simply allowed it to hit him. It caught him in the left thigh and had no effect. In retaliation he created a black mist that swirled around the dragon.

The spell clung to Thorion's scales and sank into his wings, turning them leaden and still. He cried out and tried desperately to gain altitude, but to no avail. Slowly, he began falling. Slowly, Necrovar glided after him.

Keriya, who looked on with tears in her eyes, strained to reach the glowing power inside her. She wanted to help, but all her mental advances splashed up against a barrier. Was that the block Necrovar had spoken of?

No! she thought, shaking her head furiously. She couldn't allow Necrovar's lies to spook her. She knew better than to listen to him. This wasn't a block, it was a safeguard. She thought back to what Shivnath had told her: *I will not allow you to freely access the power within you. It will be veiled until the right moment. Then it will be gone forever.*

She *would* be able to access the magic. She just needed more time.

In the hopes of distracting Necrovar, Keriya picked up a

rock that had been wrenched loose from the soil during her fight with Doru. She hurled it at his hovering body, but it fell so far short of its mark that he didn't even notice. He was busy preparing a spell, and he shot a bolt of black lightning at the drackling—a killing strike.

Thorion extended his wings to their full span, breaking the chains of mist that clung to him. He spun in the air, avoiding the worst of the blow. The necromagic grazed his feet and underside, but even that small contact was enough to sap the last of his strength. He spiraled back to the clifftop, landing with a crash.

Keriya screamed. The impact didn't seem to have damaged Thorion, but it was clear the lightning had addled him. He raised his head with difficulty and shot another spell at the Shadow, who'd touched down on the edge of the precipice. It hit him full force, and Keriya felt it might be enough to finish him. Black steam curled off his skin and sank to the ground, creating a cold, dark fog that shrouded the clearing.

Keriya stood frozen. Her uneven breathing grated against her ears, unnaturally loud in the sudden stillness.

Then the fog stirred, eddying around a disturbance, and Necrovar emerged. The side of his skull where Thorion's spell had hit was now a distorted, smoking wreckage. He glared at Thorion and the dragon shrieked in agony. Through their bond, Keriya felt an echo of his pain in her chest.

Her heart broke, releasing poisoned floods of guilt throughout her body. Thorion *had* been touched by the darksalm.

And it was her fault.

"*Powerful though you are, Thorion,*" Necrovar rasped, approaching with slow, deliberate steps, "*you are no match for me.*"

Why did Shivnath think we could do this? Keriya wondered to herself. *Why did anyone think we could? I'm useless, and Thorion is just a baby.*

"*You think if he were a thousand cycles old it would make a difference?*" Necrovar hissed. "*I faced his grandsire in the war.*

Rhusarion Sveltorious, a bonded, callous fool."

Necrovar raised a hand, causing Thorion to wail again. The dragon's glowing eyes rolled madly in his skull, his pupils contracting to narrow slivers.

"Two thousand winters had passed him by, and it took me only a heartbeat to kill him. He and his speaker thought they were a match for me. But I am the Shadow Lord and I am invincible, for the secret to my power lies far deeper than anyone knows. 'Only the Blood can give me death, where once it gave me life' – there is no one left who has the ability to kill me!"

"Not true," a familiar voice growled behind Keriya. Necrovar's gaze flickered to the speaker, and Keriya imagined she saw fear cloud his ruined face. She chanced a backward look and saw the bogspectre hovering in the trees. Its one black eye locked onto hers.

"He's wrong," it told her.

He's wrong, Keriya repeated to herself, as if realizing a fundamental truth.

It was that truth which shattered the block on Shivnath's magic. She had the power to kill Necrovar, and that power had finally come to a breaking point.

She swung the sword at Necrovar and a surge of unbridled energy erupted from her body. It slammed into the Shadow, encasing him in a sphere of magic that glowed like a miniature sun.

Heat fires sprang to life on the moss at his feet and a whirlwind whipped around them, clawing at Keriya's clothes. Necrovar's shape was just visible in the middle of the blinding mass. Over the roar of her spell, she could hear him screaming.

She didn't stop to think whether or not it was a good idea. Hefting the sword with all the strength she had left, she ran forward and sliced his body in twain. Energy erupted from his shorn figure, and he burst apart in an explosion forceful enough to blast her into the air.

Keriya was hurled into a rock on the far side of the clearing and felt her skull knock against it with a dull crack. Fighting to hang on to consciousness, she squinted against the brightness to see what had happened.

Searing blue lightning stemmed from the place where Necrovar had stood, forking into the heavens like the writhing, tangled branches of a massive tree. In the epicenter of the chaos was a black hole, a tear in the fabric of space and time that led to some unknown place.

The world began to distort, and everything shrank in toward that one point. Keriya grabbed fistfuls of moss to anchor herself to the ground, to keep from being pulled in and devoured by the spell, but she could feel it latching onto her, taking hold of her. The fires flared, the ground heaved, the howling wind reached an ear-splitting pitch, and then . . .

Then everything was nothing.

CHAPTER FORTY-ONE

THE HERO

"If you let go of what you think you are,
you become that which you might be."
~ Beledine Arowey, Second Age

She was surrounded by darkness. The empty black pressed upon her from all sides. She was surrounded, and she was alone.

Keriya had died. She had unleashed a power she couldn't control, and she had paid for it with her life.

She had failed.

No, thought a tiny voice in her head. *I didn't fail. I killed Necrovar, too. I saved Thorion.*

The thought staved off the suffocating despair that was threatening to creep in.

<Keriya.>

Keriya cringed; the mindvoice sent fire racing through her head. <Shivnath?>

Suddenly she realized that she still had her memories and she could still feel pain, which meant she couldn't be dead. As soon as that thought occurred to her the blackness fell away, coalescing into swirls of ebony fog. She became aware that she was standing on a solid surface, something tangible and real.

And there was Shivnath. Illuminated by a sourceless, omnipresent light, she glittered in the gloom like a gemstone trapped in a slab of midnight granite. Her eyes, as always, put the surrounding shadows to shame.

"Am I dead?" It was Keriya's first question, though she knew she wasn't.

"Not yet."

"So . . . where are we?" They were no longer on Selaras, she was certain of that. Shivnath had appeared to her, somewhere, somehow, in order to talk.

And oh, did they have some talking to do.

"You," said Shivnath, "are in the Etherworld."

The statement only gave rise to a hundred new questions, but for the first time, Keriya had no desire to ask them. There was only one answer she wanted.

"Shivnath, do you know what just happened?"

"I know everything."

"Necrovar said something to me. He said you sent me as a sacrifice. That you wanted him to kill me instead of Thorion."

"He said those exact words, did he?"

Keriya's heart sank. Did Shivnath's detachment indicate she thought the accusation was offensive, or just beneath her notice? Or did it indicate she was upset that her plan hadn't worked?

"I know you probably can't tell me the truth because of the binding laws," Keriya said to her feet, since she couldn't bring herself to look at the god. "But I've decided that whatever the truth is, I don't want to hear it."

There was a long silence. When Keriya could no longer bear waiting, she peeked up through her bangs.

"Is that so?" was all Shivnath said.

"Yes. If he was lying to me, then great. Everything's fine. And if he wasn't . . . I understand why you had to do that."

"Do you?"

"Yes," Keriya said again. "It was for Thorion's sake. I mean, don't get me wrong, it was still an awful thing to do. I thought we were friends."

"Friends?"

Keriya rolled her eyes. Even if the binding laws were keeping Shivnath from explaining herself, she ought to be treating this discussion a little more seriously.

"Well, I don't know what you'd call it when your mentor is a big old dragon god, but whatever. That's not my point. The point is, I know why you had to choose Thorion over me."

"You've changed since you left Aeria," said Shivnath. The edge in her voice had vanished. In its place there was a softness that hinted at respect—or perhaps an unspoken apology.

"Perhaps. But I still have one question for you."

"And what would that be?" The bite had returned to the god's tone.

"The same question as always," said Keriya, folding her arms and matching Shivnath glare for glare. "Why me?"

It was this answer that would explain everything. After all she had learned and all she had seen, Keriya could no longer believe that Shivnath had selected her randomly out of the millions of people that existed in the world.

"I give you the same answer as always: because I chose you."

Keriya buried her face in her hands and let out a growl. That answer was just as unfulfilling now as it had been when she'd first heard it. Shivnath was hiding something from her, she was sure of it.

"Any other questions?" said Shivnath.

"Yeah, why'd you bother coming here if you refuse to have a proper conversation with me?"

"Ah, I'm glad you asked."

Frowning, Keriya looked up at her. The dragon's eyes, which usually absorbed light rather than reflecting it, had an odd shine to them.

"I'd like you to give me that sword."

It took a moment for Keriya to process the request. Her frown deepened and her hand strayed to her hip—the belt was still buckled around her waist. The ancient sword was with her, resting in its scabbard.

"Why?" she wanted to know. "What does it mean to you, and to Necrovar?"

"That is not your concern," Shivnath replied in a tone that suggested she thought Keriya ought to have known better than to ask. But Keriya wasn't going to stand for that anymore.

"I think it is my concern. If you want me to travel thousands of leagues to bring it to you, I think I have a right to some answers. To just *one*."

Shivnath's beautiful, terrifying face grew dark. Her pupils thinned to needles and she bared her fangs. Keriya drew back, fearing that she'd crossed the line.

"Keriya, you don't want to be involved in this war. It is much larger and much more dangerous than you know. I want that sword. You don't deserve to hold it."

"You're wrong," Keriya countered, bristling at Shivnath's cruel choice of words. "The bogspectre gave it to me. He told me to keep it safe!"

"Like you kept Thorion safe?"

That stung like a hard slap in the face. Keriya bit down on her lip and fought off the tears that burned her throat. She raised her chin proudly, struggling to keep her composure, but Shivnath saw right through her.

"I tell you again," the dragon began, "you don't want to be involved in—"

"I didn't want to be part of this war, you *made* me part of it," Keriya interrupted. Her voice cracked, but she didn't care. It didn't matter if Shivnath saw how weak she was—she had to say her piece. "I didn't choose to start this, but I'm choosing to finish it. I will keep fighting. I will keep Thorion safe, and I'll keep the sword safe, too. You're not getting it. It's the only defense I've ever had against magic wielders."

Shivnath tilted her head. Now her face was as blank and unmoving as a stone. In a way, that was more unsettling than her anger had been.

"Are you defying me?" she said finally. "I, the god who wove a magic more powerful than you can comprehend into your soul? I, who was the first to believe in you, who gave you all the tools you needed to become the person you are today?"

Guilt stabbed at Keriya, but she held fast. "Yes. You may have given me magic, but I got here on my own. And until you decide to give me some answers, I am done with you."

As she spoke, Keriya's heart constricted with pain and her

stomach twisted with anticipation. Shivnath was the patron saint of Aeria, and Keriya had looked up to her for as long as she could remember. More than that, she now felt connected to the dragon god. She didn't want to be done with Shivnath.

But it was clear that Shivnath wasn't going to make any concessions. She studied Keriya as a snake might study an unsuspecting mouse.

"Your quest has made you wiser," the dragon observed. Keriya was taken aback—that wasn't the sort of response she'd been expecting. In fact, it was the first time Shivnath had paid her a compliment.

"Uh . . . thanks."

Shivnath dipped her snout in the barest of nods. Silence stretched between them, for Keriya had no idea what to say next. They had reached an impasse.

"So," she finally managed, "if I'm not dead, how do I get back to Selaras?"

After what seemed like a suspiciously long pause, Shivnath deigned to answer. "I imagine all you would have to do is step through the Rift."

She extended one of her leathery wings, indicating something to the right. Keriya looked and saw a band of cloudy light suspended in the black mist, carving through it like a jagged scar. Bright, sparkling fibers ran along its edges, miniature lightning bolts in a tiny cosmos.

She took a few hesitant steps toward the Rift, mesmerized by its strange beauty. This was it: the tear in the magicthreads that separated the Etherworld from the mortal realm. She reached out to touch it, and the fibers twisted toward her, sensing her approach.

"You'd better hurry. You've already spent too long here; your life-threads have assimilated to this world," Shivnath said behind her. Keriya nodded absently. She pursed her lips, then turned to face the dragon one final time.

"It was nice to see you again, Shivnath." It was an offering of peace, an attempt to part ways on good terms. Keriya stared up at Shivnath, who stared back down at her. "Usually that's a cue to tell someone it was good to see them, too."

"It was nice to see you, Keriya," Shivnath said after a moment of consideration.

"I guess this is goodbye."

"I wouldn't count on it."

Keriya smiled. Then she faced the Rift and, steeling herself, stuck her hand into the flickering filaments. It didn't hurt, as she'd thought it would; instead, a gentle tingling infused her flesh. The glowing clouds wrapped around her hand and she felt a tug.

A floating, weightless sensation spread across her body as she was drawn into the light. She was slipping into a place between dreams and reality, between consciousness and unconsciousness, between life and death. The light faded, and suddenly she was falling, tumbling head over heels through darkness.

<Keriya? Keriya, wake up.>

The mindvoice stopped her mad spiral. She felt warm breath on her cheek and dewy grass beneath her fingers. An ache began to throb on the back of her head. With great effort, she roused herself.

The wind had died, the fires had vanished, and the world had relaxed back into its normal state. Keriya blinked to clear her blurry vision and took stock of her surroundings. All that was left of Necrovar was a crater where his body had been. A sizable chunk of the cliff had crumbled away into the jungle below; the remainder of the clearing was a charred mess.

It was over.

She had actually won.

She couldn't revel in her triumph, because she felt a painless wound that no healer could ever soothe. She was empty. Her power had vanished, leaving her hollow once more.

Hollow forever, she thought sadly, remembering Shivnath's warning. The loss might have consumed her had Thorion not been there to bring her back from the brink of despair.

"You did it," he whispered. It took Keriya a dazed moment to realize he had spoken Allentrian. Was that possible? Or had she hit her head harder than she'd thought?

"I'm learning your language," he added, sensing her confusion.

She leaned over, pressing her face against the scales of his shoulder so he couldn't see the tears brimming at the corners of her eyes.

"Thank you for coming back for me," she said.

An odd hacking sound interrupted them, and they turned as one. The bogspectre hovered at the edge of the smoking crater, its dark form visible against the brightening eastern sky. Keriya's memory of the fight was hazy, the details slipping away like sand through a sieve, but she seemed to recall the bogspectre had said something to Necrovar. And Necrovar had been afraid . . . hadn't he?

She opened her mouth to thank the bogspectre for its help. What came out instead was, "Who are you?"

The bogspectre scrutinized her with its one eye. A tremor wracked its airborne body.

"Soulstar . . . Keriya Soulstar . . . watch over my sword." Before Keriya could reply, it disappeared with a swirl of its gelatinous tail.

"I will," she promised the dawn.

Another sound issued from the trees. Keriya craned her neck around and saw Max running toward her. Roxanne followed him, half-carrying Effrax. The Fironian had his arm slung over her shoulder and was limping along as fast as he could go. And behind them . . .

Max dropped to his knees when he reached Keriya, asking what had happened, checking her eyes, feeling her forehead, taking her hands in his, but she ignored him. In fact, she ignored everyone except for the hallucination that looked remarkably like Fletcher Earengale.

"I didn't think I'd ever see you again," she said faintly.

"I didn't think you cared," he admitted, crouching beside

her. "Look, Keriya—"

Keriya didn't wait for him to finish. She leaned forward and threw her arms around his neck.

"You are an idiot," she told him, thumping him on the back with her fist. "But so am I. I'd never have gotten this far without you. You stuck with me from the beginning, from all the way back in Aeria. You were there when everyone else hated me. And I never thanked you."

"Well," he said, awkwardly returning her embrace, "what else is a brother good for?"

"Not much," she laughed. There was so much she wanted to know—where had he gone? How had he found her? What had happened while they'd been apart?—but she couldn't find the words. She wished she could tell Fletcher how much he meant to her, but Fletcher seemed to know.

"It's okay," he assured her, drawing away.

"Keriya, you're bleeding." Max removed his hand from her head to show her that his fingers were stained dark red. "Can you see straight? Are you dizzy?"

"I'm fine."

"You sure?" Roxanne asked skeptically, staring around the decimated clearing. "What in the world happened here?"

"It was Necrovar," said Keriya. "We killed him."

Her announcement was met with silence. Fletcher and Roxanne exchanged incredulous glances and Effrax raised his eyebrows. He didn't look well; he was drenched in sweat and his left pant leg was torn and bloodstained, revealing a grisly wound beneath.

"That's . . . impossible," Max finally said.

"It's true," Thorion confirmed in Allentrian, with only a hint of an accent. Fletcher beamed proudly at the drackling—that was new. He'd been terrified of Thorion before they'd parted ways.

Everyone began clamoring for explanations, but Keriya wasn't in the mood for further conversation. She ached all over, and now that Max had mentioned it, she was starting to feel dizzy. She was also parched, starving, and exhausted.

Max noticed her eyelids drooping. "Enough questions," he announced. "We need to get Seba, and then we need to get everyone to a proper healer."

He put one arm around Keriya's shoulders and snaked the other beneath her knees, picking her up and carrying her away from the battleground.

The sun broke over the treetops before them. Keriya smiled as the soft light touched her. Lying in Max's arms, she couldn't help but feel safe. Safe and happy. Perhaps the happiest she'd ever been. Their ragtag team had been reunited and she had saved Thorion.

More than that, she had saved the world. She'd made her own choices and stayed loyal to Shivnath, regardless of whether or not Shivnath had actually deserved it.

That just might make me a hero, she thought to herself.

In her last waking moments she tried to recall what it had been like to wield, but it was like trying to catch a cloud in her hands. And as she slipped into the comfort of a dreamless slumber, so the memory of magic slipped away, too.

EPILOGUE

A dragon soared through the haze, its wings carving sharp trails through the clouds that shrouded the canyon. It landed on a steep path, touching down before a woman and a man.

As soon as it landed, the dragon collapsed on the ground, writhing in torment. Its screams rent the air as it thrashed about. The woman tried to help, but the man held her back.

The two of them exchanged heated words. The woman sank to her knees, sobbing. The man knelt before her and placed his hands on her shoulders.

"My feelings for you were never a lie. You saved the best part of me." He gently kissed her lips, lips which twisted into a snarl.

The woman stood, and there was darkness in her eyes. She lifted the sword over her head. The blade flashed blood-red as it caught light from the river of lava flowing sluggishly far below. She twirled it around and drove it down with all her might, down into the man's chest.

The splinter of his sternum was audible even over the dragon's anguished roars. Liquid spurted from the injury, staining his clothes black. The woman wrenched the sword free of his flesh and the man fell sideways, dead before he hit the ground.

"NO!"

With a startled cry, Seba sat bolt upright. She was shaking all over, drenched in a cold sweat. It didn't take her long to calm down, because she'd grown used to the sight of Max dying. Ever since she'd had the foresight, that vision had haunted her daydreams and nightmares alike.

Seba blinked and stared around. She was lying on a soft cot, dressed in a plain white shift. There were other cots standing in a row beside hers, but she was alone in the long, narrow room. She faced a wall filled with large windows, through which she could see a peaceful bamboo garden dusted with snow.

"Snow?" she breathed, frowning. How long had she been asleep? The last thing she could remember was sneaking through the rainforest, following Max and that miserable Keriya Soulstar.

A door banged open to her left and a wrinkled old woman wearing the white robes of a healer bustled in. The crest embroidered upon her sleeve marked her as a resident of the city of Irongarde. She took one look at Seba and let out a cry.

"Princess! You're awake!"

Seba felt like she was still dreaming. How had she gotten here? Where was Max? Her mind was fuzzy, diluted by a smog of confusion.

"Praise Zumarra you're safe! I'll let Captain Rainsword know at once—"

Seba's thoughts sharpened and another pang of fear jolted some sense into her. Wherever she was, Rainsword had somehow found her. "No, don't tell him! Please," she added in a parched and raspy voice when she saw the healer falter. "I don't feel well enough for visitors."

"But surely, Princess, we can let your father's servicemen know you've recovered from your coma—"

"You must tell no one." Seba tried to sound commanding, but that was difficult to do when it felt like she hadn't spoken in weeks. "I don't want him to know I'm awake. I—I don't want anyone to see me like this."

It was a sorry excuse, and she and the healer both knew it. But the woman also knew her place. She clasped her hands and bowed low to Seba, indicating her cooperation.

"You must be thirsty," said the woman, her healer instincts taking over. "May my assistants come in? They've been looking after you ever since you were brought here."

"How long ago was that?" Seba wanted to know.

"Nearly a month, Your Grace," the healer replied in a

breathy voice. "Prince Maxton wouldn't tell us how you came to be in this condition, so it's been difficult to treat you, not knowing what—"

"Max? He's here?" Seba perked up at once. "Is he safe?"

"Of course," said the healer, looking confused. "He's staying in Indrath Olven, but he's been busy with political meetings. He came to visit you while he was here to see the Dragon Speaker."

The happiness that had swelled in Seba's chest burst like a bubble. She gripped her sheets to keep her hands from shaking.

"The . . . dragon speaker?" she repeated, fighting to keep her voice calm.

"Yes," the healer gushed, aglow with admiration. "She's been staying in the infirmary, resting before she returns to Noryk with Lord Thorion. We've been honored to have such a hero bless our halls with her presence!"

"I see," Seba said faintly. She must have missed quite a lot while she'd been unconscious. "Thank you for the information. You may send in your assistants—but remember, no one outside of my personal healers may know I'm awake."

"Yes, princess." The healer bobbed another bow and scuttled away.

As soon as she was gone, Seba threw off her covers and slid out of the bed. Her legs shook when she put her weight on them and she nearly collapsed. She'd grown weak and frail.

Supporting herself with her hands, she stumbled across the aisle to the nearest window. She leaned upon it, her breath fogging the glass, and stared at the garden without seeing it.

How long would the healer protect Seba from Rainsword? She couldn't go back to the palace and face her father's wrath. She couldn't be trapped there forever, especially not when Max was still in danger.

The healer's assistants came in and swarmed around Seba, insisting that she return to bed. They fed her and gave her an assortment of foul-smelling potions. Seba let them fuss over her, all the while plotting her escape. As soon as she was strong enough to stand on her own, she would break out of the infirmary.

Soulstar might have everyone else fooled, but Seba saw her for what she really was. She was no hero—she was a murderer.

And Seba was prepared to kill her before she had the chance to kill Max.

END OF BOOK I

GLOSSARY &
PRONUNCIATIONS

Aeria (AIR-ee-uh):
A country on the north side of Shivnath's mountains, and childhood home to Keriya, Fletcher and Roxanne. Believed by Allentrians to be nothing more than a myth.

Aldelphia (all-DELL-fee-uh) Alderwood:
Empress of Allentria, a position widely considered to be the most powerful in the world. As empress, she also holds positions including Premier of the Union of the States and Head of the Council of Nine, among others.

Allentria (uh-LEN-tree-uh):
A large continent surrounded by water, divided into four different kingdoms that operate together under common imperial law.

Argos Moor:
The tallest mountain in Allentria, and home to Shivnath. Part of the mountain range that separates Aeria from Allentria.

Bloodmoon, the:
The smaller of the two moons which orbits Selaras; so named for its eerie, reddish hue.

Bogspectre:
An infamous monster who can possess people, absorb their souls, and rot their bodies away from the inside.

Centureling:
The draconic term for a young dragon who has reached the age marker of a hundred years.

Cezon (SEZ-on) Skyriver:
A man with a dubious, possibly criminal background, who meets Keriya, Fletcher and Roxanne when they first arrive in Allentria.

Darksalm:

A toxic and deadly substance, the main ingredients of which are dragon blood and necromagic. It has the ability to burrow into the magicsource of any mortal creature it touches, killing them slowly and sealing their soul to Necrovar after they die.

Derlei (DARE-lay):

The basic monetary unit of Allentria.

Doru Maermist:

A member of the Imperial Guard of Allentria, who is also in league with Necrovar.

Drachrheenar (DRACK-ree-nar):

The draconic term for 'dragon speaker.'

Drachvold (DRACK-vold):

A dangerous predator, native to mountainous regions of northern Allentria. Uses stomach acid to melt prey before ingesting its meals.

Drackling:

A generic term for a young dragon, one who has not yet reached magical maturity.

Effrax (EFF-racks) Nameless:

A Fironian who joins Keriya on her quest to find the last dragon.

Erastate (EHR-uh-state):

The western kingdom of Allentria, home to the empire's air wielders.

Esentia (eh-SEN-cha):

The name of the yellow star around which Selaras orbits.

Etherworld, the:

A parallel universe created by the gods to imprison Necrovar and his followers. For the sake of the magical balance, the dragons were also imprisoned there.

Evasdrin (EH-vas-drin):

A poisonous liquid, derived from an herb bearing the same name, that renders wielders incapable of using their magic.

Fironem (FEAR-oh-nem):

The southern kingdom of Allentria, home to the empire's fire wielders.

Fletcher Earengale (AIR-in-gale):

Keriya's best friend. An Aerian native who accompanies Keriya on her journey across Allentria.

Galantasa (GAL-an-TAH-sah):
The northern kingdom of Allentria, home to the empire's water wielders.

Gohrbryn (GORE-brin) Tanthflame:
Commander-General of the Imperial Guard of Allentria.

Great War, the:
The first war fought against Necrovar during the Second Age, approximately 7,000 years ago.

Grouge (rhymes with "rouge"):
A demon who lived during the time of the Great War in the Second Age, who served Necrovar.

Helkryvt (HEL-krift):
Known to the Aerians as the god of evil, and Shivnath's arch- enemy. Known to Allentrians as someone quite different.

Holden Sanvire:
Head Elder of Aeria, and father of Penelope Sanvire. Presides over the Aerian Elders with an iron fist, and truly loathes Keriya.

Iako (YAH-ko) Blackwater:
A member of Cezon Skyriver's band of criminals.

Imperial Guard, the:
Elite and powerful soldiers employed by the Imperial government, whose job it is to protect Allentrian citizens and keep the peace.

Keriya (CARE-ee-uh) Soulstar:
A young girl with no magic powers of her own; an Aerian native, she is chosen by Shivnath to journey to save the last dragon in the world. She journeys to Allentria to find and defeat Necrovar.

Magicsource:
The source of a person's magical power, often referred to as "the soul."

Magicthread:
Term used colloquially to refer to molecules of magic, and scientifically to refer to a long, cohesive strand of magic molecules, which wielders use to manipulate or create elements in the world around them.

Maxton Windharte:
Prince of the Erastate, heir to the Cloud Throne, and an expert on the subject of dragons and the rheenarae. Assigned to accompany Keriya on her quest to find the last dragon.

Mindspeak:
To telepathically communicate with another living creature.

Moorfain (MORE-fain):
A foreign country, located far to the east of Allentria, across the Waters of Chardon.

Necrocrelai (NECK-row-CREE-lie):
A large species of demon, humanoid in shape but with certain draconic characteristics, such as wings and horns. Natural-born dark wielders, they pledged themselves to Necrovar during the Great War.

Necromagic:
Term used to denote any type of magic that has been tainted by Necrovar's touch. The tainted magicthreads will turn pitch-black, thus making them easy to identify.

Necrovar (NECK-row-var):
The physical embodiment of all evil. After bonding with a human host it gained the ability to use magic and became a powerful wielder who nearly took over the world in the Second Age.

Naero (nigh-AIR-oh):
The Allentrian guardian of airmagic, and god of the Erastate. Has the form of a great white griffin.

Noryk (NOHR-ick):
The Imperial City, and capitol of Allentria, located at the geographic centre of the continent.

Oldmoon, the:
The larger of the two moons orbiting Selaras; so named because originally it was the only satellite in the sky.

Penelope Sanvire:
A young Aerian girl. Daughter of Holden Sanvire, she often bullied both Keriya and Fletcher while they lived in Aeria.

Rheenar (REE-nar):
The draconic word for 'speaker.'

Rift, the:
The tear in the magicthreads that divide the Etherworld from Selaras.

Roxanne Fleuridae (FLUE-rih-dye):
An Aerian girl who accompanies Keriya on her journey across Allentria, and a very powerful earth wielder.

Sebaris (say-BAH-riss) / Seba (SAY-ba) Wavewould:
Princess of the Galantasa; Eldest of House Ishira, the reigning royal family; and heir to the Coral Throne.

Selaras (seh-LAH-ris):
The human term for the planet; the world.

Senteir (sen-TEER):
The first Allentrian city Keriya, Fletcher and Roxanne visit, located in the northeastern part of the Smarlands.

Shädar (shay-DAR):
One of the necrocrelai who served Necrovar during the Great War. Most powerful of all the demon lords who pledged allegiance to Necrovar.

Shadow Lord, the:
A moniker for Necrovar. Also used in colloquial conversation simply as 'the Shadow.'

Shadowbeast:
Name given to Necrovar's demonic minions; dead creatures who have bartered their souls to Necrovar in exchange for a second chance at life, and been resurrected as his servants.

Shivnath (SHIV-nath):
The Allentrian guardian of earthmagic, and god of the Smarlands. She is also known by the Aerians and is worshipped as their patron saint. Has the form of a great green dragon with pitch-black eyes.

Smarlands (SMAR-lands):
The eastern kingdom of Allentria, and home to the empire's earth wielders.

Taeleia (TIE-lay-ah) Alenciae (uh-LEN-see-aye):
Representative of the Delegation of the Elves in the Allentrian Council of Nine.

Thorion (THOR-ee-on) Sveltorious (svel-TOR-ee-us):
A young, bronze-scaled dragon who is summoned by Keriya and eventually bonds with her.

Valerion (vah-LEHR-ee-on) Equilumos (eh-QUI-loo-mus):
Widely regarded as the greatest hero ever to have lived. A warrior from the Second Age who sought to defeat Necrovar and end the Great War by offering his soul to the gods of Selaras.

Valaan (vah-LAHN):

The Allentrian guardian of firemagic, and god of the Fironem. Has the form of a great phoenix bird whose fires never burn out.

Wielder:

A person who wields any type of magic.

Zumarra (zoo-MAH-rah):

The Allentrian guardian of watermagic, and god of the Galantasa. Has the form of a great blue sea serpent.

ABOUT THE AUTHOR

ELANA A. MUGDAN is a writer and filmmaker based in New York City. She is described by her friends and family as "the weirdest person I know," and wears that weirdness proudly on her sleeve. She likes dragons, as is evidenced by this book, and hopes that the world of Allentria will bring as much joy to her readers as it does to her.

www.allentria.com

If you liked *Dragon Speaker*, please consider leaving us a review on Goodreads, Barnes & Noble, or Amazon!

And don't miss

DRAGON CHILD

BOOK II OF THE SHADOW WAR SAGA
BY ELANA A. MUGDAN

For the first time ever, Keriya Soulstar is truly happy. She's a hero among the Galantrians; she's been reunited with her dragon, Thorion; she's even daring to think she's found a place she can call home. Things are good.

Unfortunately, things beyond the towering walls of Irongarde are most definitely *not* good. The Allentrian states are gearing up for war, and when a surprise attack reveals that Thorion is sick, Keriya's happy life crumbles apart.

In a race against time, Thorion's allies must delve into the past to provide hope for the future. And as Keriya uncovers unpleasant secrets about the dragons' role in the first great war against the Shadow, she realizes her battle has only just begun.

On Sale May 2019!

CPSIA information can be obtained
at www.ICGtesting.com
Printed in the USA
FFHW021308060219
50436476-55630FF